**W9-AED-570**

# *The Best* AMERICAN SHORT STORIES 2012

# The Best
# AMERICAN
# SHORT
# STORIES®
# 2012

Selected from
U.S. and Canadian Magazines
by TOM PERROTTA
with HEIDI PITLOR

*With an Introduction by Tom Perrotta*

HOUGHTON MIFFLIN HARCOURT

BOSTON • NEW YORK

ISSN 0067-6233
ISBN 978-0-547-24209-5
ISBN 978-0-547-24210-1 (pbk.)

Printed in the United States of America

DOC 10 9 8 7 6 5 4 3 2

"The Last Speaker of the Language" by Carol Anshaw. First published in *New Ohio Review,* Issue 10. Copyright © 2011 by Carol Anshaw. Reprinted by permission of the Joy Harris Literary Agency.

"Pilgrim Life" by Taylor Antrim. First published in *American Short Fiction,* Vol. 14, No. 53. Copyright © 2011 by Taylor Antrim. Reprinted by permission of the author.

"What We Talk About When We Talk About Anne Frank" by Nathan Englander. First published in *The New Yorker,* December 12, 2011. From *What We Talk About When We Talk About Anne Frank: Stories* by Nathan Englander, copyright © 2012 by Nathan Englander. Used by permission of Alfred A. Knopf, a division of Random House, Inc.

"The Other Place" by Mary Gaitskill. First published in *The New Yorker,* February 14 & 21, 2011. Copyright © 2010 by Mary Gaitskill. Reprinted by permission of Mary Gaitskill.

"North Country" by Roxane Gay. First published in *Hobart,* Issue 12. Copyright © 2012 by Roxane Gay. Reprinted by permission of Roxane Gay.

"Paramour" by Jennifer Haigh. First published in *Ploughshares,* Vol. 37, No. 4. Copyright © 2011 by Jennifer Haigh. Reprinted by permission of Jennifer Haigh.

"Navigators" by Mike Meginnis. First published in *Hobart,* Issue 12. Copyright © 2011 by Mike Meginnis. Reprinted by permission of Mike Meginnis.

"Miracle Polish" by Steven Millhauser. First published in *The New Yorker,* Novem-

# Contents

# Foreword

I THINK THAT THIS YEAR was the strongest for the short story since I began reading for this series six years ago. Far more than usual, I became thoroughly absorbed in literary journals as I sat in the corner of a waiting room or in my car outside my kids' pre-school, trying to conjure ways to stall a doctor or a dentist or my children. It turns out that the statement "I just have a few more pages" does not inspire patience in very busy or very young people.

Frankly, it's easier for me during a weaker year. The bolder, fun-nier, sadder, truer, and more deftly written stories rise immedi-ately to the surface. I struggle a little over whether to pass along a handful of those stories that fell between my "yes" and "no" piles. Then I wait while the guest editor reads. We often learn that we responded most strongly to many of the same stories. Twenty are chosen, authors are contacted. And on to the next year.

This year, trying to winnow the thousands of stories that I read down to 120 finalists felt like pushing crowds of beloved relatives from an airplane. Tom Perrotta, this year's guest editor, seemed to agree. I had the sense that after the first batch of stories that he read, he'd assembled most of the book in his mind. But then came the next batch, and with it, a host of new favorites and a complete upending of his earlier list, a process that continued right until the end.

I admit that I have a sweet spot for humor, although who doesn't, really? I found myself consistently entertained by a vast number of hilarious voices and characters, as well as happily surprised by the amount of satire. So often humor gets a bad rap, although I don't

see why. Good humor—good *timing*—in fiction is an art. To tell a
story that needs to be told, to transport the reader, to entertain,
and to be funny—these, to me, are the real challenges and, when
achieved, some of the best payoffs of my job.

I was also glad to see a greater diversity of themes this year, as
well as more direct and imaginative ways of addressing real-world
issues: the struggling economy figured more frequently, as did the
military, video game subculture, the dangers of commercialism,
and America's fascination with all things youthful.

In February, Tom and I met for lunch at a restaurant in Cambridge. We brought our long lists of final candidates and set about
trying to determine the finest twenty stories, those that balanced
humor and heft of subject matter, voice and content. He was a stellar guest editor, deeply thoughtful about what makes a good story,
as the reader will note in his excellent introduction. He valued
directness of voice and simplicity of language. Tom did not fall
for the stories with easy laughs or thinly veiled satire, with up-to-
the-minute content or zinging in-jokes—stories that, to be candid,
I myself was initially drawn to. He puzzled over each finalist story
that he and I had chosen: Did the voice hold up until the end?
Did the author take risks, and did they succeed? Did the characters need to speak—and did they say precisely what needed to
be said? We finished our lunch, ordered coffee, and continued
to ponder the lists. We paid our bill. The restaurant emptied. We
chose maybe ten stories that would appear in the book. But in the
end, it was up to Tom to head off and make the final decisions. As
we reached for our coats, I saw that we were the only people other
than the wait staff left in the restaurant. On the floor a mouse
scurried past as if to remind us that we really had stayed too long.

Tom chose a list of stories that together form a wonderfully
diverse and vibrant collection. There are stories in which humor
abuts tragedy, in which characters whose clear-eyed witness to
some new or baffling situation is irresistible. Here are stories with
premises at once unimaginable and inevitable. And in this book
are some of my favorite characters as well as some of my favorite
sentences—like this one, from Angela Pneuman's story: "He reminded Calvin of a cop, the way he could joke around and then
get serious, all of a sudden, pulling rank and leaving you feeling
like a jerk." Or this one, Lawrence Osborne's: "Growing older had
proved a formidable calamity." And, I can't help myself, one more

from the wonderful Edith Pearlman: "Alice Toomey, the headmistress, would have welcomed a rule against excessive skinniness." See if you don't come across at least one or two or ten of your own.

The stories chosen for this anthology were originally published between January 2011 and January 2012. The qualifications for selection are (1) original publication in nationally distributed American or Canadian periodicals; (2) publication in English by writers who are American or Canadian, or who have made the United States their home; (3) original publication as short stories (excerpts of novels are not knowingly considered). A list of magazines consulted for this volume appears at the back of the book. Editors who wish their short fiction to be considered for next year's edition should send their publication or hard copies of online publications to Heidi Pitlor, Houghton Mifflin Harcourt, 222 Berkeley St., Boston, Massachusetts 02116.

HEIDI PITLOR

# Introduction

WHEN I WAS a little kid, there was only one pizzeria in my hometown of Garwood, New Jersey, an unassuming place called Nick's on North Avenue. The pizza was excellent, so good that it completely validated the breathtaking boast printed on the takeout box, alongside an illustration of an insanely proud, somewhat pudgy, presumably Italian chef: *You've Tried the Rest, Now Try the Best!*

One day, though—I must have been seven or eight—my father decided to check out a pizzeria in Cranford, the next town over. I drove with him to pick up our order and was shocked—incensed, really—to discover that this unfamiliar establishment had the audacity to make the exact same claim as Nick's.

"Hey, wait a minute," I complained. "This can't be the best. Nick's is the best."

"It's a matter of opinion," my father told me. "Nobody can say for sure which one's better than the other."

I was troubled by this explanation, especially when my father added that pretty much every pizzeria in the New York area used the same box, with the same goofy-looking chef and the same rhyming slogan on the cover. It was totally illogical, not to mention unfair to Nick's pizza, which I was pretty sure *was* the best in the world. Though I had to admit, once we got home and started eating, that the pizza from Cranford was actually pretty tasty, and possibly even delicious.

Like the best pizza, an anthology of the best American short stories for a given year is nothing if not a matter of opinion. In this particular case, the operative opinions are my own, though heavily influenced by those of Heidi Pitlor, the series editor, who selected the long list of stories that I then winnowed down to the twenty included in this volume.

So where, you might ask, do my opinions come from? What are the aesthetic values underlying my decisions? I realize, of course, that not everyone's dying to know. Many readers—maybe even most, I'm not going to kid myself—will skip this introduction and head right to the stories themselves. It's possible that some of them have read my work and think they already have a pretty good idea of where I'm coming from. It's also possible that they've come to trust The Best American Series and don't worry too much about the tastes and biases of the individual editors. Or maybe they're just hungry to read some good fiction and would prefer not to get bogged down in a discussion of pizza boxes and recent literary history. That's okay with me—I'm pretty sure they won't be disappointed. By any standard, this year's batch of stories is pretty damn good.

But let's just stipulate that you're reading this introduction because you do care about what went into the quixotic task of selecting the twenty best American short stories out of the multitude published over the course of 2011. You may simply be curious, interested in getting to know your editor a little better (in which case I'm flattered), but you may also be skeptical or even mildly hostile, wondering what gives me—gives anyone, for that matter—the right to impose his or her personal tastes on the American reading public.

*Who,* I hear you wondering, *does this guy think he is?*

Since you asked, let me start with the basics. I'm a straight, white, middle-aged guy from the suburbs, married with two kids. Kind of boring on paper, and maybe not that much more exciting in the flesh. Does that matter? If so, how much? To what extent are my preferences as a reader determined by the boxes I check on a census form?

You tell me.

I'm not going to deny the importance of race or gender or age or sexual orientation, claim that I've somehow managed to transcend my circumstances or achieve some Zen-like state of detachment whereby these facts about me no longer count. I went to graduate school in the 1980s, absorbed my share of literary theory and identity politics. I understand that I'm always reading as a straight white man, even when I think I'm not or wish I wasn't, and that some cultural reflexes are so deeply ingrained, we forget they're there. So it's entirely possible—inevitable, even—that my reactions and choices have been conditioned by unconscious biases, by *who I am* rather than by the objective qualities of the fiction I'm purporting to judge. If a critic suggests that this anthology reads as if it was assembled by a heterosexual Caucasian male born during the Kennedy administration, I would have to plead no contest and throw myself on the mercy of the court.

But that can't be the whole story. A reader has to be more than the sum of his or her demographically determined reflexes. Like most writers, I actually do possess a literary aesthetic, a set of well-defined preferences that I bring to the table whenever I encounter a work of fiction. To give you an idea of where these preferences originated and how they function in real life, it might be helpful for me to talk a little about two of the most significant American writers of the past thirty years, Raymond Carver and David Foster Wallace.

I first read Carver in 1983. I was a senior in college, a working-class kid at Yale, moving uneasily between what felt to me like two very different worlds. I knew I wanted to be a writer, but I was confused about my potential audience. Was I supposed to write for my professors, who seemed to think that Thomas Pynchon was the greatest living American novelist, or should I be writing for the people I'd grown up with, the ones whose stories I was hoping to someday tell? What about my parents, who hadn't gone to college and hadn't even heard of Pynchon? Where did they fit in? These were the kinds of questions that were floating, half-formulated, in my mind when I picked up Carver's first collection, *Will You Please Be Quiet, Please?*, and read the opening lines of the story "Fat":

> I am sitting over coffee and cigarets at my friend Rita's and I am telling her about it.
>   Here is what I tell her.
>   It is late of a slow Wednesday when Herb seats the fat man at my station.

The story is short and cryptic, part workplace anecdote, part fable, about a melancholy compulsive eater gorging himself at a diner and the strange compassion he elicits from his waitress, who is telling the story to an uncomprehending friend. Later that night, when the narrator's boyfriend—a heartless chef named Rudy—forces himself on her in bed, the narrator experiences an even deeper moment of connection with her overweight customer:

> I turn on my back and relax some, though it is against my will. But here is the thing. When he gets on me I suddenly feel I am fat. I feel I am terrifically fat, so fat that Rudy is a tiny thing and hardly there at all.

It's hard for me to describe the excitement I felt when I read that story, and the ones that followed. It felt like Carver was offering an answer to my personal dilemma, proving it was possible to write sophisticated literary fiction about ordinary people in language that was both authentic and accessible. When I learned that Carver had written some of his stories while working as a night-shift janitor at a hospital, I decided that I'd found my role model, a true working-class hero.

Carver taught creative writing at Syracuse University, so that was where I went to graduate school two years later. Unfortunately for me, he retired right before I arrived, but I was lucky enough to work instead with Tobias Wolff, at the time an up-and-coming short story writer (he hadn't yet published *This Boy's Life,* the now-classic book that would make him famous and revitalize the genre of literary memoir). Fairly or not, Carver and Wolff were both closely associated with a literary movement known at the time as minimalism, or dirty realism, a style that combined pared-down, plainspoken writing with hardscrabble subject matter. I had no doubt that it was the most exciting thing happening in American fiction and was thrilled to be so close to the center of that particular universe.

During my time in grad school, the Syracuse English Department also happened to be a hotbed of Marxist and post-structuralist literary theory—Althusser, Lacan, Derrida, and the like—the kind of dense, jargon-filled criticism that seemed like a foreign language even after it had been translated into English. It was mind-boggling and comical at the same time, a supposedly revolutionary form of discourse that would have been utterly incomprehensible to the working-class people it aimed, in some mysterious way, to liberate. My exposure to this arcane academic dialect only deepened my commitment to the clarity and concision I found in Carver's work, his willingness to speak in a language everyone could understand.

I left Syracuse after an eventful three years, equipped with a set of core beliefs about fiction that has remained with me ever since: I like stories written in plain, artful language about ordinary people. I'm wary of narrative experiments and excessive stylistic virtuosity, suspicious of writing that feels exclusive or elitist, targeted to readers with graduate degrees rather than the general public, whatever that means. I sometimes think of this as a blue-collar or populist aesthetic, but it's probably better to think of it as democratic, part of an American vernacular tradition that includes Twain and Crane, Cather and Hemingway, Hammett and Chandler, and stretches all the way back to Emerson ("The roots of what is great and high must still be the common life") and Whitman ("Nothing is better than simplicity").

For the most part, I think these ideals have served me pretty well. They've helped guide and inspire my own writing—both my choice of subject matter and the kinds of sentences I write—and focus my reading too. But they've also caused me to misunderstand, or at least underestimate, writers who work from a different set of assumptions and values.

This was certainly the case with David Foster Wallace, now widely considered the most important writer of his (my) generation. When Wallace published his magnum opus, *Infinite Jest,* in 1996—it was mostly written in Syracuse, by the way, that unlikeliest of literary meccas—I couldn't help but see him as the anti-Carver, long-winded and erudite, more familiar with tennis camps and elite colleges than diners and hospitals. I found it all too easy to dismiss him as a self-indulgent postmodernist, a throwback to 1970s maximalists like Pynchon and William Gaddis, the old guard whom I believed Carver had supplanted. In some ways I was right: Wallace shared the outsized ambition, intellectual confidence, and stylistic boldness of his predecessors, along with their willingness to write exhausting, unapologetically cerebral novels that were vehicles for ideas rather than stories, riffs rather than characters. Unlike a lot of readers, I was irritated rather than charmed by the sprawling footnotes—Wallace's refusal to let you forget his presence (or his genius) for even a page or two. To my mind, his postmodern pyrotechnics were the fictional equivalent of a rock-god guitar solo that goes on for so long, you can't even remember what song you're listening to; all you can do is shake your head in weary, worshipful amazement. The Carver school was closer to indie rock, I thought, the songs tight and unpretentious, the line between the musicians and fans so blurry it sometimes vanished altogether.

It took me a long time to get past these objections and see that Wallace wasn't simply picking up where Pynchon and Gaddis had left off. It was the brilliant and wide-ranging essays in *A Supposedly Fun Thing I'll Never Do Again* that changed my mind, helped me understand that Wallace wasn't really a fiction writer in the traditional sense. Like Norman Mailer, he was more of a free-floating intelligence, a cultural observer whose methods and obsessions enabled him to notice things that were invisible to the rest of us and to diagnose the peculiar sickness of the age. No matter what he was writing—story, essay, novel—he was engaged in the same overarching project, attempting to document and embody a crisis in postmodern consciousness, the human personality breaking down under the pressure of too much information. Yes, he was guilty of literary excess, but the excess wasn't really superfluous; it was precisely the point. I felt a little stupid for missing that.

So what does all this have to do with *The Best American Short Stories 2012*? Less than I expected, actually. I've read a lot of short fiction over the past several months, and one thing I've learned is that the debate that seemed so important to me fifteen or twenty years ago —minimalism versus maximalism, populism versus elitism, realism versus experimentalism, Carver versus Wallace, however you want to frame it—just isn't that big an issue anymore. As crucial as they are in my own personal narrative, neither Raymond Carver nor David Foster Wallace seemed to cast much of a shadow over this year's pool of stories. You might sense a vague kinship with Wallace in George Saunders's poignant and very funny "Tenth of December" or catch the homage to Carver in Nathan Englander's provocative "What We Talk About When We Talk About Anne Frank," but that's about it. This makes sense, I guess: time passes, the culture moves on, tastes evolve. Carver and Wallace are gone, both way before their time, and death has made them seem even more distinctive somehow, more stubbornly themselves, one of a kind and irreplaceable, rather than leaders of rival schools of fiction.

If there's a single writer who looms over this year's collection —over the art of the short story as it's practiced in North America right now—it would have to be Alice Munro. Munro is an acknowledged master, of course—her reputation has been growing steadily for decades—but she still hasn't gotten enough credit for the way she's expanded our sense of what stories can do and how they might be written. "Axis," the story included here, feels both typical of her work and quietly remarkable—typical in its choice of subject matter (rural Canadian girls hoping to escape their drab small-town lives) and remarkable for its combination of amplitude and compression, its ability to encompass multiple decades and points of view in a handful of tightly focused scenes. Edith Pearlman's creepy and powerful "Honeydew" has a similar complexity—it's composed of three intricately braided perspectives—as does Saunders's "Tenth of December," the two-sided chronicle of a chance encounter between a lonely boy and a sick man, both of whose inner lives are fully accessible to the reader.

When I was in graduate school—not that long ago, I swear —it was considered highly unorthodox for a story to be written like this. Out of curiosity, I looked back at the *Best American Short Stories 1986*, edited by none other than Raymond Carver—it's an amazing collection, a snapshot of an unusually rich moment in American fiction, with stellar contributions by Richard Ford, Amy Hempel, and Mona Simpson, among others—and confirmed my suspicion: there's not a single story in the anthology that switches its point of view. It just wasn't done, at least not in the literary mainstream: back then, you had your main character, and you had your central event or situation, and that was that. The fact that it's no longer considered risky, or even especially noteworthy, to tell a story from multiple perspectives—or to range freely across the expanse of a character's life, as Julie Otsuka does in her haunting "Diem Perdidi"—owes a lot to Munro's formal daring, her insistence on smuggling the full range of novelistic techniques into the writing of her short fiction, and the influence she's had on her contemporaries.

But maybe that's just inside baseball, gossip for the MFA crowd. Form and technique matter, of course, but we read fiction to satisfy a more basic need—to imagine our way into other lives, to explore characters and situations that tell us something new about the world, and maybe about ourselves, or to remind us of something important that we may have forgotten. If that's what you're looking for, I humbly suggest that you've opened the right book.

As always, this year's stories come from prestigious publications (*The New Yorker, The Paris Review, Tin House*) as well as obscure ones (at least to me) such as *Fifth Wednesday Journal* and *New Ohio Review;* oddly enough, two come from a single issue of a magazine called *Hobart.* You'll find work from some of our finest writers—Mary Gaitskill, Kate Walbert, Steven Millhauser, and Jennifer Haigh, among others—and discover new voices such as Taiye Selasi, Taylor Antrim, Adam Wilson, and Mike Meginnis. You'll enounter bizarre scenarios—please check out "Beautiful Monsters" by Eric Puchner and "Volcano" by Lawrence Osborne—as well as a variety of intriguing, sometimes challenging characters: the homeless drunk trying to be a good dad in Jess Walter's "Anything Helps"; a black woman who teaches structural engineering at an obscure technical college in Roxane Gay's "North Country"; a young boy jealous of his dying brother in Sharon Solwitz's "Alive"; a lesbian single mom who works at Home Depot in Carol Anshaw's "The Last Speaker of the Language"; and a sewage inspector who wanders into dangerous moral territory in Angela Pneuman's "Occupational Hazard." Some of these stories are funny and some are heartbreaking—my own personal favorites somehow manage to be both at once—while others are angry or disturbing. There are a couple of sexy ones too, though fewer than I might have expected. But all of them took me somewhere I didn't expect to go and jolted me into that state of heightened alertness and emotional receptivity that's one of the great rewards of reading good fiction.

Inevitably, I had to leave out some stories I really enjoyed and admired, and I'm sorry about that. There were just so many good ones to choose from, so many different ways to envision the final list. There will undoubtedly be critics who disagree with my selections, skeptics who think I was the wrong person for the job or believe that they could have chosen more wisely. To them I say, with all due respect, I'm sure your pizza would be pretty tasty, and possibly even delicious, but mine is clearly the best.

It says so right on the box.

TOM PERROTTA

*The Best*
AMERICAN
SHORT
STORIES
2012

CAROL ANSHAW

# The Last Speaker of the Language

FROM *New Ohio Review*

ALL *RIGHT*. HERE we go.

Darlyn teeters high on a swayback wooden ladder she has
dragged in from her mother's garage. From here she can reach
around blindly on top of the kitchen cabinets. She has struck pay
dirt—a tidy arrangement of small, flat bottles. She doesn't have to
look to know they will all be pints of Five O'Clock Vodka.

She backs down the ladder, finds a grocery bag, goes back up,
and tosses in every bottle she can reach. Then she moves the ladder farther along the way and clears out the bottles above those
cabinets. She pours the liquor down the drain in the sink. Five
O'Clock is not for the amateur drinker. When she has the presence of mind, Darlyn's mother filters it through a Brita, then
mixes it with lime juice and ice and ginger ale, her version of a
Suffering Bastard. After a while, though, she drops the lime and
the niceties and in the end skips even the glass.

All this poking around her mother's hiding places and finding
a few handles of Five O'Clock in the bottom of the laundry basket
and tidying up a little but not dealing with a huge meal-moth situation in the pantry takes maybe an hour, but when she is done
her mother is still passed out on the floor of the bathroom. Darlyn needs to use the toilet, which her mother is sort of propped
against, like a bad doll. She takes her by an arm and a leg, and
pulls her sideways by her sweatshirt over a ways toward the wall,
lifts her head onto a folded towel. Then, while she is sitting on
the toilet, she sinks into the special sorrow of peeing while your

mother is out cold on the floor next to you. There are probably heavy drinking cultures, she thinks—maybe in rural eastern Europe—where they have a specific word for this emotion.

She leaves Jackie where she lies. She will ask Russ to go over later, when their mother will be more wakeable. He can put her through a home-style Valium detox they use to avoid the punishments of the emergency room. Jackie has a ton of Valium, also pain pills—jumbo scrips from a collection of sketchy doctors around the city. In the pursuit of euphoria and numbness, she is a busy and resourceful person. At one point, she even had money to fund her downfall, a surprise inheritance from an aunt, almost all of it gone in just a few years to the Five O'Clock company, and in the early, flush days of her roll, to the Stolichnaya family. Also to phone scammers who preyed on her until Darlyn got her mother's number changed, twice. Now Jackie drinks without her phone friends and their tantalizing investments. If she wants bad company, she has to go out for it.

Darlyn does not have enough money to support her mother. This is a problem that weighs on her, what will happen when Jackie runs out. And so she makes these futile gestures toward getting her to sober up, maybe even get a job. Jackie is only in her late sixties. Early on she was a bookkeeper, but of course that's a computerized business now. Done in offices where no one chain-smokes.

Lake is making dinner. At seven she was queen of the Easy-Bake Oven. At ten she is queen of the microwave. When she turns twelve, she will get to use the stove without supervision. Darlyn sees from the empty cartons on the counter that tonight it's going to be Señora Garcia's Enchiladas and Rice. Lake is sliding the contents of two black plastic trays onto actual plates, then sprinkling chopped cilantro over the small, dark, oily masses, so it won't be obvious that dinner is an off-brand frozen entrée. Then she uses her frosting funnel to squeeze a swirl of sour cream onto the rims of the plates. Lake watches a lot of Food Network programming and is big into side dollops and drizzles and sometimes, like tonight, decorative foams.

"Wow, this looks so good," Darlyn says, and hopes she sounds sincere.

Lake is the name her daughter chose for herself last year. She wasn't happy with Mary. Darlyn's thinking was to give her the plainest name possible. She herself has suffered her whole life with one that makes anyone using it sound like they're calling over a truckstop waitress. It just never occurred to her that she was allowed to change it. So, good for Mary. Good for Lake.

They sit across the breakfast bar from each other.

"Mmm, this green—"

"Lemon-avocado foam," Lake says in a grave way accompanied by a small frown of concentration, then tastes some, judging.

"Listen. We're pulling the plug on the phone tonight. Your Uncle Russ is helping me with Grandma, and at some point in the middle of the night he's going to throw up his hands and call here for help. I have to open the store tomorrow so I have no time for your grandmother's monkey business. I need solid sleep."

"Is she going to be all right?" For no reason Darlyn can see, Lake is crazy about her grandmother.

"Oh, I can't imagine that, but I don't want you ruining your childhood worrying about her."

"Can I cook this weekend?"

"I'm working Saturday while you and your Uncle Russ are at *Wicked*. But Sunday I'm all yours. What're you going to make?"

"Arctic char with a crust of crushed macadamia nuts and ancho chilies."

"Wow."

"You'll take me to Trader Joe's for my ingredients?"

"Sure." Because the child she wound up with is Lake, single parenthood is turning out to be the easiest part of Darlyn's life.

At 2:24 A.M., the phone starts ringing. Darlyn forgot to pull the plug.

"Fuck." She gets up, yanks the cord from the wall, then falls back into bed.

"That's going right into your locker," she tells Brad Wiggins first thing Friday morning in reference to his glitter T-shirt. She hands him an orange Home Depot polo. "You got the word about pushing the Butterscotch Heather stain-resistant nylon? We've got a big overstock situation. Big."

"The thing is, it's really a total violation of my professional ethics to put that crap carpet in a client's home."

"You don't have clients. *We* have customers. This is Home Depot, not the Mart. You're just a beginning gay guy, not a cutting-edge Manhattan decorator." She can say stuff like this, being technically queer herself.

Her cell has been ringing in her pocket since she got to work. It's Russ. When she can duck into the break room, she calls him back.

"How was she when you got there?"

"Well, that's the thing. That's why I've been calling you *seven hundred* times. She wasn't home when I got there and I still haven't been able to find her."

"You went to Umpire's?"

"And Corey's."

Darlyn fishes around for an idea on her mother's whereabouts, but comes up blank. "We'll just have to wait until she calls. And hope she hasn't gotten hold of a new credit card."

"Looking particularly minxy today, D."

This is Norm Homer, head of Décor and Darlyn's immediate supervisor. ("Hey dude," Brad Wiggins likes to say, when Norm is not around, "get a real last name.")

What is minxy even? He appears to have no awareness at all of workplace sexual harassment. Although he is in his fifties, Norm still lives with his parents. For the employee picnic last summer, his big idea—for the five seconds until it got shot down—was a kissing booth to raise money for a cure for something. Darlyn and the cashiers were supposed to take turns, charging five dollars a kiss. So what is she going to do, report him and get him fired so he can sit home with his parents, bewildered? Plus she doesn't want to raise a ruckus. She is lucky to have this job. Her two closest friends plus her brother have all lost theirs. They are totally demoralized. They are in a private prison, the lockdown of failure.

The woman in the shower with Darlyn is married. The shower is in the bathroom of Room 17 at the Diplomat Motel up on Lincoln. No one in the diplomatic service of any country has ever stayed there.

Darlyn is too in love with this woman. Christy, this is the woman's name. She holds no place in Darlyn's life, and Darlyn holds no place in hers. Christy is never going to leave her husband. What she and Darlyn have is totally compartmentalized. This particular compartment is an hour and fifteen minutes between Darlyn leaving work and having to pick up Lake at swim practice. This hugely circumscribed affair is the reason she thinks of herself at the moment as only technically queer. She would like to be a lot queerer, but that's not happening.

"You know what I imagine as I go to sleep?" Christy is very soapy at the moment, kissing along Darlyn's hairline, the top of her ear. She always kisses Darlyn in such a gentle, specific way, as though she can't believe how lucky she is to be able to do this, to have Darlyn. "I imagine us on vacation in Spain. It's sunny and hot in the street outside, but we're in a room with shutters and it's cool as can be. We're in bed planning where to go for dinner, what we're going to wear."

Darlyn doesn't say anything. Her own fantasy is that they go grocery shopping together. As unlikely as the vacation in Spain.

Her attraction to Christy isn't just about the sex, or even just about love. It's also about life being so much bigger than Darlyn previously thought, a bigness just out of reach.

It's almost Lake's bedtime and she is perched at the front of her chair, deep into whatever's happening on the desktop screen, moving the mouse around as fast as a real one. She smells of chlorine. Sometimes Darlyn worries that the municipal pool is half chlorine, half toddler pee.

"What're you doing?"

"Playing Palomino."

In Palomino Playland, horse avatars have adventures in an imaginary land of mountains and forests, as opposed to a bungalow neighborhood on the northwest side of Chicago. The Palomino site is designed to appeal to preteen girls. Darlyn worries that her daughter is the only ten-year-old playing. That all the other horses—Wind Warrior and Light Beam and especially Old Red—are, behind the Internet scrim, pedophiles in crusty sweats. She has laid down the law: no meeting up with anyone Lake meets online. Darlyn's fears of the Web are huge.

"I forgot to tell you. While you were in the basement? Grandma called."

"How'd she sound?" Darlyn hates the answer to this question before she even hears it. Whatever, it will mean calling in for a personal day tomorrow, Saturday, the biggest day of the week at the Depot—the day management especially hates absenteeism—then wasting that day rescuing Jackie.

"She sounded really really happy. She's going to take me to Disney World. She wants you to call. I wrote down the number."

"This is the worst thing about America," Darlyn tells her brother as she drives down the Skyway into Indiana on Saturday morning. He is wedged into the passenger seat of her old Civic. His thigh overlaps the emergency brake and part of the space Darlyn needs to shift gears. "That they give fresh, new credit cards to total drunks."

"No, the worst thing about America," Russ says, "is that they don't have a padded cell you can put people like Ma into. For like six months, maybe a year. Until they get their mind right. They got rid of all the padded cells. Big mistake."

"That's it, I bet! It looks like a giant ship!" Lake is excited in the back seat. As though this is a fun family expedition. She is such a wonderful person even at ten that she hasn't once complained that rescuing her grandmother means missing *Wicked*, which she has been delirious about for weeks. Darlyn is not happy that Lake is along for this little intervention, but she couldn't find a sitter on short notice.

Early on, back when Indiana required gambling to be offshore, the casino *was* a fake ship. The gangplank would be hauled up and the casino would move into the harbor—that is, about a foot from the dock. You couldn't get on when it was "at sea." You had to wait an hour until it "came back to port." Now the law is more lenient and the ship disguise pretty much forgotten and gamblers can just come and go as they please.

Jackie isn't in the casino. She is in the hotel, where the management has apparently provided her with a complimentary room. Darlyn finds this out from the flirty woman at the concierge desk, who got her job in spite of a snake tattoo peeking out from under the white cuff of her shirt. Darlyn doesn't flirt back, not even a little. She has plenty enough aching sorrow without going under that cuff.

On the seventh floor of the hotel, she holds Lake's hand while Russ knocks on the door. Which Jackie throws open as though there's a big party inside and she's the hostess. A heavy smell of dead smoke rolls out from inside. Like a battleground the morning after the war. Jackie is wearing an outfit blaring color and shine, with little beaded tassels on the sleeves. She's only a little drunk, a lull in her bender.

"I don't think I've seen this blouse before." Darlyn tugs at one of the tassels.

"I got it downstairs. They have some really nice shops. Come in everybody. Oh, Mary sweetie, nice of your mother to bring you."

"Lake," Lake corrects her.

"Have some fruit, honey." Like she's Lady Bountiful. Like she's a nutritionist. She waves at a giant basket on the table, exotic fruits nestled in green excelsior, an orchard from another planet. "The fruit comes with the room. And the room is *comped*."

"Mangosteen," Lake says, picking something out of the basket, studying it. Then something else. "Dragonfruit."

Darlyn doesn't like that her mother is now using vocabulary like "comped." "How did you even get out here?" Darlyn asks.

"I took the gambler bus from Broadway and Lawrence. It's all old Vietnamese guys and me. Listen, I made a lot of money last night." She opens her purse on the dresser and pulls out four thick, banded packets of hundred-dollar bills. "They want me to come back down and play in the Winner's Circle. It's a special honor."

"They want their money back is all," Russ says. "They'd club you to death in the parking lot except it would be bad publicity. So they have to get you to lose it."

Darlyn only realizes the room is a suite when an old guy in his underwear comes through a doorway off to the side. He's in a wheelchair.

"Hey everybody," he says, rubbing his hair with the heel of one hand, waking himself up, dislodging dandruff onto his shoulder. "Anyone up for brunch?"

"This is Billy," Jackie says. "A new friend."

"A sleepover friend," Lake helps her.

"Whoa! This gentleman will be leaving immediately." Russ grabs the handles on the back of the wheelchair and pushes it into the hallway. "Somebody get him his clothes. We're done here. We're all going home, Ma. Darlyn will bring the car around."

On the way back, they make a pit stop for cheap underwear at the outlet mall, which is only a short ways from the casino ship, both situated in the shadow of a nuclear reactor.

Russ waits in the car with Jackie, who makes a big show of blowing her smoke out the window to keep the in-car environment healthy.

"I love when we can all get together like this," she says as Darlyn and Lake climb out and head for the Jockey outlet.

The mall is paved with concrete, featureless except for a tragic circus-themed Sno-Cone stand and two little bucking-bronco rides by the restrooms. Inside, the stores all have the same smell, what Darlyn thinks of as "Third World Factory." The salespeople have a shy, unsure look, as though they have been hired from an employee outlet.

"These are cool," Lake says, holding up some totally unsuitable underpants.

"You can have those later. When you're twenty-seven."

Jackie's winnings add up to a little over $40,000; once again a surprise bundle of money has dropped down on her. This time, Darlyn and Russ are taking charge. At home, they sit side by side in front of the computer, looking over CD rates on bank websites. Darlyn spots a new site on the browser's Favorites menu. Tiddly Winkles. She can't remember seeing Lake playing this, but how could it not be a molestation hotbed?

"One percent doesn't seem that great," Russ says. They have little experience dealing with large chunks of cash. A few years back, before they found out Jackie was just running through the windfall from her Aunt Toots, before they knew about the bogus brokers, when they still believed Jackie's malarkey about 75 percent returns or whatever, they thought their mother was an investment genius. Hahahahahahahaha.

"The way she spends, this won't last her six months, even factoring in the interest." Darlyn gets depressed just saying these words. Russ tries to help.

"Maybe we should take her back out to the ship. I mean it could be she's just naturally lucky and we could take her out there every few months and build her account back up."

It is thinking like this that has kept Russ from finding success in the real world.

Now he says, "I'm tired of money. It's such a boring problem, worrying about it. I hate money and education and skills. I really hate skills."

"Skill sets," Darlyn says. "I especially hate those."

The two of them, how they put it is they sort of forgot to go to college. It didn't seem necessary at the time. They both got good enough jobs without going to that much trouble. They hadn't factored in a big recession and a whole long line of newer, younger people with degrees, eager to work for a pittance.

Lake puts two bags of buckwheat flour in the cart. She has with her a list of ingredients for supper, also for her big dessert recipe: Caramel-Cashew-Coconut Cobbler topped with pineapple sorbet. She is sure she is going to win the dessert division of America's Top Junior Chefs, also that she will be able to take Darlyn on a vacation to Pittsburgh in March for the finals. Darlyn, who has already spent a number of hours supervising Lake's test-baking of this item, now has an image in place, of using up a week of her vacation to sit on a folding chair between overbearing mothers of other contestants, in the ballroom of the Pittsburgh Sheraton, rooting for a cobbler. She knows it's bad to have a complaint about the world's most wonderful child, but it would have been so great if Lake was interested in, say, tango, or European architecture. She was prepared for a few genetic wild cards, though, having used an anonymous sperm donor (how she thinks of the person with whom she had a two-night stand during the death throes of her heterosexuality).

In the checkout line, Darlyn's phone pings. A text from her mother: WHERES MY MONEY¿¿

Some girls who hang out at Umpire's have taught Jackie how to text. Apparently she accidentally hit some Spanish option key.

In response to the question: DELETE THIS THREAD? Darlyn presses YES.

As if it was that easy.

*

At the bank on Monday, the receptionist jumps a little when she looks up and sees them waiting. A response to Russ; this happens. Darlyn tells the woman they want to buy a CD.

"I'm going to need to see some identification," the woman says.

This gets Darlyn's hackles right up. "Why do you need identification when *we're* giving the money to *you?*"

"I'm still going to need to see some identification."

Darlyn nods toward the woman's Jurassic-era beige computer. "Are you hooked up there with Interpol?"

A message is sent, maybe through one of those under-the-counter robbery buzzers. A financial planner guy comes out to see what's up. He turns out to be a reasonable guy, and within the hour they are done, having invested the $40,000 in something better than a CD, a "portfolio" of three mutual funds. Jackie will get small, regular dividends.

"And that's all she's getting," Darlyn says. "The money stays in there, growing."

Russ says, "Right. For when she's still a drunk, but also nonambulatory and demented." Before he was laid off (in truth, probably not having much to do with the recession; apparently he frightened some of the patients), Russ was a certified nursing assistant in a retirement home. He has no illusions about old age. He belongs to a society that will come around when he decides it's time, put a hood over his head, and fill it with helium. Adios.

"I'm seeing rolls of Prairie Rust, rolls of Williamsburg Blue going out off the loading dock. What I'm not seeing is Butterscotch Heather."

Darlyn hates being lectured by Norm. She stares at his *Manager* name tag to avoid eye contact. Eye contact is something she hopes never to have with him.

Her cell starts ringing in the pocket of her Depot apron. The ringtone she has for Christy is Kelly Clarkson singing "The Trouble with Love Is." This song plays with mind-shredding frequency over the store's sound system and so the ring goes unnoticed in the ambient din. The system they have is Darlyn opens the phone inside her pocket so Christy knows she's there. Then Darlyn goes into the deserted area of the stockroom where off-season merchandise is stored. Today she sits between two pallets of antifreeze.

"Here's the saddest thing." Christy is calling from the Bluetooth inside her Lexus. "It was on NPR." (Christy lives in the NPR-listener, Lexus-driver demographic.) "This woman just died. She was the last speaker of her language. Bo. That was the language. The sad part was when the second-to-last speaker of Bo died four years before. So for her last four years, this woman had no one in the world she could talk with."

"I don't think that's the saddest thing. I think the saddest thing is me being in love with you."

"Don't say that."

"You're the only one I can speak Bo with."

Between their furtive assignations, Darlyn lives her real life with all its little pieces locking into one another, a seemingly complete picture. But this is an illusion. Lift up one of the pieces and you'd be looking into an entire universe tumbling with color and light. Sometimes Darlyn will be at work, or waiting to pick up Lake after swim practice, and a whiff of something Christy-like—floral and potent—will come in through the window, and Darlyn's heart will be torn suddenly by cruel and giant hands. She dreams vividly, then can't call up the dreams on waking, but carries through the day their emotional tone, an echo from the blackout chasm of Darlyn's free fall. She can hear her soft scream as she tumbles down again and again. This is the harrowing/fabulous form in which love has come to her.

"It's so shiny." The customer is small, frail, soft-spoken. Her whole manner begs for a little bullying.

"That's the Stain Sergeant coating. You'll never have to worry, even about chocolate, or red wine. It'll all wipe right off." Darlyn envisions oppressed Chinese workers in Shanghai stirring giant, toxic vats of Stain Sergeant.

"Are you sure this is a neutral shade?"

Darlyn would ordinarily answer this by rote, telling her that butterscotch is the new gray. Today, though, she stops to pour some good into the cosmic karma pool, so maybe she can ladle some out later. Something good like Christy getting out of her lousy marriage.

"You know, on second thought, I think it might be a little too buttery," she tells the woman, envisioning the huge bolts of But-

terscotch Heather gathering dust at the back of the carpet warehouse. She presses on, though. "I'm thinking maybe you're right
about the blue-gray. And skip the Stain Sergeant. You don't want
the shine, and you can always have the blue-gray washed. It's cotton."

"I want more." This, of course, is Darlyn, at the Diplomat, with
Christy. This is the first time they have been here in time for the 9
to 11 A.M. Early Bird Special. A long silence has settled on them,
but gently, like fog. They don't really have time for long silences,
or lingering moments. Darlyn rushed over here in the middle of a
work morning, something unprecedented in the two years they've
been doing this, since the day Christy came slumming into the
Depot because it was the only place she could think of where she
might get grass-green indoor-outdoor carpeting. Her son is a soccer nut and wanted this for his bedroom. Christy has never asked
for this sort of emergency meeting before. Darlyn thinks maybe
it's a signal.

"You just *think* you want more," Christy says. She is kneeling on
the floor, the top half of her face-down across the mattress, only
her face isn't really down, it's turned toward Darlyn. Most of their
conversations take place naked and in positions they can't remember having gotten themselves into—post-sex exhaustion positions.
"But if we moved out of this space, into real life, two tons of rubble
would come crashing down on us."

"I've already thought about the rubble. I don't care." The silence that follows is so long Darlyn is sure she was wrong about
today being different, that the conversation has dead-ended in exactly the same place it always does. She is reaching for her bra, to
get dressed and going, when Christy says,

"Well, okay then. Let's do it."

"Just like that?" Something invisible begins to beat against Darlyn's chest with a mallet, a mallet wrapped in a towel, but it still
hurts in a sensational way. Sensational. The most exquisite anguish
imaginable.

Afterward, on her way in from the parking lot, she fist-bumps
Terri, who runs the hot-dog cart at the Depot's north entrance.
Two dollars a dog. She sells about a billion a day. She makes a lot
more money than people think.

"What're you so happy about?" Terri opens the metal lid of her cart, letting the steam of mysterious meat and soft bread billow up between them. "You want one? On the house?"

"I'm in love" is Darlyn's reply to the hot-dog offer. The first time she has told anyone. It feels like jumping off a cliff in a hang glider, something she actually used to do in her twenties, before she had Lake to be responsible for.

Gary the Husband isn't who Darlyn expected. Of course she only has about fifteen minutes for really focused expectation, the minutes since getting a call from Christy, totally flipped out, saying, "I tried to stop him, but—" Darlyn knows Gary runs marathons and so she has formed an image of someone small and thin, like those Kenyan runners, only white and a neurologist. But when he shows up just before midnight, he turns out to be stocky, with a big vein popping in and out along the side of his neck. They stand at the front door. She has told Lake to stay in her room, that she will explain later, but not to be afraid. And Darlyn finds she's not afraid either, even though right away he gets red and starts shouting. All Darlyn hears is blahblah-fuckingfreak-blahblah-lesbohomewrecker. It doesn't matter what he says. It's all just air coming out of a tire going flat. All she can feel is elation. His standing here means Christy didn't lose her nerve; she told him and hung tough. Their plan is fragile, but it's Friday, a whole day after they made it, and the plan is still alive.

Gary has begun poking his index finger into Darlyn's chest to make his big points. She puts her hand up to stop this, which leaves him poking her palm. Much better. She is only waiting for her brother to show up and apply a little reasonability to the situation. Russ is very good for this purpose. He is actually hopelessly out of shape, but no one tests that fact, given that he could kill you just by falling on you.

"I'm already there," he told her on the phone. And now, over Gary's shoulder she can see Russ getting out of a cab, paying the driver slowly, with coins from his change purse. And then he is behind Gary, tapping him on the shoulder and saying, "I think this conversation has come to an end." Russ knows some judo tricks from his bouncer days. One of his hands wraps over Gary's shoulder, the other pinches a nerve at the base of Gary's thick neck, causing him to wince and lock his teeth. "No more poking or shouting," Russ tells him, and Gary's response is something like "Kghhgk."

Sunday is the longest day of this year. Russ is nailing a plywood ramp over the steps to Jackie's side door. Lake is inside making everyone Gruyère omelets. Jackie and Billy's presence in the kitchen probably can't be fully counted as supervision, but they *are* adults, sort of. The omelets have to be eaten sequentially as Jackie has only one usable frying pan; the others, veterans of much inebriated cooking, look as though they've been smelted in a forge. When Russ stands up and rubs the small of his back, he's kind of alarmingly flushed with the effort. "Do you think you could talk to her, you know, about no more quickie marriages? I feel one coming on."

Darlyn, who measured and cut the plywood and brought it over, says, "The wheelchair doesn't seem to be an obstacle. It might even be a feature. She says the best part is being able to park right in front of any store. That's the best part." Through the open window she can hear her mother and Billy discussing the almost certain guilt of the latest Tot Mom on *Nancy Grace,* a show they both keep up with. The rhythms of the conversation have a definite in-the-bag quality.

"I'm going to have to get Lake out of the cocktail lounge pretty soon."

But then any urgency to progress to whatever comes next vanishes, replaced by a delicious stillness. Darlyn sets her omelet plate on the windowsill and picks up an open box of nails and smells inside. Like spring, wet and elemental.

"You're not even listening to me, are you?" Russ says after saying something she didn't listen to. "You're not receiving outside information at the moment. You think this romance is going to change your life. But it won't."

"Why are you being mean?"

"I'm not. I'm trying to save you from heartbreak when she misses the Lexus or can't get custody of her kids, when that pricky little husband starts fighting her with all his money, and she just caves."

"Of course she will. You think I don't know that?" Darlyn says, then lowers her voice. "It's just about—even for a day—being this purely happy. Like, happy to be a carbon-based life form."

Russ doesn't say anything. Then Darlyn doesn't say anything. They just stand in the light haze of thirdhand cigarette smoke drifting out through the window screen until the silence is suddenly cut with the sparky flap of cards being shuffled and Billy telling Lake, "The idea is to go higher than the dealer without going over twenty-one."

## *Pilgrim Life*

FROM *American Short Fiction*

BY THURSDAY I STILL hadn't said word one about the accident. My roommate Rand would be the guy, and this would be the moment: he and I sitting on our narrow balcony, legs shot through the railings, nighttime, glittery San Francisco laid out below us. September 22, 1999. "Know what Hardar Jumpiche says about giving away good feelings?" he asked.

Took me a second to realize who he meant: the author of *Today's the Day*. That and *Buddhism for Dummies* had appeared on the back of the toilet after Rand sold his startup to WestLab. The incubator's stock had since been on a tear—up 6 percent this month—which had left Rand worth, more or less, $12 million. Twelve *mill*-ion. *Twelve* million. It was like trying to speak French. Rand of the Quiksilver backpack, the weed habit, the SAE beer-opener key chain.

"Shed the ego and feel what's left," Rand said.

*Tell him.*

But I'd just burned my mouth on a molten marijuana brownie, so I didn't—and maybe, I suddenly thought, *don't*. The rudiments of a different plan came together as I stood to collect that backpack from where it lay on the floor of the apartment.

"Breathe out the ego and breathe in, what is it . . . ?" Rand asked when I returned to the balcony. He sat bolt upright, a palm open on each knee—a fair approximation of Jumpiche's author photo.

I'd read a few pages of *Today's the Day* in the bathroom. "Charity," I said, tonguing the stinging roof of my mouth, building out my idea. A loan was too humiliating; Rand had been carrying the rent since July. But what about an *investment?* "You said 3rdBase is sitting on some dough? Research and development?"

"Charity," Rand repeated, pondering the word.

Rand had run down the problem for me a few nights before: Two million in a Wells Fargo money market doing no one any good. WestLab had delivered the funding, earmarked for R&D, just as Rand's ideas guy, Stanford summa cum laude, went missing on what was supposed to be a weeklong sex vacation to the Philippines. Rand needed to phone somebody—the embassy?—but just as pressing, in his view, was spending that two million. WestLab wanted new ideas by the week. Baby startups like 3rdBase had to shovel money out the door. "Shows people you're serious," Rand had told me.

"What's the latest with your mom?" he asked me now. "Home from the hospital?"

I didn't want to talk about it. "Listen." I conjured a pitch: the *Wine Gazette* could create a subscription site. "Wholesalers, restaurant and retail buyers. Chomping at the bit to get access to our wine ratings. Nothing to get it started. A few hundred thousand." What I was looking for in his backpack was his laptop, to which we could connect the DSL cable and perform some online banking transactions. What I found, quaintly, was a company checkbook and a pen.

"You don't want to talk about it. Totally understand. Let the thoughts go and feel what's left," Rand said.

I meditated with him a moment, both of us sitting there inhaling and exhaling like monks. The colors in our two-bedroom soaked and bleared. I'd eaten two brownies. I would spend the night huddled under the covers, wondering if I'd ever see Claire again, recalling the man she'd hit, his puppet legs, his body jackknifed around a boulder. The accident.

*Tell him.*

Below us the J Church shrieked along its rails, following its oxbow turn. The apartment's air tasted lightly of cocoa and sugar —brownie mix. The plastic checkbook cover felt like buttery calfskin. "Mom's depressed," I said, because this was the latest, via voicemail, from my brother.

"She'll make it."

"Could be big," I said. "The Wine Gazette dot-com. And what do you say about money?"

"Speaking of—you never told me how you and Claire made out at Stateline."

His startup's logo appeared in the check's upper-left corner, a miniature Louisville Slugger knocking the leather off a baseball. I was going to drop his shovel-it-out-the-door line, but at the last minute changed course: "Like a shark, you said. You said this to me during Shark Week."

Sort of heartless, mentioning Shark Week: his sister was that pro surfer who'd lost her arm to a tiger shark in Maui two years before. She was an inspiration, still competing, still winning, but Rand had taken the incident hard. Whenever the Discovery Channel rolled out the great whites for a ratings boost, he logged sick days in front of the TV, stoned and weeping.

He gathered his hands into his lap; his frame shook with bottled feeling. I felt bad. Rand was nice to me. The rent. The parties he invited me to. He was, face it, the reason I had a social life, the reason I met Claire. He genuinely wanted to know about Mom's cancer. But Rand's money would get Claire the best lawyer in San Francisco, get her to return my phone calls, vanquish my recalcitrant guilt. How much? I closed my eyes and let a number take shape in the ether. I made the check out to myself and handed him the pen.

A check! A $500,000 check! My degree in comp lit told me it was just one more unreliable signifier along a chain of Late Capitalist meanings, but when I folded the slip of paper into a dart-shaped airplane, then an origami swan, then gave myself a nasty cut on its edge the next morning, it felt like the thing itself: as intrinsically precious as buried gold.

Ten A.M. sharp and I was stepping through the door at the *Gazette,* where I earned $23,000 a year as an assistant editor with zero health insurance. Just a half-hour earlier, in the shower, I'd doubled down on my plan: the *Gazette* really did need a pay site, so why not play rainmaker for the magazine, secure a raise, maybe a Kaiser Permanente card, *and* get Claire the best lawyer in town? Handle this right, I told myself, striding through the railcar space lined with scalloped wine racks, hearing my boss, the associate publisher, at his desk, behind his pair of folding Chinese screens. Handle this right, I told myself, and in three months that guy Claire hit might still be in a coma, and no way would we be together, but my guilt over making a bad situation worse would fade, and I'd be free to achieve dharma, *bodhicitta*, serenity—one of those versions of paradise in Rand's books.

"Big news," I said, sliding the check out of my wallet and placing it on Marv's keyboard. My boss gave me an arrowed look. Breakfast for him was three boiled eggs and a chocolate creatine shake —lunch was a bucket of lo mein from the joint down the street —but the retrovirals he popped like breath mints kept the meat off of him. His face was cadaverous; I could pinch his cheekbones between my fingers.

I pointed at the well-creased check, but he wouldn't look at it. "Know a Detective Sanchez?" he asked.

"Who?"

"South Lake Tahoe Police Department. Wants your phone number. You're, apparently, unlisted."

"Did you give it to him?"

"I said I wanted to speak to you first."

"Go ahead. I'm no lawyer, but how's the guy in the passenger seat guilty of anything?"

"You're no lawyer."

The words had just dropped out of my mouth. *Passenger seat.*

"Lewis, have you committed a crime?"

"Marv, do you want the whole sordid story?"

"Jesus, no."

Marv reported so many details about his life, major and minor —how he liked to unwind in the evenings (low-volume porn on his plasma, the *Wall Street Journal,* a tumbler of pizza wine), his HIV status, what he ate for breakfast every day, his abusive father, the electrician he'd fucked on Saturday night. Were we friends? I wanted us to be—he was the age my father would be if he'd lived past twenty-five (I never knew the man)—but I got the queasy sense he'd tell this stuff to anyone he shared an office with.

"You remember Claire, right?" I asked him. "The pourer from Grief Vineyards I've been seeing?"

"So I told Sanchez all I had was your cell phone."

"I thought you wanted to speak to me first."

"Why don't you take a day or two off? Settle this?"

The Sheetrock walls were thin. I heard the game developers we shared the floor with clacking away on their keyboards. I heard their coffeemaker gurgling.

And then I was staring at the copy of the 3rdBase check still lying there on Marv's keyboard. Up until that moment, I hadn't noticed the overlong signature, the way it spilled past the line and piled up at the check's edge. Rand had signed it *How stoned do you think I am?*

My cell phone buzzed—a blocked number. I pressed the green button, still feeling hopeful enough to say "Claire."

But it wasn't Claire.

About six weeks ago I hit on Claire Baldessari while watching her place her plastic knife and fork at the four o'clock position. Table manners! What a turn-on, especially given the setting: a potluck dinner in a Dolores Street apartment of a friend of Rand's, dim lighting, Chinet plates on laps, Indian-style seating, and three different cannabis-laced casseroles (tuna, zucchini, eggplant) on the menu. I couldn't place Claire, though I knew I'd seen her before. College friend? I'd gone to a small, extremely expensive private college in Washington State because it was situated in the opposite corner of the country from my hometown, because it had a friendly-sounding name, because it was that or Florida State—everywhere else rejected me—and because I could afford it, thanks to the education trust fund my grandmother left me in her will. I'd even stayed there an extra year to collect my master's. And now here I was, living three-figure paycheck to paycheck. Whenever I thought of that emptied-out trust, I doubled over in pain.

"Come here often?"

"You're the guy who brought the bad wine?" Claire asked. I nodded. The *Gazette* received a flood of California, Oregon, and Washington reds and whites; every other month the tweedy, be-spectacled Master of Wine editor in chief flew out from New York and convened a panel of local sommeliers to sample and rate the best of it; the bottles he refused to taste went to me. I'd become reasonably popular in Rand's circle by arriving at every social event clutching four by the neck in each hand.

"How do you know the wine's bad?"

Claire told me she did a bit of marketing and all the appointment tastings for a small winery in the East Bay. Boring job, she said, but check this out: "Nineteen ninety-four Contra Costa Petite, ninety-year-old head-trimmed vines, ultra-low yield, cold-soaked, hand-punched, one hundred percent new French oak." The assistant winemaker who'd hired her was a scratch golfer, so in addition to all that, he'd tutored her in the names of a good twenty or twenty-five top players on the PGA tour.

"Grief Vineyards?" I asked. Kind of a niche category, East Bay wineries. Grief had these dourly memorable all-black labels.

"Wine's not really my thing," she said, nodding. "But I've tasted enough to know what's bad." She had lank brown hair and a beauty mark on the left side of her chin. I asked for her number, and she hesitated for a moment and then wrote it on my wrist. I'd never been over to Grief; I realized where I'd seen her before —at a birthday party for one of Rand's 3rdBase partners. On a dare, she and another girl had stripped to their bras and done an interpretive dance to some dirge-y Arab Strap song on the kitchen table. I took a chance and told her about it. "You were really sexy," I said.

"Yeah, I guess I'm trying to get my life together now," she said, not at all embarrassed. She took a small bite of food, put her plastic utensils at four o'clock, and I went hot.

The question is: what kind of snob gets turned on by table manners? Trust me, I'm not. In a room of blue bloods, I'm so intimidated I can't speak. I grew up in a Pensacola split-level, my single mom supporting my brother and me on an elementary school teacher's salary and a bit of grudging assistance from Grandmother. But my *mom* was raised rich, so she kept us from putting our elbows on the table, reaching for the ketchup, or chewing with our mouth open. You're Pilgrim stock, she liked to say. She proved it at the public library, with birth records, and one or two times she dragged both of us off to some *Mayflower* ancestry association lunch in Florida. At the last one, over Christmas, my paunchy lawyer brother played the prince, chitchatting his way around the room, shaking palsied hands, helping the geriatrics into chairs. I slugged five glasses of sherry (all they had) and asked the caterer to give me a hand job in the bathroom.

I don't know what's wrong with me. I make bad decisions. In a tight spot, I lose perspective. All of the sudden I'm behind the wheel of a rented Mazda, flooring the accelerator, a body in my rearview.

Mom says the Plymouth Colony Pilgrims were brave and fair-minded and industrious and that they were searching for spiritual freedom. The last part feels like me—at least since I started reading my roommate's books, warming to their foggy, upbeat slogans. *Our deepest fear is that we're powerful beyond measure; the present moment is the only moment that ever is.* But brave, fair-minded, et cetera? That's not me at all. Maybe Mom's gilding the lily. After her cancer came back, I logged a little library time myself, thinking she might like talking on the phone about our ancestry. (By the way: the San Francisco Public Library? A homeless shelter with bookshelves.) The part about the Plymouth Colony that grabbed me had to do with their justice system. Even before the Puritans in Salem kicked off their famous trials, the goodhearted denizens of Plymouth would tie a girl up, throw her in the water, and if she managed to get herself untied before she drowned, she was a witch. If she drowned, she was innocent. Trials by ordeal, those pretty little travesties of logic were called.

So—some of those brave, fair-minded, and industrious Pilgrims were messed-up cowards like me. I didn't drift into the shoulder and hit the guy, but I talked Claire into the shotgun seat, and I slid behind the wheel, and I got us racing downhill on Route 50 again. I told her I loved her and that not one car had passed—as if either of those facts mattered. I wasn't that drunk, but negotiating the downhill grade and S-curves took all of my concentration. By the time I finally hit a straightaway, I had more happy-ending nonsense prepped and ready. But when I turned my head, Claire was nodding toward a Shell station, saying she had to throw up. I pulled in. She entered the mini-mart, spoke to the clerk, and pointed back up the dark mountain.

"Son, did you know leaving the scene's a category B felony?" Detective Sanchez asked in his rich, movie-actor voice.

"I was hoping you were someone else," I said, back at my *Gazette* desk, cell phone warm on my ear. September sunlight angled through our small-paned windows and pooled around wine bottles I'd unboxed yesterday, now waiting to be logged in. Why bother? It was Central Valley cabernet, cheap stuff the New York editor would never consent to taste.

"Talking about in-car-ceration."

I touched Rand's check with my finger, feeling hopeful, wistful —and then seriously foolish.

"Who were you hoping I was, son?"

I told him. "But she didn't leave the scene. Or only to use a pay phone."

"You were there?"

"Nope," I said, and then helplessly, plaintively: "Claire won't return my calls."

A faint *thunk,* and then a crackle on the line. Was Sanchez recording the conversation? *Passenger seat:* I might say those words to him as easily as I'd said them to Marv. But if I put myself in the car, I might expose Claire as a liar. Unless she'd already told Sanchez that I'd been with her and that it had been *my* idea to drive away. Impossible to know without talking to her first.

*In-car-ceration.*

I hadn't seriously weighed jail time, for either of us. In fact, I still routinely heard the animal *thud-thud* along the door and thought *deer.* In the darkest corner of my brain, well away from wherever my conscience lived, I still believed Claire *had* hit a deer, and the man around the rock had been sleeping or passed out drunk. I hadn't investigated very carefully. I'd simply opened the door, stood, got a glimpse of his bearded chin, his unlaced boots, and shards of a bottle glinting in the gravel, saw his chest rise and fall with breath, and thought, *back in the car.*

"Son, let me ask you something."

"Call me Lewis," I said.

"You want to see your pretty girlfriend do five to twenty?"

My desktop monitor's screen saver became a scarlet funnel opening in the center. "She couldn't get cell coverage. She went to the nearest—"

"*Were* you there? Yes or no," Sanchez asked.

"No," I said, knowing how unconvincing I sounded.

And full of guilt. Because I'd gone along with Claire's plan. *It's cleaner if I leave you here and go back up alone.* She said this to me after dialing 911 from the pay phone attached to the side of the Shell station.

"Has he died?" I asked Detective Sanchez. Tuesday's *Sacramento Bee* (I bought it at the newsstand near the courthouse) reported an unidentified hitchhiker, fifty-four, in a coma at a local hospital after a collision on U.S. 50. One sentence, in the police blotter. And nothing on Wednesday or Thursday.

"Better hope he don't. You have yourselves a disagreement that night?"

I clamped my lips shut. Sanchez was doing his detective thing, shaking me down a little.

His laugh had tinny menace, like a handful of gravel flung against a screen.

I *wanted* to tell him yes. I wanted to tell him that I'd kept my mother's cancer from Claire because I loved her and because I was afraid she didn't love me and would force me to go to Florida. Sanchez wouldn't care about any of that, would focus on the one thing—my driving away—and call that a criminal act. Which I suppose it was. But here's my perspective: I'm twenty-three, stalled out, stuck between the middling student I've been and the adult I'm meant to become. That night I was on a mad comet of feeling. I wanted to sling us off that mountain and into the innocent, waiting dark.

I had to get off the phone. I had to talk to Claire, find out what she'd told him. Claire lived in a Mission District three-bedroom with two other girls. She rode the BART to and from work. She said she didn't care about money—but she was lying. Everybody cares about money. So if I told her voicemail I had *a half-a-million-dollar check* and that I wanted to give her the money for legal fees, or whatever, just give it to her, surely that would win me a callback.

I apologized to Sanchez: I was at work and had an important meeting. Could we talk later? No, he started to say, but I hit the red button and set the phone down.

Out on Brannan, veils of fog had moved in, spoiling an otherwise perfect blue-sky September day. I shivered through the hanging wet, walking west, past an empty conference hall, past a bail bonds storefront, past a no-sign restaurant with blacked-out windows that Marv told me was a leather bar. It was still early; if Claire was working at Grief today, she wouldn't have left yet. I tried her cell.

"Hey, it's me." Voicemail. "Look, I—" Traffic stacked up beside the sidewalk, in the right-hand lane that led to the U.S. 101 ramp. I increased my pace, letting my gaze trip past one stuck, solo driver after another. "Just received some distressing news. My mom's got —well, she's sick, and I need to go see her in Florida, but I'm not leaving, obviously, before I know what's going on with our situation."

I held my phone away from me and instructed myself: *No, Lewis. No.* How low can a person sink? I thought: *Re-record that sucker. Just say you love her and you want to take your share of the blame.* I forced my thumb to the pound key.

Then I walked into this no-coverage pocket, Brannan at Eighth —the city was full of them—and my phone dropped the call.

Here's the story: Back in July my mom's breast cancer returned after a fifteen-year remission, and my brother Brian called to put in this request I couldn't quite deal with—come home and help him take care of her.

"I just don't think I can this minute," I told him.

"Why not?"

"Did you even actually sprain your stupid ankle?" I asked. That was his story: he had injured his ankle scrimmaging in his lawyer soccer league and couldn't drive, and Mom needed rides to and from her chemo appointments; she needed someone to pitch in with the shopping and cooking.

"Mr. California would prefer we hire a nurse?" Brian said on the phone.

"I can't just leave. I have a *job*."

"Allegedly."

I didn't take the bait; I suspected Brian, single, living in a carriage apartment above Mom's garage, envied my life out here and wanted to spoil it, even though he'd never admit that.

"Guarantee my firm lets you paralegal for double whatever you're making now," he said. "Dude, look." He softened his voice. "Mom's depressed. She took three sick days in a row last week. Gully had to scramble for subs. She won't tell him what's up." Mom taught fourth grade at the elementary school we'd both gone to. Principal Guthrie, "Gully," smoked brown cigarillos and wore a ruby pinkie ring and those glasses that tinted automatically when he walked outside.

Brian and I were less than two years apart and had never gotten along. We'd been opposites in school: me—zitty, introverted, painfully self-conscious; Brian—jockish, confident, varsity soccer captain. In high school I went along with Mom to all his soccer games, sat in the buggy heat on folding camp chairs and helped her count his assists and goals. When I made cross country, she did drag Brian to one of my meets, but I cramped and finished tenth, and Brian proclaimed it a loser sport, and she never made him come again. I'd gotten better grades, but he'd gone to law school—FSU—and taken a job at a small law firm in Pensacola. He was constantly tan, drove a jacked-up Blazer with a dancing bear sticker on the bumper, and walked around with a Deke baseball cap carabinered to his belt loop. And he was telling me to grow up.

Actually, I should feel sorry for the guy. On my last visit to Pensacola, over the holidays, we spent most of Christmas Day sitting on Mom's back stoop, watching carpenter ants munch away at the rotting picnic table in the palm-shaded yard. It was as close to a fraternal moment as we got: I asked him how things were going, even though I could pretty much tell. He'd gained at least twenty pounds and was maybe some kind of alcoholic. All morning he'd been taking nips from a Sheetz to-go mug filled with Wild Turkey. "I can tell you this," he said. "Twenty-five and living in Mom's garage ain't the end of the fucking rainbow." He dropped his chin, dug a fat knuckle into his eye socket, and spat into the crabgrass.

Move out, I'd thought. But all his life he'd stuck by her, and she by him. In high school, for instance, he told the soccer team I was gay, wrote poetry, and had tried to kill myself. When I complained, Mom helpfully pointed out that the poetry part was true. That was why I'd gone to college so far away—to shake this feeling that they were arrayed against me, that I was the family's third wheel.

I hung up on Brian, and called Mom. Nothing to worry about, she said. They'd caught it early, and the chemo would be mild. She'd be absolutely fine. Mom was using her authoritative voice, the one that could silence a room of hyperactive nine-year-olds. Visit at Thanksgiving, she said, not sounding the least bit depressed. The Florida Mayflower Society was doing a dinner; we'd go.

And then a couple days later, I met Claire Baldessari at that potluck and got her to write her phone number on my wrist. We went out, and she wore this clingy, long-sleeved yellow top and her hair in a pair of girlish braids, and after dinner in a dark corner of a bar on Mission, I moved to kiss her, and she let me but also said, into my teeth, that she had to take things slow. "I'm in a weird place," she said. I nodded as if I understood and snaked my hands up underneath that tight top. We had sex back at my place on our second date, and afterward she told me that she'd been dumped by a forty-something Venezuelan restaurant owner who'd been busted by the cops for a cinder-block-sized brick of cocaine in the trunk of his Porsche. He'd posted bail and taken off for Mexico, but not before knocking Claire up. After the abortion she'd checked into a clinic in Marin with serious depression: "a bad time," her words. Abortion, depression. Four months before. She said all of this with her back to me, sitting on the edge of my bed, hunting on the floor for her bra. She was trying to warn me off, but I was a late bloomer, girl-wise, finally losing my virginity during junior year in college, and at twenty-three I thought about sex all the time. And Claire had this way of seeming detached and unattainable—she didn't look at me, even as she let me pull her back into bed for another round.

I forced myself not to call her as much as I wanted to. We went out again, and then again, and like that, we were maybe dating, and I was happier than I'd ever been in my life—I couldn't read, watch TV; I couldn't focus on my work. I'd be logging wines into the database and close my eyes for a moment and see Claire on my balcony tip her head back to exhale a column of smoke straight up. I'd imagine biting that smooth, vulnerable length of her neck. She smoked, she said, to keep from eating, to lose the weight she'd gained on lithium. What weight? I wondered. And what softness there was—around her hips, the back of her thighs, her breasts —that was where I loved to grip and squeeze and suck.

We hadn't had a talk about being exclusive or anything, but when she went over to the house of the guy she worked with, the guy who'd taught her about golf—Chad—to watch Tiger Woods edge Sergio García for the PGA tournament, I was insanely jealous. And, plus, she sort of seemed to be holding herself back in bed. The Prozac blunted her libido, she said, but her libido seemed fine to me. There was something else getting in the way. I'd go down on her—I loved doing that—and she'd start breathing heavy and strain against me. But then she'd hoist me up like she didn't want to come. "Makes me dizzy," she'd say, by way of apology. Dizzy good? Dizzy bad? With Claire I felt the opposite

—the still center of a turning world, the frictionless bearing inside
a rotating axle. As far away as I could be from some impetuous act.
I wanted the rest of my life to be like that.

Brian kept calling, but I didn't want to talk to him. By this point
I was trying to get Claire to go away for a weekend—a big step for
us. Rand's friend owned a house near South Lake Tahoe, not far
from the casinos over the border in Stateline. Claire liked blackjack, and she said a trip up there sounded like fun, but we hadn't
set a date, and I feared it would never happen. One thing was
for sure: this young, knock-kneed relationship wouldn't survive my
leaving for Florida.

I didn't tell Claire about Mom. She *adored* her mother, an ex-
hippie who ran a couple of baby-wear boutiques in Portland—no-
bleach-cotton jammy pants, seven brands of African-style slings.
They spoke every day. And when I let drop at a taqueria one night
that I'd moved out to the West Coast to sort of get away from my
mother and brother, she gave me a look of disappointment that
made me wish I hadn't said anything at all. Claire had been a total
terror to her mom for years—but guess who'd come through for
her when she'd needed help getting an abortion and some time
at a psychiatric clinic? "Mom pretty much saved my life," Claire
told me, gravely, reaching across the bowl of pickled carrots and
peppers and taking my hands. It was the first time I noticed the
jagged, arrow-shaped scars pointing up her forearms. "That's what
mothers do," Claire said.

Meanwhile, my brother's messages were these mini-lectures
about family responsibility, about *time to grow up*. I laid it all out to
Rand, who had family trouble of his own—a dad in Phoenix constantly asking him for money, a born-again mom who called only
to beg him to get saved. We were in the apartment, watching the
Giants get roughed up by the Dodgers, 5–0, bottom of the fourth,
middle of August.

"Is your mother going to die?" he asked flatly.

I passed my hand through the air—as if the question was a bug
or a bad smell. When I was in fifth grade, a few rounds of chemo
had wiped her cancer out; she'd said there was nothing to worry
about. I told him I didn't actually know.

With two on and a full count, Jeff Kent struck out looking. Rand
grimaced, hit mute, and said we should sit on the floor and medi-
tate on the question. So we sat Indian style, and I closed my eyes

and breathed deep and slow. My first thought was about all those reassuring miles between San Francisco and Pensacola. Then I thought of the scars I'd seen on Claire's arms. Then I asked myself a question: apart from college tuition and a hard-on for table manners, what had my family ever given me?

"Dude," Rand said. His back was rigid, his hands splayed open on his knees, and his face had turned white. He whistled air through his teeth.

"What? Are you okay?"

He shook both hands as if trying to dry them in the air. "Some powerful energy, amigo."

"You look really freaked out."

Rand snapped the TV off and stood on shaky legs to go into his bedroom. He came back rolling a joint, eyes wide. "Like, this solid *wave* of premonition." Twice previous he'd experienced the same —right before his sister got her arm bitten off and days before WestLab had made an offer on 3rdBase. "So it could be a positive or a negative thing."

"Could be Mom dying?"

He shrugged, exhaling smoke. "*So* totally out of your control. The forces of the universe, my man. You and I? Mice. Plankton."

Rand was a good guy, but he smoked a lot of pot. And the Giants rung up the Dodgers for eight in the bottom of the ninth that night—a crazy-unlikely come-from-behind victory that Rand wouldn't shut up about for days. A couple of nights later over take-out sushi (his treat), I asked him if *that* could have been what his premonition was about. He stared at me, apparently stunned by the idea.

He said he'd put $5,000 on the Giants through his bookie.

"You have a bookie?"

"I have a problem," he said, stuffing his mouth with ahi.

A squad car passed by on my walk between work and Claire's apartment. And then another. And then another. Later I'd realize—*of course*—it was the same one, circling around, but I didn't look closely because I couldn't have imagined at the time that I was, in fact, being tailed. I'd discover later that Sanchez had interviewed the Shell station attendant who'd told him that Claire had been with a young man that night, and that they'd split up, and the guy had set off down Route 50 on foot. SFPD tipped him that

Claire Baldessari's boyfriend was a wanted money-laundering Venezuelan drug dealer, thought to be residing in Rosarito, Mexico. Possible fatal hit-and-run was already a big case for Sanchez, but nabbing an international fugitive could get him serious press attention. He'd put a couple of SFPD street cops on me Tuesday morning, received word that I didn't match the Venezuelan's description, but Sanchez stubbornly decided I was the man in question, or if not, Claire had a taste for bad guys, and I was some other brand of criminal. Bottom line: I'd hit the guy; I'd sped off the mountain; she was protecting me by claiming she was responsible. *In-car-ceration*.

It would be a mess my lawyer (well, Rand's lawyer) would have to sort out. At that time, 11:15 A.M. or so on a Friday, I blamed my repeated sightings of slow, sharking cop cars on the neighborhood—the pastel-painted South Van Ness housing projects and the Muni Plaza at Mission and Eighteenth, with its encamped homeless and open-air drug deals. I gripped my phone, expecting it to ring any second, expecting Claire to speak sympathetic words into my ear about my mother, even as I was ashamed of having told her. The fog banked away, and the blue bowl of sky came into view, the sun, hot and huge, shining down on me like a spotlight. The warmth felt so good and calming that I stood there with my face turned up, blocking sidewalk traffic.

"Fuck out of my way." This solid-framed black guy wearing a Warriors tank threw his shoulder into me and flicked a pair of scratch-off lottery tickets into my face. One flapped harmlessly off the side of my nose, but the other caught me corner-on in the eye.

A couple of seconds basking in a private ray of sun and see what you get?

This is the hardest part for me to tell.

Rand's friend's Tahoe house was an A-frame enclosed in a grove of trees, overlooking the boat launch at Fallen Leaf Lake. It had been a long, grueling drive from San Francisco, and Claire had been strangely noncommunicative the whole time, so I was drained and tense. I really wanted this weekend to go well. And when I stepped out of the car, saw the house, caught a view of moonlight flashing on the lake below, and breathed in the crisp, weightless mountain air, I felt certain, for the first time, that it

would. I even started fantasizing about staying past the weekend
—turning a two-day getaway into a new and better kind of life. You
could grow hillside zinfandel on the ferociously sunny, cool slopes
of the Sierra, a thousand feet or so below us. We had enough wine-
world contacts; we could get some land, plant vines, make a little
name for ourselves, and live up here where the air tasted so good
and no cell phones worked.

When I gave a little fist pump of pleasure, Claire broke into her
first smile since San Francisco and kissed me and told me she was
glad she'd come—as if she'd been debating the question.

Inside, I slept a hard, dreamless ten hours under scratchy sheets
and heavy camp blankets. In the morning, first thing, I wanted to
hike a trail above the house, and so we climbed to a rocky ridge
and lay together on a flat table-sized rock in brilliant morning sun-
shine. Claire pulled her T-shirt up to her armpits to get some sun
on her stomach, then took the shirt off completely. Her nipples
stood up through the sports bra. I brushed the back of my hand
against her thigh, but she gently pushed me off. Someone might
see us, she said.

She was fast and strong getting back down the trail, and mis-
interpreting this as horniness, I half-jogged after her, excited,
bursting through the door and lifting her to the kitchen counter.
Claire's lips were warm, her neck salty, and I clutched her to me
hungrily. She flattened her hand on my chest. "Breakfast," she
said. "There's nothing here."

Apart from half a box of Ritz crackers and a six-pack of Sierra
Nevada, that was true. So sex would have to wait for a grocery store
run into the town of South Lake. As I crossed the Safeway lot, my
phone found a signal and beeped with a stored voicemail message
from Brian. If I even cared, he said, the doctor says Mom has to
lose the breast. She'd go into the hospital next week. Maybe now I
would come home?

Bacon, Goldfish, two cans of tuna, and multigrain English muf-
fins went into the shopping cart. I got back to the house; Claire
looked in the bag and asked me what the hell was wrong with me.

Taking her in my arms, I told her I was distracted—the truth. I
buried my face in her hair, kissed her beauty mark. I pulled down
her shorts and smacked her plump butt. She yelped and arched
her back, and so I did it again, harder, a blow that stung my hand.

"Easy," she said.

I ran my fingers into her hair and bunched it in my fist.

"Stop," she said, breathless. "Stop. Lewis."

It was cool in the house, but sweat had broken out along her brow and in the hollow of her neck.

"What's wrong?" I asked, with a severity and an impatience that surprised me.

She turned her body away from mine, ran the tap, and cupped water into her mouth. She'd been talking to her therapist, she said, about how her ex had treated her. Her therapist had said it was important to maintain a sense of serenity; gentleness was what she needed.

So we did it in the bed, and I was slow and careful, and she brought herself off with her fingers. That fucking guy, I thought the whole time. I hadn't been in a fight since seventh grade, but I wanted to teach the ex in Mexico a lesson. Knock him over. Get in his face.

I calmed down after I'd come and eaten a bacon sandwich and taken a shower. Claire was out on the deck, reading some Robin Cook paperback she'd found by the couch and smoking a cigarette. I munched Goldfish and watched her tip her head back to exhale. I remembered that fight in seventh grade: a gang of eighth-graders—Brian's friends—who'd pulled me into a stand of magnolia trees and held me down and rabbit-punched my arms and legs until they were numb. Not so much a fight as a beating.

The plan was cocktails, slots, blackjack—goofy, sleazy fun! But Stateline is a sad place: four shabby casinos squatting on the Nevada side of U.S. 50. Pulling into Harrah's—the least depressing-looking of the four—idling behind a jumbo bus disgorging a parade of seventy-somethings, Claire and I considered driving back to our cozy house in the woods, lighting the gas fire, and drinking that six-pack.

But we'd come all this way. So in we went and straight to the buffet, where a stump of prime rib, steam trays of crusty mashed potatoes, and traffic-cone-colored mac-and-cheese put us off dinner. Claire led me back to the casino floor and squeezed in between two old men in cowboy hats at a $5-bid table. I brought her a gin and tonic, got myself two, and watched Claire turn $60 into $300 and then into $40, at which point she pushed back from the table and suggested quarter slots. I kept thinking of how she'd looked on the flat rock under the blue sky, her skin white as paper. I was drinking more than I should—because the gin kept the depressing chill of Harrah's off me, and because drinks were half price, thanks to a mess in the middle of the gaming floor: a chandelier had come down on a roulette table, and there was yellow police tape around the debris. Wires dangled out of a jagged hole in the ceiling.

Over at the quarter slots, I worked through $20 in about six minutes—all I wanted to spend. Claire hit a few times: spinning lights, a siren, and a clattering waterfall of coins. Staring at her half-full bucket, I thought of how, when we were kids, Brian used to savor his bowl of ice cream after I'd plowed through mine, and then would taunt me with how much he had left. I was feeling resentful that Claire had brought up her ex. I could feel my poor judgment take over, like a powerful muscle, a delicious feeling of coiled intent.

I rattled the single quarter in my bucket. I swiveled on my slot machine stool and said, "If this one hits, you have to marry me."

"You're on," Claire said. She shook her own bucket of quarters and blew her bangs straight up. She'd had a few drinks herself.

"I'm infatuated with you."

"I know. It's really sweet."

"Every time I think my life is falling apart—boom, there you are."

"Boom," she mimicked. "What do you mean falling apart?"

I stuck the quarter in, pulled the knob, and came up Bar, Lemon, Cherries.

"Lucky guy," she said, teasingly. "You know, there's a wedding chapel upstairs. I would have held you to it."

That got me down on my knee.

"You're cute," she said, and then a sad awareness spread across her face.

"Claire Baldessari." I took her hands in mine and looked into her fearful brown eyes.

"Lewis, stop. You're not thinking."

"You don't know what I'm going to ask you."

"Seriously. I'll say no."

By this point I'd attracted a little audience, a pair of old ladies in matching pink blouses and mesh cowgirl hats. A guy running a floor waxer, who snapped off the noisy machine to see what I was going to say.

"I've been in touch with him," Claire blurted. "He wants me to come down there."

"Who?" And then: *Oh*.

She stared gloomily at the slot machine. She drank her gin and tonic in one long go. "Sometimes I think I'm getting better," she said. "Other times?" She wiped her chin.

The cowgirls turned their heads. The guy switched his waxer back on.

I drove us back to the A-frame in silence. I opened the door and kicked off my shoes. Claire said she had to pee, and after ten minutes or so, she hadn't returned. I went into the bedroom to look for her.

"What are you doing?"

She was packing her bag. "I don't want to have to in the morning."

I tried to find the lake through the bay window, but it was a cloudy night, and the view was a texture map of trees and leaves. "Maybe we should just go now," I said. "Go home."

I didn't mean it. I was tired. Neither of us was equipped to drive the five hours to San Francisco, but Claire nodded, evidently relieved. She said she'd take the first shift at the wheel.

She rode the shoulders, straddled the center line through the S-curves. I didn't see him. I heard Claire's cry of alarm and felt the car fishtail sideways.

*Thud thud. Deer.*

Claire's hands hovered above the wheel. I got out of the car and saw a man sprawled face-down behind a rock, legs splayed. Couldn't see his face, only a glimpse of bearded chin. Boots, no laces, one half off, revealing a dingy wool sock. Unconscious, breathing—not dead. Shards of a bottle winking at me in the gravel. Blood? I didn't actually go look. The highway was dead still.

Call it a trial, and twenty-three-year-old me with a choice to make. Except I didn't see the choice. Untie the rope, pull for the surface. *Back in the car.*

*

At the Shell station, after calling 911, Claire told me what her story to the cops would be: we'd had a fight back at the house in South Lake, and she'd taken off in the car without me. She'd driven away after the accident only because her cell didn't work, and she needed to call for help.

"That's crazy," I said. "I'm going back up there with you."

She shook her head. I'd never seen her so calm and settled. There was a roadside motel less than a mile away I could walk to, she said. Get a room for a few hours' sleep, and if she could, she'd pick me up in the morning—or better probably just to call a Sacramento taxi service and catch a bus back to San Francisco on my own. She had no idea how long this would take.

"C'mon," she said. "I've got to go."

No, no way, I said, but she looked at me as if I knew as well as she did that this was the best plan. Still I said no, but the forcefulness dropped out of my voice. Eventually I exited the car, and Claire arranged herself behind the wheel, hitched the seat forward, and started the engine. She reversed the car—no visible dents anywhere—then blew me a kiss through the open window and told me to take care of myself. "Take care of yourself, Lewis," like that, and a long, consoling smile—a final goodbye if I've ever seen one. But I was slow on the uptake. I simply thought: big fine, license suspended. The guy had practically been standing in the road, on the downhill shoulder of a four-lane mountain highway, at midnight. The word *manslaughter* looped through my head one or two times, but I chased it away.

I caught a ride all the way to Sacramento with an old Mexican guy in a Ford F-150. Thankfully, he didn't want to talk. I camped out at the Sacramento bus terminal and bought a ticket for the first Greyhound to San Francisco.

"You're home early," Rand said when I came through the door. "Did you win rent?" He was sprawled on the couch, wrapped in a sleeping bag, watching the 49ers lose and drinking orange juice straight from the carton. The look on my face made him wince. "That's a joke. Look, no pressure. I know you're good for it. Want some of this?"

I went straight to the bedroom to charge my phone. It had been dead for hours, and I was sure it was stacked with voicemails from Claire.

I lay on my bed and stared up at the water-stained stucco and thought of my mother and brother in Pensacola and how contemptuous I could be about their small, provincial lives. A line of ants climbed a stack of magazines beside the bed. There weren't any messages. I felt homesick for the first time in five years.

By the time I'd reached Claire's apartment on Dolores Street, my eye still hurt, and my vision was watery and out of focus. I climbed to her doorbell, punched it, and heard heavy footsteps inside— unmistakably male. I could have turned around and taken cover down the block, but I didn't, and the door opened, and I was facing a sandy-haired guy in his late thirties with a leather cuff on his wrist and grapevine tattoos on his arms.

Behind him, up the interior stairs, were Claire's legs, just a glimpse of them, her shins and the base of her right knee.

"Hey, brother," Chad the golfer said. He smelled like her perfume. "Can't let you in."

"Claire?" I called past him.

Chad stepped through the door and pulled it closed behind him. "You want to help her? Tell the police you were in the car, tell them whose idea it was to drive away."

"What's this?" I asked, wiping my eye. "Are you two—what?"

"She's messed up in the head. Cops are threatening her with felony leaving-the-scene 'cause they think she's covering up for Mr. Venezuela. And she won't put you in the car. She thinks this is what she deserves for treating you the way she did," Chad said, in a reasonable voice. "Felony, brother. Girl is sinking into something."

"You're her new boyfriend?"

Chad just gave me a bewildered look. He had lines around his eyes, a shell necklace. I swayed on my feet, and he put a hand on my arm. I was oddly grateful for the contact and support. "Talk to the police, and it'll be better for both of you. You want to do the right thing, don't you?"

"Claire!"

Success! The door started to open, and I readied myself to charge past Chad, scoop her up, and carry her off. But what I saw stopped me. It's not like I'd been having a great week, but at least I'd been eating, bathing, venturing outside. Claire, on the other hand—her face was rinsed of color, her hair matted, her legs spindly and frail; she squinted and lifted a trembling hand to shield her eyes from the sun. Fresh bandages on her forearms.

"Heads up," Chad said, nodding over my shoulder.

The squad car that had passed me three times on the way here had pulled to the curb, its lights spinning. A single whoop of siren got my attention.

In Pensacola the sun stays low through the short January afternoons, and the light skims across the gulf. From the office where I now work, I watch pelicans hang hungrily in the air. I watch them gather themselves and bomb into the drink.

My job is to create payment spreadsheets and invoices for the lawyers at Brian's firm. I'm basically a secretary, but guess what? McMillian, Yates, and Brewer *is* in fact paying me twice what I was making at the *Wine Gazette*. Overpaying me actually, given how baggy my days are, how much time I have to stare through the homey gingham window treatments near my desk and watch the action (Jet Skis, sailboats, seagulls, those pelicans) on the gulf.

Mom's doing okay. Not great. She lost the breast, and now she's on a new cycle of chemo because the doctor found another small tumor. He thinks the chemo will take care of it, but that's what he said before the mastectomy. She's lost most of her hair and is tired all the time, but likes having her sons close by. Brian or I will try to help her off the sofa, and she'll wave us off. "I'm hardy," she'll say, hauling herself up. "Pilgrim stock." Brian's glad I'm here, though he won't admit that. I know because he's got a girlfriend, a tattooed cocktail waitress named Sally, who told me. She comes over and cooks chowders and oyster stews mild enough that Mom can eat them. Surprisingly, Mom likes Sally, and Brian seems to be laying off the bourbon, has dropped some weight, and is playing soccer again.

We don't talk much, Brian and me, though I catch rides with him to the firm. I like to walk home along the water. It's two or three miles to our house, but I enjoy the exercise. I ask myself why I fell so hard for a girl who didn't fall for me. Why I proposed to her. Why I left an injured man on the side of the road. Sometimes asking these questions makes me think I've changed—grown up a little—and then I'll see boat masts tipping back and forth in the harbor like metronome needles, and I get this overwhelming urge to try to steal one of them and set sail for, like, Havana.

Amazing: Rand actually invested $250,000 of WestLab money in www.thewinegazette.com—specifically Marv's subscription database. After my community service hours were done, and before I left San Francisco, I helped Marv write a proposal and business plan and hand-delivered it to Rand, who stuffed it in his Quiksilver backpack. Long shot, I told Marv. But Rand emailed the other day to tell me the news and to offer me a consulting fee of $5,000. Yes, please.

Samuel Gaerig came out of his coma; his broken ribs and broken leg healed. Rand's lawyer, who took my case (pro bono), got his name for me, and I've been calling the halfway house in Sacramento where he's supposed to be living to see how he's doing. Not well. Gaerig is a drug addict (heroin and crack), as well as an alcoholic. He had dementia before the accident. He keeps running off, disappearing for days. Claire is the liable party for any injury suit Mr. Gaerig brings, but Brian says given his mental problems, she could get out of it with a good lawyer. Claire pled no contest to the felony hit-and-run but avoided jail. She lost her license, got two years supervised probation, and a $1,000 fine. This news came to me via my lawyer.

I pled guilty to misdemeanor failure to lend assistance and spent ninety hours dressed in a green jumpsuit in Golden Gate Park, wielding one of those pincher tools, picking up soda cans, junk food wrappers, and more used condoms than anyone wants to hear about. Did your time, Brian says. Put the whole thing behind you.

But I have these nightmares—not about that night on Route 50, about small stuff. A couple of papers I'd plagiarized in college. This lie I told my mother to get her to send me $500 (trip to dentist, three fillings needed). A six-pack I stole from the corner store near my old apartment in San Francisco. I wake up, jaw tight, covers and sheets thrashed to the floor, desperate to tell someone, anyone, I'm sorry.

Rand's latest email had an attached news story: five westerners suspected of sex tourism gunned down by an Islamic group in an alley behind a hotel in Manila. He thinks his ideas guy was one of them and wonders if I want to come back to San Francisco to be his new number two. It's easy, he says. Mostly just reading CNET and *Fast Company* and *Red Herring* and writing memos about possible avenues for expansion. "You don't even have to write the memos," he writes. "Just keep shoveling the money out the door."

I haven't emailed him back. I don't know what to do. I know this: if I leave Pensacola, I'll never come back.

*Boom-splash.* The pelicans take these kamikaze plunges into the water. The way they hit, not one should survive—but of course, they all do. They come up with their beaks full of fish.

NATHAN ENGLANDER

# What We Talk About When We Talk About Anne Frank

FROM *The New Yorker*

THEY'RE IN OUR HOUSE maybe ten minutes and already Mark's lecturing us on the Israeli occupation. Mark and Lauren live in Jerusalem, and people from there think it gives them the right.

Mark is looking all stoic and nodding his head. "If we had what you have down here in South Florida," he says, and trails off. "Yup," he says, and he's nodding again. "We'd have no troubles at all."

"You do have what we have," I tell him. "All of it. Sun and palm trees. Old Jews and oranges and the worst drivers around. At this point, we've probably got more Israelis than you." Debbie, my wife, puts a hand on my arm—her signal that I'm either taking a tone, interrupting someone's story, sharing something private, or making an inappropriate joke. That's my cue, and I'm surprised, considering how often I get it, that she ever lets go of my arm.

"Yes, you've got everything now," Mark says. "Even terrorists."

I look at Lauren. She's the one my wife has the relationship with—the one who should take charge. But Lauren isn't going to give her husband any signal. She and Mark ran off to Israel twenty years ago and turned Hasidic, and neither of them will put a hand on the other in public. Not for this. Not to put out a fire.

"Wasn't Mohamed Atta living right here before 9/11?" Mark says, and now he pantomimes pointing out houses. "Goldberg, Goldberg, Goldberg—Atta. How'd you miss him in this place?"

"Other side of town," I say.

"That's what I'm talking about. That's what you have that we don't. Other sides of town. Wrong sides of the tracks. Space upon space." And now he's fingering the granite countertop in our kitchen, looking out into the living room and the dining room, staring through the kitchen windows at the pool. "All this house," he says, "and one son? Can you imagine?"

"No," Lauren says. And then she turns to us, backing him up. "You should see how we live with ten."

"Ten kids," I say. "We could get you a reality show with that here in the States. Help you get a bigger place."

The hand is back pulling at my sleeve. "Pictures," Debbie says. "I want to see the girls." We all follow Lauren into the den for her purse.

"Do you believe it?" Mark says. "Ten girls!" And the way it comes out of his mouth, it's the first time I like the guy. The first time I think about giving him a chance.

Facebook and Skype brought Deb and Lauren back together. They were glued at the hip growing up. Went all the way through school together. Yeshiva school. All girls. Out in Queens till high school and then riding the subway together to one called Central in Manhattan. They stayed best friends until I married Deb and turned her secular, and soon after that Lauren met Mark and they went off to the Holy Land and shifted from Orthodox to *ultra*-Orthodox, which to me sounds like a repackaged detergent—OR-THODOX ULTRA®, now with more deep-healing power. Because of that, we're supposed to call them Shoshana and Yerucham now. Deb's been doing it. I'm just not saying their names.

"You want some water?" I offer. "Coke in the can?"

"'You'—which of us?" Mark says.

"You both," I say. "Or I've got whiskey. Whiskey's kosher too, right?"

"If it's not, I'll kosher it up real fast," he says, pretending to be easygoing. And right then he takes off that big black hat and plops down on the couch in the den.

Lauren's holding the verticals aside and looking out at the yard. "Two girls from Forest Hills," she says. "Who ever thought we'd be the mothers of grownups?"

"Trevor's sixteen," Deb says. "You may think he's a grownup, and he may think he's a grownup—but we are not convinced."

Right then is when Trev comes padding into the den, all six feet of him, plaid pajama bottoms dragging on the floor and T-shirt full of holes. He's just woken up, and you can tell he's not sure if he's still dreaming. We told him we had guests. But there's Trev, staring at this man in the black suit, a beard resting on his belly. And Lauren, I met her once before, right when Deb and I got married, but ten girls and a thousand Shabbos dinners later —well, she's a big woman, in a bad dress and a giant blond Marilyn Monroe wig. Seeing them at the door, I can't say I wasn't shocked myself.

"Hey," he says.

And then Deb's on him, preening and fixing his hair and hugging him. "Trevy, this is my best friend from childhood," she says. "This is Shoshana, and this is—"

"Mark," I say.

"Yerucham," Mark says, and sticks out a hand. Trev shakes it. Then Trev sticks out his hand, polite, to Lauren. She looks at it, just hanging there in the air.

"I don't shake," she says. "But I'm so happy to see you. Like meeting my own son. I mean it." And here she starts to cry, and then she and Deb are hugging. And the boys, we just stand there until Mark looks at his watch and gets himself a good manly grip on Trev's shoulder.

"Sleeping until three on a Sunday? Man, those were the days," Mark says. "A regular little Rumpleforeskin." Trev looks at me, and I want to shrug, but Mark's also looking, so I don't move. Trev just gives us both his best teenage glare and edges out of the room. As he does, he says, "Baseball practice," and takes my car keys off the hook by the door to the garage.

"There's gas," I say.

"They let them drive here at sixteen?" Mark says. "Insane."

"So what brings you here after all these years?" I say.

"My mother," Mark says. "She's failing, and my father's getting old—and they come to us for Sukkot every year. You know?"

"I know the holidays."

"They used to fly out to us. For Sukkot and Pesach, both. But they can't fly now, and I just wanted to get over while things are still good. We haven't been in America—"

"Oh, gosh," Lauren says. "I'm afraid to think how long it's been. More than ten years. Twelve," she says. "With the kids, it's just impossible until enough of them are big."

"How do you do it?" Deb says. "Ten kids? I really do want to hear."

That's when I remember. "I forgot your drink," I say to Mark.

"Yes, his drink. That's how," Lauren says. "That's how we cope."

And that's how the four of us end up back at the kitchen table with a bottle of vodka between us. I'm not one to get drunk on a Sunday afternoon, but, I tell you, when the plan is to spend the day with Mark I jump at the chance. Deb's drinking too, but not for the same reason. I think she and Lauren are reliving a little bit of the wild times. The very small window when they were together, barely grown up, two young women living in New York on the edge of two worlds.

Deb says, "This is really racy for us. I mean, *really* racy. We try not to drink much at all these days. We think it sets a bad example for Trevor. It's not good to drink in front of them right at this age when they're all transgressive. He's suddenly so interested in that kind of thing."

"I'm just happy when he's interested in something," I say.

Deb slaps at the air. "I just don't think it's good to make drinking look like it's fun with a teenager around."

Lauren smiles and straightens her wig. "Does anything we do look fun to our kids?"

I laugh at that. Honestly, I'm liking her more and more.

"It's the age limit that does it," Mark says. "It's the whole American puritanical thing, the twenty-one-year-old drinking age and all that. We don't make a big deal about it in Israel, and so the kids, they don't even notice alcohol. Except for the foreign workers on Fridays, you hardly see anyone drunk at all."

"The workers and the Russians," Lauren says.

"The Russian immigrants," he says, "that's a whole separate matter. Most of them, you know, not even Jews."

"What does that mean?" I say.

"It means matrilineal descent, is what it means," Mark says. "With the Ethiopians there were conversions."

But Deb wants to keep us away from politics, and the way we're arranged, me in between them and Deb opposite (it's a round table, our kitchen table), she practically has to throw herself across to grab hold of my arm. "Fix me another," she says.

And here she switches the subject to Mark's parents. "How's the visit been going?" she says, her face all somber. "How are your folks holding up?"

Deb is very interested in Mark's parents. They're Holocaust survivors. And Deb has what can only be called an unhealthy obsession with the idea of that generation being gone. Don't get me wrong. It's important to me too. All I'm saying is there's healthy and unhealthy, and my wife, she gives the subject a *lot* of time.

"What can I say?" Mark says. "My mother's a very sick woman. And my father, he tries to keep his spirits up. He's a tough guy."

"I'm sure," I say. Then I look down at my drink, all serious, and give a shake of my head. "They really are amazing."

"Who?" Mark says. "Fathers?"

I look back up and they're all staring at me. "Survivors," I say, realizing I jumped the gun.

"There's good and bad," Mark says. "Like anyone else."

Lauren says, "The whole of Carmel Lake Village, it's like a D.P. camp with a billiards room."

"One tells the other, and they follow," Mark says. "From Europe to New York, and now, for the end of their lives, again the same place."

"Tell them that crazy story, Yuri," Lauren says.

"Tell us," Deb says.

"So you can picture my father," Mark says. "In the old country, he went to *heder*, had the *peyes* and all that. But in America a classic *galusmonger*. He looks more like you than me. It's not from him that I get this," he says, pointing at his beard. "Shoshana and I—"

"We know," I say.

"So my father. They've got a nice nine-hole course, a driving range, some greens for the practice putting. And my dad's at the clubhouse. I go with him. He wants to work out in the gym, he says. Tells me I should come. Get some exercise. And he tells me" —and here Mark points at his feet, sliding a leg out from under the table so we can see his big black clodhoppers—"'You can't wear those Shabbos shoes on the treadmill. You need the sneakers. You know, sports shoes?' And I tell him, 'I know what sneakers are. I didn't forget my English any more than your Yiddish is gone.' So he says, *'Ah shaynem dank dir in pupik.'* Just to show me who's who."

"Tell them the point," Lauren says.

"He's sitting in the locker room, trying to pull a sock on, which is, at that age, basically the whole workout in itself. It's no quick business. And I see, while I'm waiting, and I can't believe it—I nearly pass out. The guy next to him, the number on his arm, it's three before my father's number. You know, in sequence."

"What do you mean?" Deb says.

"I mean the number tattooed. It's the same as my father's camp number, digit for digit, but my father's ends in an eight. And this guy's, it ends in a five. That's the only difference. I mean, they're separated by two people. So I say, 'Excuse me, sir.' And the guy just says, 'You with the Chabad? I don't want anything but to be left alone. I already got candles at home.' I tell him, 'No. I'm not. I'm here visiting my father.' And to my father I say, 'Do you know this gentleman? Have you two met? I'd really like to introduce you, if you haven't.' And they look each other over for what, I promise you, is minutes. Actual minutes. It is—with *kavod* I say this, with respect for my father—but it is like watching a pair of big beige manatees sitting on a bench, each with one sock on. They're just looking each other up and down, everything slow. And then my father says, 'I seen him. Seen him around.' The other guy, he says, 'Yes, I've seen.' 'You're both survivors,' I tell them. 'Look. The numbers.' And they look. 'They're the same,' I say. And they both hold out their arms to look at the little ashen tattoos. To my father I say, 'Do you get it? The same, except his—it's right ahead of yours. Look! Compare.' So they look. They compare." Mark's eyes are popping out of his head. "Think about it," he says. "Around the world, surviving the unsurvivable, these two old guys end up with enough money to retire to Carmel Lake and play golf every day. So I say to my dad, 'He's right ahead of you. Look, a five,' I say. 'And yours is an eight.' And my father says, 'All that means is he cut ahead of me in line. There same as here. This guy's a cutter. I just didn't want to say.' 'Blow it out your ear,' the other guy says. And that's it. Then they get back to putting on socks."

Deb looks crestfallen. She was expecting something empowering. Some story with which to educate Trevor, to reaffirm her belief in the humanity that, from inhumanity, forms.

But me, I love that kind of story. I'm starting to take a real shine to these two, and not just because I'm suddenly feeling sloshed.

"Good story, Yuri," I say, copying his wife. "Yerucham, that one's got zing."

Yerucham hoists himself up from the table, looking proud. He checks the label of our white bread on the counter, making sure it's kosher. He takes a slice, pulls off the crust, and rolls the white part against the countertop with the palm of his hand, making a little ball. He comes over and pours himself a shot and throws it back. Then he eats that crazy dough ball. Just tosses it in his mouth, as if it's the bottom of his own personal punctuation mark —you know, to underline his story.

"Is that good?" I say.

"Try it," he says. He goes to the counter and pitches me a slice of white bread, and says, "But first pour yourself a shot."

I reach for the bottle and find that Deb's got her hands around it, and her head's bowed down, like the bottle is anchoring her, keeping her from tipping back.

"Are you okay, Deb?" Lauren says.

"It's because it was funny," I say.

"Honey!" Deb says.

"She won't tell you, but she's a little obsessed with the Holocaust. That story—no offense, Mark—it's not what she had in mind."

I should leave it be, I know. But it's not like someone from Deb's high school is around every day offering insights.

"It's like she's a survivor's kid, my wife. It's crazy, that education they give them. Her grandparents were all born in the Bronx, and here we are twenty minutes from downtown Miami but it's like it's 1937 and we live on the edge of Berlin."

"That's not it!" Deb says, openly defensive, her voice super high up in the register. "I'm not upset about that. It's the alcohol. All this alcohol. It's that and seeing Lauren. Seeing Shoshana, after all this time."

"Oh, she was always like this in high school," Shoshana says. "Sneak one drink, and she started to cry. You want to know what used to get her going, what would make her truly happy?" Shoshana says. "It was getting high. That's what always did it. Smoking up. It would make her laugh for hours and hours."

And, I tell you, I didn't see it coming. I'm as blindsided as Deb was by that numbers story.

"Oh, my God," Deb says, and she's pointing at me. "Look at my big bad secular husband. He really can't handle it. He can't handle his wife's having any history of naughtiness at all—Mr. Liberal Open-Minded." To me she says, "How much more chaste a wife can you dream of than a modern-day yeshiva girl who stayed a virgin until twenty-one? Honestly. What did you think Shoshana was going to say was so much fun?"

"Honestly-honestly?" I say. "I don't want to. It's embarrassing."

"Say it!" Deb says, positively glowing.

"Honestly, I thought you were going to say it was something like competing in the Passover Nut Roll, or making sponge cake. Something like that." I hang my head. And Shoshana and Deb are laughing so hard they can't breathe. They're grabbing at each other so that I can't tell if they're holding each other up or pulling each other down.

"I can't believe you told him about the nut roll," Shoshana says.

"And I can't believe," Deb says, "you just told my husband of twenty-two years how much we used to get high. I haven't touched a joint since before we were married," she says. "Have we, honey? Have we smoked since we got married?"

"No," I say. "It's been a very long time."

"So come on, Shosh. When was it? When was the last time you smoked?"

Now, I know I mentioned the beard on Mark. But I don't know if I mentioned how hairy a guy he is. That thing grows right up to his eyeballs. Like having eyebrows on top and bottom both. So when Deb asks the question, the two of them, Shosh and Yuri, are basically giggling like children, and I can tell, in the little part that shows, in the bit of skin I can see, that Mark's eyelids and earlobes are in full blush.

"When Shoshana said we drink to get through the days," Mark says, "she was kidding about the drinking."

"We don't drink much," Shoshana says.

"It's smoking that she means," he says.

"We still get high," Shoshana says. "I mean, all the time."

"Hasidim!" Deb screams. "You're not allowed!"

"Everyone does in Israel. It's like the sixties there," Mark says. "It's the highest country in the world. Worse than Holland and India and Thailand put together. Worse than anywhere, even Argentina—though they may have us tied."

"Well, maybe that's why the kids aren't interested in alcohol," I say.

"Do you want to get high now?" Deb says. And we all three look at her. Me, with surprise. And those two with straight longing.

"We didn't bring," Shoshana says. "Though it's pretty rare anyone at customs peeks under the wig."

"Maybe you guys can find your way into the glaucoma underground over at Carmel Lake," I say. "I'm sure that place is rife with it."

"That's funny," Mark says.

"I'm funny," I say, now that we're all getting on.

"We've got pot," Deb says.

"We do?" I say. "I don't think we do."

Deb looks at me and bites at the cuticle on her pinkie.

"You're not secretly getting high all these years?" I say. I really don't feel well at all.

"Our son," Deb says. "He has pot."

"Our son?"

"Trevor," she says.

"Yes," I say. "I know which one."

It's a lot for one day, that kind of news. And it feels to me a lot like betrayal. Like my wife's old secret and my son's new secret are bound up together, and I've somehow been wronged. Also, I'm not one to recover quickly from any kind of slight from Deb—not when there are people around. I really need to talk stuff out. Some time alone, even five minutes, would fix it. But it's super apparent that Deb doesn't need any time alone with me. She doesn't seem troubled at all. What she seems is focused. She's busy at the counter, using a paper tampon wrapper to roll a joint.

"It's an emergency-preparedness method we came up with in high school," Shoshana says. "The things teenage girls will do when they're desperate."

"Do you remember that nice boy that we used to smoke in front of?" Deb says. "He'd just watch us. There'd be six or seven of us in a circle, girls and boys not touching—we were so religious. Isn't that crazy?" Deb is talking to me, as Shoshana and Mark don't think it's crazy at all. "The only place we touched was passing the joint, at the thumbs. And this boy, we had a nickname for him."

"Passover!" Shoshana yells.

"Yes," Deb says, "that's it. All we ever called him was Passover. Because every time the joint got to him he'd just pass it over to the next one of us. Passover Rand."

Shoshana takes the joint and lights it with a match, sucking deep. "It's a miracle when I remember anything these days," she says. "After my first was born, I forgot half of everything I knew. And then half again with each one after. Just last night, I woke up in a panic. I couldn't remember if there were fifty-two cards in a deck or fifty-two weeks in a year. The recall errors—I'm up all night worrying over them, just waiting for the Alzheimer's to kick in."

"It's not that bad," Mark tells her. "It's only everyone on one side of your family that has it."

"That's true," she says, passing her husband the joint. "The other side is blessed only with dementia. Anyway, which is it? Weeks or cards?"

"Same, same," Mark says, taking a hit.

When it's Deb's turn, she holds the joint and looks at me, like I'm supposed to nod or give her permission in some husbandly anxiety-absolving way. But instead of saying, "Go ahead," I pretty much bark at Deb. "When were you going to tell me about our son?"

At that, Deb takes a long hit, holding it deep, like an old pro.

"Really, Deb. How could you not tell me you knew?"

Deb walks over and hands me the joint. She blows the smoke in my face, not aggressive, just blowing.

"I've only known five days," she says. "I was going to tell you. I just wasn't sure how, or if I should talk to Trevy first, maybe give him a chance," she says.

"A chance to what?" I ask.

"To let him keep it as a secret between us. To let him know he could have my trust if he promised to stop."

"But he's the son," I say. "I'm the father. Even if it's a secret with him, it should be a double secret between me and you. I should always get to know—even if I pretend not to know—any secret with him."

"Do that double part again," Mark says. But I ignore him.

"That's how it's always been," I say to Deb. And, because I'm desperate and unsure, I follow it up with "Hasn't it?"

I mean, we really trust each other, Deb and I. And I can't remember feeling like so much has hung on one question in a long time. I'm trying to read her face, and something complex is going on, some formulation. And then she sits right there on the floor, at my feet.

"Oh, my God," she says. "I'm so fucking high. Like instantly. Like, like," and then she starts laughing. "Like, Mike," she says. "Like, kike," she says, turning completely serious. "Oh, my God, I'm really messed up."

"We should have warned you," Shoshana says.

As she says this, I'm holding my first hit in, and already trying to fight off the paranoia that comes rushing behind that statement.

"Warned us what?" I say, my voice high, and the smoke still sweet in my nose.

"This isn't your father's marijuana," Mark says. "The THC levels. One hit of this new hydroponic stuff, it's like if maybe you smoked a pound of the stuff we had when we were kids."

"I feel it," I say. And I do. I sit down with Deb on the floor and take her hands. I feel nice. Though I'm not sure if I thought that or said it, so I try it again, making sure it's out loud. "I feel nice," I say.

"I found the pot in the laundry hamper," Deb says. "Leave it to a teenage boy to think that's the best place to hide something. His clean clothes show up folded in his room, and it never occurs to him that someone empties that hamper. To him, it's the loneliest, most forgotten space in the world. Point is I found an Altoids tin at the bottom, stuffed full." Deb gives my hands a squeeze. "Are we good now?"

"We're good," I say. And it feels like we're a team again, like it's us against them. Because Deb says, "Are you sure you guys are allowed to smoke pot that comes out of a tin that held non-kosher candy? I really don't know if that's okay." And it's just exactly the kind of thing I'm thinking.

"First of all, we're not eating it. We're smoking it," Shoshana says. "And even so, it's cold contact, so it's probably all right either way."

"'Cold contact'?" I say.

"It's a thing," Shoshana says. "Just forget about it and get up off the floor. Chop-chop." And they each offer us a hand and get us standing. "Come, sit back at the table," Shoshana says.

"I'll tell you," Mark says. "That's got to be the number-one most annoying thing about being Hasidic in the outside world. Worse than the rude stuff that gets said is the constant policing by civilians. Everywhere we go, people are checking on us. Ready to make some sort of liturgical citizen's arrest."

"Strangers!" Shoshana says. "Just the other day, on the way in from the airport. Yuri pulled into a McDonald's to pee, and some guy in a trucker hat came up to him as he went in and said, 'You allowed to go in there, brother?' Just like that."

"Not true!" Deb says.

"It's not that I don't see the fun in that," Mark says. "The allure. You know, we've got Mormons in Jerusalem. They've got a base there. A seminary. The rule is—the deal with the government—they can have their place, but they can't do outreach. No proselytizing. Anyway, I do some business with one of their guys."

"From Utah?" Deb says.

"From Idaho. His name is Jebediah, for real—do you believe it?"

"No, Yerucham and Shoshana," I say. "Jebediah is a very strange name." Mark rolls his eyes at that, handing me what's left of the joint. Without even asking, he gets up and gets the tin and reaches into his wife's purse for another tampon. And I'm a little less comfortable with this than with the white bread, with a guest coming into the house and smoking up all our son's pot. Deb must be thinking something similar, as she says, "After this story, I'm going to text Trev and make sure he's not coming back anytime soon."

"So when Jeb's at our house," Mark says, "when he comes by to eat and pours himself a Coke, I do that same religious-police thing. I can't resist. I say, 'Hey, Jeb, you allowed to have that?' People don't mind breaking their own rules, but they're real strict about someone else's."

"So are they allowed to have Coke?" Deb says.

"I don't know," Mark says. "All Jeb ever says back is 'You're thinking of coffee, and mind your own business, either way.'"

And then my Deb. She just can't help herself. "You heard about the scandal? The Mormons going through the Holocaust list."

"Like in *Dead Souls*," I say, explaining. "Like in the Gogol book, but real."

"Do you think we read that?" Mark says. "As Hasidim, or before?"

"They took the records of the dead," Deb says, "and they started running through them. They took these people who died as Jews and started converting them into Mormons. Converting the six million against their will."

"And this is what keeps an American Jew up at night?" Mark says.

"What does that mean?" Deb says.

"It means—" Mark says.

But Shoshana interrupts him. "Don't tell them what it means, Yuri. Just leave it unmeant."

"We can handle it," I say. "We are interested, even, in handling it."

"Your son, he seems like a nice boy."

"Do not talk about their son," Shoshana says.

"Do not talk about our son," Deb says. This time I reach across and lay a hand on her elbow.

"Talk," I say.

"He does not," Mark says, "seem Jewish to me."

"How can you say that?" Deb says. "What is wrong with you?" But Deb's upset draws less attention than my response. I'm laughing so hard that everyone turns toward me.

"What?" Mark says.

"Jewish to you?" I say. "The hat, the beard, the blocky shoes. A lot of pressure, I'd venture, to look Jewish to you. Like, say, maybe Ozzy Osbourne, or the guys from Kiss, like them telling Paul Simon, 'You do not look like a musician to me.'"

"It is not about the outfit," Mark says. "It's about building life in a vacuum. Do you know what I saw on the drive over here? Supermarket, supermarket, adult bookstore, supermarket, supermarket, firing range."

"Floridians do like their guns and porn," I say. "And their supermarkets."

"What I'm trying to say, whether you want to take it seriously or not, is that you can't build Judaism only on the foundation of one terrible crime," Mark says. "It's about this obsession with the Holocaust as a necessary sign of identity. As your only educational tool. Because for the children there is no connection otherwise. Nothing Jewish that binds."

"Wow, that's offensive," Deb says. "And closed-minded. There is such a thing as Jewish culture. One can live a culturally rich life."

"Not if it's supposed to be a Jewish life. Judaism is a religion. And with religion comes ritual. Culture is nothing. Culture is some construction of the modern world. It is not fixed; it is ever changing, and a weak way to bind generations. It's like taking two pieces of metal, and instead of making a nice weld you hold them together with glue."

"What does that even mean?" Deb says. "Practically."

Mark raises a finger to make his point, to educate. "In Jerusalem we don't need to busy ourselves with symbolic efforts to keep our memories in place. Because we live exactly as our parents lived before the war. And this serves us in all things, in our relationships too, in our marriages and parenting."

"Are you saying your marriage is better than ours?" Deb says. "Really? Just because of the rules you live by?"

"I'm saying your husband would not have the long face, worried his wife is keeping secrets. And your son, he would not get into the business of smoking without first coming to you. Because the relationships, they are defined. They are clear."

"Because they are welded together," I say, "and not glued."

"Yes," he says. "And I bet Shoshana agrees." But Shoshana is distracted. She is working carefully with an apple and a knife. She is making a little apple pipe, all the tampons gone.

"Did your daughters?" Deb says. "If they tell you everything, did they come to you first, before they smoked?"

"Our daughters do not have the taint of the world we grew up in. They have no interest in such things."

"So you think," I say.

"So I know," he says. "Our concerns are different, our worries."

"Let's hear 'em," Deb says.

"Let's not," Shoshana says. "Honestly, we're drunk, we're high, we are having a lovely reunion."

"Every time you tell him not to talk," I say, "it makes me want to hear what he's got to say even more."

"Our concern," Mark says, "is not the past Holocaust. It is the current one. The one that takes more than fifty percent of the Jews of this generation. Our concern is intermarriage. It's the Holocaust that's happening now. You don't need to be worrying about some Mormons doing hocus-pocus on the murdered six million. You need to worry that your son marries a Jew."

"Oh, my God," Deb says. "Are you calling intermarriage a Holocaust?"

"You ask my feeling, that's my feeling. But this, no, it does not exactly apply to you, except in the example you set for the boy. Because you're Jewish, your son, he is as Jewish as me. No more, no less."

"I went to yeshiva too, Born-Again Harry! You don't need to explain the rules to me."

"Did you just call me 'Born-Again Harry'?" Mark asks.

"I did," Deb says. And she and he, they start to laugh at that. They think "Born-Again Harry" is the funniest thing they've heard in a while. And Shoshana laughs, and then I laugh, because laughter is infectious—and it is doubly so when you're high.

"You don't really think our family, my lovely, beautiful son, is headed for a Holocaust, do you?" Deb says. "Because that would really cast a pall on this beautiful day."

"No, I don't," Mark says. "It's a lovely house and a lovely family, a beautiful home that you've made for that strapping young man. You're a real *balabusta*," Mark says.

"That makes me happy," Deb says. And she tilts her head nearly ninety degrees to show her happy, sweet smile. "Can I hug you? I'd really like to give you a hug."

"No," Mark says, though he says it really politely. "But you can hug my wife. How about that?"

"That's a great idea," Deb says. Shoshana gets up and hands the loaded apple to me, and I smoke from the apple as the two women hug a tight, deep, dancing-back-and-forth hug, tilting this way and that, so, once again, I'm afraid they might fall.

"It is a beautiful day," I say.

"It is," Mark says. And both of us look out the window, and both of us watch the perfect clouds in a perfect sky, so that we're both staring out as the sky suddenly darkens. It is a change so abrupt that the ladies undo their hug to watch.

"It's like that here," Deb says. And the clouds open up and torrential tropical rain drops straight down, battering. It is loud against the roof, and loud against the windows, and the fronds of the palm trees bend, and the floaties in the pool jump as the water boils.

Shoshana goes to the window. And Mark passes Deb the apple and goes to the window. "Really, it's always like this here?" Shoshana says.

"Sure," I say. "Every day. Stops as quick as it starts."

And both of them have their hands pressed up against the window. And they stay like that for some time, and when Mark turns around, harsh guy, tough guy, we see that he is weeping.

"You do not know," he says. "I forget what it's like to live in a place rich with water. This is a blessing above all others."

"If you had what we had," I say.

"Yes," he says, wiping his eyes.

"Can we go out?" Shoshana says. "In the rain?"

"Of course," Deb says. Then Shoshana tells me to close my eyes. Only me. And I swear I think she's going to be stark naked when she calls, "Open up."

She's taken off her wig is all, and she's wearing one of Trev's baseball caps in its place.

"I've only got the one wig this trip," she says. "If Trev won't mind."

"He won't mind," Deb says. And this is how the four of us find ourselves in the back yard, on a searingly hot day, getting pounded by all this cool, cool rain. It's just about the best feeling in the world. And, I have to say, Shoshana looks twenty years younger in that hat.

We do not talk in the rain. We are too busy frolicking and laughing and jumping around. And that's how it happens that I'm holding Mark's hand and sort of dancing, and Deb is holding Shoshana's hand, and they're doing their own kind of jig. And when I take Deb's hand, though neither Mark nor Shoshana is touching the other, somehow we've formed a broken circle. We've started dancing our own kind of hora in the rain.

It is the silliest and freest and most glorious I can remember feeling in years. Who would think that's what I'd be saying with these strict, suffocatingly austere people visiting our house? And then my Deb, my love, once again she is thinking what I'm thinking, and she says, face up into the rain, all of us spinning, "Are you sure this is okay, Shoshana? That it's not mixed dancing? I don't want anyone feeling bad after."

"We'll be just fine," Shoshana says. "We will live with the consequences." The question slows us, and stops us, though no one has yet let go.

"It's like the old joke," I say. Without waiting for anyone to ask which one, I say, "Why don't Hasidim have sex standing up?"

"Why?" Shoshana says.

"Because it might lead to mixed dancing."

Deb and Shoshana pretend to be horrified as we let go of hands, as we recognize that the moment is over, the rain disappearing as quickly as it came. Mark stands there staring into the sky, lips pressed tight. "That joke is very, very old," he says. "And mixed dancing makes me think of mixed nuts, and mixed grill, and *insalata mista.* The sound of 'mixed dancing' has made me wildly hungry. And I'm going to panic if the only kosher thing in the house is that loaf of bleached American bread."

"You have the munchies," I say.

"Diagnosis correct," he says.

Deb starts clapping at that, tiny claps, her hands held to her chest in prayer. She says to him, absolutely beaming, "You will not even believe what riches await."

The four of us stand in the pantry, soaking wet, hunting through the shelves and dripping on the floor. "Have you ever seen such a pantry?" Shoshana says, reaching her arms out. "It's gigantic." It is indeed large, and it is indeed stocked, an enormous amount of food, and an enormous selection of sweets, befitting a home that is often host to a swarm of teenage boys.

"Are you expecting a nuclear winter?" Shoshana says.

"I'll tell you what she's expecting," I say. "You want to know how Holocaust-obsessed she really is? I mean, to what degree?"

"To no degree," Deb says. "We are done with the Holocaust."

"Tell us," Shoshana says.

"She's always plotting our secret hiding place," I say.

"No kidding," Shoshana says.

"Like, look at this. At the pantry, with a bathroom next to it, and the door to the garage. If you sealed it all up—like put drywall at the entrance to the den—you'd never suspect. If you covered that door inside the garage up good with, I don't know—if you hung your tools in front of it and hid hinges behind, maybe leaned the bikes and the mower against it, you'd have this closed area, with running water and a toilet and all this food. I mean, if someone sneaked into the garage to replenish things, you could rent out the house. Put in another family without their having any idea."

"Oh, my God," Shoshana says. "My short-term memory may be gone from having all those children—"

"And from the smoking," I say.

"And from that too. But I remember from when we were kids," Shoshana says, turning to Deb. "You were always getting me to play games like that. To pick out spaces. And even worse, even darker—"

"Don't," Deb says.

"I know what you're going to say," I tell her, and I'm honestly excited. "The game, yes? She played that crazy game with you?"

"No," Deb says. "Enough. Let it go."

And Mark—who is utterly absorbed in studying kosher certifications, who is tearing through hundred-calorie snack packs and eating handfuls of roasted peanuts, and who has said nothing since we entered the pantry except "What's a Fig Newman?"—he stops and says, "I want to play this game."

"It's not a game," Deb says.

And I'm happy to hear her say that, as it's just what I've been trying to get her to admit for years. That it's not a game. That it's dead serious, and a kind of preparation, and an active pathology that I prefer not to indulge.

"It's the Anne Frank game," Shoshana says. "Right?"

Seeing how upset my wife is, I do my best to defend her. I say, "No, it's not a game. It's just what we talk about when we talk about Anne Frank."

"How do we play this non-game?" Mark says. "What do we do?"

"It's the Righteous Gentile game," Shoshana says.

"It's Who Will Hide Me?" I say.

"In the event of a second Holocaust," Deb says, giving in. "It's a serious exploration, a thought experiment that we engage in."

"That you play," Shoshana says.

"That, in the event of an American Holocaust, we sometimes talk about which of our Christian friends would hide us."

"I don't get it," Mark says.

"Of course you do," Shoshana says. "It's like this. If there was a Shoah, if it happened again—say we were in Jerusalem, and it's 1941 and the Grand Mufti got his way, what would Jebediah do?"

"What could he do?" Mark says.

"He could hide us. He could risk his life and his family's and everyone's around him. That's what the game is: would he—for real—would he do that for you?"

"He'd be good for that, a Mormon," Mark says. "Forget this

pantry. They have to keep a year of food stored in case of the Rapture, or something like that. Water too. A year of supplies. Or maybe it's that they have sex through a sheet. No, wait. I think that's supposed to be us."

"All right," Deb says. "Let's not play. Really, let's go back to the kitchen. I can order in from the glatt kosher place. We can eat outside, have a real dinner and not just junk."

"No, no," Mark says. "I'll play. I'll take it seriously."

"So would the guy hide you?" I say.

"The kids too?" Mark says. "I'm supposed to pretend that in Jerusalem he's got a hidden motel or something where he can put the twelve of us?"

"Yes," Shoshana says. "In their seminary or something. Sure."

Mark thinks about this for a long, long time. He eats Fig New-mans and considers, and you can tell that he's taking it seriously — serious to the extreme.

"Yes," Mark says, looking choked up. "Jeb would do that for us. He would risk it all."

Shoshana nods. "Now you go," she says to us. "You take a turn."

"But we don't know any of the same people anymore," Deb says. "We usually just talk about the neighbors."

"Our across-the-street neighbors," I tell them. "They're the per-fect example. Because the husband, Mitch, he would hide us. I know it. He'd lay down his life for what's right. But that wife of his."

"Yes," Deb says. "Mitch would hide us, but Gloria, she'd buckle. When he was at work one day, she'd turn us in."

"You could play against yourselves," Shoshana says. "What if one of you wasn't Jewish? Would you hide the other?"

"I'll do it," I say. "I'll be the Gentile, because I could pass best. A grown woman with an ankle-length denim skirt in her closet — they'd catch you in a flash."

"Fine," Deb says. And I stand up straight, put my shoulders back, like maybe I'm in a lineup. I stand there with my chin raised so my wife can study me. So she can decide if her husband really has what it takes. Would I have the strength, would I care enough — and it is not a light question, not a throwaway question — to risk my life to save her and our son?

Deb stares, and Deb smiles, and gives me a little push to my chest. "Of course he would," Deb says. She takes the half stride that's between us and gives me a tight hug that she doesn't release. "Now you," Deb says. "You and Yuri go."

"How does that even make sense?" Mark says. "Even for imagining."

"Sh-h-h," Shoshana says. "Just stand over there and be a good Gentile while I look."

"But if I weren't Jewish I wouldn't be me."

"That's for sure," I say.

"He agrees," Mark says. "We wouldn't even be married. We wouldn't have kids."

"Of course you can imagine it," Shoshana says. "Look," she says, and goes over and closes the pantry door. "Here we are, caught in South Florida for the second Holocaust. You're not Jewish, and you've got the three of us hiding in your pantry."

"But look at me!" he says.

"I've got a fix," I say. "You're a background singer for ZZ Top. You know that band?"

Deb lets go of me so she can give my arm a slap.

"Really," Shoshana says. "Look at the three of us like it's your house and we're your charges, locked up in this room."

"And what're you going to do while I do that?" Mark says.

"I'm going to look at you looking at us. I'm going to imagine."

"Okay," he says. "*Nu*, get to it. I will stand, you imagine."

And that's what we do, the four of us. We stand there playing our roles, and we really get into it. I can see Deb seeing him, and him seeing us, and Shoshana just staring at her husband.

We stand there so long I can't tell how much time has passed, though the light changes ever so slightly—the sun outside again dimming—in the crack under the pantry door.

"So would I hide you?" he says. And for the first time that day he reaches out, as my Deb would, and puts his hand to his wife's hand. "Would I, Shoshi?"

And you can tell that Shoshana is thinking of her kids, though that's not part of the scenario. You can tell that she's changed part of the imagining. And she says, after a pause, yes, but she's not laughing. She says yes, but to him it sounds as it does to us, so that he is now asking and asking. But wouldn't I? Wouldn't I hide you? Even if it was life and death—if it would spare you, and they'd kill me alone for doing it? Wouldn't I?

Shoshana pulls back her hand.

She does not say it. And he does not say it. And of the four of us no one will say what cannot be said—that this wife believes her husband would not hide her. What to do? What will come of it? And so we stand like that, the four of us trapped in that pantry. Afraid to open the door and let out what we've locked inside.

MARY GAITSKILL

# The Other Place

FROM *The New Yorker*

MY SON, DOUGLAS, loves to play with toy guns. He is thirteen. He loves video games in which people get killed. He loves violence on TV, especially if it's funny. How did this happen? The way everything does, of course. One thing follows another, naturally.

Naturally, he looks like me: shorter than average, with a fine build, hazel eyes, and light brown hair. Like me, he has a speech impediment and a condition called "essential tremor" that causes involuntary hand movements, which make him look more fragile than he is. He hates reading, but he is bright. He is interested in crows because he heard on a nature show that they are one of the only species that are more intelligent than they need to be to survive. He does beautiful, precise drawings of crows.

Mostly, though, he draws pictures of men holding guns. Or men hanging from nooses. Or men cutting up other men with chainsaws—in these pictures there are no faces, just figures holding chainsaws and figures being cut in two, with blood spraying out.

My wife, Marla, says that this is fine, as long as we balance it out with other things—dinners as a family, discussions of current events, playing sports, exposure to art and nature. But I don't know. Douglas and I were sitting together in the living room last week, half watching the TV and checking email, when an advertisement from a movie flashed across the screen: it was called *Captivity* and it showed a terrified blond girl clinging to the bars of a cage, a tear running down her face. Doug didn't speak or move. But I could feel his fascination, the suddenly deepening quality of it. I don't doubt he could feel mine. We sat there and felt it together.

And then she was there, the woman in the car. In the room with my son, her black hair, her hard laugh, the wrinkled skin under her hard eyes, the sudden blood filling the white of her blue eye. There was excited music on the TV and then the ad ended. My son's attention went elsewhere; she lingered.

When I was a kid, I liked walking through neighborhoods alone, looking at houses, seeing what people did to make them homes: the gardens, the statuary, the potted plants, the wind chimes. Late at night, if I couldn't sleep, I would sometimes slip out my bedroom window and just spend an hour or so walking around by myself. I loved it, especially in late spring, when it was starting to be warm and there were night sounds; crickets, certain birds, the whirring of bats, the occasional whooshing car, some lonely person's TV. I loved the mysterious darkness of trees, the way they moved against the sky if there was wind—big and heavy movements, but delicate too, in all the subtle, reactive leaves. In that soft, blurry weather, people slept with their windows open; it was a small town and they weren't afraid. Some houses—I'm thinking of two houses in particular, where the Legges and the Myers lived, respectively—I would actually hang around in their yards late at night. Once when I was sitting on the Legges' front porch, thinking about stealing a piece of their garden statuary, their cat came and sat with me. I petted him, and when I got up and went for the statuary, he followed me with his tail up. Their statues were elves, not corny, cute elves, but sinister, wicked-looking elves, and I had thought that one would look good in my room. But they were too heavy, and so I just moved them around the yard.

I did things like that, dumb pranks that could only irritate those that noticed them. Rearranging statuary, leaving weird stuff in mailboxes, looking into windows to see where the family had dinner or left their personal things lying around—or, in the case of the Legges, where their daughter, Jenna, slept. She was on the ground floor, her bed so close to the window that I could watch her chest rise and fall the way I watched the grass on their lawn stirring in the wind. The worst thing I did, probably, was putting a giant marble in the Myers' gas tank, which could've really have caused a problem if it had rolled over the gas hole while one of the Myers was driving on the highway, but I guess it never did.

Mostly, though, I wasn't interested in causing that kind of problem. I just wanted to sit and watch, to touch other people's things, to drink in their lives. I suspect that it's some version of these same impulses that makes me the most successful real estate agent in the Hudson Valley now: the ability to know what physical objects and surroundings will most please a person's sense of identity and make him feel at home.

I wish that Doug had this sensitivity to the physical world, and the ability to drink from it. I've tried different things with him; I used to throw the ball with him out in the yard, but he got tired of that; he hates hiking and likes biking only if he has to get someplace. What's working now a little bit is fishing; fly-fishing hip deep in the Hudson. An ideal picture of normal childhood.

I believe I had a normal childhood. But you have to go pretty far afield to find something people would call abnormal now these days. My parents were divorced, and then my mother had boyfriends—but this was true of about half the kids I knew. She and my father fought, in the house when they were together, and they went on fighting, on the phone, after they were separated—loud, screaming fights sometimes. I didn't love it, but I understood it; people fight. I was never afraid that he was going to hurt her, or me. I had nightmares occasionally, in which he turned into a murderer and came after me, chasing me, getting closer, until I fell down, not able to make my legs move right. But I've read that this is one of those primitive fears that everybody secretly has; it bears little relation to what actually happens.

What actually happened: he forced me to play golf with him for hours when I visited on Saturday, even though it seemed only to make him miserable. He'd curse himself if he missed a shot and then that would make him miss another one and he would curse himself more. He'd whisper, "Oh, God," and wipe his face if anything went wrong, or even if it didn't, as if just being there was an ordeal. He'd make these noises sometimes, these painful grunts when he picked up the sack of clubs, and these noises put me on edge and even disgusted me.

Though now, of course, I see it differently. I remembered those

Saturdays when I was first teaching Doug how to cast, out in the back yard. I wasn't much good myself yet, and I got tangled up in the bushes a couple of times. I could feel the boy's flashing impatience; I felt my age too. And then we went to work disentangling and he came closer to help me. We linked in concentration, and it occurred to me that the delicacy of the line and the fine movements needed to free it appealed to him the way drawing appealed to him, because of their beauty and precision.

Besides, he was a natural. When it was his turn to try, he kept his wrist stiff and gave the air a perfect little punch and *zip*—great cast. The next time, he got tangled up, but he was speedy about getting unstuck so he could do it again. Even when the tremor acted up. Even when I lectured him on the laws of physics. It was a good day.

There is one not-normal thing you could point to in my childhood, which is that my mother, earlier in her life, before I was born, had occasionally worked as a prostitute. But I don't think that counts because I didn't know about it as a child. I didn't learn about it until six years ago when I was thirty-eight and my mother was sick with a strain of flu that had killed a lot of people, most of them around her age. She was in the hospital and she was feverish and thought she was dying. She held my hand as she told me, her eyes sad half-moons, her lips still full and provocative. She said she wanted me to know because she thought it might help me to understand some of the terrible things I heard my father say to her —things I mostly hadn't even listened to. "It wasn't anything really bad," she said. "I just needed the money sometimes, between jobs. It's not like I was a drug addict—it was just hard to make it in Manhattan. I only worked for good escort places, I never had a pimp or went out on the street. I never did anything perverted—I didn't have to. I was beautiful. They'd just pay to be with me."

Later, when she didn't die, she was embarrassed that she'd told me. She laughed that raucous laugh of hers and said, "Way to go, Marcy! On your deathbed tell your son you're a whore and then don't die!"

"It's okay," I said.

And it was. It frankly was not really even much of a surprise. It was her vanity that disgusted me, the way she undercut the confession with a preening, maudlin joke. I could not respect that even then.

I don't think that my mom's confession, or whatever it may have implied, had anything to do with what I think of as "it." When I was growing up, there was, after all, no evidence of her past, nothing that could have affected me. But suddenly, just as I was about fourteen, I started getting excited about the thought of girls being hurt. Or killed. A horror movie would be on TV, a girl in shorts would be running and screaming with some guy chasing her, and to me it was like porn. Even a scene where a sexy girl was getting her legs torn off by a shark—bingo. It was like pushing a button. My mom would be in the kitchen making dinner and talking on the phone, stirring and striding around with the phone tucked between her shoulder and chin. Outside, cars would go by, a dog might run across the lawn. My homework would be slowly getting done in my lap and this sexy girl was screaming "God help me!" and having her legs torn off. And I would go invisibly into an invisible world that I called "the other place." Where I sometimes passively watched a killer and other times became one.

It's true that I started drinking and drugging right about then. All my friends did. My mom tried to lay down the law, but I found ways around her. We would go into the woods, me and usually Chet Wotazak and Jim Bonham, and we'd smoke weed we'd got from Chet's brother, a local dealer named Dan, and drink cheap wine. We could sometimes get Chet's dad to give us a gun—in my memory he had an AK-47, though I don't know how that's possible—and we'd go out to a local junkyard and take turns shooting up toilets, long tubes of fluorescent lights, whatever was there. And then we'd go to Chet's house, up to his room, where we'd play loud music and tell dumb jokes and watch music videos in which disgusting things happened: snakes crawled over a little boy's sleeping face and he woke up being chased by a huge truck; a girl was turned into a pig and then a cake and then the lead singer bit off her head.

You might think the videos and the guns were part of it, that they encouraged my violent thoughts. But Chet and Jim were watching and doing the same things and they were not like me. They said mean things about girls, and they were disrespectful sometimes, but they didn't want to hurt them, not really. They wanted to touch them and be touched by them; they wanted that more than anything. You could hear it in their voices and see it in their eyes, no matter what they said.

So I would sit with them and yet be completely apart from them, talking and laughing about normal things in a dark mash of music and snakes and children running from psychos and girls being eaten—and be someplace my friends couldn't see, although it was right there in the room with us.

It was the same at home. My mother made dinner, talked on the phone, fought with my dad, had guys over. Our cat licked itself and ate from its dish. Around us, people cared about one another. Jenna Legge slept peacefully. But in the other place, sexy girls— and sometimes ugly girls or older women—ran and screamed for help as an unstoppable, all-powerful killer came closer and closer. There was no school or sports or mom or dad or caring, and it was great.

I've told my wife about most of this, the drinking, the drugs, the murder fantasies. She understands because she has her past too: extreme sex, vandalizing cars, talking vulnerable girls into getting more drunk than they should on behalf of some guy. There's a picture of her and this other girl wearing bathing suits, the other girl chugging a beer being held by a guy so it goes straight down her throat as her head is tipped way back. Another guy is watching, and my smiling wife is holding the girl's hand. It's a picture that foreshadows cruelty or misery, or maybe just a funny story to tell about throwing up in the bathroom later. Privately, I see no similarity between it and my death fantasies. For my wife, the connection is drugs and alcohol; she believes that we were that way because we were both addicts expressing our pain and anger in violent fantasies and blind actions.

The first time I took Doug out to fish, it was me on the hot golf course all over again. As we walked to the lake in our heavy boots and clothes, I could feel his irritation at the bugs and the brightness, the squalor of nature in his fastidious eyes. I told him that fly-fishing was like driving a sports car as opposed to the Subaru of rod and reel. I went on about how anything beautiful had to be conquered. He just pulled down his mouth.

He got interested, though, in tying on the fly; the simple elegance of the knot (the "fish-killer") arrested him. He laid it down the first time too, placing the backcast perfectly in a space between trees. He gazed at the brown, light-wrinkled water with satisfaction. But when I put my hand on his shoulder, I could feel him inwardly pull away.

As I got older, my night walks became rarer, with a different, sadder feeling to them. I would go out when I was not drunk or high but in a quiet mood, wanting to be somewhere that was neither the normal social world nor the other place. A world where I could still sit and feel the power of nature come up through my feet, and be near other people without them being near me. Where I could believe in and for a moment possess the goodness of their lives. Jenna Legge still slept on the ground floor and sometimes I would look in and watch her breathe, and, if I was lucky, see one of her developing breasts swell out of her nightgown.

I never thought of killing Jenna. I didn't think about killing anyone I actually knew—not girls I didn't like at school, not the few I had sex with. The first times I had sex, I was so caught up in the feeling of it that I didn't even think about killing—I didn't think about anything at all. But I didn't have sex much. I was small, awkward, too quiet; I had that tremor. My expression must've been strange as I sat in class, feeling hidden in my other place, but outwardly visible to whoever looked—not that many did.

Then one day I was with Chet's brother, Dan, on a drug drop; he happened to be giving me a ride because the drop, at the local college, was on the way to wherever I was going. It was a guy buying, but when we arrived, a girl opened the door. She was pretty and she knew it, but whatever confidence that knowledge gave her was superficial. We stayed for a while and smoked the product with her and her boyfriend. The girl sat very erect and talked too much, as if she was smart, but there was a question at the end of everything she said. When we left, Dan said, "That's the kind of lady I'd like to slap in the face." I said, "Why?" But I knew. I don't remember what he said, because it didn't matter. I already knew. And later, instead of making up a girl, I thought of that one.

I forgot to mention: one night, when I was outside Jenna's window, she opened her eyes and looked right at me. I was stunned, so

stunned that I couldn't move. There was nothing between us but
a screen with a hole in it. She looked at me and blinked. I said,
"Hi." I held my breath; I had not spoken to her since third grade.
But she just sighed, rolled over, and lay still. I stood there trembling for a long moment. And then, slowly and carefully, I walked
through the yard and onto the sidewalk, back to my house.

I cut school the next day and the next because I was scared that
Jenna would've told everybody and that I would be mocked. But
eventually it became clear that nobody was saying anything, so I
went back. I looked at Jenna cautiously, then gratefully. But she
did not return my look. At first this moved me, made me consider
her powerful. I tried insistently to catch her eye, to let her know
what I felt. Finally our eyes met, and I realized she didn't understand why I was looking at her. I realized that although her eyes
had been open that night, she had been asleep. She had looked
right at me, but she had not seen me at all.

And so one night, or early morning, I got out of bed, into my
mother's car, and drove to the campus to look for her—the college girl.

The campus was in a heavily wooded area bordering a nature
preserve. The dorms were widely scattered, though some, resem-
bling midsized family homes, were clustered together. The girl
lived in one of those, but though I remembered the general location, I couldn't be sure which one it was. I couldn't see into
any of the windows because even the open ones had blinds pulled
down. While I was standing indecisively on a paved path between
dorms, I saw two guys coming toward me. Quickly, I walked off
into a section of trees and underbrush. I moved carefully through
the thicket, coming to a wide field that led toward the nature preserve. The darkness deepened as I got farther from the dorms. As
I walked, I could feel things coming up from the ground—teeth
and claws, eyes, crawling legs, and brainless eating mouths. A song
played in my head, an enormously popular romantic song about
love and death that had supposedly made a bunch of teenagers
kill themselves.

Kids still listen to this same song—I once heard it coming from
the computer in the family room. When I came in and looked
over Doug's hunched shoulder, I realized the song was being used
as the soundtrack for a graphic video about a little boy in a mask

murdering people. It was spellbinding, the yearning, eerie harmony of the song juxtaposed with terrified screaming. I told Doug to turn it off. He looked pissed, but he did it and went slumping out the door. I found it and watched it by myself later.

I went back to the campus many times. I went to avoid my mother as much as anything. Her new boyfriend was an asshole, and she whined when he was around. When he wasn't around, she whined about him on the phone. Sometimes she called two people in a row to whine about exactly the same things he'd said or done. Even when I played loud music so I couldn't hear her, I could *feel* her. When that happened, I'd leave my music on so she'd think I was in my room and I'd go to the campus. I'd follow female students as closely as I could, and I'd feel the other place running against the membrane of the world, almost touching it.

Why does it make sense to put romantic music together with a little boy murdering people? Because it did make sense—only I don't know how. It seems dimly to have to do with justice, with some wrong being avenged, but what? The hurts of childhood? The stupidity of life? The kid doesn't seem to be having fun. Random murder just seems like a job he has to do. But why?

Soon enough I realized that the college campus was the wrong place to think about making it real. It wasn't an environment I could control; there were too many variables. I needed to get the girl someplace private. I needed to have certain things there. I needed to have a gun. I could find a place; there were deserted places. I could get a gun from Chet's house; I knew where his father kept his. But the girl?

Then, while I was in the car with my mom, we saw a guy hitchhiking. He was middle-aged and fucked-up-looking and my mom —we were stopped at a light—remarked that nobody in their right mind would pick him up. Two seconds later, somebody pulled over for him. My mom laughed.

I started hitchhiking. Most of the people who picked me up were men, but there were women too. No one was scared of me. I was almost eighteen by then, but I was still small and quiet-looking. Women picked me up because they were concerned about me.

I didn't really plan to do it. Mostly I just wanted to feel the gun in my pocket and look at the woman and know I *could* do it. There was this one; a thirtyish blond with breasts I could see through her open coat. But then she said she was pregnant and I started thinking, What if I was killing the baby?

Doug had a lot of nightmares when he was a baby, by which I mean between the ages of two and four. When he cried out in his sleep it was usually Marla who went to him. But one night she was sick and I told her to stay in bed while I went to comfort the boy. He was still crying "Mommy!" when I sat on the bed, and I felt his anxiety at seeing me instead of his mother, felt the moment of hesitation in his body before he came into my arms, vibrating rather than trembling, sweating and fragrant with emotion. He had dreamed that he was home alone and it was dark, and he was calling for his mother, but she wasn't there. "Daddy, Daddy," he wept, "there was a sick lady with red eyes and Mommy wouldn't come. Where is Mommy?"

That may've been the first time I truly remembered her, the woman in the car. It was so intense a moment that in a bizarre intersection of impossible feelings, I got an erection with my crying child in my arms. But it lasted only a moment. I picked Doug up and carried him into our bedroom so that he could see his mother and nestle against her. I stayed awake nearly all night watching them.

The day it happened was a bright day, but windy and cold, and my mom would not shut up. I just wanted to watch a movie, but even with the TV turned up loud—I guess that's why she kept talking; she didn't think I could hear—I couldn't blot out the sound of her yakking about how ashamed this asshole made her feel. I whispered, "If you're so ashamed, why do you talk about it?" She said, "It all goes back to being fucking molested." She lowered her voice; the only words I caught were "fucking corny." I went out into the hall to hear. "The worst of it was that he wouldn't look at me," she said. I could almost hear her pacing around, the phone tucked between shoulder and chin. "That's why I fall for these passive-aggressive types who turn me on and then make me feel ashamed." Whoever she was talking to must've said something funny then, because she laughed. I left the TV on and walked out. I took the gun, but more for protection against perverts than the other thing.

I gave my boy that dream as surely as if I'd handed it to him. But I've given him a lot of other things too. The first time he caught a fish, he responded to my encouraging words with a bright glance I will never forget. We let that one go, but only after he held it in his hands: cold and quick, muscle with eyes and a heart, scales specked with yellow and red, and one tiny orange fin. Then the next one, bigger, leaping to break the rippling murk—I said, "Don't point the rod at the fish. Keep the tip up, keep it up"—and he listened to me and he brought it in. There is a picture of it on the corkboard in his room, the fish in the net, the lure bristling in its crude mouth. And I have another picture too of him holding it in his hands, smiling triumphantly, its shining, still-living body fully extended.

She was older than I'd wanted, forty or even forty-five, but still good-looking. She had a voice that was strong and lifeless at the same time. She had black hair and she wore tight black pants. She did not have a wedding ring, which meant that maybe nobody would miss her. She picked me up on a lightly traveled forty-five-miles-an-hour road. She was listening to a talk show on the radio and she asked if I wanted to hear music instead. I said no, I liked talk shows.

"Yeah?" she asked. "Why?"

"Because I'm interested in current events."

"I'm not," she said. "I just listen to this shit because the voices relax me. I don't really care what they're talking about."

They were talking about a war somewhere. Bombs were going off in markets where people bought vegetables; somebody's legs had been blown off. We turned onto a road with a few cars, but none close to us.

"You don't care?"

"No, why should I? Oh, about this?" She paused. There was something about a little boy being rushed to an overcrowded hospital. "Yeah, that's bad. But it's not like we can do anything about it." On the radio, foreign people cried.

I took the gun out of my pocket.

I said, "Do you have kids?"

"No," she said. "Why?"

"Take me to Old Post Road. I'm going to the abandoned house there."

"I'm not going by there, but I can get you pretty close. So why do you care about current events? I didn't give a shit at your age."

"Take me there or I'll kill you."

She cocked her head and wrinkled her brow, as if she was trying to be sure she heard right. Then she looked down at the gun, and cut her eyes up at me; quickly, she looked back at the road. The car picked up speed.

"Take the next right or you'll die." My voice at that moment did not come from me but from the other place. My whole body felt like an erection. She hit the right-turn signal. There was a long moment as we approached the crucial road. The voices on the radio roared ecstatically.

She pulled over to the shoulder.

"What are you doing?"

She put the car in park.

"Turn right or you die!"

She unbuckled her seat belt and turned to face me. "I'm ready," she said. She leaned back and gripped the steering wheel with one hand, as if to steady herself. With her free hand she tapped herself between the eyes—bright blue, hot, rimmed with red. "Put it here," she said. "Go for it."

A car went by. Someone in the passenger seat looked at us blankly. "I don't want to do it here. There's witnesses. You need to take me to the place."

"What witnesses? That car's not stopping, nobody's going to stop unless the emergency lights are on and they're not, look."

"But if I shoot you in the head, the blood will spray on the window and somebody could see." It was my own voice again: the power was gone. The people on the radio kept talking. Suddenly I felt my heart beating.

"Okay, then do it here." She opened her jacket to show me her chest. "Nobody'll hear. When you're done, you can move me to the passenger seat and drive the car wherever."

"Get in the passenger seat now and I'll do it."

She laughed, hard. Her eyes were crazy. They were crazy the

way an animal can be crazy in a tiny cage. "Hell, no. I'm not going to your place with you. You do it here, motherfucker."

I realized then that her hair was a wig, and a cheap one. For some reason that made her seem even crazier. I held my gun hand against my body to hide the tremor.

"Come on, honey," she said. "Go for it."

Like a star, a red dot appeared in the white of her left eye. The normal place and the other place were turning into the same place, quick but slow, the way a car accident is quick but slow. I stared. The blood spread raggedly across her eye. She shifted her gaze from my face to a spot somewhere outside the car and fixed it there. I fought the urge to turn and see what she was staring at. She shifted her eyes again. She looked me deep in the face.

"Well," she said, "are you going to do it or not?"

Words appeared in my head, like a sign reading I DON'T WANT TO.

She leaned forward and turned on the emergency flashers. "Get out of my car," she said quietly. "You're wasting my time."

As soon as I got out, she hit the gas and burned rubber. I walked into the field next to the road, without an idea of where I might go. I realized after she was gone that she could call the police, but I felt in my gut that she would not—in the other place there are no police, and she was from the other place.

Still, as I walked I took the bullets out of the gun and scattered them, kicking snow over them and stamping it down. I walked a long time, shivering horribly. I came across a drainage pipe and threw the empty gun into it. I thought, I should've gut-shot her, that's what I should've done. And then got her to the abandoned house. I should've gut-shot the bitch. But I knew why I hadn't. She'd been shot already, from the inside. If she had been somebody different I might actually have done it. But somehow the wig-haired woman had changed the channel and I don't even know if she meant to.

The fly bobbing on the brown, gentle water. The long grasses so green that they cast a fine, bright green on the brown water. The primitive fish mouth straining for water and finding it as my son released it in the shallows. Its murky vanishing.

The blood bursting in her eye, poor woman, my poor mother.

My mother died of colon cancer just nine months ago. Shortly after that it occurred to me that the woman was wearing that awful wig because she was sick and recovering from chemo. Though of course I don't know.

The hurts of childhood that must be avenged: so small and so huge. Before I grew up and stopped thinking about her, I thought about that woman a lot. About what would've happened if I'd gotten her there, to the abandoned house. I don't remember anymore the details of these thoughts, only that they were distorted, swollen, blurred: broken face, broken voice, broken body left dying on the floor, watching me go with dimming, despairing eyes.

These pictures are faded now and far away. But they can still make me feel something.

The second time I put my hand on Doug's shoulder, he didn't move away inside; he was too busy tuning in to the line and the lure. Somewhere in him is the other place. It's quiet now, but I know it's there. I also know that he won't be alone with it. He won't know I'm there with him because we will never speak of it. But I will be there. He will not be alone with that.

ROXANE GAY

# North Country

FROM *Hobart*

I HAVE MOVED to the edge of the world for two years. If I am
not careful, I will fall. After my first department meeting, my new
colleagues encourage me to join them on a scenic cruise to meet
more locals. The *Peninsula Star* will travel through the Portage Canal, up to Copper Harbor, and then out onto Lake Superior. I am
handed a glossy brochure with bright pictures of blue skies and
calm lake waters. "You'll be able to enjoy the foliage," they tell me,
shining with enthusiasm for the Upper Peninsula. "Do you know
how to swim?" they ask.

I arm myself with a flask, a warm coat, and a book. At the dock,
there's a long line of ruddy Michiganders chatting amiably about
when they expect the first snow to fall. It is August. I have moved
to the Upper Peninsula to assume a postdoc at the Michigan Institute of Technology. My colleagues, all civil engineers, wave to me.
"You came," they shout. They've already started drinking. I take a
nip from my flask. "You're going to love this cruise," they say. "Are
you single?" they ask.

We sit in a cramped booth, drinking Rolling Rocks. Every few
minutes one of my colleagues offers an interesting piece of Upper
Peninsula trivia such as the high incidence of waterfalls in the area
or the three hundred inches of snow the place receives annually. I
take a long, hard swallow from my flask. I am flanked by a balding,
overweight tunnel expert on my right and a dark-skinned hydrologist from India on my left. The hydrologist is lean and quiet and
his knee presses uncomfortably against mine. He tells me he has a
wife back in Chennai but that in Michigan, he's leaving his options

open. I am the only woman in the department and as such, I am a double novelty. My new colleagues continue to buy me drinks and I continue to accept them until my ears are ringing and I can feel a flush in my cheeks, sweat dripping down my back. "I need some fresh air," I mumble, excusing myself. I make my way, slowly, to the upper deck, ignoring the stares and lulls in conversation.

Outside, the air is crisp and thin, the upper deck sparsely populated. Near the bow, a young couple makes out enthusiastically, loudly. A few feet away from them a group of teenagers stand in a huddle, snickering. I sit on a red plastic bench and hold my head in my hands. My flask sits comfortably and comfortingly against my rib cage.

"I saw you downstairs," a man with a deep voice says.

The sun is setting, casting that strange quality of light rendering everything white, nearly invisible. I squint and look up slowly at a tall man with shaggy hair hanging over his ears. I nod.

"Are you from Detroit?"

I have been asked this question twenty-three times since moving to the area. In a month, I will stop counting, having reached a four-digit number. Shortly after that, I will begin telling people I have recently arrived from Africa. They will nod and exhale excitedly and ask about my tribe. I don't know that in this moment, so there is little to comfort me. I shake my head.

"Do you talk?"

"I do," I say. "Are you from Detroit?"

He smiles, slow and lazy. He's handsome in his own way—his skin is tan and weathered and his eyes are almost as blue as the lake we're cruising on. He sits down. I stare at his fingers, the largest fingers I've ever seen. The sweaty beer bottle in his hand looks miniature. "So where are you from?"

I shove my hands in my pockets and slide away from him. "Nebraska."

"I've never met anyone from Nebraska," he says.

I say, "I get that a lot."

The boat is now out of the Portage Canal and we're so far out on the lake, I can't see land. I feel small.

"I better get back to my colleagues," I say, standing up. As I walk away, he shouts, "My name is Magnus." I throw a hand in the air but I don't look back.

*

In my lab, things make sense. As a structural engineer, I design concrete mixes, experiment with new aggregates like fly ash and other energy byproducts, artificial particulates, kinds of water that might make concrete not just stronger but unbreakable, perma- nent, perfect. I teach a section of Design of Concrete Structures and a section of Structural Dynamics. I have no female students in either class. The boys stare at me, and after class, they linger in the hallway just outside the classroom. They try to flirt. I remind them I will assess their final grades. They make inappropriate comments about extra credit.

At night, I sit in my apartment and watch TV and search for fac- ulty positions and other career opportunities closer to the center of the world. There's a pizza restaurant across the street and above the restaurant, an apartment filled with loud white girls who play rap loudly into the middle of the night and have fights with their boyfriends who play basketball for the university. One of the girls has had an abortion and another isn't speaking to her father and the third roommate has athletic sex with her boyfriend even when the other two are awake; she has a child but the child lives with her father. I do not want to know any of these things.

Several unopened boxes are sitting in my new apartment. To unpack those boxes means I will stay. To stay means I will be trapped in this desolate place for two years, alone. I rented my new home—a former dry-cleaning business converted into an apartment—over the phone. There are no windows, save for the one in the front door. The apartment, I thought, as I walked from room to room when I moved in, was like a jail cell. I had been sentenced. My new landlady, an octogenarian Italian who ran the dry cleaner's for more than thirty years, gasped when she met me. "You didn't sound like a colored girl on the phone," she said. I said, "I get that a lot."

The produce is always rotten at the local grocery store—we're too far north to receive timely food deliveries. I stand before a dis- play of tomatoes, limp, covered in wrinkled skin, some dotted soft white craters ringed by some kind of black mold. I consider the cost to my dignity if I move in with my parents, until I feel a heavy hand on my shoulder. When I spin around, struggling to maintain my balance, I recognize Magnus. I grab his wrist between two fin- gers and step away. "Do you always touch strangers?"

"We're not strangers."

I make quick work of selecting the least decomposed tomatoes and move on to the lettuce. Magnus follows. I say, "We have different understandings of the word *stranger.* You don't even know my name."

"I like the way you talk," he says.

"What is that supposed to mean?"

Magnus reddens. "Exactly what I said. Unless we have different understandings of the words *I, like, the, way, you,* and *talk.*"

I bite the inside of my cheek to keep from smiling.

"Can I buy you a drink?"

I look at the pathetic tomatoes in my basket and maybe it's the overwhelming brightness of the fluorescent lighting or the Easy Listening being piped through the store speakers, but I nod before I can say no. I say, "My name is Kate." Magnus says, "Meet me at the Thirsty Fish, Kate." On the drive there, I stare at my reflection in the rearview mirror and smooth my eyebrows. At the bar, Magnus entertains me with the silly things girls like to take seriously. He buys me lots of drinks and I drink them. He flatters me with words about my pretty eyes. He says he can tell I'm smart. I haven't had sex in more than two months. I haven't had a real conversation with anyone in more than two months. I'm not at my best.

In the parking lot, I stand next to my car, holding on to the door, trying to steady myself. Magnus says, "I can't let you drive home like this." I mutter something about the altitude affecting my tolerance. He says, "We're not in the mountains." He stands so close. The warmth from his chest fills the short distance between us. Magnus takes my keys and as I reach for them, I fall into him. He lifts my chin with one of his massive fingers and I say, "Fuck." I kiss him, softly. Our lips barely move but we don't pull apart. His hand is solid in the small of my back as he presses me against my car.

When I wake up, my mouth is thick and sour. I groan and sit up, and hit my head against something unfamiliar. I wince. Everything in my head feels loose, lost.

"Be careful. It's a tight fit in here."

I rub my eyes, trying to swallow the panic bubbling at the base of my throat. I clutch at my chest.

"Relax. I didn't know where you lived, so I brought you back to my place."

I take a deep breath, look around. I'm sitting on a narrow bed. I see Magnus through a narrow doorway standing near a two-burner stove. My feet are bare. A cat jumps into my lap. I scream.

Magnus lives in a trailer, and not one of those fancy double-wides on a foundation with a well-kept garden in front, but rather an old, rusty trailer that can be attached to a truck and driven away. It is the kind of trailer you see in sad, forgotten places that have surrendered to rust and overgrown weeds and cars on cinder blocks and sagging laundry lines. The trailer, on the outside, is in a fair amount of disrepair, but the inside is immaculate. Everything has its proper place.

"You should eat something," he says.

I extricate myself from the cat and walk into the galley area. Magnus invites me to sit at the table and he sets a plate of dry scrambled eggs and a mug of coffee in front of me. My stomach rolls wildly. I wrap my hands around the coffee mug and inhale deeply. I try to make sense of the trajectory between rotten tomatoes and this trailer. Magnus slides onto the bench across from me. He explains that he lives in this trailer because it's free. It's free because his trailer sits on the corner of a parcel of land his sister Mira and her husband, Peter, farm. The farm is twenty minutes outside of town. There's no cell phone reception. I can't check my email, he tells me, as I wave my phone in different directions, desperate for a signal. I ask him why he lives this way. He says he has a room in his sister's house he rarely uses. He likes his privacy.

"You took my shoes off."

Magnus nods. "You have nice feet."

"Can you take me to my car?"

Magnus sighs, quickly drains the rest of his coffee into the small sink.

On the drive back to town I sit as far away from Magnus as possible. I try to re-create the events that happened between standing in the parking lot and waking up in a trailer with a cat in my lap. I refuse to ask Magnus to fill in the blanks. At my car, he grips the steering wheel tightly. I thank him for the ride and he hands me my keys. He says, "I'd love your phone number."

I force myself to smile. I say, "Thank you for not letting me drive last night." I say, "I don't normally drink much, but I just moved here." He says, "Yes, the altitude," and waits until I drive away. I remember the pressure of his lips against mine, their texture.

In my lab, things make sense. The first snow falls in late September. It will continue to fall until May. I tell my mother I may not survive. I tell her this so many times, she starts to worry. I test cement fitness. I fill molds with cylinders of concrete. I experiment with saltwater and bottled water and lake water and tap water. I cure and condition specimens. I take detailed notes. I write an article. I turn down three dates with three separate colleagues. The hydrologist from Chennai reaffirms the openness of his options in the United States. I reaffirm my lake of interest in his options. I administer an exam that compels my students to call me Battle-Ax. I attend a campus social for single faculty. There are seven women in attendance and more than thirty men. The hydrologist is there too. He doesn't wear a wedding ring. I am asked thirty-four times if I am from Detroit, a new record for a single day. I try to remember where Magnus lives and all I recall is a blurry memory of being drunk, burying my face into his arm as we drove, and him, singing along to Counting Crows. I love Counting Crows.

There once was a man. There is always some man. We were together for six years. He was an engineer too. Some people called him my dissertation adviser. When we got involved, he told me he would teach me things and mold me into a great scholar. He said I was the brightest girl he had ever known. Then he contradicted himself. He said we would marry and thought I believed him. A couple of years passed and he said we would marry when he was promoted to full professor and then it was when I finished my degree. I got pregnant and he said we would marry when the baby was born. The baby was stillborn and he said we would marry when I recovered from the loss. I told him I was as recovered as I was ever going to be. He had no more excuses and I no longer cared to marry him. I spent most of my nights awake while he slept soundly, remembering what it felt like to rub my swollen belly and feel my baby kicking. He told me I was cold and distant. He told me I had no reason to mourn a child that never lived. He amused himself with a new lab assistant who consistently wore insensible shoes and short skirts even though we spent our days working with sand and cement and other dirty things. I found them fucking, the lab assistant bent over a stack of concrete bricks squealing like a debutante porn star, the man thrusting vigorously, literally fucking the lab assistant right out of her high heels, his fat face red and shiny. He gasped in short, repulsive bursts. The scene was so common, I couldn't even get angry. I had long stopped feeling anything where he was concerned. I returned to my office, accepted the postdoc position, and never looked back. I would have named our daughter Emma. She would have been beautiful despite her father. She would have been four months old when I left.

Snow has been falling incessantly. The locals are overjoyed. Every night, I hear the high-pitched whine of snowmobiles speeding past my apartment. There are things I will need to survive the winter —salt, a shovel, a new toilet seat, rope—so I brave the weather and go to the hardware store. I am wearing boots laced high over my calves, a coat, gloves, hat and scarf, thermal underwear. I never remove these items unless I am home. It takes too much effort. I wonder how these people manage to reproduce. I see Magnus standing over a display of chainsaws. I turn to walk away but then I don't. I stand still and hope he notices me. I realize that dressed as I am, my own family wouldn't recognize me. I tap his shoulder. I say, "What do you plan on massacring?"

He looks up slowly, shrugs. "Just looking," he says.

"For a victim?"

"Aren't you feeling neighborly?"

"I thought I would say hello."

Magnus nods again. "You've said hello."

I swallow, hard. My irritation tastes bitter. I quickly tell him my phone number and go to find a stronger kind of rope. As I pull away, I notice Magnus watching me from inside the store. I smile.

In my lab things make sense. I teach my students how to make perfect concrete cylinders, how to perform compression tests. They crush their perfect cylinders and roar with delight each time the concrete shatters and the air is filled with a fine dust. There's a lot to love about breaking things.

Everyone I meet dispenses a bit of wisdom on how to survive the "difficult" winters—embrace the outdoors, drinking, travel, drinking, sun lamps, drinking, sex, drinking. The hydrologist offers to prepare spicy curries to keep me warm, offers to give me a taste of his very special curry. I decline, tell him I have a delicate constitution. Nils, my department chair, stops by my office. He says, "How are you holding up?" I assure him all is well. He says, "The first year is always the hardest." He says, "You might want to take a trip to Detroit to see your family." I thank him for the support.

I am walking around the lab, watching students work, when Magnus calls. I excuse myself and take the call in the hallway, ignoring the students milling about, with their aimless expressions.

My heart beats loudly. I can hardly hear Magnus. I say, "You didn't need to take so long to call me."

"Is this a lecture?"

"Would you like it to be?"

"Can I make you dinner?"

I ignore my natural impulse to say no. He invites me back to his trailer, where he prepares steak and green beans and baked potatoes. We drink beer. We talk, or rather, I talk, filling his trailer with all the words I've kept to myself since moving to the North Country, longer. I complain about the weather. At some point, he holds his hand open and I slide my hand in his. He traces my knuckles with his thumb. He is plainspoken and honest. His voice is strong and clear. He talks about his job as a logger and his band —he plays guitar. When we finally stop talking he says, "I like you," and then he stands and pulls me to my feet. I stand on his boots and wrap my arms around him. He is thick and solid. When we kiss, he is gentle, too gentle. I say, "You don't have to be soft with me," and he grunts. He clasps my neck with one of his giant hands and kisses me harder, his lips forcing mine open. He brushes his lips across my chin. He sinks his teeth into my neck and I grab his shirt between my fists. I try to remain standing. I say, "My neck is the secret password." He bites my neck harder and I forget about everything and all the noise in my head quiets.

In the morning, I want to leave quickly even though I can still feel Magnus in my skin. As I sit on the edge of the bed and pull my pants on, he says, "I want to see you again." I say yes but explain we have to keep things casual, that we can't become a *thing*. He traces my naked spine with his fingers and I shiver. He says, "We're already a thing." I stand, shaking my head angrily. "That's not even possible." He says, "Sometimes, when I'm miles deep in the woods, looking for a new cutting site, it feels like I'm the first man who has ever been there. I look up and the trees are so thick I can hardly see the sky. I get so scared, but the world somehow makes sense there. Being with you feels like that." I shake my head again, my fingers trembling as I finish getting dressed. I feel nauseated and dizzy. I say, "I'm allergic to cats." I say, "You shouldn't talk like that." I recite his words over and over for the rest of the day, the week, the month.

Several weeks later, I'm at Magnus's trailer. We've seen each other almost every night, at his place, where he cooks and we talk and we have sex. We're lying naked in his narrow bed. I say, "If this continues much longer, we're going to have to sleep at my place. I have a real bed and actual rooms." He smiles and nods. He says, "Whatever you want." After Magnus falls asleep, I stare up at the low ceiling, then out the small window at the clear winter sky. Just as I'm falling asleep, his alarm goes off. Magnus sits up, rubbing his eyes. Even in the darkness I can see his hair standing on end. He says, "I want to show you something." We dress, but he tells me I can leave my coat. Instead, he hands me a quilt. Outside, a fresh blanket of snow has fallen. The moon is still high. Everything is perfect and silent and still. The air hurts but feels clean. He cuts a trail to the barn and I follow in his footsteps. As Magnus walks, he stares up into the sky. I tell myself, "I feel nothing." Inside the barn, I shiver and dance from foot to foot trying to stay warm. He says, "We have to milk the cows." He nods to a small campstool next to a very large cow. I say, "There is absolutely no way." Magnus leads me to the stool and forces me onto it. He hunches down behind me, and he pats the cow on her side. He hasn't shaved yet, so the stubble from his beard tickles me. He kisses my neck softly. He places his hands over mine, and I learn how to milk a cow. Nothing makes sense here.

Hunting season starts. Magnus shows me his rifle, long, polished, powerful. He refers to his rifle as a "she" and a "her." I tell him my father hunts and Magnus gets excited. He says, "Maybe someday your father and I can hunt together." I explain that my father hunts pheasant, and by hunt, I mean he rides around with his friends on a four-wheeler but doesn't really kill much of anything and often gets injured in embarrassing accidents. I say, "You and he hunt differently." He says, "I still want to meet your father." "I introduce only serious boyfriends to my family," I say. Magnus holds my chin between two fingers and looks at me hard. It makes me shiver. This is the first time I've seen real anger from him. I wonder how far I can push. He says, "You won't see me for a few days, but I'm going to kill a buck for you." Five days later, Magnus shows up at my apartment still wearing his camouflage and Carhartt overalls. His beard is long and unkempt. He smells rank. He is dirty. I recognize only his eyes. Magnus steps inside and pulls me into a muscular hug that makes me feel like he is rearranging my insides. I inhale deeply. I am surprised by the sharp twinge between my thighs. When he kisses me, he is possessive, controlling, salty. He moans into my mouth and turns me around, pinning my arms over my head. He fucks me against the front door. I smile. Afterward, we both sink to the floor. He says, "The buck is in the car." He says, "I missed you." I want to say something, the right thing, the kind thing. I slap his thigh. I push. I say, "Please take a shower."

I visit my parents in Florida for Thanksgiving and my mother asks why I don't call as often. I explain how work has gotten busy. I explain how snow has fallen every single day for more than a month and how everyone thinks I'm from Detroit. My mother says I look thin. She says I'm too quiet. We don't talk about the dead child or the father of the dead child. There is "this life" and "that life." We pretend "that life" never happened. It is a mercy. Magnus calls every morning before he leaves for work and every night before he falls asleep. One afternoon he calls and my mother answers my phone. I hear her laughing as she says, "What an unusual name." When she hands me my phone, she asks, "Who is this Magnus? Such a nice young man." I push. I say he's no one important. I say it a little too loudly. When I put my phone to my ear, I can only hear a dial tone. Magnus doesn't call for the rest of my trip. We won't speak until the end of January.

In my lab things make sense but they don't. I can't concentrate. I want to call Magnus, but my repeated bad behavior overwhelms me. The weather has grown colder, sharper. The world grows and I shrink. My students work on final projects. I have a paper accepted at a major conference. The semester ends; I return to Florida for the holidays. My mother says I look thin. She says I'm too quiet. When she asks if I want to talk about my child, I shake my head. I say, "Please don't ever mention her again, not ever." My mother holds the palm of one hand to my cheek and the palm of the other over my heart. I send Magnus a card and a letter and gift and another letter and another letter. He sends me a text message: I'M STILL ANGRY. I send more letters. He writes back once and I carry his letter with me everywhere. I try to acquire a taste for venison. The new semester starts. I have another paper accepted at a conference, this one in Europe. A new group of students tries to flirt with me while learning about the wonder of concrete. I get a research grant and my department chair offers me a tenure-track faculty position with the department. He tells me to take as much time as I need to consider his offer. He says the department really needs someone like me. He says, "You kill two birds with one stone, Katie." I contemplate placing his head in the compression-testing machine. I say, "I prefer to be called Kate."

The hydrologist corners me in my lab late at night and makes an inappropriate advance that leaves me unsettled. For weeks, I will feel his long, skinny fingers, how they grabbed at things that weren't his to hold. Even though it's after midnight, I call Magnus. My voice is shaking. He says, "You hurt my feelings," and the simple honesty of his words makes me ache. I say, "I'm sorry. I never say what I really feel," and I cry. He asks, "What's wrong?" I tell him about the married hydrologist, a dirty man with a bright pink tongue who tried to lick my ear and who called me Black Beauty and who got aggressive when I tried to push him away and how I'm nervous about walking to my car. Magnus says, "I'm on my way." I wait for him by the main entrance and when I recognize his bulky frame trudging through the snow toward me, everything feels more bearable. Magnus doesn't say a word. He just holds me. After a long while, he punches the brick wall and says, "I'm going to kill that guy." I believe him. He walks me to my lab to get my things.

At my apartment, I hold a bag of frozen corn against Magnus's scraped knuckles. I say, "I shouldn't have called." He says, "Yes, you should have." He says, "You have to be nicer to me." I straddle his lap and kiss his torn knuckles and pull his hands beneath my shirt.

\*

Magnus starts picking me up from work every night, and if I have to work late, he sits with me, watching me. He tells me about trees and everything a man could ever know from spending his days among them. He often smells like pine and sawdust.

In March, winter lingers. Magnus builds me an igloo and inside, he lights a small fire. He says, "Sometimes, I feel I don't know a thing about you." I am sitting between his legs, my back to his chest. Even though we're wearing layers of clothing, it feels like we're naked. I say, "You know I'm not very nice." He kisses my cheek. He says, "That's not true." He says, "Tell me something true." I tell him how I hold on to the idea of Emma even though I shouldn't, how she's all I really think about, how she might be trying to walk now or say her first words. He brings my cold fingers to his warm lips. He fills all the hollow spaces.

JENNIFER HAIGH

# *Paramour*

FROM *Ploughshares*

THE TRIBUTE WAS held downtown, far away from the theater
district. Christine crossed the street gingerly, on four-inch heels
thin as pencils—Ivan had always loved women in high heels—and
checked the address against the invitation in her purse. The building was new and modern, the front window lettered with Cyril-
lic characters and a boldface translation: UKRAINIAN CULTURAL
CENTER. She'd forgotten, nearly, that he was born in that country.
To her he'd been a New Yorker, nothing else.

The upstairs gallery was large, the wood floors gleaming. A hundred chairs were arranged in a horseshoe, facing an improvised
stage. At the door, a girl handed out programs—shyly, as if embarrassed by her unflattering but perhaps authentically Ukrainian
hairstyle, a long braid wrapped around her head.

In the front row—RESERVED FOR BORYSENKO FAMILY AND
FRIENDS—a woman sat alone. Christine studied her plump
shoulders, her blond hair twisted into a loose chignon. *Beth,* she
thought. The wife's name was lodged in her memory like a bullet that could not be removed. Ivan's marriage, its happiness or
unhappiness, had once consumed her completely. On his desk,
he'd kept a single photograph: the mysterious Beth sitting nude,
her back to the camera, a naked infant asleep on her shoulder, a
wash of pale hair hanging down her back. Now she wore a batik
sundress. Her cleavage was deep and freckled, skin that had spent
forty or fifty summers in the sun.

The room filled, hummed, quieted. A half-dozen men took

seats on the stage. Finally Ivan came striding down the aisle with a girl on his arm. The crowd burst into applause.

He'd aged, of course. His hair, still longish and wavy, was now more gray than black. He whispered something to the girl—a round-faced brunette, impossibly young, squeezed into a clinging dress.

"Let me guess. You were his favorite student."

Christine turned, startled by the intimacy. The man had leaned in close to her ear. For a second she'd felt his breath on her neck.

"I'm Martin, by the way." He was her own age, handsome like a pirate—shaved head, a deeply suntanned face.

"Christine. How did you know I was his student?"

"Ivan is nothing if not consistent." The man spoke in an unfamiliar accent. "He's always had an eye for blondes."

Christine glanced at the front row, where Ivan and the girl sat shoulder to shoulder. "It seems his tastes have changed."

Martin followed her gaze.

"Darling, that's Pia," he said. "Ivan's daughter."

Ivan Borysenko had been her teacher, a visiting professor at the small, good upstate college she'd attended on scholarship. He'd come from the city on a one-year appointment to teach playwriting, a subject that hadn't interested her in the slightest until he appeared.

She'd been a mercurial student, prone to infatuations: philosophy to French lit, Rousseau and Voltaire to Sartre and Genet. She'd studied these subjects with roughly equal aptitude, a generalist excelling at nothing, until Ivan came along.

He pronounced his name distinctly, with a soft roll of the *r*. *Borrysenko*. "It's Ukrainian," he'd explain, to blank stares. The Soviet Union had not yet crumbled; American students were unaware, still, of the many countries it comprised: the multitude of languages, plosive and sibilant; the lumbering syllables of those impenetrable names.

Christine's first effort, a surrealistic one-act, had piqued his interest—and Ivan's interest, she learned, was an irresistible force. She felt caught by him, mounted like a butterfly, held fast for his consideration and delight. Her nineteen-year-old self appeared to fascinate him completely—Christine, who had never fascinated anybody in her life. He selected her play for a student production and taught her to run auditions and rehearsals. They were assumed to be lovers, a misconception she didn't correct. She was not, strictly speaking, a virgin. With her best friend, a boy named Tommy, she had suffered two attempts—one failed, one nominally successful; both awkward and crushingly sad. In the end, Tommy dropped out of school to be the lover of a wealthy man, surprising no one but Christine, who would love him the rest of his days. That he had loved but not desired her was a truth she confided to no one. She carried the shame like a disfiguring scar.

Ivan's attentions, in private, were fierce and febrile, but it was his public devotion that thrilled her. As they crossed the campus together, she felt lit up from inside. This handsome older man, brilliant and sophisticated, had chosen Christine Mooney, wanted, and had her: this belief was etched on her classmates' faces. To Christine, at nineteen, it was more than enough.

The tribute lasted two hours: glowing testimonials by writers and directors, a charismatic Irish actor she'd seen, a lifetime ago, onstage. They spoke of Ivan's lasting imprint on the New York theater, the generations of students he'd molded and shaped. His twenty-year marriage to Beth, his rock and muse; his famous devotion to Pia, who was born remarkable and became more extraordinary—it was agreed—with each passing year.

In the front row, Ivan sat between them, an arm around each.

After the final applause, the standing ovation, he was caught in a scrum of well-wishers. "He'll be stuck here for an hour," Martin predicted, guiding Christine through the crowd, his hand hovering lightly at her back.

She and Martin shared a cab to Paramour, the Soho restaurant where the after party would be held. "South African," Martin said, when she asked about his accent. He was a dramaturge at Circle Rep, a job Ivan had helped him secure. Christine nodded and smiled, asked pertinent questions, and barely registered his answers, her mind elsewhere.

Paramour was already crowded, samba music nearly lost in the conversational roar. Christine stood in a corner, waiting for Martin to bring their drinks. Waiters circulated, precariously wielding trays of appetizers. All around her, strangers stood back to back, elbow to elbow—New Yorkers accustomed to crowds, to chaos. Old friends shrieked greetings; acquaintances made small talk at the top of their lungs. No one seemed to find this unsettling or strange.

She recognized a few faces from the tribute. At the bar, two playwrights shouted past each other. Across the room, Ivan's daughter told a story to a rapt audience. The evening's speeches had established that Pia was used to the spotlight. (At four she'd sat for a renowned Polish photographer, a portrait now hanging in the Guggenheim. She'd inspired a series of children's books written by a friend of Ivan's, and by her tenth birthday was eligible for an Equity card.) Christine watched her keenly, an ordinary-looking teenage girl, flushed and happy, tugging occasionally at her slinky dress. Her audience—a well-dressed couple, the Irish actor, a woman in a fedora—seemed captivated, their eyes bright and encouraging, as though watching a baby's first steps. In Christine's family, such attention was not lavished on children. Her mother would have called Pia a show-off. Christine found her marvelous.

She glanced out at the patio. A gray-haired man in Armani stood smoking, talking into a headset clipped to his ear. He stopped speaking when a pretty boy asked him for a light. The boy was blond and very young. He wore a silky shirt, blue paisley, that lay like paint on his skin.

*I could never live anywhere else,* Ivan had often said. To Christine, at nineteen, New York had seemed not merely the height of civilization but its actual center, the most vital point on earth. Later —after Tommy's illness, his slow wasting—the city became a cemetery, a vast and teeming grave. His final month had been spent in a downtown hospice. His wealthy lover had paid for his care, but it was Christine who'd slept in a chair by his bed.

A kiss landed on her bare shoulder, Martin returning with their drinks. "Bold, I know. I would have tapped your shoulder, but my hands are full." He handed her a wineglass. "No sign of the great man?"

"Not yet." Outside, the man and the boy leaned against the brick wall, their faces hidden in shadow. They tossed away their cigarettes and lit two more. This time the boy leaned in close, holding the man's hand to steady the flame.

Martin waved to someone in the distance. "Everyone bores me," he said. "Tell me about you and Ivan."

Christine colored. "I haven't seen him in fifteen years. I have no idea why I'm here." Astonishingly, the invitation had arrived in the mail. She'd moved a half-dozen times since college—to France on a Fulbright, to grad school, back to France. She'd touched down briefly in Chicago for a visiting professorship. Now, once again, her possessions were crossing the country in a moving van.

"My own parents can't keep track of me," she said. "I can't imagine where he got my address."

Martin frowned. "Beth didn't invite you?"

"I've never met her in my life." Again Christine glanced out the window. The man and the boy had disappeared. She felt a flash of disappointment and then, a sudden jolt. Ivan was crossing the patio—alone, his hands in his pockets, as though she'd conjured him from the air.

The room seemed suddenly quiet.

"Excuse me," she whispered, and pushed her way through the crowd.

She had never gone to bed with him. In truth, she hadn't considered it: his wedding ring, the wife and baby waiting for him in New York. What they'd done instead had seemed harmless—less serious, anyway, than *adultery*. There was still enough parochial school in her to make her blanch at the word.

Later she understood how gravely she'd miscalculated. That with every lover for the rest of her life, Ivan Borysenko would hover in the room.

She'd sat for him as a model sits for an artist. This was how he'd explained it the first time—a weeknight, late, after a long rehearsal. In his apartment, he'd watched intently as she took off her clothes. She hesitated over her bra and panties.

Everything, he said. I need to see it all.

Naked, she awaited further instruction. She lay sometimes on the floor of his apartment, sometimes the bed or the living room couch. His bed was made, always, with crisp white sheets. She lay on her back, gazing up at him. He watched her for a long time, his eyes half closed, his arms crossed. When asked, she turned on her side or belly, raised her arms or opened her legs. He did not touch her, or himself.

"Thank you, my love," he would say finally, her signal to dress and disappear. To leave him alone with the fresh memory of her.

\*

They sat together on the dark patio. "Tell me everything," Ivan said, "about your life."

Quickly she rattled off the details: the Ph.D. in French lit, the Fulbright, her new tenure-track job in California.

He lit a cigarette. "It's a pity you stopped writing. I was sure you'd continue. You were a great talent."

Her face went hot with pleasure.

"I tried for a while," she admitted. "Then I gave up and went to grad school. It's okay," she added hastily. And then, not sure if it was true: "I'm happy."

"I'm not. It shocks me that you have defected from the theater."

It was a script she remembered from long ago: Ivan playing the wounded prima donna. Her role, now, was to placate him. "I haven't defected entirely," she said. "I teach Racine and Corneille."

He looked incredulous. "Your students are still interested in classicism? Even today?"

"I'm not sure how interested they are in literature, period."

"Literature is something one reads," he snapped. "Racine and Corneille never intended their work to be read."

He stared at her a long moment, the avid dark eyes she remembered. In the shadow of his apartment they'd seemed to be all pupil. "What became of your friend Tommy?" he asked. "He was a great talent."

Her smile faded. *A great talent.* The words, she realized, were meaningless, a stock phrase he used to flatter his former students. How many times would he say it this evening? That noisy room was filled, probably, with great talents.

"I don't know." She lied. "We lost touch years ago."

"Daddy!"

Christine turned. Pia was crossing the patio in their direction, a wineglass in her hand.

"Darling." Ivan rose. "Christine, I'd like you to meet my greatest creation. My daughter, Pia."

Pia offered her hand, moist from the glass. "Nice to see you." It was the neat phrase everyone used nowadays, to greet a stranger one perhaps ought to recognize but didn't quite recall. Christine marveled at her composure. She tried to imagine herself at seventeen, out late on a school night in such a dress, drinking wine in full view of her parents. Teenage Christine celebrated in public, praised and flattered, the shining object of adult attention. The image refused to materialize. Her mind could not conceive of it.

Ivan kissed Pia's forehead. "It's eleven o'clock. You're going to turn into a pumpkin."

"Another hour," she said. "I'll be gone by midnight. Poof!"

"You won't miss a thing. The party will fizzle without you." His gaze was tender, his tone nearly flirtatious. Christine's stomach cramped violently, a wave of sickness. Jealousy was a bodily emotion. It lived in the entrails, a malevolent parasite.

They watched the girl walk away, teetering on high heels.

"She's taking the SATs in the morning," Ivan said. "She was supposed to leave at eleven."

"How will she get home?" It seemed necessary to feign interest, to partake in the general fascination with Pia. Though in fact she'd already heard more about Ivan's daughter—much, much more—than she wanted to know.

"Beth's parents bought her a car. Her boyfriend is the designated driver. He doesn't drink." Ivan pointed to a corner of the patio, where Pia was sharing a cigarette with the blond boy in the blue paisley shirt.

"Him?" Christine said.

(Possibly her perspective was skewed. Possibly—in New York, the memory of Tommy clutching her like a lonely ghost—she saw hustlers everywhere.)

"Where are you staying?" Ivan asked.

When she named the hotel, he nodded thoughtfully. "I'll meet you later. We can have a drink."

His dark eyes cut through her like a laser, as though he could see through her skin. Of course, it was the reason she had come: to be looked at in this way.

Her heart worked loudly inside her. "What about your wife?"

He shrugged elaborately, gracefully, like a dancer stretching.

"It was Beth who made the guest list. She knows I love surprises." He took her hand in both of his. "It's my night, after all. You're a present for me."

Inside, the air conditioning was going full force. Christine took a seat at the bar, shivering in the cold. She flagged a waiter passing with a tray of appetizers and took one of everything, a tiny quiche, a skewer of grilled chicken, a pile of tomatoes on toast. Eating, she thought back to the shadowy afternoons with Ivan, his bare off-campus apartment, the shades pulled to the sills, his hungry gaze clicking like a camera. After he sent her away, what had he done with the images in his head? She'd believed, always, that the pictures were for him alone. Now she imagined him calling his wife in the city. *The girl was here. She sat for me.*

Beth had known all along.

Christine, in her innocence, had never imagined such a thing: that her secret afternoons with Ivan were no secret, those burning hours that had marked her like a brand. That in actual fact she'd been part of his marriage, covered under the contract. Ivan loved women. His work took him to Los Angeles and London, to theaters and college campuses. His wife, pragmatic, had granted him certain freedoms. *Look, but don't touch.*

"There you are." Martin laid a hand on her shoulder. She felt herself leaning into it, the living heat of his hand.

"I saw you outside with Ivan. I considered joining you, but he would have torn me apart with his teeth. You're freezing," he said, rubbing her arm.

He took an olive from her plate.

"Alex Tinsley is here. His play is getting fabulous reviews. Have you seen it?"

"I haven't seen anything," she said.

"How refreshing. I'm sick to death of the theater." His eyes wandered. "Let me nab Tinsley before he leaves. Don't move. I don't want to lose you again."

She watched him cut through the crowd of great talents: actors performing at each other, directors thinking aloud, playwrights testing out speeches, auditioning their own words. Theater people were born to be looked at, though it occurred to Christine—not for the first time—that they were more impressive from a distance, observed from the mezzanine, the house lights dimmed. Their intricate private lives—Ivan's and Beth's, Tommy's—were best left in shadow. Only Racine and Corneille, dead three centuries, could be safely studied, their strange passions consigned to the past.

"Thank Jesus. A chair."

Christine turned. Pia sat heavily next to her and removed a shoe. "My feet are killing me. How do you walk in those?" She looked bleary, a little drunk, her makeup smeared.

"Never stand when you don't have to. Seriously. Try to spend the whole night sitting down." An errant bra strap slid down the girl's shoulder. Christine resisted the urge to adjust it, as her mother would have done.

"Have you seen Justin?"

A moment passed before she understood that Justin was the boyfriend. Famous since birth, Pia assumed—usually correctly—that everyone in her orbit knew the details of her life.

"He's supposed to drive me home? To Montclair? That looks so good. I'm off carbs." She eyed the toast on Christine's plate. "For this dress. I haven't had bread in a week."

"The night is over," Christine said, handing her the plate.

Pia took it, smiling gratefully. Her hands were plump as a toddler's. She ate the toast in two bites. Hungry baby, Christine thought, and wished she had more to feed her, an entire loaf of bread.

She watched Pia lurch away, teetering in her shoes, and thought, *Seventeen. That's what seventeen looks like.* She'd been just two years older, a college sophomore, when she sat for Pia's father.

By one o'clock the crowd had dwindled. Christine watched Ivan from across the room, ambushed again and again by well-wishers.

"I've had enough," she told Martin.

"Likewise," he said quickly, draining his glass. "Let's go."

For years afterward she'd wonder how the night might have unfolded if she'd simply gone back to her hotel to wait for Ivan. Would she have sat for him as she'd done before—still and silent, untouched and unloved? What, exactly, were the terms of Beth's gift?

Instead, in the taxi, she kissed Martin passionately. Let the ghosts hover: his body was a tangible thing, arms and hands and shoulders. His mouth felt warm and alive. *Yes to everything,* she thought. *Do everything to me.*

Later, lying awake in Martin's bed, she imagined Ivan appearing at her hotel in midtown, waiting as the front desk rang her room. She found out, later, that he'd turned off his cell phone and missed the call when it came. A New Jersey state trooper had found Pia's car on the Garden State Parkway, nosed into a concrete barrier, Pia unconscious behind the wheel. A generation ago, before airbags, she would have been thrown through the windshield.

Instead, the giant cushion rose up to receive her, holding her fast. Her injuries were not serious, but the SATs took place without her. She spent two days in a private hospital room filled with flowers. By day she entertained a constant stream of visitors. At night her father kept vigil beside her bed.

# Navigators

FROM *Hobart*

AFTER THEY FOUND the metal boots but before the dirt clod, Joshua's father bought graph paper at Wal-Mart. Unfurled and pinned on the wall where his mother's family pictures had once hung, it stood six feet high by seven feet wide. The paper was hung in three rows, each printed with thousands of small gray squares. If Joshua crossed his eyes, the squares seemed to rise from the page. He crossed his eyes and then uncrossed them, watching the squares rise and fall. "It's time we started a map," his father had said. "Or we'll never finish this game."

This was the logical culmination of his father's theory of The Navigator. In games, where it was so often so easy to lose perspective, but also in life. When Joshua played their game, it was his father's job to keep watch, to tell him when he was doubling back, to remind him where he meant to go, and how. When Joshua's father had the controller, these were Joshua's jobs.

Their game was *Legend of Silence,* or *LoS. LoS* was different from their other games; whereas in *Metroid* or *Zelda* the player character became more powerful as he explored, the heroine of *LoS* was diminished by every artifact she found. The manual still called them Power Ups, but this was, father and son agreed, misleading: they should be called Power Downs, or Nerfs, or Torments, because this was what they did. The goal of the game was to lose everything so that one could enter Nirvana, where the final boss lay in wait, enjoying all the ill-gotten fruits of not being and not knowing. It was their favorite game, so much so that they often discussed what they would do when it was over. What they meant was what *could* they do. It was impossible to imagine After.

Joshua's father had not played any of their other games since *LoS*. Not even *Contra*, which had previously been their favorite, because it had a two-player mode and because they could not beat it: when one died, the other soon followed. He had tried to talk to other fathers about it at Boy Scout barbecues and overnight camps, but they did not listen.

After Joshua's father smoothed the graph paper to the wall, it exhaled softly and came unstuck, sagging. He took their respective pencil boxes from the top of a pile of R-rated VHS cassettes on the TV stand. Inside were markers, highlighters, and colored pencils, watercolor pencils and pink erasers, and ballpoint pens, and number-two mechanicals.

"We'll use sixty-four squares for every screen," said his father. "That's eight by eight. Starting here, in the middle. Here." Using a red marker and a number-two mechanical, he sketched the first room of the labyrinth: its gold and velvet throne, its many crystal chandeliers, its candelabras. At the right edge of the chamber he drew a purple pillow on a white pedestal, where the heroine would lay her crown to rest if you pressed the B button. This opened the exit, which led to the next room. Joshua's father drew this from memory because they could never see it again without restarting their game. Once you left the throne room, the guards wouldn't let you come back. They did not recognize their queen without her crown.

"If we map the whole world," said his father, "we can stop getting lost. Then we'll really get cooking. We'll be through in a month." There were, his father had said, maps you could buy. But this would defeat the point, which was the journey.

You always started outside the throne room no matter how much farther you explored. The hall outside was like a decayed palace, hung with rotting standards, walls collapsing, suits of armor disassembled and scattered over the floor, brown with rust. The stern guards at the door to the throne room were responsible for preventing the rot from coming inside, in addition to keeping you out. Of course, much of this was open to interpretation, rendered in simple arrangements of squares. Sometimes Joshua thought this hallway was more like a palace waiting to be born than one dying. It was full of small monsters—green rodents, yellow bats. The first time Joshua walked this hallway, when his heroine was at the height of her powers, these enemies were trivial to kill. A single shot from the blaster, a blow with the sword. Now each journey through the hallway became more difficult as the heroine withered; it served as an index of her progress toward not being, not knowing. Sometimes, recently, father and son couldn't even make it through.

Joshua made the heroine struggle through the hallway. His father stole bites of peanut butter jelly and drank from his Big Gulp with one hand as he drew what they saw with the other. Sixty-four squares for every screen. Joshua struggled not to tell him there was cheese-puff dust in his beard.

Tuesday nights were grilled cheese, but when Joshua came home, the gas was off again. You could make grilled cheese in the microwave, but the bread would come out wrong—first soft and hot, and then too hard. He took the American cheese from the refrigerator and sat down at the television, which still worked. Sometimes he played their game without his father. Today he was upset enough about grilled-cheese night that he didn't want to play alone. He watched the cartoon channel. The map had grown again. It loomed in his periphery, slowly consuming the wall with its red, purple, forest green tendrils. Doors sprung up all over like a dalmatian's spots, doorknobs like lidless eyes. His father played without him too. Joshua unwrapped a slice of cheese and ate it in strips. He deleted all their messages, even the new ones, without listening. He unwrapped another slice.

His father came home with an envelope, unopened, in his fist. "They shut off the gas," he said through gritted teeth.

"Sorry," said Joshua.

"We can make grilled cheese in the microwave."

"No," said Joshua. "That doesn't work."

The electric bill was paid through Friday. They could still play their game. Joshua's father changed into his home pants.

Her name was Alicia. That was, in Joshua's opinion, the second most beautiful name in the world. The first most beautiful name was Trudy. Then third was his own name. Then his father's, Dustin. Alicia was not only a queen in the beginning but also a bird girl.

She had large brown wings speckled with flecks of silver and white. After her crown and throne room, these were the next things she gave up. She flew to the top of a very tall room (eight squares by fifty-four on the map) and found a door leading to a smaller room, a single screen, housing the metal boots and otherwise empty. These boots sat on a white pedestal like the one they had given their crown. At this point in the game father and son did not properly understand its principles—they thought the throne room was an interesting fluke. Joshua's father had made Alicia step into the boots. They couldn't tell what the metal boots were supposed to do. Joshua's father led Alicia out of the room, and he made her jump out into the emptiness of the very tall room. She fell to the floor, flapping her wings without effect. The weight of her boots was too much. Her wings bent and warped from the effort as she fell through seven screens. Then she crumpled on the floor, half-dead, and enemies nosed her body, gnawed, and further drained her life points. Her wings would slowly atrophy from disuse, shrinking, curling inward, dropping feathers in clots for the rest of the game, until there was nothing left. These feathers being pixels, of course—two each, twisting and angling this way and so on, such that the viewer could see what they were meant to be. Then father and son understood the game. Joshua's father said, "This is a REAL game."

It was some time before they found the Elixir of Ice. This was a blue potion that poured from the mouth of a gargoyle who looked like Alicia, but with horns and healthy wings. The Elixir of Ice made crystals in her blood and other body fluids so she couldn't run as fast as she used to, or swing her sword as well, or draw her gun as quickly. Joshua could move the same way if he tensed all his muscles painfully.

Once they were up until two in the morning, exploring the dark caves in the bottom-right corner of the map, which were riddled with hungry purple mole-men and waxy stalactites dripping fat drops of poisonous water. The boss of this area was a worm with sticky skin, which collected various enemies and hazards—spikes, mole-men. Joshua could not kill the worm because without Alicia's wings it was difficult to leap over the many differently shaped obstacles that clung to it. Joshua's father pulled him into his lap, took the controller from his hands, and finished the fight with her sword. In the next room there was only darkness and a large blue stone. They thought they would have to leave their sword there, a gift for King Arthur. When Joshua's father pressed B, Alicia struck the stone instead, which shattered the sword, leaving only a small length of blade and the hilt. The exploded fragments hung twisting in the air like stars or a junkyard mobile.

"How will we kill the enemies?" said Joshua.

"We still have the gun," said his father, chest rumbling against Joshua's back, voice low and wooden in his ear.

"We'll lose that too," said Joshua.

"Then we'll run away," said his father. Joshua saw he was losing his hair. His skin was waxy like the stalactites.

They tried to cook together. They made meatloaf with 73/27 beef and Great Value saltines. They stirred the raw beef and the rest with their bare hands, then wiped them with paper towels and washed away the pink sticky residue, Joshua feeling all this time like the worm. The ketchup and brown-sugar glaze scorched and made a black, brittle shell on the meatloaf.

They made stir-fry with bits of egg and too much soy sauce, too much salt. They made macaroni casserole and forced themselves to eat the cheddar scabs. They made pizza bagels: marinara, mozzarella, pepperoni slices. Three days in a row it was peanut butter jellies. Joshua took to sleeping on the couch while his father mapped the game. They were searching for the dirt clod.

"What do you think she'll do with it?" said Joshua.

"I don't know," said his father. "She could eat it."

"Why would it matter if she ate it?"

"You ever eaten dirt, Joshie?"

Joshua shook his head no.

"It could make her sick, for one," said his father. "That's just for a start."

"I think she'll cover her eyes with it," said Joshua. "Or maybe she'll put it in her mouth, but she'll hold it there, and plug her nose with it, so she can't scream, and she tastes it all the time." He imagined his mouth packed full.

"Like being buried alive," said his father. He patted Joshua's head. "You feeling okay, buddy?"

"Sure," said Joshua. "You want me to draw this room into the map?"

His father said yes.

His father said, "We've got seventy percent of the game mapped, but we still don't have half the items."

His father fell asleep on the couch. The TV screen was reflected in his glasses, and the game's movement made him seem awake. Joshua sat down in his lap, took over. He found the dirt clod beneath a false floor in the Chamber of Commerce, where dollars and coins flew at Alicia from all sides and clung to her body, briefly rebuilding her wings in their own green image. The dirt clod was on the floor, among several other dirt clods that looked identical, but smaller. "Wake up," said Joshua to his father. His father opened his eyes.

"You found it."

Here is what she did with the dirt clod:

She dirtied herself, browning and smearing her clothes, removing their luster. Clouds of filth hovered around her.

"Huh," said his father. He fell back asleep.

Joshua examined their clothes—his father's, his own. Both were crusted with cheese-puff dust and stained with cranberry juice cocktail. It had been nearly a month since they'd done the laundry. Joshua did not like folding the clothes, but he didn't like it when people looked at him either, at school or anywhere. His jeans were wearing thin in the knees and the groin, and the cuffs were already ragged. He paused the game and went to the kitchen for something to eat.

The sink was full of dishes slick with grime. The table was piled with pop cans, some empty, some half-full. There were coupons on the table for Gold's Gym and LA Fitness, fanned out like playing cards. The cupboard was empty except for macaroni and pumpkin pie filling.

The phone rang twice before Joshua could get to it. He thought he had known it would ring before it did ring, which was why—he thought—he looked at the phone when he did.

"Hello?" said Joshua.

"I'm sorry," said a woman's voice. "I have the wrong number."

"Who was that?" said his father, awake again.

"Some lady," said Joshua. "Wrong number."

"Crazy bitch," said his father. He closed his eyes.

Joshua would stay up for the next hour, trying to find the old answering machine tape, or something else with his mother's voice, to see if it sounded the same.

The next morning they ate off-brand Cap'n Crunch for breakfast. Joshua's father spilled droplets of milk on the gym coupons. They wrinkled and turned gray. They would stick to the table like glue. Holes would open in the paper. His father said, "We're going to move into a smaller apartment."

Joshua nodded.

His father said, "Lower rent."

Joshua nodded.

His father said, "More money to play with."

In the concert hall at the top left of the map they found the oozing earplugs inside the conductor's podium, which they broke open after killing the orchestra. When Alicia put in the earplugs, the game went quiet. Her footsteps and the footsteps of her enemies made no sound. The music was no music. Joshua fired her gun. The shots did not burble as they used to.

"Do you think it's going to stay this way?" said Joshua.

"Yes," said his father.

They moved into the new apartment. None of his father's friends could make it to help. They shared a jug of blue Gatorade as they unloaded the borrowed pickup truck. First thing, Joshua's father taped their map over the sliding glass door that was their western wall, or most of it. The map was growing. It cast a dark, faintly colored shadow on the blank carpet, like a bruise. Then it draped the couch, which they pushed against the southern wall. They set the TV up opposite, and loaded the refrigerator with everything left from the old one. A jar of mayonnaise. Several pickles. Lipton tea, still soaking the bags. A bag of potatoes. White bread. His father said, "Do you want the couch or the bedroom?"

Joshua searched his father's face for the answer. It wasn't there. It was possible there was no answer. It was possible he could say what he wanted. He said, "I'll take the couch."

His father said, "Okay."

They moved his father's weights into the bedroom, his still-boxed ab roller, his clothes, and several shoeboxes, all duct-taped shut.

They plugged in their game as the sun set. It shone brightly through the map, casting a grid over the kitchen and their faces, and in that grid a brighter bruise, or a fog, like melted crayons. Joshua's father was blue and yellow in the face, from water and

poisonous acid. Joshua's hands were green and brown from the
plant zone. The throne room was cast on the refrigerator's side.

They guided Alicia from the throne room's exit, down through
one of the gateways opened by the dirt on her clothes, and then
others unlocked by other infirmities. Joshua wanted to open some
chips, but his father said they should save them for later. Soon they
found the chamber of the orange cork. Joshua's father pressed the
B button and Alicia took the cork. She drew her gun, solemn as
pixels can. She fitted the cork inside the gun, pushing hard until
it stuck out only a little—a flare at the end.

"Now it won't fire?" said Joshua.

His father shook his head.

"She's defenseless."

His father nodded.

Their game became one of evasion. Alicia could still duck,
could still jump. They spent the rest of the night running from
enemies, seeking alternate routes—climbing previously neglected
ladders, ducking behind rocks. When they could not duck the
monsters, they ran into them head-on, took the hit, and then used
the brief invulnerability this granted to escape into the next room,
where they would do it again. Joshua's father paused often. He
offered the controller to his son, who refused it every time. They
were both sweating.

Some hours later Joshua woke up. He wiped his drool from the
knee of his father's home pants.

"You're up," said his father. "Look what I found."

"She's on the floor," said Joshua.

"I found the lead belt. You see?" It was a narrow band of pixels on Alicia's waist. She was propped up on her elbows, and her
legs were bent at the knees. The belt's buckle (unseen, but Joshua
knew it from the manual and the attract mode) was pressed firmly
to the floor. This was the weight that held her down. "This is all
that happens when I try to attack," said his father, and she pushed
her arm up feebly, the blunted remains of her sword outstretched.
It seemed less an assault than an offering. "And she can crawl." He
made her crawl.

"We are so screwed," said Joshua. "Dad, we're never going to get
anywhere like this, and we still need the sunglasses."

"Maybe we can't win," said his father. "That's life too, I guess."

It was not clear how they could leave the chamber.

After some crawling around on the floor, they discovered there were bricks in the wall, low bricks that could be destroyed with her blunted sword. The world of their game was riddled and undermined all over with tunnels just large enough for crawling. These tunnels were sometimes visible to the players, but often not. Often they were obscured by rock or tree roots, or a lava flow, or water. The only way to know she still moved was the slow scrolling of the screen. Joshua said, "Where do you think the tunnels came from?"

"I bet the sticky worm made them," said his father.

Trees rolled by, and their stumps. Ever-burning candles. Caverns and rock formations. They saw what they had seen before from new angles. Joshua drew the tunnels onto the map, which now filled most of the graph paper. They were black lines, spiraling toward the center of the map as his father made his way. But there were many dead ends in the tunnels. Father and son knew they had hit a dead end when the scrolling stopped. Then they turned back.

When Joshua woke again, he was alone on the couch. His legs were tangled in his lone wolf blanket, his shoes and socks removed. He wiped the drool from his chin and nose. The arm of the couch was crusted with his snot. He went to the bathroom. The previous tenant had left a framed picture of Greta Garbo, smoking, on the wall. There was a small peacock feather in her hat. She looked happy.

Joshua's father talked about places they could go for vacation. Santa Claus, Indiana, was a top contender. They had Holiday World, which was also a water park now. "World's biggest wooden roller coaster," said his father.

"No kidding," said Joshua.

It turned out having "money to play with" meant paying the utilities on time.

Father and son experimented with a mostly vegetarian diet. Peanut butter jellies were the same, and so were chips, but no hamburgers and no fish sticks, except on Friday, which was Hardee's night. They could afford to rent two videos a week at Blockbuster. One was always a Dad movie, rated R. One was a Joshua movie, rated PG-13 or lower. The Dad movie was usually new, from the shelves that lined the walls and circled the rest. The Joshua movie came from the inside shelves.

Sometimes Joshua's father called relatives and talked about Joshua's mother, though he tried not to let on. He thought he was speaking in code. "The Queen," he would call her. "The Duchess." Joshua listened carefully for clues as to where she was, what she was doing. "(Something something) pay phones," said his father. "(Something something) Atlanta."

Atlanta was the capital of Georgia. It was a big city. This was not nearly enough. Joshua couldn't even find his own way through *Legend of Silence.*

Their map was almost complete. The sun cast it on their coffee table, on their shoes, and on the clothing they scattered on the floor. Soon they would be done with their game. His father connected the NES through the VCR and bought a blank tape so they could record the game's ending.

His father offered wisdom at strange times. Joshua was on the toilet when his father knocked on the door. "It's busy," he said.

His father said, "Never settle for less than you deserve. But whatever you can get, understand that you'll have to give it all up someday. Prepare yourself for that, as much as you can."

"Okay," said Joshua.

"Okay," said his father. "Do you think you should have an allow-ance?"

"I don't think you can afford to give me one."

"Okay."

They were near the center of the map, just above the throne room, when they found the sunglasses. This was the last thing they needed. Joshua's father pulled him onto his lap. He put the controller in Joshua's hands. Joshua pressed B. Alicia put on the glasses. The screen dimmed. She crawled farther toward the center of the map. As she crawled, the colors faded to black. She passed through a gate, which she unlocked with how nothing she was, how faded, how silent, how crawling. She fell through a hatch into what had been the throne room. It was no longer the throne room.

"It's changed," said his father. "I'll have to change the map."

He would use the black Sharpie. The screen was black now.

A white, blinking cursor at the screen's center, as in a word processor. After a moment's hesitation, it made blocky white text on the screen.

*You are in Nirvana,* it said. *You are not in Nirvana.*

*You have come here to destroy your enemy. Your enemy has been waiting for you in Nirvana. Is your enemy in Nirvana? Yes or No.*

"No," said Joshua's father. Joshua chose no.

*No,* said the game. *Your enemy is not in Nirvana, and neither are you. There is no you.*

"What's happening," said Joshua.

His father held him close. He rubbed Joshua's tummy through his Ninja Turtles shirt.

*You might pursue your enemy,* said the game. *Do you want to pursue your enemy? Yes or No.*

"What do you think?" said Joshua's father.

"No," said Joshua. "We should not pursue our enemy."

"Good," said Joshua's father. Joshua chose no.

*No,* said the game. *You have no enemy. You have no you. The labyrinth is gone. The weight falls from your body. Your body falls from your soul. Your soul falls from your absence. The absence is not yours. Do you fear? Yes or No.*

"Are we afraid?" said his father.

"Yes," said Joshua.

*You will forget fear. Do you love?*

"Yes," said his father.

"Yes," said Joshua.

*You will forget love.*

*Congratulations. You win.*

"Game over?" said Joshua.

"I guess so."

His father squeezed him tight. Joshua wondered what they would do now. The need he felt was like when he stepped on the sliver of glass, and his mother pulled at the skin with her tweezers, and pushed them inside, until she found the glass. It was like when she told him to get ready, to squeeze his father's hand. Clenching his teeth, closing his eyes, waiting.

STEVEN MILLHAUSER

# Miracle Polish

FROM *The New Yorker*

I SHOULD HAVE said no to the stranger at the door, with his
skinny throat and his black sample case that pulled him a little to
the side, so that one of his jacket cuffs was higher than the other,
a polite no would have done the trick, no thanks, I'm afraid not,
not today, then the closing of the door and the heavy click of the
latch, but I'd seen the lines of dirt in the black shoe creases, the
worn-down heels, the shine on the jacket sleeves, the glint of des-
peration in his eyes. All the more reason, I said to myself, to send
him on his way, as I stepped aside and watched him move into
my living room. He looked quickly around before setting his case
down on the small table next to the couch. I'd made up my mind
to buy something from him, anything, a hairbrush, the Brooklyn
Bridge, buy it and get him out of there, I had better things to do
with my time, but there was no hurrying him as he slowly undid
each clasp with his bony fingers and explained in a mournful voice
that this was my lucky day. In the suddenly opened case I saw six
rows of identical dark-brown glass bottles, each a bit smaller than
a bottle of cough medicine. Two things struck me: the case must
have been very heavy, and he must not have sold anything in a
long time. The product was called Miracle Polish. It cleaned mirrors with one easy flick of the wrist. He seemed surprised, even
suspicious, when I said I'd take one, as if he had wandered the
earth for years with the same case filled to bursting with unsold
bottles. I tried not to imagine what would drive a man to go from
house to house in a neighborhood like this one, with porches and
old maples and kids playing basketball in driveways, a neighbor-

hood where Girl Scouts sold you cookies and the woman across the street asked you to contribute to the leukemia drive, but no strangers with broken-down shoes and desperate eyes came tramping from door to door lugging heavy cases full of brown bottles called Miracle Polish. The name exasperated me, a child could have done better than that, though there was something to be said for the way it sat there flaunting its fraudulence. "Don't trust me!" it shouted for all to hear. "Don't be a fool!"

When he tried to sell me a second bottle, he understood from my look that it was time to go. "You've made a wise choice," he said solemnly, glancing at me and looking abruptly away. Then he clicked his case shut and hurried out the door, as if afraid I'd change my mind. Lifting a slat of the half-closed blinds, I watched him make his way along the front walk with the sample case pulling him to one side. At the sidewalk he stopped, put down his case next to the sugar maple, wiped his jacket sleeve across his forehead, and gazed up the block as if he were the new boy in school, getting ready to cross the school yard, where faces were already turning to stare at him. For a moment he looked back at my house. When he saw me watching him, he grinned suddenly, then frowned and jerked his head away. With a sharp snap I let the blind-slat drop.

I had no interest in mirror polish. I placed the bottle in a drawer of the hutch, where I kept extra flashlight batteries, packages of light bulbs, and an unused photograph album, and gave no more thought to it.

Early one morning, a week or so later, I stepped over to the oval mirror in the upstairs hall, as I did every morning before leaving for work. As I tugged down the sides of my suit jacket and smoothed my tie, I noticed a small smudge on the glass, near my left shoulder. It had probably been there for years, ever since I'd brought the mirror down from my parents' attic, along with a faded armchair and my grandmother's couch with the threadbare arms. I tried to recall whether I had ever cleaned the oval mirror before, whether I had ever bothered to dust the old mahogany frame carved with leaves and flowers. I understood that I was having these thoughts only because of the stranger with the bony fingers and the worn-down heels, and as I went down to the hutch I felt a burst of irritation as I heard him say, "This is your lucky day."

Upstairs I pulled a tissue from the box in the bathroom and

unscrewed the top of the brown bottle. On the dark glass, in white capital letters, stood the words MIRACLE POLISH. The liquid was thick, slow, and greenish white. I applied a bit to the tissue and wiped the smudge. When I lifted my hand I was almost disappointed to see that the spot was gone. I was aware of another thing: the rest of the mirror looked dull or tarnished. Had I really never noticed it before? With another dab of polish I set to work wiping the entire surface, right up to the curves of the frame. It was done quickly; I stepped back for a look. In the light from the overhead bulb with its old glass shade, mixed with sunlight from the window on the nearby landing, I saw myself reflected clearly. But it was more than that. There was a freshness to my image, a kind of mild glow that I had never seen before. I looked at myself with interest. This in itself was striking, for I wasn't the kind of man who looked at himself in mirrors. I was the kind of man who spent as little time as possible in front of mirrors, the kind of man who had a brisk and practical relation to his reflection, with its tired eyes, its disappointed shoulders, its look of defeat. Now I was standing before a man who resembled my old reflection almost exactly but who had been changed in some manner, the way a lawn under a cloudy sky changes when the sun comes out. What I saw was a man who had something to look forward to, a man who expected things of life.

That afternoon when I returned from work, I went up to the oval mirror. In the polished glass I was struck again by a sense of freshness. Had the mirror really been so deeply in need of cleaning? There were three other mirrors in the house: the mirror over the sink in the upstairs bathroom, the mirror over the sink in the downstairs half bath, and the small circular mirror with a wooden handle that hung on a hook beside the upstairs-bathroom window. None of them had seemed to need cleaning before, but when I was through with them I saw my new reflection glowing back at me from all three. I looked at the brown bottle of Miracle Polish in my hand. It seemed an ordinary bottle, a bottle like any other. If the polish had made me look younger, if it had made me handsome, if it had smoothed my skin and fixed my teeth and changed the shape of my nose, I'd have known it was some horrible mechanical trick, and I'd have smashed those mirrors with my fists rather than allow myself to be taken in like a fool. But the image in the mirror was unmistakably me—not young, not good-looking, not anything in particular, a little slumped, heavy at the waist, pouchy under the eyes, not the sort of man that anyone would ever choose to be. And yet he looked back at me in a way I hadn't seen for a long time, a way that made the other things all right. He looked back at me—the thought sprang to mind—like a man who believed in things.

The next morning I woke before my alarm and hurried over to the oval mirror in the hall. My image glowed back at me; even my rumpled pajamas had a certain jaunty look. In the polished glass the dull walls seemed brighter, the bedroom door a richer brown. In the bathroom mirror I shone forth; the whiteness of the sink burned in the glass; the towels looked fuller. Downstairs, the re-flected window in the half bath showed part of a brilliant curtain, beyond which lay the green grass of childhood summers. All day at work I thought of nothing but those shining surfaces, like coins catching the sun, and when I came home I went from mirror to mirror, striking poses, turning my head from side to side.

Because I prided myself on never having false hopes, on never permitting myself to imagine that things were better than they were, I asked myself whether I might be allowing the mirrors to deceive me. Maybe the greenish-white polish contained a chemi-cal that, upon contact with glass, produced an optical distortion. Maybe the words *miracle polish* had caused cells in my brain to fire in a series of associations that affected the way I saw the reflected world. Whatever was happening, I knew that I needed another opinion, from someone I could trust. It was Monica who would set me straight, Monica who would know—Monica, who looked at the world through large, kind, skeptical eyes, darkened by many disappointments.

Monica arrived, as she did twice a week after work, once on Tuesdays and once, with her overnight bag, on Fridays, and as al-ways when I greeted her I was careful not to look too closely at her, for Monica was likely to draw back and say "Is something wrong?" while raising her hand anxiously to her hair. She had a habit of assessing her looks mercilessly: she approved of her eyes, liked the shape of her wrists and the length of her fingers, put up with her calves, but was unforgiving about her thighs, her chin, her biggish knees, her hips, her upper arms. She fretted over any imperfection in her skin, like a mosquito bite or a heat rash or a tiny pimple, and often wore a hidden Band-Aid on a shoulder or calf, holding some ointment in place. She wore long skirts that came down to her ankles, with plain blouses over plain white bras; she liked to mix dark greens, dark browns, and dark grays. Her shoulder-length brown hair was usually straight and parted in the middle, though sometimes she pulled it back and gathered it in a big dark clip that looked like an enormous insect. She inspected herself in front of any mirror, searching for flaws like a teenage girl before a big party. In fact she was forty and worked as an administrative assistant at the local high school. For years we had edged toward each other without moving all the way. I liked how she hesitated a little before easing into a smile; liked the slight heaviness of her body, its faint awkwardness, its air of mild tiredness; liked how, when she took off her shoes and placed her feet on the hassock, she would wiggle her toes slowly and say, crinkling her eyes, "That feels really, really good." Sometimes, in a certain light, when she held her body a certain way, I would see her as a woman for whom things had not worked out as she had hoped, a woman sinking slowly into defeat. Then a burst of fellow feeling would come over me, for I knew how difficult it was, waiting for something better, waiting for something that was never going to happen.

I took her upstairs to the oval mirror and switched on the light. "Look at that!" I said, and swept out my arm in a stagy way. It was a gesture meant to imply that what I had to show her was nothing much, really, nothing to be taken seriously. I had hoped the reflection in the polished mirror would please her in some way, but I hadn't expected what I saw—for there she was, without a touch of weariness, a fresh Monica, a vibrant Monica, a Monica with a glow of pleasure in her face. She was dressed in clothes that no longer seemed a little drab, a little elderly, but were handsomely understated, seductively restrained. Not for a moment did the mirror make her look young, or beautiful, for she was not young and she was not beautiful. But it was as if some inner constriction had dissolved, some sense of her drifting gradually into unhappiness. In the mirror she gave forth a fine resilience. Monica saw it; I saw her see it; and she began turning her body from side to side, smoothing down her long skirt over her hips, pulling her shoulders back, arranging her hair.

Now in the mornings I rose with a kind of zest and went directly to the hall mirror, where even my tumbled hair gave me a look of casual confidence, and the shadowy folds under my eyes spoke of someone in the habit of facing and overcoming obstacles. In my cubicle I worked with concentration and with an odd lightness of heart, and when I returned home in the late afternoon I looked at myself in all four mirrors. It struck me that before I could reach the oval mirror in the upstairs hall, I had to pass through the front hall, cross the dusky living room with its sagging couch, walk the length of the kitchen, and climb two sets of creaking stairs, the long one up to the landing and the short one up to the hall. One night after dinner I drove to the outskirts of town, where the old shopping center faced off against the new mall in a battle of slashed prices. In the aisle after blenders and juicers I came to them. I saw tall narrow mirrors, square mirrors framed in oak and dark walnut, round mirrors like gigantic eyeglass lenses, cheval mirrors, mirrors framed in coppered bronze, mirrors with rows of hooks along the bottom. Avoiding my reflections as well as I could, for these mirrors showed only a tired man with a look of sorrow in his eyes, I chose a rectangular mirror with a cherrywood frame. At home I opened a drawer of the hutch and took out the brown bottle. With a few careful swipes of a cloth I polished the mirror. I hung it in the front hall, across from the closet and next to the boot tray with its old slippers and gardening shoes, and stepped back. In the light of the ceiling bulb I saw my reflection, standing with a cloth over his shoulder and looking out at me as if ready to hurl himself into whatever the day might bring. The sight of him standing there with his sleeves pushed up and his cloth over his shoulder and his look of readiness—all this made me smile, and the smile that came back to me seemed to stream out of the glass and into my arms, my chest, my face, my blood.

The next day after work I stopped at a furniture store and bought another mirror. At home I polished it and hung it in the kitchen, facing the table. As I ate my dinner I was able to look up whenever I liked and see the oak table, the gleaming plate with its chicken leg and baked potato, the glowing silverware, and my reflection looking up alertly, like someone whose attention has been called to an important matter.

On Friday, Monica entered the front hall and stopped sharply when she saw the mirror. She glanced at me and seemed about to say something, then turned her face away. In front of the mirror she stared at herself thoughtfully for a long while. Without turning back to me, she said she supposed it wouldn't be such a bad idea to be able to check her hair and blouse before entering the living room, especially when it was pouring down rain, or when the wind was blowing. I said nothing as I watched her reflection push her hair boldly from her cheek. Together she and Monica moved toward the edge of the mirror and disappeared into the living room.

In the kitchen I saw Monica's lips pull into a little tight circle. It was an expression I'd never cared for, with its combination of petulance and stubborn severity, but in the new mirror I saw only a flirtatious pout. "It's just an experiment," I said. "If you really don't like it—" "But it's your house," she said. "But that isn't the point," I said. She threw me a look and lowered her eyes; it was a way she had of protesting silently. She sat with her back to the mirror as I brewed her a pot of herb tea. Seated across from her, I was able to look beyond her strained face to the back of her head, the back of her blouse collar showing through her hair, the top of her shoulder blades. They all seemed to be enjoying themselves as she talked to me about her troubles with the lawn man. Once, when she turned to look out the window, I saw in the mirror the curved line of her forehead, the upward slant of the bottom of her nose, the little slope between her nostrils and her upper lip, and I was struck by the fine liveliness of her profile.

I let a day pass, but the next day I bought a large dark-framed mirror for the living room and hung it across from the couch. I took out my brown bottle and polished the mirror well, and when I stepped back I admired the new room that sprang into view in the polished depths. Monica would, of course, push her lips together, but she would come to see it was all for the best. The mirrors of my house filled me with such a sense of gladness that a room without one struck me as a dark cell. I brought home a full-length mirror for the TV room, a rectangular mirror with a simple frame for the upstairs bedroom, an identical one for the guest room down the hall. At a yard sale I bought an old shield-shaped mirror that I hung in the cellar, behind the washer and dryer. One evening when I entered the kitchen a restlessness seized me, and when I returned from the mall I hung a second mirror in the kitchen, between the two windows.

Monica said nothing; I could feel her opposition hardening in her like a muscle. I wasn't unaware that I was behaving oddly, like a man in the grip of an obsession. At the same time, what I was doing felt entirely natural and necessary. Some people added

windows to brighten their homes—I bought mirrors. Was it such
a bad thing? I kept seeing them at yard sales, leaning against rickety tables piled with pink dishes, or hanging in hallways and bed-
rooms at estate sales at the fancy end of town. I added a second
one to the living room, a third to the upstairs bath. In the front
hall, on the back of the front door, I hung a mirror framed in a
dark wood that matched the color of the umbrella stand. When
I passed by my mirrors, when I caught even a glimpse of myself
as I walked into a room, I felt a surge of well-being. What was
the harm? Now and then Monica tried to be playful about it all.
"What?" she would say. "Only one mirror on the landing?" Then
her expression would change as she saw me sinking into thought.
Once, she said, "You know, sometimes I think you like me better there"—she pointed to a mirror—"than here"—she pointed
to herself. She said it teasingly, with a little laugh, but in her look
was an anxious question. As if to prove her wrong, I turned my full
attention to her. Before me I saw a woman with a worried forehead
and unhappy eyes. I imagined her gazing out at me from all the
mirrors of my house, with eyes serene and full of hope, and an
impatience came over me as I looked at her dark brown sweater,
at the hand nervously smoothing her dark green skirt, at the lines
of tension in her mouth.

In order to demonstrate to Monica that all was well between us,
that nothing had changed, that I was no slave to mirrors, I proposed a Saturday picnic. We packed a lunch in a basket and took a
long drive out to the lake. Monica had put on a big-brimmed straw
hat I had never seen before, and a new light-green blouse with a
little shimmer in it; in the car she took off her hat and placed it
on her lap as she sat back with half-closed eyes and let the sunlight
ripple over her face. A tiny green jewel sparkled on her earlobe.
At the picnic grounds we sat at one of the sunny-and-shady tables
scattered under the high pines that grew at the edge of a small
beach. It was a hot, drowsy day; the smoke of grills rose into the
branches; a man stood with one foot on his picnic-table bench, an
arm resting on his thigh as he held a can of beer and stared out at
the beach and the water; kids ran among the tables; on the beach,
three boys in knee-length bathing trunks were playing catch with
enormous baseball gloves and a lime-green tennis ball; a plump
mother and her gaunt teenage son were hitting a volleyball back
and forth; young women in bikinis and men with white hair on

their chests strolled on the sand; in the water, a few people were splashing and laughing; a black dog with tall ears was swimming toward shore with a wet stick in its mouth; farther out, you could see canoes moving and oars lifting with sun flashes of spray; and when I turned to Monica I saw the whole afternoon flowing into her face and eyes. After the picnic, we walked along a trail that led partway around the lake. Here and there, on narrow strips of sand at the lake edge, people lay on their backs on towels in the sun. We made our way down to the shore, through prickly bushes; on the sand Monica pulled off her sandals, and lifting up her long skirt she stepped into the water and threw back her head to take in the sun with closed eyes. At that moment it seemed to me that everything was possible for Monica and me; and going up to her I said, "I've never seen you like this!" With her eyes still closed she said, "I'm not myself today!" She began to laugh. Then I began to laugh, because of what we had both said, and because of her laughter and the sun and the sky and the lake.

On the ride home she fell asleep with her head against my shoulder. The long outing had tired me too, though not in the same way. In the course of the afternoon an uneasiness had begun to creep into me. The glare of the sun on the water hurt my eyes; the heat pressed down on me; there was a slowness in things, a sluggishness; Monica seemed to walk with more effort, as if the air were a hot heaviness she was pushing her way through. The two of us, she in her straw hat and I in my cargo shorts, seemed to me actors playing the part of ordinary people, enjoying a day at the lake. In fact I was a man weighed down with disappointment, a man for whom things had not worked out the way he had once imagined, a quiet man, cautious in his life, timid when you came right down to it, though content enough to drift along through the little rituals of his day. And Monica? I glanced over at her. The back of her hand lay on her leg. The four fingers were leaning to one side, the thumb hung in front of them—and something about those fingers and that thumb seemed to me the shape of despair.

But when I opened my front door and stepped into the hall behind Monica, then the good feeling returned. In the mirror we stood there, she in her shimmering green blouse and I with a glow of sunburn on my face. Deep in the shine of the polished glass, her hand rose in a graceful arc to remove her straw hat.

In the living room I snatched glimpses of her in both mirrors as she walked buoyantly toward the kitchen. In the sunny kitchen her cheerful reflection picked up a pitcher of water that caught the light. I looked at the second mirror, where she began to raise a glass of shining water, paused suddenly, and opened her mouth in a lusty yawn. "I'd like to lie down," Monica said. I turned my head and saw her tight lips and tired eyelids. I followed her as she made her way slowly up the stairs and past the new mirror on the landing. For a moment her hair glowed at me from the glass. At the top of the stairs she walked sternly and without a glance past the oval mirror and into the bedroom, where I watched her bright reflection lie down on the bed and close her eyes. I too was tired, I was more than tired, but the sheer pleasure of being home filled me with a restless energy that drove me to stride through all the rooms of the house. From time to time I stopped before a polished mirror to turn my head this way and that. It was as if my house, with its many mirrors, drew all the old heaviness and weariness from my body; and in a sudden burst of inspiration I took out the bottle of Miracle Polish, which was still two-thirds full, and went down to the cellar, where I applied it to a new mirror that had been leaning against the side of the washing machine, waiting for me to decide where to hang it.

Later that evening, as we sat in the living room, Monica still seemed tired, and a little moody. I had led her to the couch and tried to position her so that she could see her good-humored reflection, but she refused to look at herself. I could feel resistance coming out of her like the push of a hand. In the mirror I admired a shoulder of her blouse. Then I glanced over at the other Monica, the one sitting stiffly and very quietly on the couch. I had the sense of a sky darkening before a storm. "Can't," I thought I heard her say, so softly that I wondered if she had spoken at all; or perhaps she had said "Can."

"What did you—" I breathed out, barely able to hear my own words.

"I can't," she said, and now there was no mistaking it. "Such a perfect day. And now—this." She raised her arm in a weary sweeping motion that seemed to include the entire room, the entire universe. In the mirror her reflection playfully swept out her arm. "I can't. I tried, but I can't. I can't. You'll have to—you'll have to choose."

"Choose?"

Her answer was so hushed that it seemed barely more than an exhalation of air. "Between me and—her."

"You mean . . . her?"

"I hate her," she whispered, and burst into tears. She immediately stopped, took a deep breath, and burst into tears again. "You don't look at me," she said. "But that's not—" I said. "I have to go," she said, and stood up. She was no longer crying. She took another deep breath and rubbed her nostrils with the back of a bent finger. She reached into a pocket of her skirt and pulled out a tissue that crumbled into fuzz. "Here," I said, holding out my handkerchief. She hesitated, took it from me, and dabbed at her nostrils. She handed back the handkerchief. She looked at me and turned to leave. "Don't," I said. "Me or her," she whispered, and was out the door.

During the next week I flung myself into my work, which was just complicated enough to require my full attention, without interesting me in the least. At five o'clock I came directly home, where I felt soothed in every room. But I was no child, no naive self-deceiver intent on evading a predicament. I wanted to understand things; I wanted to make up my mind. From the beginning there had been a deep kinship between Monica and me. She was wary, trained to expect little of life, grateful for small pleasures, on her guard against promises, accustomed to making the best of things, in the habit of both wanting and not daring to want something more. Now Miracle Polish had come along, with its air of swagger and its taunting little whisper. Why not? it seemed to say. Why on earth not? But the mirrors that strengthened me, that filled me with new life, made Monica bristle. Did she feel that I preferred a false version of her, a glittering version, to the flesh-and-blood Monica with her Band-Aids and big knees and her burden of sorrows? What drew me was exactly the opposite. In the shining mirrors I saw the true Monica, the hidden Monica, the Monica buried beneath years of discouragement. Far from escaping into a world of polished illusions, I was able to see, in the depths of those mirrors, the world no longer darkened by diminishing hopes and fading dreams. There, all was clear, all was possible. Monica, I understood perfectly, would never see things as I did. When she looked in the mirrors, she saw only a place that kept pulling me away from her and, in that place, a rival of whom she was desperately jealous.

I felt myself moving slowly in the direction of a dangerous decision I did not wish to make, like someone swerving on an icy road toward an embankment.

It wasn't until another week had passed that I knew what I was going to do. Summer was in its fullness; on front porches, neighbors fanned themselves with folded newspapers; sprinklers sent arcs of spray onto patches of lawn and strips of driveway, which shone in the sun like black licorice; at the top of a ladder, a man in a baseball cap moved a paintbrush lazily back and forth. It was Saturday afternoon. I had called Monica that morning and told her I had something important to show her. She was to meet me on the front porch. We sat there drinking lemonade, like an old married couple, watching the kids passing on bicycles, a squirrel scampering along a telephone wire. A robin was pecking furiously at the roadside grass. After a while I said, "Let's go inside." She turned to me then, as if she were about to ask a question. "If that's what you want," she finally said, and turned both hands palm up.

When we stepped into the front hall, Monica stopped. She stopped so abruptly that it was as if someone had put a heavy hand on her shoulder. I watched her stare at the place where the mirror had hung. She looked at me, and looked again at the wall. Then she turned and looked at the back of the front door. Its dark panels shone dully under the hall light. Monica reached out and touched her fingers to my arm.

I took her through every room of the house, stopping before familiar walls. In the living room a photograph of my parents looked out at us from the wall where one mirror had hung. The other place was bare except for two small holes in the faded wallpaper, with its pattern of tall vases filled with pale flowers. In the kitchen a new poster showed many kinds of tea. In place of the oval mirror in the upstairs hall, there was a framed painting of an old mill beside a brown pond with two ducks. New bathroom cabinets with beveled-edge mirrors hung over the upstairs and downstairs sinks. I could see the gratitude rushing into Monica's cheeks. When the tour was over, I led her to the drawer in the hutch and removed the brown bottle. In the kitchen she watched me pour the thick greenish-white liquid into the sink. I washed out the empty bottle and dropped it into the garbage pail next to the stove. She turned to me and said, "This is the most wonderful gift that you—"

"We're not done yet," I said, with a touch of excitement in my

voice, and led her through the kitchen door and down the four
wooden steps into the back yard.

Against the back of the house all the mirrors stood lined up,
slanted at different angles. There it was, the oval mirror from
the upstairs hall, leaning over a cellar window. There they were,
the two front-hall mirrors, the kitchen mirrors in their wooden
frames, the shield-shaped mirror from the cellar, the living room
mirrors, the bedroom mirrors, the full-length mirror from the TV
room, a pair of guest-room mirrors, the upstairs-bathroom mirror removed from its cabinet, the mirror from the landing, the
downstairs-bathroom mirror, and other mirrors that I had bought
and polished and stored in closets, ready to be hung: square mirrors and round mirrors, swivel mirrors on wooden stands, a mirror
shaped like a four-leaf clover. In the bright sun, the polished mirrors gleamed like jewels.

"Here they are!" I said, throwing out my hand. I began walking
along in front of them, from one end to the other. As I passed
from mirror to mirror slanted against the house, I could see different parts of me: my shoes and pant cuffs, my belt and the bottom
of my shirt, my sudden whole shape in the tall mirror, my swinging
hand. Now and then I caught pieces of Monica's rival, standing
back on the green, green grass. "And now," I said, as if I was addressing a crowd—and I paused for dramatic effect. I glanced at
Monica, who stood there with a look that was difficult to fathom,
a worried look, it seemed to me, and I wanted to assure her that
there was nothing to worry about, I was doing it all for her, everything would soon be fine. I bent over behind a broad mirror at the
end of the row and withdrew a hammer. And, raising the hammer
high, I swung it against the glass. Then I walked back along that
row of mirrors, swinging the hammer and sending bright spikes of
glass into the summer air. "There!" I cried, and smashed another.
"See!" I shouted. I swung, I smashed. Lines of wetness ran along
my face. Bits of mirror clung to my shirt.

It was over faster than I'd thought possible. All along the back
of the house, broken mirror-glass lay glittering on the grass. Here
and there, an empty frame showed triangles of glass still clinging to the wood. I looked at the hammer in my hand. Suddenly
I threw it across the yard, hurled it high into the row of spruces
at the back. I could hear the hammer falling slowly through the
needly branches.

"There!" I said to Monica. I made a wiping gesture with both hands, the way you do when you're done with something. Then I began walking up and down in front of her. A terrible excitement burned in me. I could feel my blood beating in my neck. I imagined it bursting through the skin in brilliant gushes of red. "She's gone! That's what you wanted! Isn't it? Isn't it? All gone! Bye-bye! Are you happy now? Are you?" I stopped in front of her. "Are you? Are you?" I bent close. "Are you? Are you? Are you?" I bent closer still. I bent so close that I couldn't see her anymore. "Are you? Are you? Are you? Are you? Are you?"

Monica did the only thing she could do: she fled. But first she stood there as if she were about to speak. She stared at me with the look of a woman who has been struck repeatedly across the face. There was hurt in that look, and tiredness, and a sort of pained tenderness. And along with it all came a quiet sureness, as of someone who has made up her mind. Then she turned and walked away.

There is a restlessness so terrible that you can no longer bear to sit still in your house. You walk from room to room like someone visiting a deserted town. Every day I mourned for my mirrors with their gleam of Miracle Polish. Where they'd once hung I saw only patterns in wallpaper, framed paintings, door panels, lines of dust. One day I drove out to the mall and came home with an oval mirror in a plain dark frame, which I hung in the upstairs hall; I used it strictly for checking my suit jacket. Once, when the doorbell rang, I rushed downstairs to the front door, but it was only a boy with a jar, collecting money for a new scout troop. I could feel grayness sifting down on me like dust. A bottle of Miracle Polish —was it so much to ask? One of these days the stranger is bound to come again. He'll walk toward my house with his heavy case tugging him to one side. In my living room he'll snap open the clasps and show me the brown bottles, row on row. Mournfully he'll tell me that it's my lucky day. In a voice that is calm, but decisive and self-assured, I'll tell him that I want every bottle, every last one. When I close my eyes, I can see the look of suspicion on his face, along with a touch of slyness, a shadow of contempt, and the beginnings of unbearable hope.

ALICE MUNRO

# Axis

FROM *The New Yorker*

FIFTY YEARS AGO, Grace and Avie were waiting at the university gates, in the freezing cold. A bus would come eventually, and take them north, through the dark, thinly populated countryside, to their homes. Forty miles to go for Avie, maybe twice that for Grace. They were carrying large books with solemn titles: *The Medieval World, Montcalm and Wolfe, The Jesuit Relations.*

This was mostly to establish themselves as serious students, which they were. But once they got home, they would probably not have time for such things. They were both farm girls who knew how to scrub floors and milk cows. Their labor as soon as they entered the house—or the barn—belonged to their families.

They weren't the sort of girls you usually ran into at this university. There was a large School of Business, whose students were nearly all male, and several sororities, whose members studied Secretarial Science and General Arts and were there to meet those men. Grace and Avie had not been approached by sororities—one look at their winter coats was enough to tell you why—but they believed that the men who were not on the lookout for sorority girls were more apt to be intellectuals, and they preferred intellectuals anyway.

They were both majoring in history, having won scholarships enabling them to do so. What would they do when they were finished? people asked, and they had to say that they would probably teach high school. They admitted that they would hate that.

They understood—everybody understood—that having any

sort of job after graduation would be a defeat. Like the sorority girls, they were enrolled here to find somebody to marry. First a boyfriend, then a husband. It wasn't spoken of in those terms, but there you were. Girl students on scholarships were not usually thought to stand much of a chance, since brains and looks were not believed to go together. Fortunately, Grace and Avie were both attractive. Grace was fair and stately, Avie red-haired, less voluptuous, lively, and challenging. Male members of both their families had joked that they ought to be able to nab somebody.

By the time the bus came, they were nearly frozen. They worked their way to the back, so they could smoke what would be their last cigarettes until after the weekend. Their parents would not be suspicious if they smelled it on them. The smell of cigarettes was everywhere in those days.

Avie waited until they were comfortable to tell Grace about her dream.

"You must never tell anybody," she said.

In the dream, she was married to Hugo, who really was hanging around as if he hoped to marry her, and she had a baby, who cried day and night. It howled, in fact, till she thought she would go crazy. At last she picked up this baby—picked *her* up, there never was any doubt that it was a girl—and took her down to some dark basement room and shut her in there, where the thick walls ensured that she wouldn't be heard. Then she went away and forgot about her. And it turned out that she had another girl baby anyway, one who was easy and delightful and grew up without any problems.

But one day this grown daughter spoke to her mother about her sister hidden in the basement. It turned out that she had known about her all along—the poor warped and discarded one had told her everything—and there was nothing to be done now. "Nothing to be done," this lovely, kind girl said. The abandoned daughter knew no way of life but the one she had and, anyway, she did not cry anymore; she was used to it.

"That's an awful dream," Grace said. "Do you hate children?"

"Not unreasonably," Avie said.

"What would Freud say? Never mind that, what would Hugo say? Have you told him?"

"Good God, no."

"It's probably not as bad as it seems. You're probably just worried again about being pregnant."

It had been Avie, really, who had persuaded Hugo that they should sleep together, or have sex, as people would later say. She thought it would make him seem more manly, more assured. He was a nice-looking, eager boy with dark hair flopping over his forehead, and he had a tendency to pick out people he could worship. A professor, a brilliant older student, a girl. Avie. If they slept together, she thought, she might fall in love with him. After all, neither of them had ever had that experience with anybody else. But what sex had led to, chiefly, was fright about certain accidents, worry about late periods, and the monstrous possibility that she might be pregnant.

The truth was that she would rather have had Grace's boyfriend, Royce, who was a veteran of the Second World War. Unlike Avie, Grace was in love. She believed that her virginity and her refusal to let Royce dispose of it—not what he was used to—was a way of keeping him interested. But at times he was ready to give up on her, and to divert him from such bad moods she had learned to distract him with gossip or jokes about people like Hugo, whom he rather despised. In fact, Grace had got into the habit of making up stories about Hugo that weren't anywhere near true. Both legs in one pant leg, after a session of harried lovemaking—nonsense like that. She hoped that Avie would never find out.

In the early summer, Royce got on a bus and went to visit Grace on her parents' farm. The bus had to pass the town where Avie lived, and by chance from his window he saw Avie, standing on the sidewalk of the main street, talking to somebody. She was full of animation, whipping her hair back when the wind blew it in her face. He remembered that she had quit college just before her exams. Hugo had graduated and got a job teaching high school in some northern town, where she was to join him and marry him.

Grace had told Royce that Avie had had a bad scare, and it had caused her to come to this decision. Then it had turned out to be all right—she wasn't pregnant—but she had decided she might as well go ahead anyway.

Avie didn't look like anybody trapped by a scare. She looked carefree, and in immensely good spirits—prettier, more vivid, than he ever remembered seeing her.

He had an urge to get off the bus and not get on again. But, of course, that would land him in more trouble than even he could contemplate. Avie was sashaying across the street in front of the bus now anyway, disappearing into a store.

They had waited supper half an hour for him, at Grace's house, and even at that it was only five-thirty. "The cows are boss around here, I'm afraid," Grace's mother said. "I suppose you're quite a stranger to farm life."

She looked nothing like Grace, or Grace looked nothing like her, thank God. Scrawny, cropped gray hair. She scurried around so, she didn't ever seem to get a chance to straighten up.

A schoolteacher, she had been, and she looked it. A school-teacher watching out for whatever wrong thing she hasn't caught you doing yet. The father seemed anxious to get to the cows. The grown son wore a sneer. So did the younger sister, who was supposed to be a genius on the piano. Grace sat mute and shamed, but lovely, flushed from the cooking.

What were his plans, the mother wanted to know, his plans now that he had graduated? (Grace must have told them that lie; she must have concealed the fact that he'd walked out on his last exam because the questions were idiotic. Had she thought that mere bravado?)

Right now, he said, he was driving a taxi. There was not much to do with a degree in philosophy. "Unless I decide to become a priest."

"You a Catholic?" the father said, so startled he almost choked on his food.

"Oh. Do you have to be?"

Grace said, "Just kidding." But she sounded as if all the kidding had gone out of her.

"Philosophy," the mother said. "I didn't know you could study just that for four years."

"Slow learner," Royce said.

"Now you're joking."

He and Grace washed the dishes in silence, then went for a walk in the lane. Her face was still rosy from embarrassment or the kitchen heat, and her teasing nature seemed to have turned to lead.

"Is there a late bus?" he said.

"They're just nervous," she said. "It'll be better tomorrow."

He looked up at some feathery, slightly Oriental-looking trees, and asked her if she knew what they were.

"Acacia. Acacia trees. They're my favorite trees."

Favorite trees. What next? Favorite flower? Favorite star? Favorite windmill? Did she have a favorite fence post? About to inquire, he figured it would hurt her feelings.

Instead, he asked what they would be doing the next day. Maybe a picnic in the woods, he hoped. Somewhere he could get her alone.

She said that they would be making strawberry jam all day.

"You don't choose here," she said. "You just deal with what's ready. Follow the seasons."

He had counted on helping with some farm work. He was good with machinery, which surprised people, and he had a real interest in how others earned a living, even though he shied away from making a commitment of that kind himself.

In fact, it had occurred to him—of all things—that the father might be getting past it and the brother would prove to be some sort of dunce (Grace had spoken of him scornfully) and that he, Royce, right now at loose ends and neither stupid nor lazy, might slip into a bucolic life amid picturesque dumb animals and bursting orchards, with time on his hands all winter to cultivate his mind. Sabine farm.

But he could tell that the father and the brother were not going to be keen to have him around. No time for him. And they wouldn't think of farming, even efficient farming, as a restorative for the soul. He would be stuck with the strawberries. Unless the younger sister, the genius piano player, hauled him in to turn her pages.

"All my children have their gifts," the mother had said to him, as they got up from the table, and the pianist was excused from the dishes. "Ruth has her music, Grace has her history, and Kenny, of course, is the one for agriculture."

In the lane he tried putting his arm around Grace, but the embrace was awkward, with some stumbling in the narrow ruts of the track.

"Is this how it's going to be?" he said.

"Never mind," she said. "I have a plan."

He couldn't see what that could be. The room where he would sleep was off the kitchen. The window was stuck about a quarter of the way up—it didn't open far enough for him to sneak out.

"Tomorrow we make the jam," Grace said. "All day, likely. Ruth will be practicing—she'll drive you crazy, but never mind. Next day, Mother has to take her into town for her examination. Then all the kids who have been examined have to sit and wait till the last one's done, and that's when they give out the results to everybody. See?"

"I don't see your mother agreeing to leave us alone," Royce said. "Or isn't this the plan I'm thinking it is?"

"It is," Grace said. "I have to go and see my friend Robina. Robina Shoemaker. I'll have to go on my bike, so it'll take a while. She lives on the other side of the highway. We've been friends since we were little, and now for two years she's been crippled. A horse stepped on her foot."

"Good Christ," he said. "Rural calamities."

"I know," she said, not seeming to care about matching his tone. "So I am supposed to be going to see her, but I actually won't be. After Mother and Ruth are gone, I'm turning the bike around and coming back and we'll have the house to ourselves."

"And this exam is long?"

"I promise you. Long. And then they are going to take some strawberries to Grandma, and that always takes at least an hour. Are you following me?"

"I hope so."

"Can you be good all day tomorrow? Don't be sarcastic to Mother."

"Sorry," he said. "I promise."

But he had to wonder. Why now rather than any of those times last winter when he could easily have gotten her up to his room and arranged for his roommate to be out? Or last spring, when she drove him crazy in the dark corners of the park? What about her vaunted virginity?

"I have pads," she said. "How many do you usually need?"

To his surprise, he had to say he didn't know.

"Virgins aren't my cup of tea."

She hugged herself, laughing, the way he was used to her.

"I didn't mean to be funny." Really he hadn't.

Her mother was sitting on the side steps, but surely she couldn't have heard. She asked if they'd had a nice walk and said that she herself always looked forward to the cool of the evening.

"We're lucky here—not holed up in the heat like you city folks."

When he woke up in the morning he thought that he had ahead of him one of the longest days of his life, but in fact it went easily. The jugs were lowered in their racks into the bubbling hot water. The strawberries were hulled and heated till they boiled and developed a pink froth like midway candy. The work was organized amiably, with the three of them quick to see when another needed help lifting a pot or coming to another's aid with a handy movement of the strainer. The kitchen was murderously hot, and first Royce, then Grace, then Grace's mother thrust their faces under the cold-water tap and came up dripping.

"Why did I never in my life think of that before?" the mother said, standing there with witch tails stuck to her forehead. "It takes a man to think of things that smart, doesn't it, Grace?"

The piano was being played all day long by the child who was to be examined, reminding each of them, in their different ways, of the trials and promises of the day to come.

At the end of the afternoon Royce was given the keys to the car and drove five miles to the nearest store, where he bought sliced ham and ice cream and ready-made potato salad for supper. It seemed that potato salad not made at home was something unknown in that house.

Warm jam was poured over the ice cream.

The mother in her water-spotted dress was fairly giddy with the labor and the achievements of the day.

"Royce here is the type to spoil a woman," she said. "Anybody with him around would be getting the work done whiz-bang and then be enjoying ice cream every day. We'd be spoiled."

The brother said that Grace was spoiled already—she thought she was smart because she had went to college.

"Gone," the mother said.

Grace threatened to dump a spoonful of potato salad down his shirt. He grabbed it away and ate it from his fingers.

Grace said, "Yuck."

The mother warned them.
"Manners."

The next day the father and the brother were stooking early oats in the acres they owned on the other side of the highway. They took lunch with them, and counted on the woman who rented the place to supply them with drinking water. All this Grace had figured out.

Ruth was made to stand very still while her mother fixed her hair up with braids and ribbons to set off her doomed expression. She said she couldn't eat anything. The mother said, "Nerves," and wrapped up some soda biscuits in waxed paper. Just a few minutes before the car drove away, Grace got on her bicycle and waved goodbye. The mother said to give her love to the girl who was crippled. A jar of the fresh jam was wrapped up to keep it safe in the bicycle's basket, to provide a treat for her.

Royce had been told that he deserved a day off, after yesterday's work. But the tall brick house, so impressive from the outside, had not a scrap of grace or comfort within. The furniture was simply stuck here and there, as if nobody had ever had time for a plan. The front door was partly blocked by Ruth's piano. At least there were books to read in the living room. He took *Don Quixote* from a shelf of classics, behind glass, and yelled "Knock 'em dead!" to Ruth, who didn't answer. His ears followed the car down the lane, then heard it turn toward the highway. He read a few words, letting the house change over, switch itself to his side. The pattern of the oilcloth on the kitchen table seemed to be conspiring, the flypapers were as fresh as Ruth's curls, the radio turned off, everything waiting. Without any haste, he walked to the room off the kitchen, where he felt it proper to tidy the bed and hang up his few clothes. He pulled the blind down to the sill, took off everything he had on, and got under the quilt.

He had not come unequipped, even knowing that his chances might be slim. No lack of readiness now. The hush felt momentous. How far would she think it necessary to go before she turned back?

The kitchen clock struck one, the time that Ruth was due at the music teacher's. Now surely, surely.

He heard the bike on the gravel. But the kitchen door did not open as soon as he expected. Then he understood that she was pushing the bike around to the back of the house, to hide it.

Good girl.

Her footsteps entered, very lightly, as if not to waken anyone sleeping in the house. Then a shy movement of the door, which, as he had already noted, had no locks of any kind. He stayed quite still, his eyes open just a slit. He gave her time. He had thought she might get into bed with her clothes on, but no. She was taking off every stitch in front of him, head bowed, lips pressed together, then moistened with her tongue. Very serious.

What a darling.

They were far enough advanced not to have heard the car. At first he had made quite an effort to be quiet, not because he believed in any danger but just because he meant to go easy, be very gentle with her. This notion, however, was on the point of being left behind. She didn't seem to require such care. They were making enough noise themselves not to hear anything outside.

They would not have heard the car anyway—it had been left a distance down the driveway. Likewise, the footsteps must have been soft, the kitchen door carefully opened.

If they had heard even the kitchen door they might have had a moment to prepare. But as it was, the door of the room was flung open before they could understand that such a thing had happened. And, in fact, it took them a minute to stop and register the mother's face gaping, somehow huge, right at the foot of the bed.

She was not able to speak. She shook. She stuttered. She steadied herself by holding the bed frame.

"I cannot," she said when she could. "Cannot. Cannot. Believe."

"Oh, shut up," Royce said.

"Do you—do you—do you have a mother?"

"None of your business," Royce said. He heaved Grace to one side without looking at her, reached down for his pants on the floor, and worked them on under the quilt before he got out of the bed. His movements kicked Grace away from him. He could not help that, hardly noticed it. She had her head buried in the sheets, her bare buttocks now somehow exposed.

"What have you done?" the mother said. "We take you into our family. We make you welcome in our home. Our daughter—"

"Your daughter makes up her mind for herself."

"You hear him?" the mother cried at Grace's buried head, her hands clutching at the dress she had put on specially for the piano examination. There wasn't anywhere for her to sit down, except for the bed, and she couldn't sit on that.

Royce responded to this by gathering the things that belonged to him, tidied up in Grace's honor. Once he had to say "Excuse me" to the mother, but his tone was brutal.

When Grace heard him zip up his bag she turned over and put her feet on the floor. She was perfectly naked.

She said, "Take me. Take me with you."

But he had gone out of the room, out of the house, as if he hadn't even heard her.

He walked out to the road in such a rage that he could not think where to turn for the highway. When he found it, he hardly remembered to keep to the gravel, out of the way of the cars that might come along on the paved road. He knew he'd have to hitch, but for the moment he could not slow down to do it. He didn't think he'd be able to talk to anybody. He remembered whispering to Grace the day before when they were doing the strawberries, kissing under the rush of cold water when her mother's back was turned. Her fair hair turning dark in the stream of water. Acting as if he worshiped her. How at certain moments that had been true. The insanity of it, the insanity of letting himself be drawn. That family. That mad mother rolling her eyes to heaven.

When he got weary enough and sane enough, he slowed down and put out his thumb for a ride. There was little conviction in the gesture, but a car did stop for him.

He continued to be lucky during the day, though most of the rides were fairly short. Farmers wanting a bit of company on their way to town or their way home. There was general conversation. One farmer at the end of a ride said to him, "Say, can't you drive?"

Royce said sure. "Just recently I've been driving taxis."

"Well, aren't you getting a bit old, then, to be hitching rides? You got through college and all—aren't you of the opinion that you should be getting a real job?"

Royce considered this, as if it were a truly novel idea.

He said, "No."

Then he got out, and he saw across the road in the cut of the highway a tower of ancient-looking rock that seemed quite out of place there, even though it was capped with grass and had a small tree growing out of a crack.

He was on the edge of the Niagara Escarpment, though he did not know that name or anything about it. But he was captivated. Why had he never been told anything about this? This surprise, this careless challenge in the ordinary landscape. He felt a comic sort of outrage that something made for him to explore had been there all along and nobody had told him.

Nevertheless, he knew. Before he got into the next car, he knew that he was going to find out; he was not going to let this go. Geology was what it was called. And all this time he had been fooling around with arguments, with philosophy and political science.

It wouldn't be easy. It would mean saving money, starting again with pimpled brats just out of high school. But that was what he would do.

Later, he often told people about the trip, about the sight of the escarpment that had turned his life around. If asked what he'd been doing there, he'd wonder and then remember that he'd gone up there to see a girl.

Avie was near campus for one day in the fall, picking up a few books that she had left behind at her former boarding house. She went up to the university to see if she could turn them in at the secondhand bookshop there, but found that she didn't really want to. She was surprised at first not to meet anyone she knew. Then she ran into a girl who had sat next to her in her Decisive Battles of Europe class. Marsha Kidd. Marsha told her that they had all been shocked that Avie wasn't coming back.

"You and Grace, it's such a shame," Marsha said.

Avie had written Grace a letter during the summer. Then she'd worried that the letter was somewhat too frank on the subject of her doubts about getting married, and she had written a second letter that was quite witty in denying the doubts of the first. There had been no answer to either one.

"I sent her a card," Marsha said. "I thought maybe she and I could get a room together. When I heard you weren't going to be around. Not that I ever got any reply."

Avie remembered that she and Grace had made jokes about Marsha, whom they saw as the sort of dim and tiresome girl who would not even mind becoming a high school teacher and would never have a man after her in her life.

"Somebody said she had colitis," Marsha said. "That's when you get all swollen, isn't it? That would be miserable."

Avie went home and wrote thank-you notes, which she had been neglecting to do. She mailed the presents that were going to Kenora. Hugo had his first teaching job there, in the high school. He had rented an apartment for them to live in. Perhaps in a year they could get a house.

In the summer, when he was working at Labatt, they'd had one of their pregnancy scares, but it had turned out to be all right. So they'd gone camping on Civic Holiday weekend, to celebrate, and for the first time it had seemed that they were truly in love. It was also the first time that they had really gotten pregnant, and they had announced that they would be getting married in Kenora very soon, before she began to show.

They were not unhappy about it.

In what was once called the club car, on the train from Toronto to Montreal, Avie is on her way to visit one of her daughters. She and Hugo had six children in the end, all grown now. Hugo has been dead for a year and a half. Except for those couple of years in Kenora, he spent his entire teaching career in Thunder Bay. Avie never had a job, and nobody expected her to have one, with all those children. But she had more spare time than anybody would have thought, and she spent most of it reading. When the great switch came in women's lives—when wives and mothers who had seemed content suddenly announced that it was not so, when they all started sitting on the floor instead of on sofas, and took university courses and wrote poetry and fell in love with their professors or their psychiatrists or their chiropractors, and began to say "shit" and "fuck" instead of "darn" and "heck"—Avie was never tempted to join in. Maybe she was too fastidious, too proud. Maybe Hugo was just too much of a sitting duck. Maybe she loved him. At any rate, she was as she was, and reading Leonard Cohen wouldn't be any help to her.

Since being widowed, however, she has read less. She has stared out of windows more. Her children say that she is withdrawing into herself. On this train ride she hasn't bothered much with her book, though it is a good one.

The man across from her has glanced at her a couple of times and is now studying her quite openly. He says, "Avie?"

It's Royce. He doesn't look so different, after all.

Their conversation is easy, covering at first the usual ground. The six children are marveled at. He says that you'd never know it to look at her. He didn't remember Hugo's name but is sorry to hear that he's dead. He's surprised at the idea that you can live a whole life in Port Arthur. Or Thunder Bay, as it is now called.

They drink gin and tonics. She tells him that Hugo had no apprehensions at all. He died sitting in his chair, watching the news.

Royce has traveled. Lived in various places. He taught geology, though he is now retired.

Did he marry?

No. Oh, no. And no children that he knows of.

He says this with the slight twinkle that usually accompanies this statement, in Avie's experience.

Now he has a peach of a retirement job. The best job ever, except for geology. In eastern Ontario, as it turns out. Where he is heading now. Gananoque.

He describes the old fort there, the fort built at the mouth of the St. Lawrence River to withstand the American invasion that never came. The most important of the chain of forts along the Rideau Canal. It has been preserved intact, not as a replica but as the thing itself. He shows people around, gives them a history lesson. It's shocking how little people know. Not just the Americans, of whom you expect it. Canadians too.

He has written a little book about the Rideau. It's for sale in the Gananoque fort. He managed to get a good deal of the geology into it as well as the history. He went into the field a bit late to make his mark. But why not try to tell people about it? Now he is coming home from a trip he made to Toronto, to try to interest some booksellers there. Some of them took a few copies on spec.

Avie says that one of her daughters works for a publisher in Toronto.

He sighs.

"It's uphill, really," he says abruptly. "People don't always see in it what you see yourself. But you're okay, I guess. You've got your kids."

"Well, after a point," Avie says, "after a point, you know, they're just people. I mean, they're yours, of course. But they're really —they're people you know."

God strike me dead, she thinks.

"I remember something," he says, much more cheerfully. "I remember I was on a bus, and I was going through the town where you lived. I don't know if I knew beforehand that it was where you lived, but there I saw you on the street. I just happened to be on the right side of the bus to see you. I was going farther north. I was going to see a girl I knew then."

"Grace."

"That's right. You were friends with her. Anyway, I saw you there on the sidewalk talking to somebody and I thought you looked just irresistible. You were laughing away. I wanted to get right off the bus and speak to you. Make a date with you, actually. I couldn't very well not turn up where I was expected, but I could meet you on my way back. I thought, That's what I could do—make a date to meet you on the way back. I actually did know something about you, now that I think of it. I knew that you were going around with somebody, but I thought, Well, make a try for it."

"I never knew," Avie says. "I never knew you were there."

"And then, as it happened, I didn't come back the same way, so I wouldn't have been wherever you were waiting, so it would have been botched all round."

"I never knew."

"Well, if you had known, would you have agreed? If I'd said, 'Be at such-and-such a place, such-and-such a time,' would you have been there?"

Avie doesn't hesitate. "Oh, yes," she says.

"With the complications and all?"

"Yes."

"So it's a good thing? That we didn't make contact?"

She does not even try for an answer.

He says, "Water under the bridge." Then he leans back into the headrest and closes his eyes.

"Wake me up before we're into Kingston if I've gone to sleep," he says. "There's something I want to be sure to show you."

Not so far off from giving her automatic orders, like a husband.

He wakens without any prompting from her, if he ever was asleep. They sit in the train at the Kingston station while people get on and off, and he tells her it's not yet. When the train starts up again, he explains that all around them are great slabs of limestone packed in order, one on top of the other, like a grand construction. But in one spot this gives way, he says, and you can see something else. It's what is known as the Frontenac Axis. It is nothing less than an eruption of the vast and crazy old Canadian Shield, all the ancient combustion cutting through the limestone, pouring over, messing up those giant steps.

"See! See!" he says, and she does see. Remarkable.

"Remember to watch for that if you come through again," he says. "You can't really look at it from a car—there's too much traffic. Why I take the train."

"Thank you," she says.

He doesn't answer but turns away, nods a little with what seems to be important assent.

"Thank you," she says again. "I'll remember."

Nods once more, doesn't look at her. Enough.

When that first pregnancy was well advanced, around Christmastime, Avie had received a brief letter from Grace.

"I hear you are married and expecting. You may not have heard I have dropped out of college, due to some troubles I have had with my health and my nerves. I often think of our talks and particularly the dream you told me about. It still scares the daylights out of me. Love, Grace."

Avie remembered then the conversation with Marsha. The colitis. The tone of Grace's letter seemed off kilter, with some pleading note in it that made her put off answering. She herself was feeling quite happy at the time, full of practical concerns, light-years away from whatever stuff they had talked about in college. She didn't know if she could ever find her way back there or find a way to talk to Grace as she was now. And later, of course, she got too busy.

She asks Royce if he heard anything from Grace, ever.

"No. No. Why should I?"

"I just thought."

"No."

"I thought you might have looked her up later on."

"Not a good idea."

She has disappointed him. Prying. Trying to get at some spot of live regret right under the ribs. A woman.

# *Volcano*

FROM *Tin House*

SIX MONTHS AFTER she divorced her husband, Martha Fink packed her bags and flew to Honolulu to attend a lucid-dreaming seminar at the Kalani resort on the Big Island of Hawaii. She had discovered the faithless Donald in the same position that the wife of Samuel Pepys had discovered the London diarist in, three hundred years before: copulating with the family maid. "I was deep inside her cunny," Pepys admitted that night in his diary, "and indeed I was at a wondrous loss to explain it."

Martha filed for divorce. She collected the apartment on Central Park West and a considerable sum of money, then went to counseling. Lovers did not materialize to replace the discarded husband. She became yet more enraged, went on Zoloft, and finally decided that her eighteen years of therapy and dietary rigor had not, in the end, helped her very much to face the endgame of biology itself. Growing older had proved a formidable calamity.

Nothing saves you from it, she realized. Not irony, certainly, or dieting or gyms or drugs or the possession of children and priceless friends. Nothing saves the declining human from the facts of her decline except the promises of work. And that had not saved her either, because, unluckily, she hated her work. She detested it more and more. A lawyer, she now realized, should always maintain extracurricular passions, and she had not. Her lifelong practicality and good humor had not sustained her either, and her fine skin and aristocratic profile felt to her increasingly insufficient, if not wasted. There was now just Hawaii and dreams. The resort, run by two gay dancers, was next to an active volcano.

She spent a night on Waikiki in a high-rise hotel called the Aston. The city seemed compressed, airless and suffocating. A nightmare of dullness and saturation, of Burberry and Shiseido, of families braying on the far side of thin walls. Her room was filled with red neon.

She wept all night, strung out on sleeping pills. In the morning, she went to the old Sheraton for coffee in a courtyard of banyans and squabbling pintails. It was now called the Manoa Surfrider, and there was Soviet-looking architecture all around. She sat there for some hours. She felt herself coming apart. The sun did not cheer her up; there was no charm whatsoever in the colonial affect of her surroundings, a style that could be called New Jersey Tropical.

She went to Pearl Harbor in the afternoon. Sappy music played, and the crowd was hustled along like cattle. "Each visitor can contemplate his innermost responses and feelings." In the bus back to Waikiki, she saw a poster for Dr. Rosa Christian Harfouche, a preacher selling Signs, Wonders, and Miracles. The streets were full of federal detention centers and ukulele stores. Not a single attractive human. Suddenly she felt years older than forty-six.

She waited tensely for her flight to Hilo.

From the air, the islands regained their beauty. They seemed far-flung again, imposing, like sacred statues lying on their sides. The sea was immense, like a visual drug that could calm the most turbulent heart. Not America, then, but Polynesia, though it was difficult to remember. She slept, and her tears subsided into her core.

A driver from Kalani was there to meet her. They drove down to Pahoa through a landscape of lava rock and papaya groves. In town, they had a milk shake in a "French café" and sat outside for a while, looking up at silver clouds shaped like anvils, static above the volcano. The driver told her, as if it was a detail she might relish, that he had transported fourteen people so far from the airport to Kalani for the Dream Express seminar. Most of them, he said cattily, were middle-aged women who looked like they were having a bad time.

"A bad time?" she said tartly. "Do I look like I'm having a bad time?"

"No, ma'am. You look real eager."

Eager, was she that? In a way, she was. A wide freeway swept

down to the southern coast and lava flats and cliffs, above which
Kalani stood in its papaya woods. As the sea appeared, she felt a
keen relief. The road dipped up and down past affluent hippie
resorts, yoga retreats, and fasting centers. A few flabby joggers shot
by, all ponytails and tattoos. At the gates of Kalani, lanterns had
been lit for the evening.

The resort was a considerable estate made up of groups of
traditional spherical Hawaiian houses raised off the ground. In
the thatched communal meeting place, everyone ate a macrobi-
otic, vegetarian buffet dinner, courtesy of the resort. The owners
and the dancers were dressed in Hawaiian skirts and performing
a votive dance to the volcano goddess, Pu'ah. They danced and
clapped to welcome the new residents, jiggling their hips, rolling
their fingers, and hailing the volcano itself, which lay only a few
miles distant and had become active only two weeks before. At
sundown, a dull red glow stretched across the horizon.

Kalani hosted four different seminars at a time. The Dream Express group was indeed, she saw at once, highly populated with
middle-aged women wearing tense and confused expressions. Her
heart might have sunk right then if she hadn't determined not to
let it. She braced herself for these sad, bewildered specimens, who
were likely capable of comradeship and kindness. Her eyes sorted
through them, but she was unable to keep from disapproving. The
seminar leader, Dr. Stephen DuBois, was a Stanford psychiatrist
who supplemented his academic income with dream seminars
in alternative health centers. It was he who had devised a way to
"wake" the dreamer inside her dream and make her conscious of
it, through a daily routine of herbs and nightly use of a special pair
of goggles that shot regulated beams of light into the eyes during
the deepest periods of REM sleep. With these methods, one could
enter a state of "lucid dreaming" and consciously direct the flow
of the dream itself. It was a common technique of dream therapy
but rarely used in a controlled environment like Kalani, a context
from which normal reality had been almost entirely subtracted.
DuBois claimed to be able to alter each participant's relationship
to her own dreams by the use of the herb galantamine. Aside from
being a popular treatment for Alzheimer's, polio, and memory dis-
orders, galantamine, derived from Caucasian snowdrop flowers,
was said to induce exceptionally intense and memorable dreams

by deepening REM sleep. It looked like a white powder, like very pure cocaine.

DuBois introduced them all to one another: a psychiatrist from Rome at the end of a long nervous breakdown, a married couple from Oregon working through their difficulties, a female stock-broker from London who already possessed a "friend" inside her dreams who flew with her across vast oneiric landscapes. There were a few Burning Man types from the Bay Area who came every year, young and wide-eyed, and two New York basket cases fleeing their catastrophic jobs and marriages. All in all, they were what she had expected. Bores and beaten-down shrews in decline and kooks. She didn't mind, particularly. People are what they are and they were no more broken down by life's disappointments than she herself was. She was sure that half the women had faithless husbands who had run off with younger women. They had that archetypal event inscribed upon their faces.

"It's very simple," DuBois explained from the head of their trestle table. The volcano dance had wound down, and a group of new-age square dancers arrived at the adjoining table. "Every night we'll take a capsule of galantamine and go to bed at a rea-sonable hour. We'll put on our goggles before we go to sleep. If the infrared beam wakes us up, we'll leave the goggles on and go back to sleep. Hopefully, though, we won't wake up at all. We'll simply become conscious inside our dreams."

"Really?" said the Italian psychiatrist.

"Certainly. When that happens, you all have to remember a few basic things. To change your dream, simply reach out and rub a rough surface. A wall is perfect. The dream will change immedi-ately and you can enjoy the next one. If you want to fly, simply start turning on the spot. You'll start flying."

They all began to smile, to nod. It would be like hours of en-tertainment every night. Like cinema inside their heads. And, be-cause of the powdered snowdrop, they would remember it all.

"Every morning, we'll tell each other what we dreamed. It'll help us remember everything, and it'll help us write our dream journals. The dream journal will be a book we can take back with us when we have finished here. Something permanent and life-changing."

Now they would get acquainted and then return to their

thatched cabanas and prepare for the first night of lucid dreaming. It seemed to Martha a simple enough plan, and she was still tired from the long flight. The resort owners stopped by the table, still in their skirts: handsome, tan, muscular gay men whom you could imagine vigorously fucking in hot tubs and saunas. Shaking their hands gave her a twinge of arousal.

"Look over there," one of them said. He pointed to the glow visible above the tree line. "Looks like lava on the move."

Across the smooth, rolling lawns, Martha could see naked men strolling down toward the hot tubs surrounding the swimming pool. The resort was nudist after 9 P.M. After a cup of chamomile tea and a few desultory chats, she said good night to the group and walked back to her cabana. A high moon illumined the edge of the jungle.

She took the galantamine capsule, lay under the mosquito nets of her bed, and attuned herself to the rhythmic chirping of the tree frogs. She put on the cumbersome goggles and adjusted the strap so that it did not squeeze her face too tightly. Then her exhaustion took over. She was too tired to care that the goggles were uncomfortable or that the frogs were loud because the windows had no glass. She slept without thinking about sleeping, and soon the REM cycle had swept her up.

She began to dream at once, but later she could not remember it as clearly as she had hoped. She did recall that in this dream she was standing in a hotel bar, drinking a glass of port. Rain was falling outside, and behind her there seemed to be a roaring fire. When she turned to look at it, she felt the fire's heat touch her face, and the piercing red beam of the machine inside the goggles flooded her consciousness with its color. Unused to this intrusion, she awoke immediately and tore off the goggles.

The first thing she heard was the frogs. The moon had moved position and shone directly into the room, touching the foot of the bed. She was drenched in sweat. She got up and went to the screened window. Nightjars sang in the papayas. She felt intensely awake and therefore restless. She put on her flip-flops and a sarong and climbed down the steps of her cabana into the long, wet grass. At the end of the lawn shone the pool, wreathed with steam from the all-night Jacuzzi. She made her way to the hot tub, tiny frogs popping out of the grass around her feet, and when she reached the pool she disrobed again and sank into the water, naked. Tall palms stood around the pool. The moon shone between them.

As she floated on her back, she could feel that something in this idyllic scene was not quite right. It was too serene. Then, from far off, she heard a wild whoop of male voices. She sat up. A group of naked men ran down the lawn toward her. They approached in a line, their erections flapping about, and they headed straight for the pool. Startled, she leapt out of the water, grabbed her sarong, and darted into the dripping papaya trees on the far side of the footpath. The men, oblivious to her presence, jumped en masse into the pool and filled it with phalli and noise. She reached out and touched the rough bark of one of the trees, and as she did she found herself back in her bed, the goggles still fixed to her head. Rain was pouring down outside the window.

She tore off the goggles, gasping, her body drenched with sweat. The rain was so heavy that the frogs had fallen silent, and all she could hear was the mechanical dripping from the edge of the window frame and the rustle beyond, in the forest. She got up a second time, and her bewilderment made her reach out and touch the insect screen to see if it was real. She wrote down her dream straightaway.

In the morning, the sun returned, but there was a taste of burned wood on the air, born from afar, and a reddish dust that seemed to linger over the tree line. In the cafeteria, the group was eagerly discussing the eruption of the volcano during the night —one of a series of eruptions, it seemed.

"It kept me up all night," the London broker said, eyeing Martha up and down. "Didn't you hear it?"

"Nothing," Martha said. "Did it rain all night?"

"It rained, but there was one hour when it was pure moonlight, peaceful as can be. I went down to the pool." The broker lowered her voice. "Unfortunately, it was occupied. Men are strange, don't you think?"

The woman had bossy, aggressive green eyes that possessed a knack for mentally undressing other women.

"I slept badly," Martha admitted, rubbing her eyes. "The rain woke me up."

"Personally, the galantamine does nothing for me. You?"

Martha shrugged. "I have nothing to compare it to."

During the day, they listened to DuBois lecture in one of the rotunda meeting halls, and Martha dozed in a corner, feeling that she had not enjoyed enough sleep. It was a hot day, and after lunch she went for a walk by herself along the coast road, where the woods were thicker. She walked for miles, until she came to a gray beach under the cliffs, where sundry hippies and half-stoned locals sat drinking kava and smoking reefers. Beyond the beach lay flats of black lava that reached out into the sea. She went down onto the beach and lay in the roasting sun for a while. Her grief welled up inside her until tears flowed down her face. No one could see them there. She emptied herself out and breathed heavily until her body was reoxygenated.

Later that night, she walked down to the lava again with some of the other dream women. One of them was a mosaic artist from Missoula, Montana, and another sold hot tubs for a living. Makeshift kava cafés made of driftwood had been set up on the rock shelves, and wild travelers on motorbikes appeared out of nowhere, racing across the lava with their lights blazing. The women drank kava and seaweed honey out of small paper cups and watched the red glow of the volcano in the distance; three divorced women, two of them long into middle age, waiting for improbable turns of events. Aging European hippies in feather earrings, with names like Firewind and Crystal Eye, tried to pick them up. Martha felt supremely detached from everyone. She didn't want to talk about the love lives of the other women. Everyone's love life, she thought, was more or less the same, and to be disgusted one only had to remember that seventy million women were saying exactly the same things to their friends at that very same moment.

"I left him only six months ago," one of the women was saying, as if they had all known each other for years. "He never gave me cunnilingus either. I know he was sleeping around—"

"They're *all* sleeping around."

"Does a fling every two years count as sleeping around?"

"Maybe we could fuck one of those filthy hippies. Firewind is quite sexy."

They drank the kava and became more stoned.

"Mine never gave me cunnilingus either. They get lazy after a while. No one stays with anyone, ever, unless they're Christians."

"I wouldn't sleep with Firewind. He has blue fingernails."

"You wouldn't notice in the dark."

"Yes, but feather earrings?"

To Martha, the red glow in the night sky was more compelling than the conversation. It seemed incomprehensible that a volcano was active so close to them and yet there was no outward concern. The more distant molten lava must be moving down to the sea. The scene must be one of terror and grandeur, yet no one saw it. She thought about it as they licked salty seaweed honey off their fingers.

She dreamed of her husband that night. She was cutting his toenails in a sea of poppies, and his toes were bleeding onto her scissors. He laughed and writhed as she ripped his toes with the blades. The galantamine made her remember it vividly. In the morning, she skipped the dream seminar, which no longer held much interest for her, and rented a motorbike from the front desk. She took a night bag and some money and decided to play the day by ear. She drove to Pahoa and on through Kurtistown until she reached Route 11, which turned west toward Volcanoes National Park. Soon she was rising through the Ola'a Forest.

At the top of the rising road stood the strange little town of Volcano. It was a cluster of houses on the edge of one of the craters, lush with rain forest. She parked by a large hotel and walked into a wonderful old lobby with a fireplace and oil paintings of volcanic eruptions on the walls. There was no one there. She wandered around the room for a while, admiring the native Hawaiian artifacts, then noticed a spacious bar on the far side of the reception desk. She went in.

Enormous windows wrapped around the room. Through them, the entire crater could be seen. It was a pale charcoal color, a vast field of uneven rock scored with ridges from which glittering steam rose hundreds of feet into the air. A pair of antlers hung above the bar itself, next to a "volcano warning meter," a mocking toy with a red arrow that pointed to various states of imminent catastrophe.

At the bar sat an elderly gentleman in a flat-cloth cap, dipping his pinky into a dry martini. He looked up at her with watery, slightly bloodshot eyes in which there was a faint trace of lechery. He wore a windowpane jacket of surpassing ugliness and a dark brown tie with a gold pin in it. The barman was the same age, a sprightly sixty or so, and his eyes contained the same sardonic and predatory glint of sexual interest in a forty-six-year-old woman entering their domain unexpectedly.

"Aloha," the barman said, and the solitary drinker repeated it. She echoed the word and, not knowing what to do, sat down at the bar as well.

"Going down to the crater?" the capped man asked.

"Yes. I just wanted a stiff drink first."

"A good idea. I recommend the house cocktail. The Crater."

"What is it?"

"White rum, pineapple juice, cane sugar, Angostura bitters, a grapefruit segment, a dash of Cointreau, a cherry, dark rum, a sprig of mint, an egg white, and a hint of kava," said the barman.

"I'll have a glass of white wine."

"The Crater'll set you up better."

She looked at the volcano paintings, the flickering fire, the inferno landscape smoldering beyond the windows, and finally she noticed that the man in the cap was halfway through a Crater. Oh, why the fuck not?

"Okay," she said, "I'll have one."

They all laughed.

"Try walking across that crater after one of those," the drinker said. "The name's Alan Pitchfork. No, it's not my real name, but hey, we're at the Volcano Hotel in Volcano, so who the hell cares?"

She took off her scarf and sunglasses.

"I'm Martha Prickhater. That is my real name."

"Oh, is it now?"

Alan leaned over to touch her glass with his. Her eyes strayed up to the ancient clock underneath the antlers, and she was surprised to see that it was already 2 P.M.

"Are you a local?" she asked politely.

"Moved here from Nebraska in 1989. Never looked back. Retired geologist."

"How nice. Did you come here with your wife?"

"Died in Nebraska, 1989."

"Ah, I see. I'm sorry."

"Long time ago, not to worry."

"Well, cheers."

She sipped the amazing brew. It tasted like the effluent from a chewing gum factory.

"Cheers," the man said, and did nothing.

"Staying at the hotel?" he went on, eyeing her. "Nice rooms

here. Traditional style. African antiques in some of them. Views over the volcanoes."

"I hadn't thought about it."

"Well, you should think about it. You get a good night's sleep up here in Volcano, if a good night's sleep is what you want."

"I'll bear it in mind," she said testily.

"You should. Bear it in mind, I mean. There's no better spot for watching the sunset."

She finished her drink, said her farewells, and went back into the sunlight of the parking lot, where her bike stood, the only vehicle there. She drove down the lonely road to the trails that led to the crater. She chained up the bike and wandered down, through the rain forest dripping with water from a shower she apparently had not noticed. The trail led to the edge of the lava crater, which smelled of sulfur. She walked out into the middle of the stone plain.

In the sun, the wreaths of rising steam looked paler, more ethereal. She lay down and basked, taking off her shoes and pushing her soles into the slightly warm rock. Looking up, she could not see the hotel at all. To the south, the sky was hazed by the continuing eruption of the neighboring crater and soon, she could tell, that haze would reach the sun and eclipse it. She was tipsy and slow and her body ached for something. A man's touch, maybe. The touch of a rogue.

It was early evening when she got back to the hotel. The fire was roaring high and yet there was still no sign of other guests. She hesitated, because she was not quite sure why she had come back at all. The barman was on a ladder, dusting one of the oil paintings. He stepped down to welcome her back.

"Want a room?" he said hopefully.

"Not exactly."

"I can give you thirty percent off."

It was clear the place was empty.

"Dinner?" he tried, stepping gingerly around her. "A drink at the bar? Two for one?"

She peered into the bar and saw that the same drinker was still there, a little the worse for wear but still upright on his seat, another Crater in front of him. He caught her eye and winked. Behind him, the windows had dimmed, and only the outline of the crater could still be made out, illumined by the red glow that never seemed to diminish. The men told her the hotel's clientele had vanished after the volcano warnings had been issued two nights earlier.

"Volcano warnings?" she said, sitting down again at the bar.

"Red alert." Alan smiled, raising his glass.

The barman began to prepare a Crater without her asking for it.

"Yeah," he drawled. "They run like ants as soon as there's a red alert. But Alan here and I know better. We've seen a hundred red alerts, haven't we, Alan?"

"A thousand."

"See?" The barman garnished her drink with a yellow paper parasol. "It's perfectly safe to stay the night if you so wish."

"I wasn't thinking of it."

"It's a long ride back to Kalani," the geologist remarked. "In the dark, I mean."

She let it go.

*I can do it,* she thought.

They turned and watched the fireworks display outside for a while. The eruption had intensified, and it was easy to imagine the flows of lava dripping into the sea only a few miles away. The glow cast itself against the walls of the bar, turning the room a dark red. She gripped her drink and tilted it into her mouth, watching the geologist drum his fingers on the bar. Who was he and where did he live? He never seemed to leave the hotel bar. He asked her how she had found the crater, and he added that he had watched her cross it from this same window.

Soon she was tipsy again. Something inside her told her that a motorbike ride back to Kalani at this hour would be suicidal. That "something" was simultaneously a desire to cave in, to book a room upstairs with African antiques and a view of the eruption. But it seemed, at the same time, inexpressibly vulgar to do so. To be alone in a hotel like this with two decrepit old men. She tossed back the dregs of her disgusting drink and ordered another.

"That's the spirit," the barman said. "It's on me."

Alan disputed the right to buy the drink and soon she was obliged to thank him.

"Shall we go sit by the fire?" he said.

In the main room, where the fire crackled and hissed, the Ha-

waiian masks had taken on a lurid uniqueness. They stared down
at the odd couple sinking into the horsehair armchairs. The geologist put his drink down on a leather-surfaced side table and told
her a long story about the last major eruption, when he had spent
a week alone in Volcano, smoking cigars at the bar and enjoying
the view. People were cowards.

"Personally, I'm not afraid of lava. It's a quick death, as good as
any other, if not better."

"That's philosophical of you."

"I'm a geologist. You have beautiful legs, by the way. If I may
say."

She started with surprise and displeasure and instinctively
pulled her skirt down an inch or so.

"No, don't cross them," he went on. "Don't feel awkward."

Instead of feeling awkward, she felt warm and insulted. Her
face began to flush hot and she wanted to throw her drink in his
face. She controlled herself, however, and tried to smile it off.

"Thank you, if that's a compliment."

He said it was, and he wasn't going to apologize for it. His
scaly, wrinkled skin seemed to shine under the equally antiquated
lamps. After a while, she heard a quiet but insistent pitter-patter
against the windows that was not rain. The man smiled. It was ash
falling.

"Sometimes," Alan said, "I swear it's like the last days of Pom-
peii."

As the evening wore on, it became obvious that she would have
to stay overnight. The barman told her that she could have the
Serengeti Suite at half price. She agreed. He served them sandwiches with Hawaiian relishes, and more Craters. Martha began to
see double. Eventually, she decided to go up to her room and lock
the door. It was safer that way. She got up and staggered to the
stairwell, while the geologist sat back and watched her radiant legs
take her there. They said good night, or at least she thought he
did, and she pulled herself up the squeaky stairs with a pounding
head.

The suite was cold, and she left the main light off while she
lit the glassed-in gas fire. Then she opened the curtains and let
the red glow invade the rooms. On the horizon, beyond the extinct crater's rim, globs of white light seemed to shine behind a
frazzled line of trees. She lay on the damp bed and kicked off

her shoes. There were Zulu shields on the walls and pictures of Masai spearing black-maned lions under the suns of long ago. The chairs looked like something from a luxury safari lodge. She lay there and grew subtly bored, discontented with her solitude. She wondered what they would be doing at Kalani right then. Dancing in skirts to the volcano goddess, sitting around a fire and drinking their kava with marshmallow, or doing Personhood Square Dancing in the woods, with paper hats. She lay there for an hour, fidgeting and feeling her emptiness and loneliness well up within her, then got up again and went to the bathroom to rebrush her hair. The antagonizing red light filled her with restless anxiety, but also an itching desire not to be alone. She looked at herself in the mirror and saw, for once, what was actually there: a lean, pale, frightened-looking little girl of forty-six. She put some salve on her lips and dusted her face with powder.

The hotel creaked like an old ship. Wind sang through empty rooms. She went out into the corridor with its thick, red carpet and felt her way along the hallway, listening carefully. She could hear a man singing to himself in one of the rooms, no doubt the repulsive geologist. She thought of his slack gray skin and his leering eyes, and she felt a moment's quickening lust-disgust. What was arousing to her was that she was alone and no one could ever discover what she was doing. She ran her finger along each door as she passed. As if responding to her telepathic signal, one of them finally opened and the familiar face, with its leprechaun eyes, popped out.

"So there you are," Alan said. He put a finger to his lips so that she wouldn't reply.

His room was exactly the same as hers, but it was plunged in complete darkness, as if he had been prepared to go to bed. She sat down on the bed. Soon his hands were all over her, the scaliness visible only by the light of the volcano. His dry, slightly perfumed skin was against hers, though she refused to look at his face. Instead, she kept her eye on the red glow and on the Zulu shields on the walls. He told her they were alone, as he put it, "on a live volcano," and the thought seemed to make him smile. All these years sitting in that damn bar, he said, and hoping that a beautiful woman like her would walk in. Up to then she never had. No sir, not until then. She had walked into the bar and he knew, he said, as soon as he laid eyes on her, that she would sleep with him.

"You did?" she whispered.

"I saw it in your face. You would sleep with an ugly old man like me."

He gripped her shoulders and kissed them slowly, as if there were kiss spots arranged in a predetermined line along them. His mouth was dry and papery, but not untitillating, precisely, because it was a human mouth. She could accept it in the dark. From behind, he slipped a hand between her legs, and she let herself roll to one side, sinking into sheets scented by contact with inferior cologne. He pulled her arms behind her and, perhaps for the first time in a year, she forgot that her treacherous ex-husband existed. The geologist closed greedily around her, and before long he was inside her, desperate and voracious and relaxed at the same time, and although she knew it was a dream, she was not sure how to terminate it or change it. She reached out and stroked the wooden surface of the bedstead, then the cold surface of the wall, but still the old man held her pinned down and pumped away at her. *The goggles,* she thought. When was the beam of red light going to wake her? And soon she heard rain, or was it ash, pitter-pattering on the windows and tinkling like falling sand on the sills. The man gnawed her neck, her shoulder blades, and told her he was going to penetrate her all night long. His perspiration dropped onto her face. She flinched, but still she didn't wake up.

JULIE OTSUKA

# *Diem Perdidi*

FROM *Granta*

SHE REMEMBERS HER name. She remembers the name of the president. She remembers the name of the president's dog. She remembers what city she lives in. And on which street. And in which house. *The one with the big olive tree where the road takes a turn.* She remembers what year it is. She remembers the season. She remembers the day on which you were born. She remembers the daughter who was born before you—*She had your father's nose, that was the first thing I noticed about her*—but she does not remember that daughter's name. She remembers the name of the man she did not marry—Frank—and she keeps his letters in a drawer by her bed. She remembers that you once had a husband, but she refuses to remember your ex-husband's name. *That man,* she calls him.

She does not remember how she got the bruises on her arms or going for a walk with you earlier this morning. She does not remember bending over, during that walk, and plucking a flower from a neighbor's front yard and slipping it into her hair. *Maybe your father will kiss me now.* She does not remember what she ate for dinner last night, or when she last took her medicine. She does not remember to drink enough water. She does not remember to comb her hair.

She remembers the rows of dried persimmons that once hung from the eaves of her mother's house in Berkeley. *They were the most beautiful shade of orange.* She remembers that your father loves peaches. She remembers that every Sunday morning, at ten, he takes her for a drive down to the sea in the brown car. She remembers that every evening, right before the eight o'clock news, he sets out two fortune cookies on a paper plate and announces to her that they are having a party. She remembers that on Mondays he comes home from the college at four, and if he is even five minutes late she goes out to the gate and begins to wait for him. She remembers which bedroom is hers and which is his. She remembers that the bedroom that is now hers was once yours. She remembers that it wasn't always like this.

She remembers the first line of the song "How High the Moon." She remembers the Pledge of Allegiance. She remembers her Social Security number. She remembers her best friend Jean's telephone number even though Jean has been dead for six years. She remembers that Margaret is dead. She remembers that Betty is dead. She remembers that Grace has stopped calling. She remembers that her own mother died nine years ago, while spading the soil in her garden, and she misses her more and more every day. *It doesn't go away.* She remembers the number assigned to her family by the government right after the start of the war: *13611*. She remembers being sent away to the desert with her mother and brother during the fifth month of that war and taking her first ride on a train. She remembers the day they came home: *September 9, 1945*. She remembers the sound of the wind hissing through the sagebrush. She remembers the scorpions and red ants. She remembers the taste of dust.

Whenever you stop by to see her, she remembers to give you a big hug, and you are always surprised at her strength. She remembers to give you a kiss every time you leave. She remembers to tell you, at the end of every phone call, that the FBI will check up on you again soon. She remembers to ask you if you would like her to iron your blouse for you before you go out on a date. She remembers to smooth down your skirt. *Don't give it all away.* She remembers to brush aside a wayward strand of your hair. She does not remember eating lunch with you twenty minutes ago and suggests that you go out to Marie Callender's for sandwiches and pie. She does not remember that she herself once used to make the most beautiful pies, with perfectly fluted crusts. She does not remember how to iron your blouse for you or when she began to forget. *Something's changed*. She does not remember what she is supposed to do next.

She remembers that the daughter who was born before you lived for half an hour and then died. *She looked perfect from the outside*. She remembers her mother telling her, more than once, *Don't you ever let anyone see you cry*. She remembers giving you your first bath on your third day in the world. She remembers that you were a very fat baby. She remembers that your first word was *No*. She remembers picking apples in a field with Frank many years ago in the rain. *It was the best day of my life*. She remembers that the first time she met him she was so nervous, she forgot her own address. She remembers wearing too much lipstick. She remembers not sleeping for days.

When you drive past Hesse Park, she remembers being asked to leave her exercise class by her teacher after being in that class for more than ten years. *I shouldn't have talked so much*. She remembers touching her toes and doing windmills and jumping jacks on the freshly mown grass. She remembers being the highest kicker in her class. She does not remember how to use the "new" coffeemaker, which is now three years old, because it was bought after she began to forget. She does not remember asking your father, ten minutes ago, if today is Sunday, or if it is time to go for her ride. She does not remember where she last put her sweater or how long she has been sitting in her chair. She does not always remember how to get out of that chair, and so you gently push down on the footrest and offer her your hand, which she does not always remember to take. *Go away*, she sometimes says. Other times, she just says, *I'm stuck*. She does not remember saying to you, the other night, right after your father left the room, *He loves me more than I love him*. She does not remember saying to you, a moment later, *I can hardly wait until he comes back*.

She remembers that when your father was courting her he was always on time. She remembers thinking that he had a nice smile. *He still does*. She remembers that when they first met he was engaged to another woman. She remembers that that other woman was white. She remembers that that other woman's parents did not want their daughter to marry a man who looked like the gardener.

She remembers that the winters were colder back then, and that there were days on which you actually had to put on a coat and scarf. She remembers her mother bowing her head every morning at the altar and offering her ancestors a bowl of hot rice. She remembers the smell of incense and pickled cabbage in the kitchen. She remembers that her father always wore nice shoes. She remembers that the night the FBI came for him, he and her mother had just had another big fight. She remembers not seeing him again until after the end of the war.

She does not always remember to trim her toenails, and when you soak her feet in the bucket of warm water, she closes her eyes and leans back in her chair and reaches out for your hand. *Don't give up on me.* She does not remember how to tie her shoelaces or fasten the hooks on her bra. She does not remember that she has been wearing her favorite blue blouse for five days in a row. She does not remember your age. *Just wait till you have children of your own,* she says to you, even though you are now too old to do so.

She remembers that after the first girl was born and then died, she sat in the yard for days, just staring at the roses by the pond. *I didn't know what else to do.* She remembers that when you were born, you too had your father's long nose. *It was as if I'd given birth to the same girl twice.* She remembers that you are a Taurus. She remembers that your birthstone is green. She remembers to read you your horoscope from the newspaper whenever you come over to see her. *Someone you were once very close to may soon reappear in your life,* she tells you. She does not remember reading you that same horoscope five minutes ago or going to the doctor with you last week after you discovered a bump on the back of her head. *I think I fell.* She does not remember telling the doctor that you are no longer married or giving him your number and asking him to please call. She does not remember leaning over and whispering to you, the moment he stepped out of the room, *I think he'll do.*

She remembers another doctor asking her, fifty years ago, minutes after the first girl was born and then died, if she wanted to donate the baby's body to science. *He said she had a very unusual heart.* She remembers being in labor for thirty-two hours. She remembers being too tired to think. *So I told him yes.* She remembers driving home from the hospital in the sky-blue Chevy with your father and neither one of them saying a word. She remembers knowing she'd made a big mistake. She does not remember what happened to the baby's body and worries that it might be stuck in a jar. She does not remember why they didn't just bury her. *I wish she was under a tree.* She remembers wanting to bring her flowers every day.

She remembers that even as a young girl you said you did not want to have children. She remembers that you hated wearing dresses. She remembers that you never played with dolls. She remembers that the first time you bled, you were thirteen years old and wearing bright yellow pants. She remembers that your childhood dog was named Shiro. She remembers that you once had a cat named Gasoline. She remembers that you had two turtles named Turtle. She remembers that the first time she and your father took you to Japan to meet his family, you were eighteen months old and just beginning to speak. She remembers leaving you with his mother in the tiny silkworm village in the mountains while she and your father traveled across the island for ten days. *I worried about you the whole time.* She remembers that when they came back, you did not know who she was and that for many days afterward you would not speak to her; you would only whisper in her ear.

She remembers that the year you turned five you refused to leave the house without tapping the door frame three times. She remembers that you had a habit of clicking your teeth repeatedly, which drove her up the wall. She remembers that you could not stand it when different-colored foods were touching on the plate. *Everything had to be just so.* She remembers trying to teach you to read before you were ready. She remembers taking you to Newberry's to pick out patterns and fabric and teaching you how to sew. She remembers that every night, after dinner, you would sit down next to her at the kitchen table and hand her the bobby pins one by one as she set the curlers in her hair. She remembers that this was her favorite part of the day. *I wanted to be with you all the time.*

She remembers that you were conceived on the first try. She remembers that your brother was conceived on the first try. She remembers that your other brother was conceived on the second try. *We must not have been paying attention.* She remembers that a palm reader once told her that she would never be able to bear children because her uterus was tipped the wrong way. She remembers that a blind fortuneteller once told her that she had been a man in her past life and that Frank had been her sister. She remembers that everything she remembers is not necessarily true. She remembers the horse-drawn garbage carts on Ashby, her first pair of crepe-soled shoes, scattered flowers by the side of the road. She remembers that the sound of Frank's voice always made her feel calmer. She remembers that every time they parted, he turned around and watched her walk away. She remembers that the first time he asked her to marry him, she told him she wasn't ready. She remembers that the second time she said she wanted to wait until she was finished with school. She remembers walking along the water with him one warm summer evening on the boardwalk and being so happy, she could not remember her own name. She remembers not knowing that it wouldn't be like this with any of the others. She remembers thinking she had all the time in the world.

She does not remember the names of the flowers in the yard whose names she has known for years. *Roses? Daffodils? Immortelles?* She does not remember that today is Sunday, and she has already gone for her ride. She does not remember to call you, even though she always says that she will. She remembers how to play "Clair de Lune" on the piano. She remembers how to play "Chopsticks" and scales. She remembers not to talk to telemarketers when they call on the telephone. *We're not interested.* She remembers her grammar. *Just between you and me.* She remembers her manners. She remembers to say thank you and please. She remembers to wipe herself every time she uses the toilet. She remembers to flush. She remembers to turn her wedding ring around whenever she pulls on her silk stockings. She remembers to reapply her lipstick every time she leaves the house. She remembers to put on her anti-wrinkle cream every night before climbing into bed. *It works while you sleep.* In the morning, when she wakes, she remembers her dreams. *I was walking through a forest. I was swimming in a river. I was looking for Frank in a city I did not know and no one would tell me where he was.*

On Halloween day, she remembers to ask you if you are going out trick-or-treating. She remembers that your father hates pumpkin. *It's all he ate in Japan during the war.* She remembers listening to him pray, every night, when they first got married, that he would be the one to die first. She remembers playing marbles on a dirt floor in the desert with her brother and listening to the couple at night on the other side of the wall. *They were at it all the time.* She remembers the box of chocolates you brought back to her after your honeymoon in Paris. "But will it last?" you asked her. She remembers her own mother telling her, "The moment you fall in love with someone, you are lost."

She remembers that when her father came back after the war, he and her mother fought even more than they had before. She remembers that he would spend entire days shopping for shoes in San Francisco while her mother scrubbed other people's floors. She remembers that some nights he would walk around the block three times before coming into the house. She remembers that one night he did not come in at all. She remembers that when your own husband left you, five years ago, you broke out in hives all over your body for weeks. She remembers thinking he was trouble the moment she met him. *A mother knows.* She remembers keeping that thought to herself. *I had to let you make your own mistakes.*

She remembers that, of her three children, you were the most delightful to be with. She remembers that your younger brother was so quiet, she sometimes forgot he was there. *He was like a dream.* She remembers that her own brother refused to carry anything with him onto the train except for his rubber toy truck. *He wouldn't let me touch it.* She remembers her mother killing all the chickens in the yard the day before they left. She remembers her fifth-grade teacher, Mr. Martello, asking her to stand up in front of the class so everyone could tell her goodbye. She remembers being given a silver heart pendant by her next-door neighbor, Elaine Crowley, who promised to write but never did. She remembers losing that pendant on the train and being so angry she wanted to cry. *It was my first piece of jewelry.*

She remembers that one month after Frank joined the Air Force he suddenly stopped writing her letters. She remembers worrying that he'd been shot down over Korea or taken hostage by guerrillas in the jungle. She remembers thinking about him every minute of the day. *I thought I was losing my mind.* She remembers learning from a friend one night that he had fallen in love with somebody else. She remembers asking your father the next day to marry her. *"Shall we go get the ring?" I said to him.* She remembers telling him, *It's time.*

When you take her to the supermarket she remembers that coffee is Aisle Two. She remembers that Aisle Three is milk. She remembers the name of the cashier in the express lane who always gives her a big hug. *Diane.* She remembers the name of the girl at the flower stand who always gives her a single broken-stemmed rose. She remembers that the man behind the meat counter is Big Lou. "Well, hello, gorgeous," he says to her. She does not remember where her purse is and begins to panic until you remind her that she has left it at home. *I don't feel like myself without it.* She does not remember asking the man in line behind her whether or not he was married. She does not remember him telling her, rudely, that he was not. She does not remember staring at the old woman in the wheelchair by the melons and whispering to you, *I hope I never end up like that.* She remembers that the huge mimosa tree that once stood next to the cart corral in the parking lot is no longer there. *Nothing stays the same.* She remembers that she was once a very good driver. She remembers failing her last driver's test three times in a row. *I couldn't remember any of the rules.* She remembers that the day after her father left them, her mother sprinkled little piles of salt in the corner of every room to purify the house. She remembers that they never spoke of him again.

She does not remember asking your father, when he comes home from the pharmacy, what took him so long, or who he talked to, or whether or not the pharmacist was pretty. She does not always remember his name. She remembers graduating from high school with high honors in Latin. She remembers how to say, "I came, I saw, I conquered." *Veni, vidi, vici.* She remembers how to say, "I have lost the day." *Diem perdidi.* She remembers the words for "I'm sorry" in Japanese, which you have not heard her utter in years. She remembers the words for "rice" and "toilet." She remembers the words for "Wait." *Chotto matte kudasai.* She remembers that a white-snake dream will bring you good luck. She remembers that it is bad luck to pick up a dropped comb. She remembers that you should never run to a funeral. She remembers that you shout the truth down into a well.

She remembers going to work, like her mother, for the rich white ladies up in the hills. She remembers Mrs. Tindall, who insisted on eating lunch with her every day in the kitchen instead of just leaving her alone. She remembers Mrs. Edward deVries, who fired her after one day. *"Who taught you how to iron?" she asked me.* She remembers that Mrs. Cavanaugh would not let her go home on Saturdays until she had baked an apple pie. She remembers Mrs. Cavanaugh's husband, Arthur, who liked to put his hand on her knee. She remembers that he sometimes gave her money. She remembers that she never refused. She remembers once stealing a silver candlestick from a cupboard, but she cannot remember whose it was. She remembers that they never missed it. She remembers using the same napkin for three days in a row. She remembers that today is Sunday, which six days out of seven is not true.

When you bring home the man you hope will become your next husband, she remembers to take his jacket. She remembers to offer him coffee. She remembers to offer him cake. She remembers to thank him for the roses. *So you like her?* she asks him. She remembers to ask him his name. *She's my firstborn, you know.* She remembers, five minutes later, that she has already forgotten his name, and asks him again what it is. *That's my brother's name,* she tells him. She does not remember talking to her brother on the phone earlier that morning—*He promised me he'd call*—or going for a walk with you in the park. She does not remember how to make coffee. She does not remember how to serve cake.

She remembers sitting next to her brother many years ago on a train to the desert and fighting about who got to lie down on the seat. She remembers hot white sand, the wind on the water, someone's voice telling her, *Hush, it's all right.* She remembers where she was the day the men landed on the moon. She remembers the day they learned that Japan had lost the war. *It was the only time I ever saw my mother cry.* She remembers the day she learned that Frank had married somebody else. *I read about it in the paper.* She remembers the letter she got from him not long after, asking if he could please see her. *He said he'd made a mistake.* She remembers writing him back, "It's too late." She remembers marrying your father on an unusually warm day in December. She remembers having their first fight, three months later, in March. *I threw a chair.* She remembers that he comes home from the college every Monday at four. She remembers that she is forgetting. She remembers less and less every day.

When you ask her your name, she does not remember what it is. *Ask your father. He'll know.* She does not remember the name of the president. She does not remember the name of the president's dog. She does not remember the season. She does not remember the day or the year. She remembers the little house on San Luis Avenue that she first lived in with your father. She remembers her mother leaning over the bed she once shared with her brother and kissing the two of them good night. She remembers that as soon as the first girl was born, she knew that something was wrong. *She didn't cry.* She remembers holding the baby in her arms and watching her go to sleep for the first and last time in her life. She remembers that they never buried her. She remembers that they did not give her a name. She remembers that the baby had perfect fingernails and a very unusual heart. She remembers that she had your father's long nose. She remembers knowing at once that she was his. She remembers beginning to bleed two days later when she came home from the hospital. She remembers your father catching her in the bathroom as she began to fall. She remembers a desert sky at sunset. *It was the most beautiful shade of orange.* She remembers scorpions and red ants. She remembers the taste of dust. She remembers once loving someone more than anyone else. She remembers giving birth to the same girl twice. She remembers that today is Sunday, and it is time to go for her ride, and so she picks up her purse and puts on her lipstick and goes out to wait for your father in the car.

EDITH PEARLMAN

# Honeydew

FROM *Orion*

CALDICOTT ACADEMY, A private day school for girls, had not expelled a student in decades. There were few prohibitions. Drinking and drugging and having sex right there on the campus could supposedly get you kicked out; turning up pregnant likewise; that was the long and short of it. There was a rule against climbing down the side of the ravine on the west side of the school, where a suicide had occurred a century earlier, but the punishment was only a scolding.

Alice Toomey, headmistress, would have welcomed a rule against excessive skinniness. Emily Knapp, all ninety pounds of her, was making Alice feel enraged, and, worse yet, making her feel incompetent—she, Alice, awarded the prize for Most Effective Director two years in a row by the Association of Private Day Schools. This tall bundle of twigs that called itself a girl—Alice's palms ached to spank her.

Emily: eleventh grade, all A's, active member of various extracurricular activities, excused from sports for obvious reasons. She visited a psychiatrist once a month and a nutrition doctor once a week, who emptied her pockets of rocks and insisted that she urinate before stepping on the scale. She had been hospitalized only twice. But according to her mother, Emily was never more than two milligrams away from an emergency admission.

She displayed other signs of disorder. Hair loss. Skin stretched like a membrane over the bones of the face. A voice as harsh as a saw. But her conversation, unless the subject was her own body mass, was intelligent and reasonable.

Alice had endured a series of painful meetings with Dr. Richard Knapp, physician and professor of anatomy, and his wife, Ghiselle. The three met in Alice's dowdy office. The atmosphere was one of helplessness.

On one of those occasions, "I worry about death," Alice dared to say.

"Her death, if it occurs, will be accidental," said Emily's father evenly.

Ghiselle flew at him. "You are discussing some stranger's case history, yes?" Despite twenty-five years in Massachusetts, she retained a French accent and French syntax, not to mention French chic and French beauty.

Richard said, "It is helpful to keep a physician's distance."

Husband and wife now exchanged a look that the unmarried Alice labeled enmity. Then Richard placed his fingers on Ghiselle's chiffon arm, but it was Alice he looked at. "Emily doesn't want to die," he said.

"That is so?" scoffed Ghiselle.

"She doesn't want a needle fixed to her vein. She doesn't want an IV pole as a companion."

"That is so?"

"She doesn't want to drive us all crazy."

"What *does* she want?" said Alice; and there was a brief silence as if the heavy questions about Emily's condition and the condition of like sufferers were about to be answered, here, now, in Godolphin, Massachusetts.

"She wants to be very, very, very thin," said Richard. No shit, thought Alice. "Achhoopf," snorted Ghiselle, or something like that. She herself was very thin, again in the way of Frenchwomen —shoulders charmingly bony, neck slightly elongated. Her legs under her brief skirt—too brief for fifty? not in this case—were to die for, Caldicott students would unimaginatively have said.

"She wants to become a bug and live on air," Richard added, "and a drop or two of nectar. She thinks—she sometimes thinks —she was meant to be born an insect."

Alice shuddered within her old-fashioned dress. She wore shirtwaists, very long in order to draw attention away from her Celtic hips and bottom, and always blue: slate, cornflower, the sky before a storm. She wondered if this signature style would become a source of mockery. She was forty-three, and six weeks pregnant

—in another few months the shocked trustees would have to ask her to resign. Perhaps it would be more honorable to expel herself. "What can we do?" she asked.

"We can chain her to a bed and ram food down her throat," said Ghiselle, her accent lost in her fury. Alice imagined herself locking the chain to the headboard. Now Richard's fingers slid down the chiffon all the way to Ghiselle's fingers. Five fiery nails waved him off. The two younger Knapp daughters, their weight normal, were good students, though they lacked Emily's brilliance and her devotion to whatever interested her.

"Emily must find her own way to continue to live," said Richard, at last providing something useful and true; but by now neither woman was listening.

Though Caldicott was not a residential school, Emily had been given a room to herself. It was really a closet with a single window looking out on the forbidden ravine. Mr. da Sola, jack-of-all-trades, had lined two of the walls with shelves. Mr. da Sola was a defrocked science teacher from the public schools who had seen fit to teach intelligent design along with evolution and had paid for that sin.

"I don't need another science teacher," Alice had said, wondering where he got the nerve to sit on the corner of her desk. What dark brows he had, and those topaz eyes . . .

"That's good; I don't want to be a science teacher," he told her. He didn't tell her that no other private school had agreed to interview him. "I want to return to my first loves, carpentry and gardening." So she took him on.

On Mr. da Sola's shelves Emily had placed her specimen collection equipment; the specimens themselves, collected from the ravine and its banks; and some books, including the King James Bible and an atlas of South America. There was also a box of crackers, a box of prunes, and several liters of bottled water.

Emily was permitted to take her meager lunch here and also her study periods, for the study hall nauseated her, redolent as it was of food recently eaten and now being processed, and sometimes of residual gases loosed accidentally or mischievously. So she dined among her dead insects, admiring chitinous exoskeletons while she put one of three carrot sticks into her mouth. Chitin was not part of mammal physiology, though she had read that after death and before decomposition, the epidermis of a deceased human develops a leathery hardness, chitinlike it could be called, which begins to resemble the beetles who gorge on the decaying corpse and defecate at the same time, turning flesh into compost. The uses of shit were many. The most delightful was manna. Emily liked the story of Moses leading the starving Israelites into the desert. Insects came to their rescue. Of course the manna, which Exodus describes as a fine frost on the ground with a taste like honey, was thought to be a miracle from God, but it was really Coccidae excrement. Coccidae feed on the sap of plants. The sugary liquid rushes through the gut and out the anus. A single insect can process and expel many times its own weight every hour. They flick the stuff away with their hind legs, and it floats to the ground. Nomads still eat it—relish it. It is called honeydew.

Ah, Coccidae. She could draw them—she loved to draw her relatives—but unfortunately the mature insect is basically a scaly ball: a gut in a shell. It was more fun to draw the ant—its proboscis, pharynx, two antennae. Sometimes she tried to render its compound eye, but the result looked too much like one of her mother's jet-beaded evening pouches. She could produce a respectable diagram of the body, though: the thorax, the chest area, and the rear segment, segmented itself, which contained the abdomen and, right beside it, the heart.

Richard was pulling his sweater over his head. The deliberate gesture revealed, one feature at a time, chin, mouth, nose, eyelids closed against the woolen scrape, eyebrows slightly unsettled, broad high brow, and, finally, gray hair raised briefly into a cone.

Alice and two Caldicott teachers lived on the school grounds. Their three little houses fronted on the grassy field where important convocations were held. The backs of the houses overlooked the ravine. In the wet season the ravine held a few inches of water —enough for that determined suicide a century ago. These days it provided a convenient receptacle for an empty beer can and the occasional condom. On the far side of the ravine was a road separating Godolphin from the next town. The Knapps lived in a cul-de-sac off that road. Leaving his house, walking across the road, side-slipping down his side of the ravine and climbing sure-footed up hers—in this athletic manner Richard had been visiting Alice twice and sometimes three times a week, in the late afternoon, for the past few years. Sometimes he picked a little nosegay of wild-

flowers on his way. Alice popped them into any old glass—today
the one on her bureau. She was undressed before his sweater had
cleared his head. And so, reclining, naked thighs crossed against
her own desire, she watched the rest of the disrobing, the careful
folding of clothes. Sometimes crossing her thighs didn't work, and
she'd surrender to a first bliss while he busied himself hanging
his jacket on the chair. Not today, though. Today she managed
to keep herself to herself like the disciplined educator she was,
waited until her body was covered by his equally disciplined body;
opened her legs; and then spinster teacher and scholarly physician discarded their outer-world selves, joined, rolled, rolled back
again, each straining to become incorporated into the other, to
be made one, to form a new organism wanting nothing but to
make love to itself all day long. Perhaps some afternoon they—it
—would molt, grow wings, fly away, and, its time on earth over, die
entwined in its own limbs and crumble to dust before midnight.

Emily didn't do drugs often. Her substance of choice—her only
substance, in fact—was *bicho de taquara,* a moth grub found in the
stems of Brazilian bamboo plants, but only when they are flower-
ing. Mr. da Sola tended bamboo in one corner of the Caldicott
glass-covered winter garden. He harvested the grubs, removed
their heads, dried them, ground them up, and stored the resulting
powder in a jar labeled *rat poison.* Each year he produced about six
teaspoons of the stuff; three times a year he and Emily swallowed
a spoonful each . . .

   The Malalis, in the province of Mines, Brazil, report an ecstatic
sleep similar to but shorter than the unconscious state produced
by opium, and full of visual adventures. Emily could attest to that,
but she did not share her visions with Mr. da Sola, who enjoyed
his own private coma beside her on the floor of her little room.
In Emily's repeated dream she was attending a banquet where she
was compelled to crawl from table to table, sampling the brilliant
food: pink glistening hams, small crispy birds on beds of edible
petals, smoked fish of all colors ranging from the deep orange of
salmon to the pale yellow of butterfish. And then: salads within
whose leaves lurked living oysters recently plucked from their
shells, eager to be nibbled by Emily; the mauve feet of pigs, lightly
pickled; headcheese, the fragrance of calf still floating from its
crock. And vegetables: eggplant stewed with squash blossoms; a

pumpkin, its hat off, stuffed with crème fraîche and baked. And desserts: melons the color of peaches and peaches the size of melons, fig preserves in hazelnut cups; and, at last, a celestial version of brie en croûte, the croûte made of moth wings, for Mr. da Sola allowed a few moth grubs to hatch and mature and deposit their larvae before he gently pinched them dead and removed their new wings, and he caught butterflies too, in the outside garden, and sewed wing to wing to make several round fairy quilts and sugared and steamed them and laid them out on the carpenter's table and plopped into each a light cheese faintly curdled; and then he molded several croûtes and baked them. He did all this off-dream. Emily plunged into the pastries. When she awoke there was often white exudate on her teeth, which she removed with her forefinger. Then she rubbed her fingertip dry on the unvarnished floor of the room while watching Mr. da Sola awake from his own glorious adventure, whatever it was. She suspected Alice was its heroine.

The rest of her time in the little room, Emily studied. She was master of the ant heart—like the hearts of all insects it was a primitive tube—and had now turned her attention to the complicated stomach. She was soon to give a lecture on the ant stomach to the middle school and to anyone else who wanted to listen. Caldicott students were encouraged to share their interests. Wolfie Featherstone had recently talked about utopian societies, and her sidekick, Adele Alba, had analyzed figures of speech and the power of syntax.

And so, one Tuesday, Emily stood on a platform beside an easel where her diagrams were propped. "The abdomen is the segmented tail area of an ant," she rasped, pointing with her father's hiking stick. "It contains the heart, and would you believe it the reproductive organs too, well, you probably would believe that, and it contains most of the digestive system. It is protected by an exoskeleton. And get this"—she licked her lips and let her pointer hang vertically between her pipe-cleaner legs until it touched the floor, making her look like a starving song-and-dance man—"the ant has not one stomach but two."

"So does the cow," drawled a fat girl.

"The cow's two stomachs only serve the cow."

"Serve the cow only," corrected Adele.

"Whatever. The ant's larger stomach, called the crop, is at the service of all. As an ant collects food and eats it, the nutrient is dissolved into a liquid and stored in the crop. When a fellow ant is hungry, its antennae stroke the food-storer's head. Then the two ants put their mouths together, together, together"—she controlled her unseemly excitement with the aid of the soothing smile Mr. da Sola sent from the back of the room—"and the liquid food passes from one to the other. And in addition to the generous crop, each ant has another, smaller stomach, its 'personal belly.'"

Alice, wearing a faded denim dress, said, "Then the larger stomach belongs to the community."

"Yes!" said Emily. "And if philosophers had brains in their heads they would realize that the ant's collective pouch is the most advanced device that evolution or God if you prefer has come up with."

"A soup kitchen," interrupted the fat girl.

"And the ant feeding her associates through her mouth out of her own belly is the fundamental act from which the social life, the virtues, the morality, and the politics of the formicary—that's the word for the ant as a society—are derived." Alice saw that Emily used no notes. "Compared to this true collective, Wolfie, Brook Farm is a sandbox."

A few girls were gagging or at least making gagging sounds.

"The ant is being exploited by her pals," said the irritating fattie. Her size-six jeans were big on her and she wore her little sister's tee. A strip of pink flesh showed between the two, like a satin ribbon. "When does *she* eat?"

"She cannot be said to eat as we understand eating," said Emily severely. "She collects and stores and regurgitates. She is the lifespring of her world."

"So we evolved, and lost our second stomach," said Wolfie. "We got ourselves brains instead. A good deal."

"What's good about the brain?" said Emily. "*It* evolved to make money and war."

"Zeugma!" shouted Adele Alba.

Perhaps it was because of the only moderate success of her lecture, perhaps because of her binge at the banquet—at any rate, Emily turned up at the nutritionist that week at an unacceptable weight. She was hospitalized. She was not force-fed, but her room's bathroom had no door, and while she consumed one pea at a time she was watched by a nurse's aide with baroque curves.

"Sugar, eat," coaxed the aide.

"Honey, do," mocked Emily. But she acceded to the regimen; her work was calling her. Soon she'd gained enough to be discharged, though she'd have to see the nutritionist twice a week for a while. She was released a day earlier than planned. Her mother drove to the hospital in a downpour. She brought a present: a long, black vinyl raincoat with a hood.

"Thank you," said Emily, unsurprised at the kindness of the gift. Her mother was everything a human was entitled to be: outspoken, attached to her particular children, unacquainted with tact. Ghiselle had no concern for the superorganism—but, after all, ever since the development of the spine, the individual had become paramount, the group disregarded. Ghiselle was only following the downhill path of her species.

"There's a candy bar in the pocket of the raincoat," said Ghiselle.

"Oh."

"Wolfie and Adele can split it. *Veux-tu rentrer?*"

*"Pas encore. Laisse moi à la bibliothèque, s'il te plaît."* Emily was the only member of the family, Richard included, who had mastered enough French to converse with her mother in her mother's tongue.

Ghiselle parked and Emily got out of the car. The rain had stopped. The new coat concealed Emily's emaciation, and she had raised her hood against the suspended mist that had followed the rain, so her patchy hair was concealed too. She looked, Ghiselle thought, like any serious modern girl—bound for medical school, maybe, or a career in science.

Emily crossed the modest campus and entered the library. Ghiselle blew her nose and drove away.

"Emily is the heroine of the moment," Alice murmured into Richard's shoulder.

"Is she? They all love insects now?"

"No, they envy her monomania—"

"Polymania is more like it. Subway systems, for instance—she can diagram the underground of every major city in the world."

"And they associate it with her lack of appetite, and they associate *that* with free will. 'You can get a lot done if you choose to skip dinner,' Wolfie Featherstone told me. Richard, not eating will become a fad and then a craze and then a cult."

"Well, bulk the girls up ahead of time. Have the cook serve creamed casseroles instead of those stingy salads."

Alice groaned. "You are undermining Caldicott's famed nutrition."

"Screw nutrition. The body tends to take care of itself unless it's abused. All the girls except Emily are strong enough to beat carpets."

"Beat carpets? The maids do that once a year."

"Ghiselle does it more often."

"Ghiselle? I don't believe you. Ghiselle is a *grand dame*."

"On the surface. She's a peasant inside." He withdrew his arm gently from beneath Alice's shoulder, clasped his hands under his head. The watery light from the uncurtained window shone on him—on them both, Alice supposed, but she had lost all sense of herself except as a receptacle with grasping muscles and a hungry mouth. Only her lover was illuminated. His pewter hair swept his forehead, sprouted from his underarms, curled around his nipples, provided a restful nest for his penis, too restful maybe . . . she leaned over and blew on the nest and got things going again.

And afterward . . . well, this woman had come late to passion and had not yet learned restraint. "Do you love Ghiselle the *grand dame* or Ghiselle the peasant?"

"I love you, Alice."

"You *do?*"

"I do." He loved Ghiselle too, but he didn't burden Alice with that information. He had come to believe that monogamy was unnatural. He would like to practice polygamy, bigamy at least, but Ghiselle would run off to Paris, taking the girls . . .

"Oh, Richard," Alice was lovingly sighing. Then there was silence, and the room that had seemed so steamy grew cool like a forest brook, and she was as happy as she had ever been. They lay side by side in that silence.

"So you'll leave her," Alice ventured after a while.

". . . No."

"No!" She sat up. "You are going to stay with the bitch."

"She is not a bitch. We're a bit of a misalliance, that's all, fire and steel you might say."

"Misalliance? A disaster!"

He kissed her left nipple, and the right, and the navel; and if she'd had any sense she would have dropped the argument and lain down again. Instead, "You're going to stay with her for the sake of the children instead of divorcing her for the sake of yourself. And for the sake of me," she cried. "But Richard. Children survive this sort of thing. Sometimes I think they expect it. I've noticed at the bat mitzvahs I get invited to, and I get invited to them all, the girls with two sets of parents and a colony of half-sibs—they're the snappiest. Richard, come live with me, come live with me and be my—" He covered her mouth with his. "We belong together," she said when she got her breath, and he did it again. "You are practicing probity," she said, and this time he didn't interrupt her. "You are a prig!" She began to sob in earnest. He held her until the sobs grew less frequent, and they lay down again, and she fell asleep, and he held her for some time after that.

At five o'clock he woke her. Bleakly they dressed, back to back. Richard put on the clothes he'd folded earlier; Alice pulled on jeans and a wedgewood sweater. Then they turned. Her cheekbone touched his jaw. *We'll meet again.* Richard left by the back door, walking carefully because the rain had made the earth slick. The air was cold now. Alice, standing at the doorway, crossed her arms in front of her waist and cupped her elbows in her hands. Women have worried in that position for centuries. She watched her lover make his slippery way toward the bottom of the ravine. Maybe Paolo da Sola would marry her. She could raise his salary.

Emily was now standing on Alice's side of the ravine not far from Alice's house. She leaned against a birch. She had just left the library where she had been reading about ants' circles of death. Sometimes ants, for no apparent reason, form a spiral and run in it continuously until they die of exhaustion. What kind of behavior was that from so evolved a creature? Oh, she had much to figure out. But at the moment all she wanted to do was watch her father behaving like a boy. If he sprained an ankle, it would put a crimp in his love life. Too bad he didn't have six ankles. But with only two he did manage to leap over the little creek at the bottom of the ravine, land without incident, and start to climb the far side. He did not look up over his right shoulder or he would have seen Alice standing in her doorway, and he did not look up over his left shoulder or he would have seen Emily and her tree;

he looked straight ahead through those binocular eyes embedded in his skull. Emily herself had compound eyes, at least some of the time—the images she saw were combined from numerous ommatidia, eye units, located on the surface of the orb. These eye units, when things were working right, all pointed in slightly different directions. In a mirror she saw multiple Emilys, all of them bulging, all of them gross.

Alice wrenched her gaze from Richard's climbing form and looked sideways and saw Emily, aslant against a white tree, spying on her father. She was covered in a black, helmeted carapace. She looked as if she had attached herself to the tree for nourishment. She was a mutant, she was a sport of nature, she should be sprayed, crushed underfoot, gathered up, and laid in a coffin . . . Then rage loosened and shriveled, and Alice, in a new, motherly way, began to move toward the half sister of her child-to-be. She couldn't keep her footing in the mud, so she had to use her hands too. She would bring Emily to her house. She would offer her a weed. She would not mention food. She would whisper to the misguided girl that life could be moderately satisfying even if you were born into the wrong order.

Having safely ascended the opposite bank of the ravine, Richard turned and squinted at the artful bit of nature below: two banks of trees slanting inward as if trying to reach each other, some with pale yellow leaves, some brown, some leafless; more leaves thick at their roots; and mist everywhere. It was a view Ghiselle would appreciate, she loved pointillism, though she had decorated their house in bright abstractions for no apparent reason. For no apparent reason one of his two promising younger daughters spent her evenings in front of a television screen and the other seemed to have sewn her thumb to her BlackBerry. Perhaps it was in the nature of people to defy their own best interests. Why, look, as if to validate his insight, there was his beloved Emily, oh Lord let her live, make her live, there was Emily, plastered lengthwise to a tree like a colony of parasitic grubs; and there was his Alice, intruding like the headmistress she couldn't help being, undertaking to crawl toward Emily not on hands and knees but on toes and fingertips, her limbs as long as those of a katydid nymph. And above her body, her busybody, you might say, swayed that magnificent blue rump.

*

Some of what Alice wished for came about. She and Emily developed a cautious alliance. Emily's weight went up a bit, though her future remained worrisome. Paolo da Sola said "Sure!" to Alice's proposal of marriage. "And I don't want to know the circumstances. I've been mad about you since we met."

Richard eventually replaced Alice with an undemanding pathologist who already had a husband and children. The baby born to Alice had Paolo's dark brows and golden eyes—surprising, maybe, until you remember that all humans look pretty much alike. And when Caldicott's old-fashioned housekeeper discovered Wolfie and Adele embracing naked in Emily's little room, and failed to keep her ancient mouth shut, Alice summoned a meeting of the trustees and told them that this expression of devoted friendship was not in contravention of any rule *she* knew of. She adjusted her yawning infant on her pale blue shoulder. Anyway, she reminded them and herself, Caldicott's most important rules, even if they weren't written down, were tolerance and discretion. All the others were honeydew.

ANGELA PNEUMAN

# Occupational Hazard

FROM *Ploughshares*

ON A FRIDAY, during his inspection of the sludge containment tank at the East Winder Municipal Wastewater Treatment Plant, Calvin's foot slipped off the catwalk—it was raining, the metal was wet—and his left work boot and left leg became submerged up to the knee in treated sewage.

"Whoops," said the plant manager beside him. The plant had a history of noncompliance, and the inspection had been unscheduled, causing the manager's big-cheeked Irish face to grow and stay red as Calvin lifted samples. Now the man visibly cheered up. "Occupational hazard," he said merrily.

"Shit," said Calvin. The sludge plastered his pants to his shin, oozed underneath the tongue of his boot. The manager showed him the hose, and he rinsed most of it off, but he knew the smell —sewage sweetened with chemicals—would inhabit the interior of his battered Taurus for days.

"Fragrant truffle," said Dave Lott back at the office, sniffing thoughtfully as Calvin passed his cube. "Hints of coriander."

"Right," said Calvin.

"Eau de *toilette*," Dave Lott said.

Calvin snorted.

It was past five-thirty, and the office—twelve beige cubicles at sea in the middle of a low-ceilinged room—was nearly empty. Calvin parked himself in his cube, which shared a wall with Dave Lott's, and glumly logged on to his computer. His shin and his foot felt clammy, but he was determined to ignore it for the fifteen minutes he needed to write up his report. Sometimes discomfort sharpened his brain, he'd noticed. On Calvin's other side, Robin, the sole female inspector, stood to put on her jacket, pulling an arm's length of thin, flat red hair out from the collar and letting it slap flatly against her back. It was so long that she probably hadn't cut it in twenty years, like the missionary women Calvin had known in church as a kid. But he always liked watching her bring it up out of her jacket. It was long enough for her to sit on.

"Nuances of anise," Dave Lott said. "*An-us.* Get it?"

"Blow it up yours," Calvin said.

"Ah, poopy jokes," said Robin tiredly, on her way down the hall. "They never get old."

When she was gone, Dave Lott stood and peered at Calvin over the divider. He was a stout bald man with a gray thicket of a beard. The beard was an upside-down triangle, shaped like pubic hair, Calvin had thought more than once. But you'd never say that kind of thing to Dave Lott's face. Calvin liked the guy, but carefully. He reminded Calvin of a cop, the way he could joke around and then get serious, all of a sudden, pulling rank and leaving you feeling like a jerk. Dave Lott's eyes were as gray as his beard, small and round, tiny gravel pits above gold-speckled half-glasses. The glasses were the magnifying kind you bought at the drugstore. The kind old ladies wore, which was another thing you'd never say to Dave Lott's face.

"Grab a beer?" Dave Lott said.

"Sorry, man. Got to get home."

Dave Lott nodded and pushed up the gold glasses, ambiguously, with his middle finger.

"Got to get out of these pants," Calvin said.

It was Thursday, and Calvin's wife, Jill, had her GRE class, and he had to watch the boys. Jill hated Dave Lott, though she wouldn't use the word *hate*. Everything was *dislike*, and now even the boys only *disliked* okra and *disliked* string beans, which sounded creepy to Calvin, coming from them—too much calm specificity. Jill disliked Dave Lott. She was friends with the man's first wife in the way he'd noticed women were friends, with the need to designate an opponent so they could know they were on the same side.

"Next time," Calvin tacked on, but Dave Lott just grinned through his beard and was gone. In a few days the man would be dead, picked off the periphery of Calvin's life, and Calvin would find himself trying to remember some significant detail about this, their last exchange; but in the moment there was only the dull noise of Dave Lott's work boots on the cloudy plastic hall runners tacked over the carpet, the suck of the steel door closing behind him, the trace smell of sewage coming from Calvin's own cube.

At home, Calvin's boys were in the basement watching their favorite video, a cartoon of *The Ten Commandments*. Jill stood in the bathroom before the mirror, gripping the cordless phone between her chin and shoulder while she did her eye makeup.

"I know it," she said into the phone. Her blue eyes flicked over Calvin as he popped his head in, and then she leaned into the mirror and blinked at herself. "I know it. No kidding." She was pretty, still—not like a movie star but like women on aspirin commercials, trim, sensibly brunette, smiling much of the time. She and Calvin were at war. Jill claimed to want another child, to want to try for a girl, and Calvin had found himself boycotting sex until they talked about it reasonably, which meant, he knew she knew, until he talked her out of it. He felt—unreasonably perhaps—that this desire of hers had nothing to do with him, though he couldn't prove that, of course, and couldn't imagine trying to explain why it mattered. Whenever he caught himself admiring her, it pissed him off. Now he wished he'd gone out for a drink with Dave Lott after all.

He headed to the kitchen, opened a bottle of beer, and stared out at the back yard. A domed jungle gym rose from the grass like half a skeleton planet. Last year, Calvin had looked away for a moment to tend the grill, and Trent, then five, had fallen the wrong way. When Calvin looked back, his son had crumpled quietly to the ground, staring at his broken wrist, more confused than in pain.

Now there was a shuffle on the linoleum behind him. Trent, in the doorway, raised his skinny arms and intoned, "Thou shalt not covet."

"Hey, bud," said Calvin, crossing the floor and passing a hand over the boy's fluffy brown hair.

"What's covet, again?"

"When you want something that's not yours."

"And then you steal it."

"No, I think it's just wanting it. They're separate commandments, aren't they?"

The boy nodded. "What's that smell?"

"Wastewater," Calvin said. He knelt by his son, palmed the boy's bony chest. Trent smelled a little too, kind of fruity, like he was due for a bath, but Calvin liked it.

"Can I sip your beer?"

"Nope."

"Can I hold it?"

Calvin handed him the bottle and took it back when Trent's lips fitted over the top, moving like a feeding fish.

"What did I say," said Calvin, standing. "Honor thy father and mother."

"Drinking's a sin," Trent challenged.

"Drinking's an *indulgence*. It's like sugar. It's fine if you don't overdo it."

"Sugar's a treat," Jill called from the hallway. "Drinking's a habit." Now she was standing in the doorway behind Trent, hands on her hips.

"Anything can be a habit," Calvin said.

"You'd know," Jill said.

"I'm sure that's supposed to mean something," Calvin said, "but you lost me."

Jack, their four-year-old, called Trent from the basement and the older boy backed out of the doorway and disappeared. At the counter, Jill began silently assembling her sandwich. Calvin watched the side of her face as she spread peanut butter carefully to the edges of one slice of bread, then matched up the top slice, crust to crust, as if it took great concentration.

Two nights ago, he overheard her tucking in the kids at bedtime. She told them that she loved them more than anything else in the world. "More than Daddy?" Trent said, and Calvin found himself automatically curious about how she might answer, and then abruptly not curious at all. He moved quickly on past the door.

Jill looked up from the sandwich and narrowed her eyes. "What's that smell?"

Calvin extended his foot toward her. His pant leg was dry and stiff. "Occupational hazard."

Jill nodded grimly. She lifted a knife from the block, carved her apple into quarters, and zipped it into a Baggie.

"Dave Lott got it worse than me," Calvin added, lying without knowing he was going to. "Up to the waist."

"Yeah, well, you know what I think about that," Jill said. "Couldn't happen to a nicer guy."

The horrible news about Dave Lott came on Saturday night, when the boys were in bed. Calvin was watching *Frontline* while Jill studied at the dining room table. "Listen to this stuff," she was saying. "Nine tracks, numbered one through nine; nine dogs, A through I. Dog A must always run in track four. Dog G must always run beside Dog B, but never beside Dog C. Dog C always runs in track eight. Just to answer one question you have to make a chart, and it's a timed test."

The phone rang, and Calvin felt the mean satisfaction of answering it instead of responding to Jill.

"Calvin?" said a woman. For a second he couldn't place her voice, then realized it was Robin, from work. She'd never called him at home before. "Listen," she said.

He said, "Sure, hi, Robin, go ahead," wanting Jill to hear how polite he was, what a good guy other people thought he was, the kind of guy people from work could call at home. And there was something about Robin's tone that made him consider the possibility of something sexual, some signals of a crush he'd missed. He felt tentatively flattered and compassionate. He anticipated telling Jill.

But then Robin kept talking, and Calvin was writing down the name of the hospital as if he needed the note to remember, as if both the boys hadn't been born there. Dave Lott was sick with an infection. A freak thing, one in a million. A fast-acting strain of strep invading his soft tissue, shutting down the circulation to his limbs, eating him into a coma.

Jill stood in front of the television as he told her, working her feet in and out of her slippers one at a time. "Oh, God," she said. "From the sludge?"

Remembering his lie, Calvin had to shrug. "He had a paper cut," he said. It could have been true, for all he knew. "He and Dora thought it was the flu, at first." Dora was the second wife, and Jill rolled her eyes at the name.

"Well, I'm sorry," Jill said. "It's awful." She stretched her mouth into a flat, frank grimace that said she was sorry Dave Lott was in bad shape but that she wasn't going to change her opinion about him just because he was in the hospital, either.

Part of Calvin respected this—what he thought of as her bottom-line nature. But he disliked this about her too, and just now he wished he could think of something nasty to say, something to wipe the grimace right off her face. Inexplicably, he got a hard-on. He crossed his arms over his lap and leaned forward.

"Don't look at me like that," Jill said. "I said I was sorry."

Calvin had always appreciated bacteria, with all their invisible processes. He liked the intricacy of their names—fecal coliform, *Escherichia coli*, the whole hardy *Bacillus* genus. Bacteria were the secret to waste management, after all, allowing humans to live virtually on top of one another. They were nature's recyclers, breaking everything down to nutrients to be reabsorbed. It irritated Calvin the way people always acted like bacteria were the bad guys, and antibiotics were the good guys, because the antibiotics—their overuse, anyway—were what was screwing up the bacterial balance, tipping the scale toward the pathogenic. He'd shut down a few conversations with this rant. He'd refused to let the doctor prescribe antibiotics for his kids' sinusitis, insisting that their bodies would take care of it, and he had been right. Sure there were harmful bacteria—everywhere, in fact. If wastewater treatment plants were a bacterial smorgasbord, so was your basic kitchen counter. So was the surface of your skin. Like dormant cancer cells, you carried around any number of things that could kill you if you got cut in the right place, if your immune system was sufficiently worn down. You couldn't blame bacteria for killing Dave Lott, who was dead by Tuesday, before Calvin had even had a chance to stop by the hospital.

When the secretary sent out the mass voicemail, Calvin was the lone inspector in the office. He stood up and peered over the divider. There was Dave Lott's dirty coffee cup. There was the picture of his daughter from a few years ago, ten or eleven, her hair pulled tightly into two ponytails. The room's emptiness felt different suddenly, and Calvin threw on his jacket and cleared out. *We weren't really friends,* he reminded himself. Even before he'd left off the occasional beer after work, that's all it had been—an occasional beer after work.

Outside, it was wet and chilly, with a substantial wind that whistled through some invisible gaps in the dash of his car. But the heater was enthusiastic, and even with the lingering sewage smell, he spent the afternoon driving two-lane roads he'd known his whole life. He turned on talk radio and didn't listen. It seemed stupid to Calvin, now, not to have had more beers after work with Dave Lott. It made him feel weak and pushed around by his wife, even though she'd never exactly told him not to. Now he imagined that Dave Lott had seen him this way, weak and pushed around. In his head, Calvin had an imaginary conversation with Jill, in which he told her in no uncertain terms that he would continue to have drinks with Dave Lott and any other friend—acquaintance—he saw fit. Then he imagined another conversation in which he told her something similar, but in a more reasonable voice. Perhaps Jill would have drawn it out into a lengthy battle. Perhaps she would have griped for a few days, then let it go. Perhaps she would have, eventually, admired his loyalty, even to a man she would forever dislike for leaving his wife, her friend.

He'd intended to surprise the Blue Ridge Treatment Plant with a brief inspection, but he found himself passing the facility and turning onto the back road that led to the small farm where he'd grown up. His folks still lived there, though they'd stopped farming and had sold off their acreage bit by bit, for income. Now, radiating from the scabby old clapboard farmhouse were five brick ranch homes for families who worked in town and wanted to build in the country. He didn't stop the car. Neither of Calvin's parents was sick, though his father had had a bout with prostate cancer. They were fine. A little shakier to get up from the table after Sunday dinner, maybe, but that was all. Now he slowed down to make sure their truck was in the driveway, and then he sped up, hoping they wouldn't see him pass if they happened to glance out the window.

Dave Lott's first wife, Pat, and their daughter, Jennifer, lived three hours away in Indiana. "Of course you'll stay with us," said Jill into the phone, and they arrived the night before the funeral.

Pat struggled to get each foot out of the car—she was a short, bulky woman—and stood up into Jill's arms. When they separated, Calvin saw that they were both dabbing at their eyes, though they'd had nothing good, between them, to say about Dave Lott when he was alive. Pat made a sound of perseverance—something like "Whoo"—and smiled over at where Calvin stood three feet back on the grass. She reached for him, and he had no choice but to step in for a hug too. "Oh," she said, patting his back with both hands, pressing herself hard into his stomach. After what seemed like an acceptable amount of time, he pushed back from her, but she gripped his upper arms. "This really brings everything back up for me," she said. "This really peels the scab off the old wound." She smiled again, bravely. She had one of those mouths where a strip of pink gum showed above her upper teeth. It was the kind of thing you couldn't not notice, once you had. She held her smile and blinked at him, hard, until he felt compelled to smile back and nod as if he understood, as if they'd all been married to Dave Lott, as if he'd let them all down and now, on top of it all, he'd gone and died.

Through the open driver's-side door, Calvin saw Jennifer in the passenger seat, picking at her chin in the lighted visor mirror. When she got out of the car, she let Jill hug her, but the girl looked as if she felt more captured than embraced.

Inside, Jill offered the guest bedroom and the couch.

"We'll share the guest bedroom," said Pat.

"I'll take the couch," said Jennifer.

Pat gave Jill a prim, significant pucker, which Calvin watched Jennifer ignore. The girl had ragged, dark bangs that fell into her eyes, and the rest of her hair had been drawn into a braid that went down the back of her head and then another inch or two down her neck. There was a name for this kind of braid, Calvin thought. He set the bags in the living room, for the time being.

"I told Jennifer she could watch the boys while the adults talk," Pat said. "That would be fun for her. Take her mind off things." She passed a hand over the girl's forehead, brushing the long bangs out of her eyes. "Right, Jennifer?"

Jennifer's head reared back from the hand, slightly, like a snake.

"Whatever you want to do, sweetie," Jill said. "They're in the basement occupied with a video. You can lie down, or read, or just hang out with us. Who wants coffee?"

"Did you hear that, Jennifer?" Pat said.

Calvin wished the woman would give her daughter a moment's peace. She seemed unable to stop addressing the girl. And touching her too. Now Pat was squeezing Jennifer's shoulders, repeating, "Whatever you feel like," as the girl hunched into herself unhappily.

*

"Are you awake?" Jill asked Calvin that night, entering their bedroom and turning on a low light. She and Pat had stayed up late, talking in the kitchen.

Calvin kept his eyes closed. He heard the zipper of her jeans, and the shushing as she pushed them down her legs. She moved, unnecessarily, to the table on his side of the bed, and rummaged in a drawer. He could smell her. Then she moved to the dresser and he knew she was slipping into one of the short nightgowns she'd taken to wearing to bed ever since she'd gone off the pill. It took two to have a baby, she'd said, and even though she couldn't force him, she'd informed him that she would no longer do her part to prevent anything.

"They're having such a hard time," Jill said. She turned off the light and got into bed. Under the covers, she pulled up the nightgown and pressed her bare breasts against his back. "Jennifer's in such a difficult stage," she said, moving her breasts against him. Her nipples grew hard, but just her intention, that she wanted something from him and was trying to get it her way, made her methods easier for him to ignore. "Dave wasn't much of a father to her, but he was all she had." She reached under the waistband of his shorts, from behind, moved her hand over his ass, and tried to work it between his legs. Calvin shifted away from her, slapping at her arm as if he were asleep.

"I know you're awake," said Jill as she rolled away. "You can't fool me."

At the funeral home, guests seemed to be dividing themselves up on either side of the aisle by who was friends with Pat, the first wife, and who was friends with Dora, the second wife. It was like a wedding, that way. Since Calvin would know everyone from work, he'd been enlisted to come early and stand toward the door at the back of the funeral parlor with the printed programs. He didn't mind this, as it kept him far from the half-open coffin. When Jill arrived with Pat and Jennifer, they all stood near him. Dora had taken her seat already, left of the aisle in the front row.

"Will you speak to her?" Jill asked Pat.

"I don't know," Pat said, then, "Don't look, honey," as Jennifer turned to find the woman. Pat pulled Jennifer close, and the girl kept her face blank. "I guess I'll have to say something." Pat turned to Calvin, as if for confirmation.

Calvin said, "Umm." What did the woman want from him?

Pat turned back to Jill. "I guess I should probably say something."

"Wait and see," Jill suggested, shooting Calvin a nasty look. "You shouldn't feel like you have to."

Visitors trickled in. Robin arrived with her husband, a thin man with an earring whom Calvin had met once before. They joined the small, stunned group of Calvin's coworkers who'd shown up early. Calvin had worked with these people for more than five years and had never seen them dressed up before. They'd all greeted Pat, then made their way to Dora, then stood at the far side of the room, inhabiting their clothes awkwardly, unsure of where to sit. Calvin had invited them all to the house afterward, for a grim sort of reception. He imagined Dora would be receiving guests at her house too.

People who hadn't seen Jennifer in the years since she and Pat had moved admired, quietly, how she'd grown. Calvin watched the girl answer questions in monosyllables. When she spoke, her lips parted to reveal a chipped upper-front tooth.

"You okay, honey?" Pat kept asking her between guests, keeping one square hand on the girl's back. "She hasn't said much since last week," said Pat to Jill. "Have you, honey."

"I've said stuff."

"Right," Pat said. "She's in that phase right now. You know, where everything I say is wrong?"

"I'm not in a phase," Jennifer said. "I just don't have anything to say."

"Last night you had something to say," said Pat. "That you hated me. Remember that?" To Jill, Pat said, "That's part of the phase too."

Jennifer rolled her eyes.

"It's hard to know what to say," Jill said. Which in itself was a great thing to say, Calvin thought, and if Jill had looked his way, he might have smiled at her.

"I know," said Pat. "I know. I just think we could give this phase a rest when something like this happens." She pushed the tips of her fingers up against her eyebrows until her eyes bugged out. When she let go, the loose arch of skin over each eye reshaped itself slowly. Calvin realized he was staring at this and looked away.

The door had been propped open with a rubber wedge. Outside, the sky was heavy and gray. It had been raining off and on all morning, and he could smell worms and wet pavement. He thought he could smell the storm drains too. There was a finger of cold in the air, as though winter hadn't given up. He watched a long blue car pull up and drop off a tiny elderly woman encased in a clear plastic rain shawl. She crept through the door with a walker and kissed Pat on the cheek.

"Oh, Miss Evelyn," Pat said. "Jennifer, this lady used to watch you when you were little."

"Do you remember me?" said the old woman.

Jennifer nodded and, in the first willing motion Calvin had seen her make, leaned down to hug the old woman. Over the woman's stooped shoulder Jennifer's face appeared suddenly nearer to Calvin's, eyes closed, nose shiny and broad. The skin on her lower jaw looked red and bumpy, and fine brown hairs were growing at the corners of her mouth, the kind Jill tweezed away in front of the bathroom mirror. As if she felt Calvin looking, Jennifer opened her eyes. They were small and gray, like her father's. Calvin felt for her. Her father dead, her mother hard to take at best. Before the funeral, at the house, while standing before the closet, looking for one of his ties, he had heard Jennifer's shower through the wall. He heard the splash and patter against the stall, the rush of water hitting the tub, the squelching of plastic bottles of shampoo and conditioner. He was stepping into his pants when he heard something more, almost not a sound, it was so faint. He parted the hanging row of shirts and realized that through the thin plaster, he was listening to the girl cry. There was also a subdued smacking sound, as if she were bringing her hand hard against her forehead.

"Jennifer's a tough case," whispered Jill as they took their seats several rows back from the first. "Pat says she said nothing the whole drive down. Five hours. Pat thinks she's still in shock."

"I don't know about shock," Calvin said. "I mean, she can talk normally enough. Shock is a real condition. With real symptoms."

"I know what shock is," Jill said.

"Pat should give the kid a break. Some space."

"Space," Jill said, her breath an explosion in his ear. "You don't give a troubled kid too much space. Did you see that chipped tooth?" Jill glanced toward Pat and Jennifer in the front row to make sure she couldn't be heard. "Pat found her eating raw macaroni for a snack. Right out of the box. Hard as rocks. And this even before Dave died."

Calvin nodded at a man and woman they knew casually from church, who lowered themselves into chairs in the row in front of him. Jill smiled at them too and grasped their hands. Then she turned back to Calvin and frowned. "Don't you think that's kind of strange?"

"Sure," Calvin said.

"Pat asked her why, and she said she liked the way it sounded in her ears. The crunching. She said she liked how sharp it was against her tongue."

"It's strange, but it doesn't seem like a huge thing."

"Pat worries," Jill said. "And now she has to deal with Dora on top of everything else. That's a hurt that's still fresh."

"She keeps it that way," Calvin said.

"What?"

"Nothing."

"I heard you," Jill hissed in his ear. "Pat didn't ask for any of this, you know."

"What?" said Calvin, as the organ playing picked up pace and volume.

"You can't even muster up the generosity to be nice. Don't think I don't see it."

"What?" said Calvin, touching his ear. He knew it was childish. "What? What?"

Jill shook her head and set her teeth.

The hymn was one Calvin recognized, "In the Sweet By-and-By," and its message was that everything would be okay after everyone was dead. In the front row, Pat's shoulders started to shake, and she reached for Jennifer's hands, clutching them to her chest. This pulled the girl's far arm awkwardly across her body, though she remained facing straight ahead, in the direction of the coffin. This and everything else seemed to Calvin to boil down to resistance—to giving in or not giving in, even when you couldn't say exactly what there was to be resisted or what made you want to.

After the funeral there was a confrontation in the parking lot. Calvin saw it coming. The second wife moving up behind Pat, Calvin's own nod to her, a woman he'd met only once, causing Pat to turn around on her heel. The second wife was already hugging Jennifer, and when the woman handed her a pocket-sized book of collected love poems, explaining that they had belonged to Dave Lott's mother, Calvin saw the girl's chin trembling.

"How thoughtful," Pat said crisply, stepping in between them, extending her hand to the woman. "Thank you."

The second wife untangled her fingers from Pat's and passed a hand over her brown bobbed hair, as if it needed smoothing. "I loved him," she said, not very nicely.

"Fine," Pat said.

"I loved him," said the woman again. She turned to Jennifer. "You should know that."

Jennifer nodded. She looked nervously at her mother, who had begun to nod too.

"You loved him," Pat said, nodding, "and you want my daughter to know that."

"That's right," said the woman.

"Let's all take it easy," said Calvin.

"Pat," said Jill, "let's go."

"You loved him," Pat said again.

"You wouldn't know the first thing about that," the woman said.

"Don't tell *me*—" Pat started to say, but the second wife turned away. "He had a *family,*" Pat called after her. "So don't tell *me.*" The woman kept walking, and Pat began to shake. Calvin thought she might be about to collapse, which wouldn't help anyone. As he helped her to her rental car, her upper arm felt so soft and old that he found himself compelled to handle her tenderly. This made him cross.

"I'm sorry," Pat said to no one in particular.

"You were nice to even try to speak with her," said Jill. "Considering."

Jennifer stood to the side, trying to fit the book into her small blue purse. Pat sat heavily in the passenger seat but kept her feet on the pavement.

"Put your head between your knees," Jill said, and helped Pat flop forward.

When she raised herself, Calvin placed his hands on her stockinged calves and folded her legs into the car.

"I'm sorry," Pat said again. She clutched Calvin's forearm and closed her eyes, leaning her head back against the headrest.

"Okay," Calvin said, his hand on the door. "We're all done here."

"I'll drive her," Jill said to Calvin, still angry and not looking at him.

"I'll go with you," Jennifer said to Calvin. It was the first thing she'd said to him, and her voice seemed light—too agreeable, like she anticipated being told she couldn't.

"Take Jennifer," Jill said, as if Jennifer hadn't suggested it. The girl was already moving toward Calvin's car.

Once they were on the road, it began to rain. The windshield clouded over and Calvin turned on the fan. Jennifer stared out the passenger window. She rolled it down several inches, moving her face toward the cool air. They drove in silence for a few blocks. Calvin was trying to decide whether it was a comfortable or uncomfortable silence. He wondered if it could be a different thing for each person or if perceptions about silence were mutual, like an odor in the room no one could ignore.

"I'm sorry about your dad," he said, finally. "I liked him."

Jennifer was still looking out the window. They passed a storage facility. Low, putty-colored buildings stretched back from the road for a good two acres. The thought of all that stuff, just sitting there, made Calvin feel heavy.

"You know how he died, right? Basically, he was eaten alive."

"He was very sick," Calvin said.

"I didn't think his job was even dangerous."

"No, no," Calvin said. "That's not it. It's not dangerous. This was just a freak thing. Hardly ever happens. He could have picked this up at the laundromat or in his own garage. Bacteria are everywhere. All kinds of bacteria."

"So then everywhere's dangerous," said the girl. She shrugged at the revised perspective, rolled down her window all the way, and stuck her face fully into the air. Calvin wondered if she was going to throw up. He wondered if he should pull over. Her long bangs lifted straight off her forehead, standing vertically in the wind. He watched her observing herself in the passenger side mirror for a block. Then she jerked her head back into the car and let it fall against the headrest. Her lips moved, and she said something way in the back of her throat. "I hate her."

"Who?"

Jennifer smiled up at the roof of the car, exposing the chipped tooth. "I do hate her," she said. The girl's chest, with her two small beginning breasts, pulsed with what could have been laughing or crying, but she was still just smiling up at the ceiling. "What are we going to do when we get back to your house anyway," the girl said. "Just stand around?"

That was exactly what would happen. Calvin thought for a moment. "We could stop by the office, first, if you want. Your dad kept a picture of you on his desk."

The girl closed her eyes. It had been the right thing to suggest or the wrong thing, but it was out there now, and he headed in the direction of work. The rain was coming down hard, and the girl felt for the knob to roll up the window. Calvin adjusted the wipers to medium. Their motion and the rain outside made everything in the car seem more still. He turned off the defogger.

"My mother said that instead of telling her I hated her, I should have taken a dagger and stabbed her in the heart. She said I should have dissolved a bottle of sleeping pills into her coffee."

"Your mother's having a hard time."

"She's a drama queen," said Jennifer. "She's always having a hard time."

This sounded about right to Calvin, but it also seemed an inappropriate thing for him to confirm. He slowed for a light. The window had begun to fog again, and he switched on the blower.

"If it makes you feel any better," he said, "everyone hates their parents once in a while. I hated my parents. My kids are going to hate me, probably."

Jennifer looked at him balefully. Calvin felt old. And depressed. He remembered something he hadn't thought about in years. "What I used to do? I would pretend my parents had been in a car accident. Not that they were seriously hurt, or anything, just one of those fender-benders. I'd be waiting at home, and maybe it would be raining out, like today, and I'd imagine that they slid off the road going really slow, and maybe hit a tree, or a fence. Just hard enough to bump their heads good. Not even any blood."

The girl was looking toward the window again, following the staggered water drops in their descending horizontal.

"Then I'd imagine them walking in the door, looking just like they always did. My father looks a little like Don Knotts. But when they greeted me, it would be different, more polite, like they were talking to someone else's kid. My mother would ask me what grade I was in. My father would ask me who I liked for the Super Bowl that year. And I didn't mind telling them. Then I'd ask them if they had any kids, and they'd look at each other and smile and say no, they hadn't been blessed with children, and I'd know that the accident had taken me right out of their memory, and it felt great. I even kind of liked them."

"How old were you?"

"What?" Calvin said, pulling into his parking spot. "I don't know. Fifteen, maybe."

"I'm fifteen," she said.

The girl wore no coat, he realized halfway between the parking lot and the door. The rain was not heavy just now, but they had no umbrella, and by the time they reached the entrance, Jennifer's hair was damp, and the fuzzy wool of her dress showed rain spots.

Inside, in the green fluorescent light, the air was chilly. The office had emptied out for the funeral. It felt like coming in to work on a Sunday. Or like Calvin remembered feeling on the days he'd stayed home sick from school, as a child. Like he'd stepped right out of time.

Jennifer shivered, but shook her head when Calvin offered his coat. She trailed him down the plastic runner toward his cube. One-quarter of a ceiling panel had grown soggy with rain, and water gathered into a drop and fell heavily into a puddle on the plastic. When Calvin's hard-soled dress shoes hit the spot, his feet slipped out from under him, and he slapped at the floor in a kind of undignified tap dance, grabbing the side of a cubicle to regain his balance. He looked back at Jennifer, but she was reading the name tags on each cubicle they passed.

Calvin tapped on Dave Lott's name tag when they reached it. "Want to sit here for a minute? Take some time?"

"Okay," said the girl. She lowered herself into her father's desk chair. She opened one of his drawers and took out an enormous ball made of rubber bands. Then she put the ball back in the drawer and closed it.

"I'm just going to be right here," Calvin said, gesturing to his own cube, but the girl didn't look up. She was moving her hands along the top of Dave Lott's desk, picking things up and putting them back down.

Calvin went through some papers. He looked at the calendar

on his computer and pulled files for the week's inspections. Then he saw that his voicemail light was on, so he listened to his messages. One was an announcement from the secretary about the funeral, closing the office for the day. Another message announced the reception at Calvin's house. When he hung up the phone, he stood and peered over the top of the cube to check on Jennifer, but she wasn't there.

He stepped out and looked down the aisle. Empty. He called, "Jennifer?" but the only sound was the dripping ceiling and the buzzing of the fluorescent lights.

At the other end of the hall, he knocked on the bathroom door, but it was empty. He stepped up onto Rex Hickman's chair, keeping a precarious balance over the wheels as he scanned the tops of all the cubes. Nothing. He called her name again, but the room gave off no resonance, the sound dead as soon as he closed his mouth, as if there had always been only the fluorescent hum of the lights and the rain worrying the flat roof. As if the girl had never been there.

He checked the secretary's office, next to the bathroom. Locked. He crossed to the other aisle, with its identical row of cubicles, and peered into each one, but they were all empty. As if everyone had died, not just Dave Lott, as if bacteria had invaded the world and he was the only, lonely one with immunity. She wasn't in their supply closet, and she wasn't in the equipment room. He left the office and stepped out into the rain to check the car, but she wasn't there either. Back in the office he checked every cubicle again. He called her name over and over. This time, when he poked his head back into the supply closet, he switched on the light and found her wedged between the wall and a stack of boxes filled with printer paper.

"What's the idea?" Calvin said. "I didn't know where you were."

Tears formed in the girl's eyes, and she wrapped her arms around her middle. The closet was on the outside wall, and it was chilly. The ceiling in here dripped too, into a large plastic bucket that sat on an empty pallet. The girl looked miserable and cold.

"Hey," Calvin said. "Forget it. It's no big deal." He reached for her shoulder and patted her awkwardly. When she didn't resist, he placed both hands on her shoulders and brought her close to him. The girl was shivering. She sobbed three times into his coat and then quieted, like she was forcing herself to stop. "It's okay," Calvin said. He moved his hand over her back and then let go, thinking of the handkerchief he kept in his suit coat pocket, a habit his father had instilled in him. But his overcoat was unbuttoned, and the girl reached her arms inside and around him, holding him at the waist. She pressed the side of her face very hard against his shirt. It was as if she were much younger, he thought, a child, or maybe much older. He moved his hand to the back of her hair, where his fingers found and followed the texture of the damp braid. The girl shivered against him, and he wrapped his raincoat around her with his arms. Against the roof, the rain came down steadily, like it was never going to stop. It rained forty days and forty nights once, Calvin's grandfather used to say when conversation lagged. Calvin was thinking of using the line himself when the girl's legs parted on either side of his thigh. He thought it might have been an awkward accident, and he shifted, attempting to reposition her hips to the side of him. Beside his face the top box on a stack had gotten wet from another leak in the ceiling. As he tilted his head back to locate the leaky panel, the girl realigned her hips frontally against him. She began moving. First almost imperceptibly, then steadily, then with more and more urgency. It was a seeking need, intense and confused.

Calvin stepped backward and felt another wall of boxes solid behind him. The girl stepped with him, into him, though he'd turned his lower body to the left, attempting to hold her and prevent her at the same time. She dropped her face to his chest again. He was only semi-erect, but she found this with the outside of one of her thin legs. He pushed her away and tried to look her in the eye, but her eyes seemed to go straight through to the back of her head. There was something vacant about her face too, like nothing you tried to do for her would make any difference. He rested his chin on top of her hair and kept her hips away from him, with his hands. She pushed her face against his shirt, rubbing it there like a cat and making wounded, wanting noises in the back of her throat. When he brought her body close, finally, it seemed like a kindness. It seemed like the only possible help. She went up and down on her tiptoes against him. After a time, still under the cover of his coat, he reached down to her knees, lifted her skirt, slipped his hand between her legs, and stroked her through her cotton panties to the rhythm of the rain until she shuddered, bleating, "I, I, I," into his shirt.

He held her for a moment more. Then he removed his coat and wrapped it around her shoulders. He tried not to think. He steered her, silently, back into the main room of the office, down the aisle of cubicles, and out the door to the parking lot. In the car, he turned on the heat. He started to speak, meaning to impress upon her how important it would be to say nothing. But the girl was blinking sleepily out the side window, the rain streaking subtle shadows across her face in the dying light, and he closed his mouth and did not disturb her.

The first guests had already arrived by the time Calvin pulled into the driveway.

"You okay?" he asked the girl before they got out of the car.

"Yeah." With the tip of her tongue, she touched the edge of her broken tooth.

Jill appeared at the door, and the memory of the storage room flipped off like a switch in his head. "Where have you been?" she asked, and when he told her, she nodded, and the tough set of her face dissolved. She was moved, and this moved him—his heart —toward her in an old way.

Jennifer entered the house ahead of him. When her mother rose, crying, from the couch to pull her close, the girl went stiff again.

"I'll get you some Kleenex," she said to her mother, and disappeared down the hall.

Calvin poured punch and made small talk with Robin and her hippie husband. When the nut bowls needed refilling, he did that. He said the same things about Dave Lott over and over. Nice things, about his sense of humor. And he shook his head with everyone else about the way he'd died. He did not picture the man in his head. The boys returned from the sitter's, and Trent stuck close to Calvin, closed-mouthed and shy around so many new adults. When Robin's husband tousled his hair, the boy drew back and leaned heavily against Calvin's legs, a neediness of the body that brought back the moments in the supply closet with the dread remembering of a bad dream. Calvin passed a hand over his own forehead. He felt Jill watching him from across the room, and when he met her tired eyes, she smiled. Calvin forced himself to smile back. He saw Jennifer approaching her mother on the couch.

"Hello," he heard her say. He thought by the way she said it —polite and kind—that she must be talking not to Pat but to the woman next to her. Then Jennifer said, formally, "I'm so sorry for your loss," and he realized she was talking to Pat after all.

Pat reached for Jennifer's hand, and the girl allowed it to be held. "Honey," Pat said.

"I'm Jennifer," she said, introducing herself to her own mother.

Pat blinked at her. Beside Calvin, Robin's husband was saying something, but Calvin wasn't listening. He watched Pat's face turn confused, with furrowed brow and pursed lips. Jennifer kept up her polite, sad, chip-toothed smile. She covered Pat's hand with her other hand.

Calvin turned back to the man next to him. From the corner of the room, he heard Pat cry out, "Jennifer, stop it."

"You all right there?" Robin's husband was saying to Calvin, whose stomach felt bad. Trent looked up at him, his dark eyes questioning.

"Go get ready for bed," Calvin heard himself say.

"Hey. Hey, Calvin," said the man. Calvin felt a strong hand on his shoulder.

"I'm okay," Calvin said. He brought his thumb and forefinger to the corners of his eyes. "I'm all right."

"You knew him pretty well, huh," said Robin's husband.

Across the room, Pat was saying, between great, ratcheting sobs, "I'm your mother." Calvin watched Jennifer, her face the picture of propriety, touch her mother's back as impersonally as a funeral employee. He thought he heard her say, "There, there." Pat dropped her face into her knees and covered her head, and Calvin lowered his eyes like every other guest in the room. He sensed, rather than saw, Jill hurrying over to help.

Calvin thought he might be sick. Then he took a deep breath and said to Robin, to her husband, "I need some air."

Outside, it was dark and cold, but the rain had stopped. Calvin sank down onto the back cement stoop. He reached behind him into the cinder block of the house's foundation where he and Jill always kept a fifth of vodka. For some reason it seemed different than keeping the hard stuff in the house.

When he'd told Jennifer about the thing he used to do with his parents, wishing amnesia on them, he hadn't told her everything. As a kid, when he kept up the fantasy of talking to his parents as if he didn't know them, something eventually reversed itself. The longer he imagined their benign responses, the more he felt uneasy instead of relieved. In his head, he'd become desperate, leading them down the hall to his room, showing them things that would prove they had a son and that the son was he. His underwear drawer, his private collection of colored chalk dust, meticulously stacked in film canisters along the floor of his closet. In his mind's eye, his parents kept nodding pleasantly, but without recognition, and this made the young Calvin suddenly, fitfully afraid. He began watching the clock, desperate for his parents to return. By the time they really did come home, he was so happy to see them that he found himself trailing them around the house, more helpful, suddenly, than was his teenage way, just to be near them, just to reassure himself that they knew him, until his mother said, one of these times, that he was behaving like a boy with a guilty conscience.

When Jill found him, sometime later, he was sprawled on the steps, staring up at the night. The sky had cleared in spots, showing stars and a very bright half-moon.

"Oh, Calvin," Jill said, taking the half-empty bottle from him. She zipped up her coat and sat on the step above him. He leaned his head back on her knees, and she brushed his hair away from his forehead, like she did at night with the boys, like she had not done with him in a long time.

"Jill," he said, but his voice came out cracked and a little wild.

She shushed him. "Just be quiet," she said, still stroking his hair. Calvin thought he would cry from the feel of her hand. "This has been a day," she said. "Pat's a mess in there. Jennifer is a strange bird. She's saying she fell at the office. She's saying she hit her head and can't remember her own mother. She's way too old to pull this stuff."

Calvin took the bottle back from her and drank again. "I didn't see her fall," he said truthfully. "I didn't know she hit her head, but maybe she did."

"Okay," said Jill. "Whatever. Only right now she's in there asking people if they've ever seen that nice woman who keeps crying. As if anyone really gets amnesia, Calvin." On his forehead, Jill's hand went still. Calvin closed his eyes. He thought if she would just ask him for something, anything, he could do it. He knew he would be willing, in this way, for a long time.

"Listen to me," he said, expelling all his breath with the words. Two ragged breaths later he tried again, but Jill moved her hand from his forehead to his mouth. "Help me," he said into her fingers. But the words were whispered, and she mistook them for a kiss, and smiled.

ERIC PUCHNER

# Beautiful Monsters

FROM *Tin House*

THE BOY IS making breakfast for his sister—fried eggs and cheap frozen sausages, furred with ice—when he sees a man eating an apple from the tree outside the window. The boy drops his spatula. It is a gusty morning, sun-sharp and beautiful, and the man's shirt flags out to one side of him, rippling in the wind. The boy has never seen a grown man in real life, only in books, and the sight is both more and less frightening than he expected. The man picks another apple from high in the tree and devours it in several bites. He is bearded and tall as a shadow, but the weirdest things of all are his hands. They seem huge, grotesque, as clumsy as crabs. The veins on them bulge out, forking around his knuckles. The man plucks some more apples from the tree and sticks them in a knapsack at his feet, ducking his head so that the boy can see a saucer of scalp in the middle of his hair.

What do you think it wants? his sister whispers, joining him by the stove. She watches the hideous creature strip their tree of fruit; the boy might be out of work soon, and they need the apples themselves. The eggs have begun to scorch at the edges.

I don't know. He must have wandered away from the woods.

I thought they'd be less . . . ugly, his sister says.

The man's face is damp, streaked with ash, and it occurs to the boy that he's been crying. A twig dangles from his beard. The boy does not find the man ugly—he finds him, in fact, mesmerizing —but he does not mention this to his sister, who owns a comic book filled with pictures of handsome fathers, contraband drawings of twinkling, well-dressed men playing baseball with their daughters or throwing them high into the air. There is nothing well-dressed about this man, whose filthy pants—like his shirt—look like they've been sewn from deerskin. His bare feet are black with soot. Behind him the parched mountains seethe with smoke, charred by two-week-old wildfires. There have been rumors of encounters in the woods, of firefighters beset by giant, hairy-faced beasts stealing food or tents or sleeping bags, of girls being raped in their beds.

The man stops picking apples and stares right at the kitchen window, as if he smells the eggs. The boy's heart trips. The man wipes his mouth on his sleeve, then limps down the driveway and stoops inside the open door of the garage.

He's stealing something! the boy's sister says.

He barely fits, the boy says.

Trap him. We can padlock the door.

The boy goes and gets the .22 from the closet in the hall. He's never had cause to take it out before—their only intruders are skunks and possums, the occasional raccoon—but he knows exactly how to use it, a flash of certainty in his brain, just as he knows how to use the lawn mower and fix the plumbing and operate the worm-drive saw at work without thinking twice. He builds houses for other boys and girls to live in, it is what he's always done—he loves the smell of cut pine and sawdust in his nose, the *fzzzzdddt* of screws buzzing through Sheetrock into wood—and he can't imagine not doing it, any more than he can imagine leaving this gusty town ringed by mountains. He was born knowing these things, will always know them; they are as instinctive to him as breathing.

But he has no knowledge of men, only what he's learned from history books. And the illicit, sentimental fairy tales of his sister's comic.

He tells his sister to stay inside and then walks toward the garage, leading with the rifle. The wind swells the trees, and the few dead August leaves crunching under his feet smell like butterscotch. For some reason, perhaps because of the sadness in the man's face, he is not as scared as he would have imagined. The boy stops inside the shadow of the garage and sees the man hunched behind the lawn mower, bent down so his head doesn't scrape the rafters. One leg of the man's pants is rolled up to reveal a bloody gash on his calf. He picks a fuel jug off the shelf and splashes some gasoline on the wound, grimacing. The boy clears his throat, loudly, but the man doesn't look up.

Get out of my garage, the boy says.

The man startles, banging his head on the rafters. He grabs a shovel leaning against the wall and holds it in front of him. The shovel, in his overgrown hands, looks as small as a baseball bat. The boy lifts the .22 up to his eye, so that it's leveled at the man's stomach. He tilts the barrel at the man's face.

What will you do?

Shoot you, the boy says.

The man smiles, dimpling his filthy cheeks. His teeth are as yellow as corn. I'd like to see you try.

I'd aim right for the apricot. The medulla. You'd die instantly.

You look like you're nine, the man mutters.

The boy doesn't respond to this. He suspects the man's disease has infected his brain. Slowly, the man puts down the shovel and ducks out of the garage, plucking cobwebs from his face. In the sunlight, the wound on his leg looks even worse, shreds of skin stuck to it like grass. He reeks of gasoline and smoke and something else, a foul body smell, like the inside of a ski boot.

I was sterilizing my leg.

Where do you live? the boy asks.

In the mountains. The man looks at his gun. Don't worry, I'm by myself. We split up so we'd be harder to kill.

Why?

Things are easier to hunt in a herd.

No, the boy says. Why did you leave?

The fire. Burned up everything we were storing for winter. The man squints at the house. Can I trouble you for a spot of water?

The boy lowers his gun, taking pity on this towering creature that seems to have stepped out of one of his dreams. In the dreams, the men are like beautiful monsters, stickered all over with leaves, roaming through town in the middle of the night. The boy leads the man inside the house, where his sister is still standing at the window. The man looks at her and nods. That someone should have hair growing out of his face appalls her even more than the smell. *There's a grown man in my house,* she says to herself, but she cannot reconcile the image this arouses in her brain with the stooped creature she sees limping into the kitchen. She's often imagined what it would be like to live with a father—a dashing giant, someone who'd buy her presents and whisk her chivalrously from danger, like the brave, mortal fathers she reads about—but this man is as far from these handsome creatures as can be.

And yet the sight of his sunburned hands, big enough to snap her neck, stirs something inside her, an unreachable itch.

They have no chairs large enough for him, so the boy puts two side by side. He goes to the sink and returns with a mug of water. The man drinks the water in a single gulp, then immediately asks for another.

How old are you? the girl says suspiciously.

The man picks the twig from his beard. Forty-six.

The girl snorts.

No, really. I'm aging by the second.

The girl blinks, amazed. She's lived for thirty years and can't imagine what it would be like for her body to mark the time. The man lays the twig on the table, ogling the cantaloupe sitting on the counter. The boy unsheathes a cleaver from the knife block and slices the melon in two, spooning out the pulp before chopping off a generous piece. He puts the orange smile of cantaloupe on a plate. The man devours it without a spoon, holding it like a harmonica.

Where do you work? the man asks suddenly, gazing out the window at the pickup in the driveway. The toolbox in the bed glitters in the sun.

Out by Old Harmony, the boy says. We're building some houses.

Anything to put your brilliant skills to use, eh?

Actually, we're almost finished, the boy says. The girl looks at him: increasingly, the boy and girl are worried about the future. The town has reached its population cap, and rumor is there are no plans to raise it again.

Don't worry, the man says, sighing. They'll just repurpose you. Presto change-o.

How do *you* know? the girl asks.

I know about Perennials. You think I'm an ignorant ape? The man shakes his head. Jesus. The things I could teach you in my sleep.

The girl smirks at her brother. Like what?

The man opens his mouth as if to speak but then closes it again, staring at the pans hanging over the stove. They're arranged, like the tail bones of a dinosaur, from large to small. His face seems to droop. I bet you, um, can't make the sound of a loon.

What?

With your hands and mouth? A loon call?

The boy feels nothing in his brain: an exotic blankness. The feeling frightens him. The man perks up, seeming to recover his spirits. He cups his hands together as if warming them and blows into his thumbs, fluttering one hand like a wing. The noise is perfect and uncanny: the ghostly call of a loon.

The girl grabs the cleaver from the counter. How did you do that?

Ha! Experts of the universe! The man smiles, eyes bright with disdain. Come here and I'll teach you.

The girl refuses, still brandishing the knife, but the boy swallows his fear and approaches the table. The man shows him how to cup his hands together in a box and then tells him to blow into his knuckles. The boy tries, but no sound comes out. The man laughs. The boy blows until his cheeks hurt, until he's ready to give up, angry at the whole idea of bird calls and at loons for making them, which only makes the man laugh harder. He pinches the boy's thumbs together. The boy recoils, so rough and startling is the man's touch. Trembling, the boy presses his lips to his knuckles again and blows, producing a low airy whistle that surprises him —his chest filling with something he can't explain, a shy arrogant pleasure, like a blush.

The boy and girl let the man use their shower. While he's undressing, they creep outside and take turns at the bathroom window, their hands cupped to the glass, sneaking looks at his strange hairy body and giant shoulders tucked in like a vulture's and long terrible penis, which shocks them when he turns. The girl is especially shocked by the scrotum. It's limp and bushy and speckled on one side with veiny bursts. She has read about the ancient way of making babies, has even tried to imagine what it would be like to grow a fetus in her belly, a tiny bean-sized thing blooming into something curled and sac-bound and miraculous. She works as an assistant in a lab where frozen embryos are kept, and she wonders sometimes, staring at the incubators of black-eyed little beings, what it would be like to raise one of them and smoosh him to her breast, like a gorilla does. Sometimes she even feels a pang of loneliness when they're hatched, encoded with all the knowledge they'll ever need, sent off to the orphanage to be raised until they're old enough for treatments. But, of course, the same thing happened to her, and what does she have to feel lonely about?

Once in a while the girl will peek into her brother's room and see him getting dressed for work, see his little bobbing string of a penis, vestigial as his appendix, and her mouth will dry up. It lasts only for a second, this feeling, before her brain commands it to stop.

Now, staring at the man's hideous body, she feels her mouth dry up in the same way, aware of each silent bump of her heart.

The man spends the night. A fugitive, the boy calls him, closing the curtains so that no one can see in. The man's clothes are torn and stiff with blood, stinking of secret man-things, so the boy gives him his bathrobe to wear as a T-shirt and fashions a pair of shorts out of some sweatpants, slitting the elastic so that they fit his waist. The man changes into his new clothes, exposing the little beards under his arms. He seems happy with his ridiculous outfit and even does a funny bow that makes the boy laugh. He tries it on the girl as well, rolling his hand through the air in front of him, but she scowls and shuts the door to her room.

As the week stretches on, the girl grows more and more unhappy. There's the smell of him every morning, a sour blend of sweat and old-person breath and nightly blood seeping into the gauze the boy uses to dress his wound. There's his ugly limp, the hockey stick he's taken to using as a cane, which you can hear clopping from every room of the house. There's the cosmic stench he leaves in the bathroom, so powerful it makes her eyes water. There are the paper airplanes littering the back yard, ones he's taught the boy to make, sleek and bird-nosed and complicated as origami. Normally, the boy and girl drink a beer together in the kitchen after work—sometimes he massages her feet while they listen to music—but all week when she gets home he's out back with the man, flying his stupid airplanes around the yard. He checks the man's face after every throw, which makes her feel like going outside with a fly swatter and batting the planes down. The yard is protected by a windbreak of pines, but the girl worries one of the neighbors might see somehow and call the police. If anyone finds out there's a man in their house, she could get fired from the lab. Perhaps they'll even put her in jail.

Sometimes the man yells at them. The outbursts are unpredictable. *Turn that awful noise down!* he'll yell if they're playing music while he's trying to watch the news. Once, when the girl answers her phone during dinner, the man grabs it from her hand and hurls it into the sink. Next time, he tells her, he'll smash it with a brick. The worst thing is that they have to do what he says to quiet him down.

If it comes to it, she will kill the man. She will grab the .22 and shoot him while he's asleep.

On Saturday, the girl comes back from the grocery store and the man is limping around the back yard with the boy on his shoulders. The lawn mower sits in a spiral of mown grass. The boy laughs, and she hisses at them that the neighbors will hear. The man plunks the boy down and then sweeps her up and heaves her onto his shoulders instead. The girl is taller than she's ever imagined, so tall that she can see into the windows of her up-stairs room. The mulchy smell of grass fills her nose. She wraps her legs around the man's neck. A shiver goes through her, as if she's climbed out of a lake. The shiver doesn't end so much as wriggle its way inside of her, as elusive as a hair in her throat. The man trots around the yard and she can't help herself, she begins to laugh as the boy did, closing her legs more tightly around his neck, giggling in a way she's never giggled before—a weird, high-pitched sound, as if she can't control her own mouth—ducking under the lowest branches of the pin oak shading the back porch. The man starts to laugh too. Then he sets her down and falls to all fours on the lawn and the boy climbs on top of him, spurring him with the heels of his feet, and the man tries in vain to buck him off, whinnying like a horse in the fresh-mown grass. The boy clutches the man's homemade shirt. The girl watches them ride around the yard for a minute, the man's face bright with joy, their long shadow bucking like a single creature, and then she comes up from behind and pushes the boy off, so hard it knocks the wind out of him.

The boy squints at the girl, whose face has turned red. She has never pushed him for any reason. The boy stares at her face, so small and smooth and freckled compared to the man's, and for the first time is filled with disgust.

The man hobbles to his feet, gritting his teeth. His leg is bleeding. The gauze is soaked, a dark splotch of blood leaking spidery trickles down his shin.

Look what you've done! the boy says before helping the man to the house.

That night, the girl startles from a dream, as if her spine has been plucked. The man is standing in the corner of her room, clutching the hockey stick. His face—hideous, weirdly agleam—floats in the moonlight coming through the window. Her heart begins to race. She wonders if he's come to rape her. The man wipes his eyes with the end of his robe, first one, then the other. Then he clops toward her and sits on the edge of the bed, so close she can smell the sourness of his breath. His eyes are still damp. I was just watching you sleep, he says. He begins to sing to her, the same sad song he croons in the shower, the one about traveling through this world of woe. *There's no sickness, toil, or danger, in that bright land to which I go.* While he sings, he strokes the girl's hair with the backs of his fingers, tucking some loose strands behind her ear. His knuckles, huge and scratchy, feel like acorns.

What's the bright land? the girl asks.

The man stops stroking her hair. Heaven, he says.

The girl has heard about these old beliefs; to think that you could live on after death is so quaint and gullible, it touches her strangely.

Did someone you know die?

The man doesn't answer her. She can smell the murk of his sweat. Trembling, the girl reaches out and touches his knee where the sweatpants end, feeling its wilderness of hair. She moves her fingers under the hem of his sweats. The man does not move, closing his eyes as she inches her fingers up his leg. His breathing coarsens. Outside the wind picks up and rattles the window screen. Very suddenly, the man recoils, limping up from the bed.

You're just a girl, he whispers.

She stares at him. His face is turned, as if he can't bear to look at her. She does not know what she is.

He calls her Sleepyhead and hobbles out of the room. She wonders at this strange name for her, so clearly an insult. Her eyes

burn. Outside her window the moon looks big and stupid, a sleeping head.

The next day, when the boy comes home from work, the house is
humid with the smell of cooking. The man is bent over the stove,
leaning to one side to avoid putting too much weight on his injured leg. It's been over a week now and the gash doesn't look
any better; in fact, the smell has started to change, an almondy
stink like something left out in the rain. Yesterday, when the boy
changed the bandage, the skin underneath the pus was yellowish
brown, the color of an old leaf. But the boy's not worried. He's
begun to see the man as some kind of god. All day long he looks
forward to driving home from work and finding this huge ducking
presence in his house, smelling the day's sweat of his body through
his robe. He feels a helpless urge to run to him. The man always
seems slightly amazed to see him, unhappy even, but in a grateful
way, shaking his head as if he's spotted something he thought he'd
lost, and though the boy can't articulate his feelings to himself, it's
this amazement that he's been waiting for and that fills him with
such restlessness at work. Ahoy there, the man says. It's not particularly funny, even kind of stupid, but the boy likes it. Ahoy, he
says back. Sometimes the man clutches the boy's shoulder while
he changes his bandage, squeezing so hard the boy can feel it like
a live wire up his neck, and the boy looks forward to this too, even
though it hurts them both.

Now the man lifts the frying pan from the stove and serves the
boy and girl dinner. The boy looks at his plate: a scrawny-looking
thing with the fur skinned off, like a miniature greyhound fried to
a crisp. A squirrel.

I caught them in the back yard, the man explains.

Disgusting! the girl says, making a face.

Would you rather go to your room, young lady? the man says.

She pushes her chair back.

No, please. I'm sorry. You don't have to eat. He looks at his
plate and frowns. My mother was the real cook. She could have
turned this into a fricassee.

What are they like? the boy asks.

What?

Mothers.

They're wonderful, the man says after a minute. Though sometimes you hate them. You hate them for years and years.

Why?

That's a good question. The man cuts off a piece of squirrel but
doesn't eat it, instead stares at the window curtain, still bright with
daylight at six o'clock. I remember when I was a kid, how hard it
was to go to sleep in the summer. I used to tell my mom to turn
off the day. That's what I'd say, *Turn off the day,* and she'd reach up
and pretend to turn it off.

The man lifts his hand and yanks at the air, as if switching off a
light.

The boy eats half his squirrel even though it tastes a little bit
like turpentine. He wants to make the man happy. He knows that
the man is sad, and that it has to do with something that happened in the woods. The man has told him about the town where
he grew up, nestled in the mountains many miles away—the last
colony of its kind—and how some boys and girls moved in eventually and forced everyone out of their homes. How they spent years
traveling around, searching for a spot where there was enough
wilderness to hide in so they wouldn't be discovered, where the
food and water were plentiful, eventually settling in the parklands
near the boy and girl's house. But the boy's favorite part is hearing
about the disease itself: how exciting it was for the man to watch
himself change, to grow tall and hairy and dark-headed, as strong
as a beast. To feel ugly sometimes and hear his voice deepen into
a stranger's. To fall in love with a woman's body and watch a baby
come out of her stomach, still tied to her by a rope of flesh. The
boy loves this part most of all, but when he asks about it, the man
grows quiet and then says he understands why Perennials want to
live forever. Did you have a baby like that? the boy asked him yesterday, and the man got up and limped into the back yard and
stayed there for a while, picking up some stray airplanes and crum-
pling them into balls.

After dinner, they go into the living room to escape the lingering smell of squirrel. Sighing, the man walks to the picture window
and opens the curtains and looks out at the empty street, where
bats flicker under the street lamps. He's told them that when he
was young the streets were filled with children: they played until
it was dark, building things or shooting each other with sticks or

playing Butts Up and Capture the Flag and Ghost in the Graveyard, games that he's never explained.

It's a beautiful evening, he says, sighing again.

The girl does not look up from her pocket computer, her eyes
burning as they did last night. She is not a child; if anything, it's
the man's head that's sleepy, as dumb as the moon. Just listening
to him talk about how nice it is outside, like he knows what's best
for them, makes her clench her teeth.

What did you do when it rained? the boy asks.

Puppet shows, the man says, brightening.

Puppet shows?

The man frowns. Performances! For our mom and dad. My
brother and I would write our own scripts and memorize them.
The man glances at the girl on the floor, busy on her computer.
He claps in her face, loudly, but she doesn't look up. Can you get
me a marker and some different-colored socks?

They won't fit you, the boy says.

We'll do a puppet show. The three of us.

The boy grins. What about?

Anything. Pretend you're kids like I was.

We'll do one for *you*, the boy says, sensing how much this would
please the man.

He goes to get some socks from his room and then watches as
the man draws eyes and a nose on each one. The girl watches too,
avoiding the man's face. If it will make the boy happy, she will do
what he wants. They disappear into the boy's room to think up
a script. After a while, they come out with the puppets on their
hands and crouch behind the sofa, as the man has instructed
them. The puppet show begins.

Hello, red puppet.

Hello, white puppet.

I can't even drive.

Me either.

Let's play Capture the Graveyard.

Okay.

In seventy years I'm going to die. First, though, I will grow old
and weak and disease-ridden. This is called aging. It was thought
to be incurable, in the Age of Senescence.

Will you lose your hair?

I am male, so there's a four in seven chance of baldness.

If you procreate with me, my breasts will become engorged with milk.

I'm sorry.

Don't apologize. The milk will feed my baby.

But how?

It will leak from my nipples.

I do not find you disgusting, red puppet. Many animals have milk-producing mammary glands. I just wish it wasn't so expensive to grow old and die.

Everyone will have to pay more taxes, because we'll be too feeble to work and pay for our useless medicines.

Jesus Christ, the man says, interrupting them. He limps over and yanks the socks from their hands. What's wrong with you?

Nothing, the girl says.

Can't you even do a fucking puppet show?

He limps into the boy's room and shuts the door. The boy does not know what he's done to make him angry. Bizarrely, he feels like he might cry. He sits on the couch for a long time, staring out the window at the empty street. Moths eddy under the street lamps like snow. The girl is jealous of his silence; she has never made the boy look like this, as if he might throw up from unhappiness. She walks to the window and shuts the curtains without speaking and shows him something on her computer: a news article, all about the tribe of Senescents. There have been twelve sightings in three days. Most have managed to elude capture, but one, a woman, was shot by a policeboy as she tried to climb through his neighbor's window. There's a close-up of her body, older even than the man's, her face gruesome with wrinkles. A detective holds her lips apart with two fingers to reveal the scant yellow teeth, as crooked as fence posts. The girl calls up another picture: a crowd of children, a search party, many of them holding rifles. They are standing in someone's yard, next to a garden looted of vegetables. The town is offering an official reward for any Senescent captured. Five thousand dollars, dead or alive. The girl widens her eyes, hoping the boy will widen his back, but he squints at her as if he doesn't know who she is.

At work, the boy has fallen behind on the house he's drywalling. The tapers have already begun on the walls downstairs. In the summer heat, the boy hangs the last panel of Sheetrock upstairs and then sits down to rest in the haze of gypsum dust. He has always liked this chalky smell, always felt that his work meant something: he was building homes for new Perennials to move into and begin their lives. But something has changed. The boy looks through the empty window square beside him and sees the evergreens that border the lot. Before long they'll turn white with snow and then drip themselves dry and then go back to being as green and silent and lonely-looking as they are now. It will happen, the boy thinks, in the blink of an eye.

There's a utility knife sitting by his boot, and he picks it up and imagines what it would be like to slit his throat.

Did you see the news this morning? his coworker, a taper who was perennialized so long ago, he's stopped counting the years, asks at lunch.

The boy shakes his head, struggling to keep his eyes open. He has not been sleeping well on the couch.

They found another Senescent, at the hospital. He wanted shots.

But it's too late, the boy says. Their cells are corrupted.

Apparently the dumbfuck didn't know that. The police promised to treat him if he told them where the new camp is.

The boy's scalp tightens. What camp?

Where most of them ended up 'cause of the fire.

Did he tell them?

Conover Pass, the taper says, laughing. The info got online. I wouldn't be surprised if there's a mob on its way already.

The boy drives home after work, his eyes so heavy he can barely focus on the road. Conover Pass is not far from his house; he would have taken the man there, perhaps, if he'd known. It's been a month since the boy first saw him in the yard, devouring apples, so tall and mighty that he seemed invincible. Now the man can barely finish a piece of toast. The boy changes his bandages every night, without being asked, though secretly he's begun to dread it. The wound has stopped bleeding and is beginning to turn black and fungal. It smells horribly, like a dead possum. When the man needs a bath, the boy has to undress him, gripping his waist to help him into the tub. His arms are thinner than the boy's, angular as wings, and his penis floating in the bath looks shriveled and weedlike. The boy leaves the bathroom, embarrassed. It's amazing to think that this frail, bony creature ever filled him with awe.

Last night the man asked the boy to put his dead body under the ground. Don't let them take it away, he said.

Shhhh, the boy said, tucking a pillow under the man's head.

I don't want to end up in a museum or something.

You're not going to die, the boy said stupidly. He blushed, wondering why he felt compelled to lie. Perhaps this was what being a Senescent was like. You had to lie all the time, convincing yourself that you weren't going to disappear. He said it again, more vehemently, and saw a gleam of hope flicker in the man's eye.

Ahoy there, the man says now when he gets home.

Ahoy.

The smell is worse than usual. The man has soiled his sheets. The boy helps him from bed and lets him lean his weight on one shoulder and then walks him to the bathtub, where he cleans him off with a washcloth. The blackness has spread down to his foot; the leg looks like a rotting log. The boy has things to do—it's his turn to cook dinner, and there's a stack of bills that need to go out tomorrow—and now he has to run laundry on top of everything else. He grabs the man's wrists and tries to lift him out of the bathtub, but his arms are like dead things. The man won't flex them enough to be useful. The boy kneels and tries to get him out by his armpits, but the man slips from his hands and crashes back into the tub. He howls in pain, cursing the boy.

The boy leaves him in the tub and goes into the kitchen, where the girl is washing dishes from breakfast. The bills on the table have not been touched.

He'll be dead in a week, the girl says.

The boy doesn't respond.

I did some math this morning. We've got about three months, after you're furloughed.

The boy looks at her. The man has become a burden to him as well—she can see this in his face. She can see too that he loves this pathetic creature that came into their life to die, though she knows just as certainly that he'll be relieved once it happens. He might not admit it, but he will be.

I'll take care of us, the girl says tenderly.

How?

She looks down at the counter. Go distract him.

The boy does not ask why. The man will die, but he and the girl will be together forever. He goes back into the bathroom; the man has tried to get out of the tub and has fallen onto the floor. He is whimpering. The boy slides an arm around his waist and helps him back to bed. A lightning bug has gotten through the window, strobing very slowly around the room, but the man doesn't seem to notice.

What do you think about when you're old? the boy asks.

The man laughs. Home, I guess.

Do you mean the woods?

Childhood, he says, as if it were a place.

So you miss it, the boy says after a minute.

When you're a child, you can't wait to get out. Sometimes it's hell.

Through the wall, the boy hears his sister on the phone: the careful, well-dressed voice she uses with strangers. He feels sick.

At least there's heaven, he says, trying to console the man.

The man looks at him oddly, then frowns. Where I can be like you?

A tiny feather, small as a snowflake, clings to the man's eyelash. The boy does something strange. He wets his finger in the glass on the bedside table and traces a T on the man's forehead. He has no idea what this means; it's half-remembered trivia. The man tries to smile. He reaches up and yanks the air.

The man closes his eyes; it takes the boy a moment to realize he's fallen asleep. The flares of the lightning bug are brighter now. Some water trickles from the man's forehead and drips down his withered face. The boy tries to remember what it was like to see it for the first time—chewing on an apple, covered in ash—but the image has already faded to a blur, distant as a dream.

He listens for sirens. The screech of tires. Except for the chirring of crickets, the evening is silent.

The boy feels suddenly trapped, frightened, as if he can't breathe. He walks into the living room, but it doesn't help. The hallway too oppresses him. It's like being imprisoned in his own skin. His heart beats inside his neck, strong and steady. Beats and beats and beats. Through the skylight in the hall, he can see the first stars beginning to glimmer out of the dusk. They will go out eventually, shrinking into nothing. When he lifts the .22 from the closet, his hands—so small and tame and birdlike—feel unbearably captive.

He does not think about what he's doing, or whether there's

time or not to do it—only that he will give the man what he wants: bury his body in the ground, like a treasure.

He walks back into the bedroom with the gun. The man is sleeping quietly, his breathing dry and shallow. His robe sags open to reveal a pale triangle of chest, bony as a fossil. The boy tries to imagine what it would be like to be on earth for such a short time. Forty-six years. It would be like you never even lived. He can actually see the man's skin moving with his heart, fluttering up and down. The boy aims the gun at this mysterious failing thing.

He touches the trigger, dampening it with sweat, and fears that he can't bring himself to squeeze it. He cannot kill this doomed and sickly creature. Helplessly, he imagines the policeboys carrying the man away, imagines the look on the man's face as he realizes what the boy has done. His eyes hard with blame. But no: the man wouldn't know he had anything to do with it. He won't get in trouble.

The boy and girl will go back to their old lives again. No one to grumble at them or cook them dinners they don't want or make him want to cry.

The boy's relief gives way to a ghastly feeling in his chest, as if he's done something terrible.

Voices echo from the street outside. The boy rushes to the window and pulls back the curtains. A mob of boys and girls is yelling in the dusk, parading from the direction of Conover Pass, holding poles with human heads on top of them. The skewered heads bob through the air like puppets. *Off to bed without your supper!* one of the boys says in a gruff voice, something he's read in a book, and the others copy him— *Off to bed! Off to bed!*—pretending to be grownups. The heads gawk at each other from their poles. They look startled to the boy, still surprised by their betrayal. One turns in the boy's direction, haloed by flies, and for a moment its eyes seem to get even bigger, as though it's seen a monster. Then it spins away to face the others. Freed from their bodies, nimble as children, the heads dance down the street.

# Tenth of December

FROM *The New Yorker*

THE PALE BOY with unfortunate Prince Valiant bangs and cub-like mannerisms hulked to the mudroom closet and requisitioned Dad's white coat. Then requisitioned the boots he'd spray-painted white. Painting the pellet gun white had been a no. That was a gift from Aunt Chloe. Every time she came over he had to haul it out so she could make a big stink about the woodgrain.

Today's assignation: walk to pond, ascertain beaver dam. Likely he would be detained. By that species that lived among the old rock wall. They were small but, upon emerging, assumed certain proportions. And gave chase. This was just their methodology. His aplomb threw them loops. He knew that. And reveled it. He would turn, level the pellet gun, intone: Are you aware of the usage of this human implement?

*Blam!*

They were Netherworlders. Or Nethers. They had a strange bond with him. Sometimes for whole days he would just nurse their wounds. Occasionally, for a joke, he would shoot one in the butt as it fled. Who henceforth would limp for the rest of its days. Which could be as long as an additional nine million years.

Safe inside the rock wall, the shot one would go, Guys, look at my butt.

As a group, all would look at Gzeemon's butt, exchanging sullen glances of: Gzeemon shall indeed be limping for the next nine million years, poor bloke.

Because yes: Nethers tended to talk like that guy in *Mary Poppins*.

Which naturally raised some mysteries as to their origin here on Earth.

Detaining him was problematic for the Nethers. He was wily. Plus could not fit through their rock-wall opening. When they tied him up and went inside to brew their special miniaturizing potion — *Wham!*— he would snap their antiquated rope with a move from his self-invented martial-arts system, Toi Foi, AKA Deadly Forearms. And place at their doorway an implacable rock of suffocation, trapping them inside.

Later, imagining them in their death throes, taking pity on them, he would come back, move the rock.

Blimey, one of them might say from withal. Thanks, guv'nor. You are indeed a worthy adversary.

Sometimes there would be torture. They would make him lie on his back looking up at the racing clouds while they tortured him in ways he could actually take. They tended to leave his teeth alone. Which was lucky. He didn't even like to get a cleaning. They were dunderheads in that manner. They never messed with his peen and never messed with his fingernails. He'd just abide there, infuriating them with his snow angels. Sometimes, believing it their coup de grâce, not realizing he'd heard this since time in memorial from certain in-school cretins, they'd go, Wow, we didn't even know Robin could be a boy's name. And chortle their Nether laughs.

Today he had a feeling that the Nethers might kidnap Suzanne Bledsoe, the new girl in homeroom. She was from Montreal. He just loved the way she talked. So, apparently, did the Nethers, who planned to use her to repopulate their depleted numbers and bake various things they did not know how to bake.

All suited up now, NASA. Turning awkwardly to go out door.
*Affirmative. We have your coordinates. Be careful out there, Robin.*
Whoa, cold, dang.

Duck thermometer read ten. And that was without wind chill. That made it fun. That made it real. A green Nissan was parked where Poole dead-ended into the soccer field. Hopefully the owner was not some perv he would have to outwit.

Or a Nether in the human guise.

Bright, bright blue and cold. Crunch went the snow as he crossed the soccer field. Why did cold such as this give a running guy a headache? Likely it was due to Prominent Windspeed Velocity.

The path into the woods was as wide as one human. It seemed the Nether had indeed kidnapped Suzanne Bledsoe. Damn him! And his ilk. Judging by the single set of tracks, the Nether appeared to be carrying her. Foul cad. He'd better not be touching Suzanne inappropriately while carrying her. If so, Suzanne would no doubt be resisting with untamable fury.

This was concerning, this was very concerning.

When he caught up to them, he would say, Look, Suzanne, I know you don't know my name, having misaddressed me as Roger that time you asked me to scoot over, but nevertheless I must confess I feel there is something to us. Do you feel the same?

Suzanne had the most amazing brown eyes. They were wet now, with fear and sudden reality.

Stop talking to her, mate, the Nether said.

I won't, he said. And, Suzanne? Even if you don't feel there is something to us, rest assured I will still slay this fellow and return you home. Where do you live again? Over in El Cirro? By the water tower? Those are some nice houses back there.

Yes, Suzanne said. We also have a pool. You should come over next summer. It's cool if you swim with your shirt on. And also, yes to there being something to us. You are by far the most insightful boy in our class. Even when I take into consideration the boys I knew in Montreal, I am just like: no one can compare.

Well, that's nice to hear, he said. Thank you for saying that. I know I'm not the thinnest.

The thing about girls? Suzanne said. Is we are more content-driven.

Will you two stop already? the Nether said. Because now is the time for your death. Deaths.

Well, now is certainly the time for somebody's death, Robin said.

The twerpy thing was you never really got to save anyone. Last summer there'd been a dying raccoon out here. He'd thought of lugging it home so Mom could call the vet. But up close it was too scary. Raccoons being actually bigger than they appear in cartoons. And this one looked like a potential biter. So he ran home to get it some water at least. Upon his return, he saw where the raccoon had done some apparent last-minute thrashing. That was sad. He didn't do well with sad. There had perchance been some pre-weeping, by him, in the woods.

That just means you have a big heart, Suzanne said.

Well, I don't know, he said modestly.

Here was the old truck tire. Where the high school kids partied. Inside the tire, frosted with snow, were three beer cans and a wadded-up blanket.

You probably like to party, the Nether had cracked to Suzanne moments earlier as they passed this very spot.

No, I don't, Suzanne said. I like to play. And I like to hug.

Hoo boy, the Nether said. Sounds like Dullsville.

Somewhere there is a man who likes to play and hug, Suzanne said.

He came out of the woods now to the prettiest vista he knew. The pond was a pure frozen white. It struck him as somewhat Switzerlandish. Someday he would know for sure. When the Swiss threw him a parade or whatnot.

Here the Nether's tracks departed from the path, as if he had contemplatively taken a moment to gaze at the pond. Perhaps this Nether was not all bad. Perhaps he was having a debilitating conscience attack vis-à-vis the valiantly struggling Suzanne atop his back. At least he seemed to somewhat love nature.

Then the tracks returned to the path, wound around the pond, and headed up Lexow Hill.

What was this strange object? A coat? On the bench? The bench the Nethers used for their human sacrifices?

No accumulated snow on coat. Inside of coat still slightly warm.

Ergo: the recently discarded coat of the Nether.

This was some strange juju. This was an intriguing conundrum, if he had ever encountered one. Which he had. Once he'd found a bra on the handlebars of a bike. Once he'd found an entire untouched steak dinner on a plate behind Fresno's. And hadn't eaten it. Though it had looked pretty good.

Something was afoot.

Then he beheld, halfway up Lexow Hill, a man.

Coatless, bald-headed man. Super skinny. In what looked like pajamas. Climbing plodfully, with tortoise patience, bare white arms sticking out of his PJ shirt like two bare white branches sticking out of a PJ shirt. Or grave.

What kind of person leaves his coat behind on a day like this?

The mental kind, that was who. This guy looked sort of mental. Like an Auschwitz dude or sad confused grandpa.

Dad had once said, Trust your mind, Rob. If it smells like shit but has writing across it that says *Happy Birthday* and a candle stuck down in it, what is it?

Is there icing on it? he'd said.

Dad had done that thing of squinting his eyes when an answer was not quite there yet.

What was his mind telling him now?

Something was wrong here. A person needed a coat. Even if the person was a grownup. The pond was frozen. The duck thermometer said ten. If the person was mental, all the more reason to come to his aid, as had not Jesus said, Blessed are those who help those who cannot help themselves, but are too mental, doddering, or have a disability?

He snagged the coat off the bench.

It was a rescue. A real rescue, at last, sort of.

Ten minutes earlier, Don Eber had paused at the pond to catch his breath.

He was so tired. What a thing. Holy moly. When he used to walk Sasquatch out here they'd do six times around the pond, jog up the hill, tag the boulder on top, sprint back down.

*Better get moving,* said one of two guys who'd been in discussion in his head all morning.

*That is, if you're still set on the boulder idea,* the other said.

*Which still strikes us as kind of fancy-pants.*

Seemed like one guy was Dad and the other Kip Flemish.

Stupid cheaters. They'd switched spouses, abandoned the switched spouses, fled together to California. Had they been gay? Or just swingers? Gay swingers? The Dad and Kip in his head had acknowledged their sins and the three of them had struck a deal: he would forgive them for being possible gay swingers and leaving him to do Soap Box Derby alone, with just Mom, and they would consent to giving him some solid manly advice.

*He wants it to be nice.*

This was Dad now. It seemed Dad was somewhat on his side.

*Nice?* Kip said. *That is not the word I would use.*

A cardinal zinged across the day.

It was amazing. Amazing, really. He was young. He was fifty-

three. Now he'd never deliver his major national speech on compassion. What about going down the Mississippi in a canoe? What
about living in an A-frame near a shady creek with the two hippie
girls he'd met in 1968 in that souvenir shop in the Ozarks, when
Allen, his stepfather, wearing those crazy aviators, had bought him
a bag of fossil rocks? One of the hippie girls had said that he, Eber,
would be a fox when he grew up, and would he please be sure to
call her at that time? Then the hippie girls had put their tawny
heads together and giggled at his prospective foxiness. And that
had never—

That had somehow never—

Sister Val had said, Why not shoot for being the next J.F.K.?
So he had run for class president. Allen had bought him a Styrofoam straw boater. They'd sat together, decorating the hatband
with Magic Markers: *Win with Eber!* On the back: *Groovy!* Allen
had helped him record a tape. Of a little speech. Allen had taken
that tape somewhere and come back with thirty copies "to pass
around."

"Your message is good," Allen had said. "And you are incredibly
well spoken. You can do this thing."

And he'd done it. He'd won. Allen had thrown him a victory
party. A pizza party. All the kids had come.

Oh, Allen.

Kindest man ever. Had taken him swimming. Had taken him
to découpage. Had combed out his hair so patiently that time he
came home with lice. Never a harsh, etc., etc.

Not so once the suffering begat. Began. God damn it. More and
more his words. Askew. More and more his words were not what
he would hoped.

Hope.

Once the suffering began, Allen had raged. Said things no one
should say. To Mom, to Eber, to the guy delivering water. Went
from a shy man, always placing a reassuring hand on your back, to
a diminished pale figure in a bed, shouting CUNT!

Except with some weird New England accent, so it came out
KANT!

The first time Allen had shouted KANT! there followed a funny
moment during which he and Mom looked at each other to see
which of them was being called KANT. But then Allen amended,
for clarity: KANTS!

So it was clear he meant both of them. What a relief.

They'd cracked up.

Jeez, how long had he been standing here? Daylight was waiting. Wasting.

*I honestly didn't know what to do. But he made it so simple.*

*Took it all on himself.*

*So what else is new?*

*Exactly.*

This was Jodi and Tommy now.

Hi, kids.

Big day today.

*I mean, sure, it would have been nice to have a chance to say a proper goodbye.*

*But at what cost?*

*Exactly. And see—he knew that.*

*He was a father. That's what a father does.*

*Eases the burdens of those he loves.*

*Saves the ones he loves from painful last images that might endure for a lifetime.*

Soon Allen had become THAT. And no one was going to fault anybody for avoiding THAT. Sometimes he and Mom would huddle in the kitchen. Rather than risk incurring the wrath of THAT. Even THAT understood the deal. You'd trot in a glass of water, set it down, say, very politely, Anything else, Allen? And you'd see THAT thinking, All these years I was so good to you people and now I am merely THAT? Sometimes the gentle Allen would be inside there too, indicating, with his eyes, Look, go away, please go away, I am trying so hard not to call you KANT!

Rail-thin, ribs sticking out.

Catheter taped to dick.

Waft of shit smell.

*You are not Allen and Allen is not you.*

So Molly had said.

As for Dr. Spivey, he couldn't say. Wouldn't say. Was busy drawing a daisy on a Post-it. Then finally said, Well, honestly? As these things grow, they can tend to do weird things. But it doesn't necessarily have to be terrible. Had one guy? Just always craved him a Sprite.

And Eber had thought, Did you, dear doctor/savior/lifeline, just say *craved him a Sprite?*

That's how they got you. You thought, Maybe I'll just crave me a Sprite. Next thing you knew, you were THAT, shouting KANT!, shitting your bed, swatting at the people who were scrambling to clean you.

No, sir.

No sirree bob.

Wednesday he'd fallen out of the med-bed again. There on the floor in the dark it had come to him: I could spare them.

*Spare us? Or spare you?*

Get thee behind me.

Get thee behind me, sweetie.

A breeze sent down a sequence of linear snow puffs from somewhere above. Beautiful. Why were we made just so, to find so many things that happened every day pretty?

He took off his coat.

Good Christ.

Took off his hat and gloves, stuffed the hat and gloves in a sleeve of the coat, left the coat on the bench.

This way they'd know. They'd find the car, walk up the path, find the coat.

It was a miracle. That he'd gotten this far. Well, he'd always been strong. Once, he'd run a half-marathon with a broken foot. After his vasectomy he'd cleaned the garage, no problem.

He'd waited in the med-bed for Molly to go off to the pharmacy. That was the toughest part. Just calling out a normal goodbye.

His mind veered toward her now, and he jerked it back with a prayer: Let me pull this off. Lord, let me not fuck it up. Let me bring no dishonor. Leg me do it cling.

Let. Let me do it cling.

Clean.

Cleanly.

Estimated time of overtaking the Nether, handing him his coat? Approximately nine minutes. Six minutes to follow the path around the pond, an additional three minutes to fly up the hillside like a delivering wraith or mercy-angel, bearing the simple gift of a coat.

That is just an estimate, NASA. I pretty much made that up.

*We know that, Robin. We know very well by now how irreverent you work.*

*Like that time you cut a fart on the moon.*

*Or the time you tricked Mel into saying, "Mr. President, what a delight-ful surprise it was to find an asteroid circling Uranus."*

That estimate was particularly iffy. This Nether being surpris-ingly brisk. Robin himself was not the fastest wicket in the stick. He had a certain girth. Which Dad prognosticated would soon trium-phantly congeal into linebackerish solidity. He hoped so. For now he just had the slight man-boobs.

Robin, hurry, Suzanne said. I feel so sorry for that poor old guy.

He's a fool, Robin said, because Suzanne was young, and did not yet understand that when a man was a fool he made hardships for the other men, who were less foolish than he.

He doesn't have much time, Suzanne said, bordering on the hysterical.

There, there, he said, comforting her.

I'm just so frightened, she said.

And yet he is fortunate to have one such as I to hump his coat up that big-ass hill, which, due to its steepness, is not exactly my cup of tea, Robin said.

I guess that's the definition of *hero*, Suzanne said.

I guess so, he said.

I don't mean to continue being insolent, she said. But he seems to be pulling away.

What would you suggest? he said.

With all due respect, she said, and because I know you consider us as equals but different, with me covering the brainy angle and special inventions and whatnot?

Yes, yes, go ahead, he said.

Well, just working through the math in terms of simple geom-etry—

He saw where she was going with this. And she was quite right. No wonder he loved her. He must cut across the pond, thereby decreasing the ambient angle, ergo, trimming valuable seconds off his catchup time.

Wait, Suzanne said. Is that dangerous?

It is not, he said. I have done it numerous times.

Please be careful, Suzanne implored.

Well, once, he said.

You have such aplomb, Suzanne demurred.

Actually never, he said softly, not wishing to alarm her.

Your bravery is irascible, Suzanne said.

He started across the pond.

It was actually pretty cool walking on water. In summer, canoes floated here. If Mom could see him, she'd have a conniption. Mom treated him like a piece of glass. Due to his alleged infant surgeries. She went on full alert if he so much as used a stapler.

But Mom was a good egg. A reliable counselor and steady hand of guidance. She had a munificent splay of long silver hair and a raspy voice, though she didn't smoke and was even a vegan. She'd never been a biker chick, although some of the in-school cretins claimed she resembled one.

He was actually quite fond of Mom.

He was now approximately three-quarters, or that would be sixty percent, across.

Between him and the shore lay a grayish patch. Here in summer a stream ran in. Looked a tad iffy. At the edge of the grayish patch he gave the ice a bonk with the butt of his gun. Solid as anything.

Here he went. Ice rolled a bit underfoot. Probably it was shallow here. Anyways he hoped so. Yikes.

How's it going? Suzanne said, trepidly.

Could be better, he said.

Maybe you should turn back, Suzanne said.

But wasn't this feeling of fear the exact feeling all heroes had to confront early in life? Wasn't overcoming this feeling of fear what truly distinguished the brave?

There could be no turning back.

Or could there? Maybe there could. Actually there should.

The ice gave way and the boy fell through.

Nausea had not been mentioned in *The Humbling Steppe*.

*A blissful feeling overtook me as I drifted off to sleep at the base of the crevasse. No fear, no discomfort, only a vague sadness at the thought of all that remained undone. This is death? I thought. It is but nothing.*

Author, whose name I cannot remember, I would like a word with you.

A-hole.

The shivering was insane. Like a tremor. His head was shaking on his neck. He paused to puke a bit in the snow, white-yellow against the white-blue.

This was scary. This was scary now.

Every step was a victory. He had to remember that. With every step he was fleeing father and father. Farther from father. Stepfarther. What a victory he was wresting. From the jaws of the feet.

He felt a need at the back of his throat to say it right.

From the jaws of defeat. From the jaws of defeat.

Oh, Allen.

Even when you were THAT, you were still Allen to me.

Please know that.

*Falling,* Dad said.

For some definite time he waited to see where he would land and how much it would hurt. Then there was a tree in his gut. He found himself wrapped fetally around some tree.

Fucksake.

Ouch, ouch. This was too much. He hadn't cried after the surgeries or during the chemo, but he felt like crying now. It wasn't fair. It happened to everyone supposedly but now it was happening specifically to him. He'd kept waiting for some special dispensation. But no. Something/someone bigger than him kept refusing. You were told the big something/someone loved you especially but in the end you saw it was otherwise. The big something/someone was neutral. Unconcerned. When it innocently moved, it crushed people.

Years ago at The Illuminated Body he and Molly had seen this brain slice. Marring the brain slice had been a nickel-sized brown spot. That brown spot was all it had taken to kill the guy. Guy must have had his hopes and dreams, closet full of pants, and so on, some treasured childhood memories: a mob of koi in the willow shade at Gage Park, say, Gram searching in her Wrigley's-smelling purse for a tissue—like that. If not for that brown spot, the guy might have been one of the people walking by on the way to lunch in the atrium. But no. He was defunct now, off rotting somewhere, no brain in his head.

Looking down at the brain slice Eber had felt a sense of superiority. Poor guy. It was pretty unlucky, what had happened to him.

He and Molly had fled to the atrium, had hot scones, watched a squirrel mess with a plastic cup.

Wrapped fetally around the tree Eber traced the scar on his head. Tried to sit. No dice. Tried to use the tree to sit up. His hand wouldn't close. Reaching around the tree with both hands, joining his hands at the wrists, he sat himself up, leaned back against the tree.

How was that?

Fine.

Good, actually.

Maybe this was it. Maybe this was as far as he got. He'd had it in mind to sit cross-legged against the boulder at the top of the hill, but really what difference did it make?

All he had to do now was stay put. Stay put by force-thinking the same thoughts he'd used to propel himself out of the med-bed and into the car and across the soccer field and through the woods: MollyTommyJodi huddling in the kitchen filled with pity/loathing, MollyTommyJodi recoiling at something cruel he'd said, Tommy hefting his thin torso up in his arms so that MollyJodi could get under there with a wash—

Then it would be done. He would have preempted all future debasement. All his fears about the coming months would be mute.

Moot.

This was it. Was it? Not yet. Soon, though. An hour? Forty minutes? Was he doing this? Really? He was. Was he? Would he be able to make it back to the car even if he changed his mind? He thought not. Here he was. He was here. This incredible opportunity to end things with dignity was right in his hands.

All he had to do was stay put.

*I will fight no more forever.*

Concentrate on the beauty of the pond, the beauty of the woods, the beauty you are returning to, the beauty that is everywhere as far as you can—

Oh, for shitsake.

Oh, for crying out loud.

Some kid was on the pond.

Chubby kid in white. With a gun. Carrying Eber's coat.

You little fart, put that coat down, get your ass home, mind your own—

Damn. Damn it.

Kid tapped the ice with the butt of his gun.

You wouldn't want some kid finding you. That could scar a kid. Although kids found freaky things all the time. Once he'd found a naked photo of Dad and Mrs. Flemish. That had been freaky. Of course, not as freaky as a grimacing cross-legged—

Kid was swimming.

Swimming was not allowed. That was clearly posted. *No Swimming.*

Kid was a bad swimmer. Real thrashfest down there. Kid was creating with his thrashing a rapidly expanding black pool. With each thrash the kid incrementally expanded the boundary of the black—

He was on his way down before he knew he'd started. *Kid in the pond, kid in the pond,* ran repetitively through his head as he minced. Progress was tree-to-tree. Standing there panting, you got to know a tree well. This one had three knots: eye, eye, nose. This started out as one tree and became two.

Suddenly he was not purely the dying guy who woke nights in the med-bed thinking, Make this not true make this not true, but again, partly, the guy who used to put bananas in the freezer, then crack them on the counter and pour chocolate over the broken chunks, the guy who'd once stood outside a classroom window in a rainstorm to see how Jodi was faring with that little red-headed shit who wouldn't give her a chance at the book table, the guy who used to hand-paint bird feeders in college and sell them on weekends in Boulder, wearing a jester hat and doing a little juggling routine he'd—

He started to fall again, caught himself, froze in a hunched-over position, hurtled forward, fell flat on his face, chucked his chin on a root.

You had to laugh.

You almost had to laugh.

He got up. Got doggedly up. His right hand presented as a bloody glove. Tough nuts, too bad. Once, in football, a tooth had come out. Later in the half, Eddie Blandik had found it. He'd taken it from Eddie, flung it away. That had also been him.

Here was the switchbank. It wasn't far now. Switchback.

What to do? When he got there? Get kid out of pond. Get kid moving. Force-walk kid through woods, across soccer field, to one of the houses on Poole. If nobody home, pile kid into Nissan, crank up heater, drive to—Our Lady of Sorrows? UrgentCare? Fastest route to UrgentCare?

Fifty yards to the trailhead.

Twenty yards to the trailhead.

Thank you, God, for my strength.

In the pond, he was all animal-thought, no words, no self, blind panic. He resolved to really try. He grabbed for the edge. The edge broke away. Down he went. He hit mud and pushed up. He grabbed for the edge. The edge broke away. Down he went. It seemed like it should be easy, getting out. But he just couldn't do it. It was like at the carnival. It should be easy to knock three saw-dust dogs off a ledge. And it was easy. It just wasn't easy with the number of balls they gave you.

He wanted the shore. He knew that was the right place for him. But the pond kept saying no.

Then it said maybe.

The ice edge broke again, but, breaking it, he pulled himself infinitesimally toward shore, so that, when he went down, his feet found mud sooner. The bank was sloped. Suddenly there was hope. He went nuts. He went total spaz. Then he was out, water streaming off him, a piece of ice like a tiny pane of glass in the cuff of his coat sleeve.

Trapezoidal, he thought.

In his mind, the pond was not finite, circular, and behind him but infinite and all around.

He felt he'd better lie still or whatever had just tried to kill him would try again. What had tried to kill him was not just in the pond but out here too, in every natural thing, and there was no him, no Suzanne, no Mom, no nothing, just the sound of some kid crying like a terrified baby.

Eber jog-hobbled out of the woods and found: no kid. Just black water. And a green coat. His coat. His former coat, out there on the ice. The water was calming already.

Oh, shit.

*Your fault.*

*Kid was only out there because of—*

Down on the beach near an overturned boat was some ignora-mus. Lying face-down. On the job. Lying down on the job. Must have been lying there even as that poor kid—

Wait, rewind.

It was the kid. Oh, thank Christ. Face-down like a corpse in a

Brady photo. Legs still in the pond. Like he'd lost steam crawling out. Kid was soaked through, the white coat gone gray with wet.

Eber dragged the kid out. It took four distinct pulls. He didn't have the strength to flip him over but, turning the head, at least got the mouth out of the snow.

Kid was in trouble.

Soaking wet, ten degrees.

Doom.

Eber went down on one knee and told the kid in a grave fatherly way that he had to get up, had to get moving or he could lose his legs, he could die.

The kid looked at Eber, blinked, stayed where he was.

He grabbed the kid by the coat, rolled him over, roughly sat him up. The kid's shivers made his shivers look like nothing. Kid seemed to be holding a jackhammer. He had to get the kid warmed up. How to do it? Hug him, lie on top of him? That would be like Popsicle-on-Popsicle.

Eber remembered his coat, out on the ice, at the edge of the black water.

Ugh.

Find a branch. No branches anywhere. Where the heck was a good fallen branch when you—

All right, all right, he'd do it without a branch.

He walked fifty feet downshore, stepped onto the pond, walked a wide loop on the solid stuff, turned to shore, started toward the black water. His knees were shaking. Why? He was afraid he might fall in. Ha. Dope. Poser. The coat was fifteen feet away. His legs were in revolt. His legs were revolting.

*Doctor, my legs are revolting.*

*You're telling me.*

He tiny-stepped up. The coat was ten feet away. He went down on his knees, knee-walked slightly up. Went down on his belly. Stretched out an arm.

Slid forward on his belly.

Bit more.

Bit more.

Then had a tiny corner by two fingers. He hauled it in, slid himself back via something like a reverse breaststroke, got to his knees, stood, retreated a few steps, and was once again fifteen feet away and safe.

Then it was like the old days, getting Tommy or Jodi ready for bed when they were zonked. You said, "Arm," the kid lifted an arm. You said, "Other arm," the kid lifted the other arm. With the coat off, Eber could see that the boy's shirt was turning to ice. Eber peeled the shirt off. Poor little guy. A person was just some meat on a frame. Little guy wouldn't last long in this cold. Eber took off his pajama shirt, put it on the kid, slid the kid's arm into the arm of the coat. In the arm were Eber's hat and gloves. He put the hat and gloves on the kid, zipped the coat up.

The kid's pants were frozen solid. His boots were ice sculptures of boots.

You had to do things right. Eber sat on the boat, took off his boots and socks, peeled off his pajama pants, made the kid sit on the boat, knelt before the kid, got the kid's boots off. He loosened the pants up with little punches and soon had one leg partly out. He was stripping off a kid in ten-degree weather. Maybe this was exactly the wrong thing. Maybe he'd kill the kid. He didn't know. He just didn't know. Desperately, he gave the pants a few more punches. Then the kid was stepping out.

Eber put the pajama pants on him, then the socks, then the boots.

The kid was standing there in Eber's clothes, swaying, eyes closed.

We're going to walk now, okay? Eber said.

Nothing.

Eber gave the kid an encouraging pop in the shoulders. Like a football thing.

We're going to walk you home, he said. Do you live near here?

Nothing.

He gave a harder pop.

The kid gaped at him, baffled.

Pop.

Kid started walking.

Pop-pop.

Like fleeing.

Eber drove the kid out ahead of him. Like cowboy and cow. At first, fear of the popping seemed to be motivating the kid, but then good old panic kicked in and he started running. Soon Eber couldn't keep up.

Kid was at the bench. Kid was at the trailhead.

Good boy, get home.

Kid disappeared into the woods.

Eber came back to himself.

Oh, boy. Oh, wow.

He had never known cold. Had never known tired.

He was standing in the snow in his underwear near an over-turned boat.

He hobbled to the boat and sat in the snow.

Robin ran.

Past the bench and the trailhead and into the woods on the old familiar path.

What the heck? What the heck had just happened? He'd fallen into the pond? His jeans had frozen solid? Had ceased being blue-jeans. Were whitejeans. He looked down to see if his jeans were still whitejeans.

He had on pajama pants that, tucked into some tremendoid boots, looked like clown pants.

Had he been crying just now?

I think crying is healthy, Suzanne said. It means you're in touch with your feelings.

Ugh. That was done, that was stupid, talking in your head to some girl who in real life called you Roger.

Dang.

So tired.

Here was a stump.

He sat. It felt good to rest. He wasn't going to lose his legs. They didn't even hurt. He couldn't even feel them. He wasn't going to die. Dying was not something he had in mind at this early an age. To rest more efficiently, he lay down. The sky was blue. The pines swayed. Not all at the same rate. He raised one gloved hand and watched it tremor.

He might close his eyes for a bit. Sometimes in life one felt a feeling of wanting to quit. Then everyone would see. Everyone would see that teasing wasn't nice. Sometimes with all the teasing his days were subtenable. Sometimes he felt he couldn't take even one more lunchtime of meekly eating on that rolled-up wrestling mat in the cafeteria corner near the snapped parallel bars. He did not have to sit there. But preferred to. If he sat anywhere else, there was the chance of a comment or two. Upon which he would then have the rest of the day to reflect. Sometimes comments were made on the clutter of his home. Thanks to Bryce, who had once come over. Sometimes comments were made on his manner of speaking. Sometimes comments were made on the style faux pas of Mom. Who was, it must be said, a real eighties gal.

Mom.

He did not like it when they teased about Mom. Mom had no idea of his lowly school status. Mom seeing him more as the paragon or golden-boy type.

Once, he'd done a secret rendezvous of recording Mom's phone calls, just for the reconnaissance aspect. Mostly they were dull, mundane, not about him at all.

Except for this one with her friend Liz.

I never dreamed I could love someone so much, Mom had said. I just worry I might not be able to live up to him, you know? He's so *good,* so *grateful.* That kid deserves—that kid deserves it all. Better school, which we cannot afford, some trips, like abroad, but that is also, uh, out of our price range. I just don't want to *fail* him, you know? That's all I want from my life, you know? Liz? To feel, at the end, like I did right by that magnificent little dude.

At that point it seemed like Liz had maybe started vacuuming.

Magnificent little dude.

He should probably get going.

Magnificent Little Dude was like his Indian name.

He got to his feet and, gathering his massive amount of clothes up like some sort of encumbering royal train, started toward home.

Here was the truck tire, here the place where the trail briefly widened, here the place where the trees crossed overhead like reaching for one another. Weave-ceiling, Mom called it.

Here was the soccer field. Across the field, his house sat like a big sweet animal. It was amazing. He'd made it. He'd fallen into the pond and lived to tell the tale. He had somewhat cried, yes, but had then simply laughed off this moment of mortal weakness and made his way home, look of wry bemusement on his face, having, it must be acknowledged, benefited from the much appreciated assistance of a certain aged—

With a shock he remembered the old guy. What the heck? An image flashed of the old guy standing bereft and blue-skinned in his tighty-whities like a POW abandoned at the barbed wire due to

no room on the truck. Or a sad traumatized stork bidding farewell
to its young.

He'd bolted. He'd bolted on the old guy. Hadn't even given
him a thought.

Blimey.

What a chickenshittish thing to do.

He had to go back. Right now. Help the old guy hobble out. But
he was so tired. He wasn't sure he could do it. Probably the old guy
was fine. Probably he had some sort of old-guy plan.

But he'd bolted. He couldn't live with that. His mind was telling
him that the only way to undo the bolting was to go back now, save
the day. His body was saying something else: it's too far, you're just
a kid, get Mom, Mom will know what to do.

He stood paralyzed at the edge of the soccer field like a scare-
crow in huge flowing clothes.

Eber sat slumped against the boat.

What a change in the weather. People were going around with
parasols and so forth in the open part of the park. There was a
merry-go-round and a band and a gazebo. People were frying food
on the backs of certain merry-go-round horses. And yet, on others,
kids were riding. How did they know? Which horses were hot? For
now there was still snow, but snow couldn't last long in this bomb.

Balm.

*If you close your eyes, that's the end. You know that, right?*

Hilarious.

Allen.

His exact voice. After all these years.

Where was he? The duck pond. So many times he'd come out
here with the kids. He should go now. Goodbye, duck pond. Although hang on. He couldn't seem to stand. Plus you couldn't
leave a couple of little kids behind. Not this close to water. They
were four and six. For God's sake. What had he been thinking?
Leaving those two little dears by the pond. They were good kids,
they'd wait, but wouldn't they get bored? And swim? Without life
jackets? No, no, no. It made him sick. He had to stay. Poor kids.
Poor abandoned—

Wait, rewind.

His kids were excellent swimmers.

His kids had never come close to being abandoned.

His kids were grown.

Tom was thirty. Tall drink of water. Tried so hard to know things. But even when he thought he knew a thing (fighting kites, breeding rabbits), Tom would soon be shown for what he was: the dearest, most agreeable young man ever, who knew no more about fighting kites/breeding rabbits than the average person could pick up from ten minutes on the Internet. Not that Tom wasn't smart. Tom was smart. Tom was a damn quick study. Oh, Tom, Tommy, Tommikins! The heart in that kid! He just worked and worked. For the love of his dad. Oh, kid, you had it, you have it, Tom, Tommy, even now I am thinking of you, you are very much on my mind.

And Jodi, Jodi was out there in Santa Fe. She'd said she'd take off work and fly home. As needed. But there was no need. He didn't like to impose. The kids had their own lives. Jodi-Jode. Little freckle-face. Pregnant now. Not married. Not even dating. Stupid Lars. What kind of man deserted a beautiful girl like that? A total dear. Just starting to make some progress in her job. You couldn't take that kind of time off when you'd only just started—

Reconstructing the kids in this way was having the effect of making them real to him again. Which—you didn't want to get that ball roiling. Jodi was having a baby. Rolling. He could have lasted long enough to see the baby. Hold the baby. It was sad, yes. That was a sacrifice he'd had to make. He'd explained it in the note. Hadn't he? No. Hadn't left a note. Couldn't. There'd been some reason he couldn't. Hadn't there? He was pretty sure there'd been some—

Insurance. It couldn't seem like he'd done it on purpose.

Little panic.

Little panic here.

He was offing himself. Offing himself, he'd involved a kid. Who was wandering the woods hypothermic. Offing himself two weeks before Christmas. Molly's favorite holiday. Molly had a valve thing, a panic thing, this business might—

This was not—this was not him. This was not something he would have done. Not something he would ever do. Except he —he'd done it. He was doing it. It was in progress. If he didn't get moving, it would—it would be accomplished. It would be done.

*This very day you will be with me in the kingdom of—*

He had to fight.

But couldn't seem to keep his eyes open.

He tried to send some last thoughts to Molly. Sweetie, forgive me. Biggest fuckup ever. Forget this part. Forget I ended this thisly. You know me. You know I didn't mean this.

He was at his house. He wasn't at his house. He knew that. But could see every detail. Here was the empty med-bed, the studio portrait of HimMollyTommyJodi posed around that fake rodeo fence. Here was the little bedside table. His meds in the pillbox. The bell he rang to call Molly. What a thing. What a cruel thing. Suddenly he saw clearly how cruel it was. And selfish. Oh, God. Who was he? The front door swung open. Molly called his name. He'd hide in the sunroom. Jump out, surprise her. Somehow they'd remodeled. Their sunroom was now the sunroom of Mrs. Kendall, his childhood piano teacher. That would be fun for the kids, to take piano lessons in the same room where he'd—

Hello? Mrs. Kendall said.

What she meant was: Don't die yet. There are many of us who wish to judge you harshly in the sunroom.

Hello, hello! she shouted.

Coming around the pond was a silver-haired woman.

All he had to do was call out.

He called out.

To keep him alive she started piling on him various things from life, things smelling of a home—coats, sweaters, a rain of flowers, a hat, socks, sneakers—and with amazing strength had him on his feet and was maneuvering him into a maze of trees, a wonderland of trees, trees hung with ice. He was piled high with clothes. He was like the bed at a party on which they pile the coats. She had all the answers: where to step, when to rest. She was strong as a bull. He was on her hip now like a baby; she had both arms around his waist, lifting him over a root.

They walked for hours, seemed like. She sang. Cajoled. She hissed at him, reminding him, with pokes in the forehead (right in his forehead), that her freaking *kid* was at *home*, near-*frozen*, so they had to *book* it.

Good God, there was so much to do. If he made it. He'd make it. This gal wouldn't let him not make it. He'd have to try to get Molly to see—see why he'd done it. *I was scared, I was scared, Mol.* Maybe Molly would agree not to tell Tommy and Jodi. He didn't like the thought of them knowing he'd been scared. Didn't like the thought of them knowing what a fool he'd been. Oh, to hell with that! Tell everyone! He'd done it! He'd been driven to do it and he'd done it and that was it. That was him. That was part of who he was. No more lies, no more silence, it was going to be a new and different life, if only he—

They were crossing the soccer field.

Here was the Nissan.

His first thought was: Get in, drive it home.

Oh, no, you don't, she said with that smoky laugh and guided him into a house. A house on the park. He'd seen it a million times. And now was in it. It smelled of man-sweat and spaghetti sauce and old books. Like a library where sweaty men went to cook spaghetti. She sat him in front of a woodstove, brought him a brown blanket that smelled of medicine. Didn't talk but in directives: Drink this, let me take that, wrap up, what's your name, what's your number?

What a thing! To go from dying in your underwear in the snow to this! Warmth, colors, antlers on the walls, an old-time crank phone like you saw in silent movies. It was something. Every second was something. He hadn't died in his shorts by a pond in the snow. The kid wasn't dead. He'd killed no one. Ha! Somehow he'd got it all back. Everything was good now, everything was—

The woman reached down, touched his scar.

Oh, wow, ouch, she said. You didn't do that out there, did you?

At this he remembered that the brown spot was as much in his head as ever.

Oh, Lord, there was still all that to go through.

Did he still want it? Did he still want to live?

Yes, yes, oh, God, yes, please.

Because, okay, the thing was—he saw it now, was starting to see it—if some guy, at the end, fell apart, and said or did bad things, or had to be helped, helped to quite a considerable extent? So what? What of it? Why should he not do or say weird things or look strange or disgusting? Why should the shit not run down his legs? Why should those he loved not lift and bend and feed and wipe him, when he would gladly do the same for them? He'd been afraid to be lessened by the lifting and bending and feeding and wiping, and was still afraid of that, and yet, at the same time, now saw that there could still be many—many drops of goodness, is how it came to him—many drops of happy—of good fellowship

—ahead, and those drops of fellowship were not—had never been
—his to withheld.

Withhold.

The kid came out of the kitchen, lost in Eber's big coat, pajama
pants pooling around his feet with the boots now off. He took
Eber's bloody hand gently. Said he was sorry. Sorry for being such
a dope in the woods. Sorry for running off. He'd just been out of
it. Kind of scared and all.

Listen, Eber said hoarsely. You did amazing. You did perfect.
I'm here. Who did that?

There. That was something you could do. The kid maybe felt
better now? He'd given the kid that? That was a reason. To stay
around. Wasn't it? Can't console anyone if not around? Can't do
squat if gone?

When Allen was close to the end, Eber had done a presenta-
tion at school on the manatee. Got an A from Sister Eustace. Who
could be quite tough. She was missing two fingers on her right
hand from a lawn-mower incident and sometimes used that hand
to scare a kid silent.

He hadn't thought of this in years.

She'd put that hand on his shoulder not to scare him but as a
form of praise. *That was just terrific. Everyone should take their work
as seriously as Donald here. Donald, I hope you'll go home and share this
with your parents.* He'd gone home and shared it with Mom. Who
suggested he share it with Allen. Who, on that day, had been more
Allen than THAT. And Allen—

Ha, wow, Allen. There was a man.

Tears sprang into his eyes as he sat by the woodstove.

Allen had—Allen had said it was great. Asked a few questions.
About the manatee. What did they eat again? Did he think they
could effectively communicate with one another? What a trial that
must have been! In his condition. Forty minutes on the manatee? Including a poem Eber had composed? A sonnet? On the
manatee?

He'd felt so happy to have Allen back.

I'll be like him, he thought. I'll try to be like him.

The voice in his head was shaky, hollow, unconvinced.

Then: sirens.

Somehow: Molly.

He heard her in the entryway. Mol, Molly, oh, boy. When they were first married they used to fight. Say the most insane things. Afterward, sometimes there would be tears. Tears in bed? Somewhere. And then they would—Molly pressing her hot wet face against his hot wet face. They were sorry, they were saying with their bodies, they were accepting each other back, and that feeling, that feeling of being accepted back again and again, of someone's affection for you always expanding to encompass whatever new flawed thing had just manifested in you, that was the deepest, dearest thing he'd ever—

She came in flustered and apologetic, a touch of anger in her face. He'd embarrassed her. He saw that. He'd embarrassed her by doing something that showed she hadn't sufficiently noticed him needing her. She'd been too busy nursing him to notice how scared he was. She was angry at him for pulling this stunt and ashamed of herself for feeling angry at him in his hour of need, and was trying to put the shame and anger behind her now so she could do what might be needed.

All of this was in her face. He knew her so well.

Also concern.

Overriding everything else in that lovely face was concern.

She came to him now, stumbling a bit on a swell in the floor of this stranger's house.

TAIYE SELASI

# The Sex Lives of
# African Girls
FROM *Granta*

BEGIN, INEVITABLY, WITH Uncle.

There you are, eleven, alone in the study in the dark in a cool
pool of moonlight at the window. The party is in full swing on
the back lawn outside. Half of Accra must be out there. In production. Some fifty-odd tables dressed in white linen table skirts,
the walls at the periphery all covered in lights, the swimming pool
glittering with tea lights in bowls bobbing lightly on the surface
of the water, glowing green. The smells of things—night-damp
earth, open grill, frangipani trees, citronella—seep in through the
window, slightly cracked. You tap the glass lightly and wave your
hand, testing, but no one looks up. They can't see for the dark. It
rained around four for five minutes and not longer; now the sky
is rich black for its cleansing. Beneath it a *soukous* band shows off
the latest from Congo, the lead singer wailing in French and Lin-
gala.

She ought to be ridiculous: little leopard-print shorts, platform
heels, hot-pink half-top, two half-arms of bangles. Instead, wet with
sweat and moon, trembling, ascendant, all movement and muscle, she is fearsome. It is a heart-wrenching voice, cutting straight
through the din of the chatter, forced laughter, clinked glasses, the
crickets. She is shaking her shoulders, hips, braided extensions.
She has the most genuine intentions of any woman out there.

And they.

Their bright *bubas* adorn the large garden like odd brilliant bulbs that bloom only at night. From the dark of the study you watch with the interest of a scientist observing a species. A small one. Rich African women, like Japanese geisha in wax-batik *geles*, their skin bleached too light. They are strange to you, strange to the landscape, the dark, with the same polished skill-set of rich women worldwide: how to smile with full lips while the eyes remain empty; how to hate with indifference; how to love without heat. You wonder if they find themselves beautiful, or powerful? Or perplexing, as they seem to you, watching from here?

The young ones sit mutely, sipping foam off their Maltas, waiting to be asked to go dance by the men in full suits, shoving cake into their mouths when they're sure no one's looking (it rained around four; no one sees for the dark). The bolder ones preening, little Aunties-in-training, being paraded around the garden, introduced to parents' friends. "This is Abena, our eldest, just went up to Oxford." "This is Maame, the lawyer. She trained in the States." Then the push from the mother, the tentative handshake. "It's a pleasure to meet you, sir. How *is* your son?" You wonder if they enjoy it. You can't tell by watching. They all wear the same one impenetrable expression: eyebrows up, lips pushed out, nostrils slightly flared in poor imitation of the 1990s supermodel. It is a difficult expression to pull off successfully, the long-suffering look of women bored with being looked at. The girls in the garden look more startled than self-satisfied, as if their features are shocked to be forming this face.

But their dresses.

What dresses. They belong on the cake trays: as bright, sweet, and frothy as frosted desserts, the lacy "up-and-downs" with sequins, tiny mirrors, and bell sleeves, the rage in Accra this Christmas. It's the related complications—tying the *gele*, the headwrap; wrapping then trying to walk in the ankle-length skirt; the troubling fact that you haven't got hips yet to showcase—that puts you off them.

You can barely manage movement in the big one-piece *buba* you borrowed from Comfort, your cousin, under duress. The off-the-shoulder neckline keeps slipping to your elbow, exposing your (troublingly) flat chest. Absent breasts, the hem drags and gets caught underfoot, a malfunction exacerbated by your footwear, also Comfort's: gold leather stilettos two sizes too small, with a thick crust of sequins and straps of no use. You've been tripping and falling around the garden all evening, with night-damp earth sucking at the heels of the shoes, the excess folds of the *buba* sort of draped around your body, making you look like a black Statue of Liberty. Except: the Statue of Liberty wears those comfortable sandals and doesn't get sent to go fetch this and that—which is how you've now found yourself alone in the study, having stumbled across the garden, being noticed as you went: little pretty thing, solitary, making haste for the house with the shuffle-shuffle steps of skinny girls in women's shoes; and why you tripped as you entered, snagging the hem with your heel, the cloth yanked from your chest as you fell to the rug.

And lay. The dry quiet a sharp sudden contrast to the wet of the heat and the racket outside. And as sharply and as suddenly, the consciousness of *nakedness.* Eve, after apple.

Your bare breastless chest.

How strange to feel naked in a room not your own, and not stepping from the bath into the humidity's embrace, but here *cold* and half naked in the leather-scented darkness, remembering the morning, the rain around four. This was moments ago (nakedness) as you lay, having fallen, the conditioned air chilly and silky against your chest. Against your nipples. Two points you'd never noticed before but considered very deeply now: nipples. And yours. The outermost boundaries of a body, the endpoints, where the land of warm skin meets the sea of cold air. Shore. You lay on your back in the dark on the floor, like that, newly aware of your nipples.

Presently, the heart-wrenching voice floating up from the garden, *"Je t'aime, mon amour. Je t'attends."* You sat up. You listened for a moment, as if to a message, then kicked off the sandals and stood to your feet. You went to the window and looked at the singer, in flight on the stage, to the high note. *"Je t'attends!"*

Indeed.

So it is that you're here at the window when, five minutes later, he enters the room, his reflection appearing dimly on the window before you, not closing the door in the silvery dark. You think of the houseboys with their lawn chairs in an oval, reading *Othello* in thick accents, Uncle watching with pride. *Demand me nothing: what you know, you know. From this time forth I never will speak word.* (Likely not. With the thing come together, the pattern emerging, the lines, circles, secrets, lies, hurts, back to this, here, the study, where else, given the fabric, the pattern, the stars. What to say?)

Enter Uncle.


## II


From the start.

The day began typically: with the bulbul in the garden, with the sound of Auntie shouting about this or about that, with your little blue bedroom catching fire with sunlight and you waking up from the dream. In it, your mother is bidding you farewell at the airport. This first part is exactly what happened that day. You are eight years old, skinny, in the blue gingham dress with a red satin bow in your braids and brown shoes. Uncle is in the terminal, presumably buying your tickets. You are waiting with your mother on the sidewalk outside. She is crouching beside you with her hand on your shoulder, a wild throng of people jostling around and against you. Her fingernails are painted a hot crimson red. You are noticing this.

Blood on your shoulder.

Meanwhile, a stranger with a camera is trying to take a picture. She doesn't know your first name so keeps calling out, "Child!" You've never once thought of yourself as this—"child"—neither *a* child nor someone's; you've always simply been *you*. A smallish human being by the side of a larger one, both with neat braids with small beads at the ends; both slim (well, one skinny) with dark knobby kneecaps; one never without lipstick, the other never allowed. In the dream, as it happened, you ignore the photographer. "Child!" she calls louder. A dark, smoker's voice. Finally you look up in the hope of some silence.

"Smile!" She, unsmiling.

You consider, but frown.

Your mother pulls you close to her, so close you can taste her, the scent of her lotion delicious, a lie. It's a sensory betrayal, the taste of this lotion, the smell on your taste buds not roses at all. A chalky taste, heavy and soapy as wax. You suck it in greedily. Swallowing it.

Her braids are tied back with an indigo scarf, the tail of which billows up, covering her face. The scarf is tied tightly, pulling her skin toward her temples, making her cheekbones jut out like a carved Oyo mask. The red on her lips contrasts with the indigo perfectly, as the man who bought the scarf would have no doubt foreseen. Not for the first time you think that your mother is the most beautiful woman in Lagos . . . well . . . quite likely in the world, but you've never left Lagos and it hasn't begun to dawn on you that you will. That Uncle is in the terminal buying only two tickets, that she's not coming with you, that she hasn't said why. You don't think to ask. At this moment, here beside you, your mother is unquestionable. You simply don't ask. In the dream, as it happened, she kisses you quickly, her lips to your ear, and says, "Do as you're told." The stranger presses a button and the flash goes off—POP!—and your mother turns—POOF!—into air.

In the liminal space between dreaming and waking (into which enters shouting, about this or about that) you started to scream but the feel of the sound taking form in your throat woke you fully.

You wet the bed.

Now the terror passed over, with the cold in your fingers, the echo of POP! and your heart pounding, hard. To almost precisely the same beat someone leaned on a horn—HONK, HONK, HONK —at the front gates outside. You fumbled for the photo you keep under your pillow as an antidote of sorts to the dream (or the waking): the sepia shot of your mother and you, with her crouched so you're both the same height, cheek to cheek. The wildness of Lagos is an odd, knee-high backdrop: passing cars, people's legs, soldiers' boots, cripples, trash. But when you look at it now, you see only your mother. The scarf blowing forward and hiding her face. She is sending you to live with your uncle "for a while." No one has heard from her since.

Still.

You wouldn't say your mother "abandoned" you exactly; it was Uncle's idea that you come. It was the least he could do, the elder brother, her only sibling, after all that she'd been through, abandoned, pregnant, and the rest. You've heard the Sad Story in pieces and whispers, from visitors from the village, whence the rumors began: that your mother got married and is living in Abuja with no thanks to Uncle and no thought of you. Not for a minute do you believe what they say. They are villagers, cruel like your grandmother.

As told to you:

Dzifa (missing mother) was born eight years after Uncle in Lolito, a village on the Volta. Their father, a fisherman, was drowned in the river the day after Dzifa was born. Their mother, your grandmother, for obvious reasons decided her daughter was cursed. Uncle, unconvinced, worshiped and adored his little sister and the two were inseparable growing up. Dzifa was beautiful, preternaturally so, shining star of the little Lolito schoolhouse. But your grandmother, believer in boys-only education and a product of the same, withdrew her daughter from school. Your mother, infuriated, ran away from Lolito and hitchhiked her way to Nigeria. In the same years Uncle won the scholarship to study in Detroit and left Ghana, himself, for a time. Dzifa found her way to, and met your father in, Lagos (a privilege—meeting your father—that you've never had). An alto saxophonist in an Afro-funk band, he left when he learned she was pregnant.

Enter you.

The brother/sister reunion came some seven years later when business brought Uncle to Lagos. You were living at the time in a thirteenth-floor hotel room, free of charge, care of the hotel proprietor. His name was Sinclair. At least that's what they called him. This may have been his surname; you were never really sure. He was ginger-haired, Scottish, born in Glasgow, raised in Jos, son of tin miners-cum-missionaries, tall and loud, freckled, fat. On the nights that he visited, at midnight or later, he'd hand you a mango, smiling stiffly. "Go and play."

It was always a mango, with perfect gold skin, which he'd pass palm to palm before tossing it to you. He was stingy with his mangoes, barking at the kitchen staff in the morning to use more orange slices and pineapple cubes in the breakfast buffet. His face blazed an unnatural pink when he shouted, like the color of his hair or his skin after visits. (You were shocked when you moved here to find mangoes more perfect growing freely on the tree in the garden.) You'd go to the pool, glowing green in the darkness. The sounds of the highway, of Lagos at night. There were no guests or hotel staff at the pool after midnight. No sweating waiters in suits with mixed drinks on silver trays. No thin women in swimsuits, their skin seared to crimson, their offspring peeing greenly in the water. Only you. Still now there is something about those nights that you miss; maybe the promise of your mother in the morning? Hard to say.

On the night Uncle found her, she was circling the lounge like the liquor fairy, topping up vodka and Scotch. You were behind the bar reading *Beezus and Ramona,* recently abandoned by some American. *Ex libris: Michelle.* It was a Friday, you remember: Fela blasting, men shouting, the lounge packed, Sinclair smiling, counting cash, your mother's laugh. Then abruptly, glass smashing, a comparative silence, the extraction of human voice from the ongoing din. The resumption of talking. You looked. There was Uncle. She was staring at him, mouth agape, shards at her feet. *"You,"* he was saying softly, then hugging her tightly. Over and over and over. "Dzifa. *You.*" You'd never seen him before that night. You wondered how he knew her name. Sinclair wondered too and rushed over now, shouting, "DON'T TOUCH HER!" while you watched, considering Uncle.

Your mother said nothing. After a moment she smiled. Too bright to be real. Too beautiful to be fake. After the hugging and weeping and telling it all, Uncle insisted she return to Ghana. She refused. A compromise. Uncle would take "the child" to Accra and when your mother was ready she would join you. You packed. Uncle and a woman, a fair-skinned Nigerian, the photographer, drove you to the airport. You'd never been. The woman smoked cigarettes. You'd seen her at the hotel once, her hands and neck darker than her bleaching-creamed face. Your mother was silent, gazing away, out the window, her eyes black and final as freshly poured tar. You were pressed up against her, so close you could breathe her, the taste of rose lotion breaking the promise of its smell.

Then Murtala Muhammed: the arriving, the departing, the begging, the crippled, the trash and the throng. Smile! Pop! Poof! Here you are three years later. End of Sad Story.

The morning.

You set down the photo and glanced out the window. The caterers had arrived with the party decor. A large painted banner on the back of their truck read *Mary Christmas!* in red and green letters. You laughed. Only then did you realize that you'd peed in the bed, as happens when the dream is most vivid. The warmth of the wet spot turned cold on the backs of your thighs.

Auntie screamed, "You illiterates!"

"Please, oh, I beg," one of the caterers said, placating.

"It's m-e-r-r-y. *Merry* Christmas."

"Yes, madame. Mary," the caterer assured her.

"No! That says Mary. The mother of Jesus."

"Jesus *is* Christmas." As if he'd heard it somewhere.

Auntie sucked her teeth. "May He help me." The voices carried up from the gates into your room as you wiped off the backs of your legs with a towel. You detached the fitted sheet from the narrow twin bed and carried it, embarrassed, to the washroom.

## III

Ruby was there, sucking her teeth at the washer. She prefers to clean clothing the old way, by hand. Auntie will hear nothing of primary-colored plastic buckets ("You're not in backwater bloody Lolito still, are you?"). Uncle bought the washer on his last trip to London, along with the blue jeans you've cut into shorts. He'd meant them for Comfort, but they didn't quite fit, as she's put on weight studying at Oxford. Auntie, who refuses to travel to Britain, waited for the delivery as for a prodigal child. (Auntie calls London "too gray" for her taste. Comfort says Auntie feels "too black" abroad. Whatever the case, none of your neighbors have machines as impressive as the one in the washroom. Ruby would say there's a reason for that but, like you, Ruby does as she's told. It was triumph enough when the washer's noisy brother, the dryer, was sold off for parts. The whirring contraption put too great a strain on the power supply, waning in Ghana.)

Ruby was dressed in the same thing as always: a T-shirt exhorting the world to *Drink Coke!*, with a thin printed *lappa* and black *chale-watas*, the flip-flops Auntie buys in bulk for staff. No one seems to mind much that you wear them also. Comfort would "nevah deign" to. (*Nevah*, without the *r*.)

"Good morning, Ruby."

Ruby said nothing. Frowning with her eyebrows but not with her eyes. She stands like this often, with her hands on her hips,

bony elbows pushed back like a fledgling set of wings. She is pretty
to you, Ruby, though her appearance is jarring, the eyes of a griot
in the face of a girl. It's an odd mix of features: pointy chin, jutting
cheekbones, tiny nose, initiation scars, village emblems. It's hard
to tell what age she is. Her eyes have the look of a century of seeing. They say she lost a child once. (Which would certainly explain
it. In the peculiar hierarchy of African households, the only rung
lower than motherless child is childless mother.)

"Fine," she said finally. She held out her hand. You gave her the
sheet, which she shoved into the washer. She closed the windowed
door and looked, scowling, at the buttons, unsure which to press,
too proud to say so. You came up beside her, pressed Gentle Cycle.
Silence. The washer, as advertised, sprang noiselessly to life. Ruby
gasped, startled, stepping back. "Eh-hehn!" You stepped back too,
to be next to her.

And stood. Shoulder to shoulder, like a couple viewing a painting. Whites in the window of the washer, sheets and shirts. The
cloth twisting beautifully like the arms and long legs of the National Theatre dancers dancing silently in soap. Ruby sucked her
teeth, repeated "Fine," and left the washroom. She returned a moment later with a clean fitted sheet. You took this, folded neatly
and smelling of Fa soap.

You said, "Thank you."

Ruby said, "Hmph." (But her eyes said, "You're welcome," and,
briefly, she smiled. She is beautiful when she smiles. It isn't often.)


## IV


From the washroom to the kitchen at the side of the house, the
sun slanting in through the windows.

The door was propped open to the buzzing of flies and the
symphony of the sounds of the houseboys in the morning: Kofi
hanging the washing Ruby brings out to dry, blasting Joy FM on his
transistor radio; Francis's little paring knife dancing on the chopping board, a staccato cross-beat to the bass lines outside; Iago, né
Yaw, soaping the Benz in the driveway with the sloshing of cloth
in the bucket of suds; and George, grumpy gatekeeper, at the end
of his duties, eating *puff-puff* he buys at the side of the road. Your
breakfast was laid on the small wooden table: one scallop-sliced

pawpaw and lime wedge as always. Francis was frying *kelewele* for Comfort (her favorite) in honor of her first morning home. She's been in Boston for an exchange program at Harvard since August. After Christmas she'll go up to Oxford again.

"Good morning, Francis."

*"Oui. C'est ça,"* his standard answer, smiling. Francis, gentle giant, six foot six, a most unlikely cook. He'd been working in Accra's finest restaurant, Chez Guy, when Uncle discovered his *pissaladière.* To the dismay of his employer, the eponymous Guy, Uncle made Francis a better offer. His parents are Ewe, his mother from Togo, his English much weaker than his French, even now. "Did you sleep good?"

"How *could* one?" Comfort. Appearing at the door in her slippers.

She padded into the kitchen, stretching her arms with a yawn. "With Mother bloody yelling—is that *kelewele* I smell?"

*"Oui. C'est ça."*

"Oh, how *good* of you, Francis." With the exaggerated British accent. Frawn-sis.

*"Je t'en pris."*

She plopped herself down at the table across from you. Reached for a slice of your pawpaw and sighed. "And you, little lady."

"Good morning."

"Good morning. As skinny as ever. She eats only fruit." Comfort picked up the lime wedge and sucked on it, rueful. "Is Daddy awake?"

Francis frowned. *"Oui. C'est ça."*

Auntie and Uncle take their breakfast on the veranda or in the dining room with linen and china and silver. Comfort and you have always eaten in the kitchen, the small one, at the rickety wood table, like this. The arrangement dates back to the morning you arrived after the short Virgin flight from Nigeria. As he tells it, Uncle ushered you proudly into the dining room for breakfast. You don't remember any of these details. You wouldn't look up from your plate, as Francis tells it; you just sat there, mute, mango on fork tines. After Uncle tried unsuccessfully to sell you on an omelet, Francis intervened, uncharacteristically. He lifted you carefully out of the dining room chair and carried you into his kitchen. Like that. Silent, he placed you at the small wooden table and returned to his work pounding yam. For the next week you refused to eat any meal at all unless seated in "Francis's kitchen," so-called. Auntie had a massive new kitchen installed off the first-floor pantry this summer. No one but Auntie much likes the new kitchen, though it's nicer, says Francis, than Guy's. Francis still insists upon preparing for meals—shelling beans, gutting fish—in "his" kitchen.

"*Bon*. We couldn't well let you *starve*," Auntie tells it. "However pedestrian to eat with the help." Comfort assumed she was missing something special, characteristically, and demanded to join you. When Auntie said no, Comfort refused to eat also, so Uncle said yes, but only breakfast.


## V


Iago appeared presently at the door to the kitchen. He is the best-looking houseboy, you think. There's been talk of a liaison between Iago and Ruby but you don't believe a word they say. First, Ruby never smiles and Iago never stops: perfect teeth, strong and white, and one dimple. Second, she lost a child. Third, you're in love. (And what would they know about love in this house?) In addition to the beauty, and there is no other word for it—he's *beautiful* in the way that a woman is, insistent—he is clever. The cleverest of all, according to Uncle, who just last Monday said as much during Reading Group.

Uncle started the Shakespeare Reading Group last winter, with the dust like fine sugar on the grass, in the air. Auntie thinks it's ridiculous—"Houseboys reading Shakespeare? I mean, *really* . . ." —but defers to him on this as on everything. Uncle's secretary, Akosua, makes the photocopies in his office then brings them to the house wrapped in paper. Kofi drags the lawn chairs into an oval by the pool, carrying out an armchair from the living room for Uncle.

They started with *Othello*. You found a copy in the study from Comfort's final year at Ghana International School. You read it in one sitting, seated cross-legged by the bookshelf. Uncle appeared so silently you didn't hear him. At some point you stopped reading and there he was. Uncle: arms folded, leaning lightly against the door frame. You uncrossed your legs quickly, fumbling to get to your feet, trying to think up an excuse for being in there. No one's forbidden you to enter the study—as you're forbidden, for example, to enter Auntie and Uncle's room—but no one's exactly invited you either. It's your favorite room in the house.

On the one occasion Auntie caught you reading, she said nothing. She was passing by your door on her way down the stairs. You were upright in bed by the window for light, reading Comfort's *House of Mirth.* She had a bottle of Scotch. She started to speak, hiding the bottle, then stopped. You pretended not to notice the bottle. She was staring at the tie-dye that's taped to your wall, as if suddenly transfixed by the pattern. You considered her. It was a new way of seeing her, your own gaze unnoticed, staring straight at her face while she gazed past, through yours. She looked young without makeup, and tired. Even soft. The cream-satin nightdress, sponge rollers.

"That's Ruby's *lappa,* isn't it." A statement, not a question.

"She gave me the cloth, for decoration," you said.

"That was kind of her," Auntie said. "Ruby . . ." Then stopped. You waited for her to finish. She didn't. She stared at the tie-dye cloth (Ruby's old *lappa,* a worn piece of wax batik, blue with white stars, sort of misshapen stars, more like starfish), saying nothing, then abruptly looked away, as if remembering you were there. She said, "You'll strain your eyes, reading in the dark like that."

You didn't mention that you don't have a lamp. "Yes, madame."

But she didn't forbid you to enter the study. You did and found the battered *Othello.* You were there sitting cross-legged when Uncle appeared at the door and you half tried to stand.

"Don't get up."

His voice was so gentle, just barely a whisper, as if speaking too loudly might cause you to rise. "Please, don't get up." He laughed softly. He sighed. "You look just like your mother." He told you to keep Comfort's copy of *Othello.* He invited you to Shakespeare Reading Group that week. You went to the garden, read the part of Desdemona. The pool brilliant blue in the late-morning light.

George read Brabantio. Francis read Roderigo. Iago read Iago. But his name then was Yaw.

The best-looking houseboy, indeed.

It's the skin that seems edible, that insists upon being looked at, less the color than the consistency, the constancy, and the

eyes. You've only ever seen such eyes on Ashanti men with slender builds. Those twinkling, inky eyes, as narrow and angled as
Asians'.

Yaw made his announcement at the end of the hour with his
hand on his packet as if the play were a Bible. "From this day forth
my name will be Iago." Uncle asked why. "He is strongest," Yaw
said.

Kofi raised his hand. "Yes, sir?" Uncle said.

Kofi looked at Yaw, almost pityingly. Sighed. "The *king* is
strongest."

"Impeccable logic. But Yaw is correct." That one dimple. "Iago
you wish to be, Iago you are."

Iago, né Yaw, in the doorway.

"Good morning," he said brightly, leaning into the kitchen. He
held out the mangoes to Francis.

"Good morning," you said softly, turning from the table to face
him, losing your breath for a moment at the sight. Comfort said
nothing, her mouth full of *kelewele,* blowing out air—"Hot, hot,
hot"—as she chewed. As a rule she isn't rude to the house staff
(like Auntie) but she doesn't "associate" either. Even to Ruby, who
was employed before Comfort was born, Comfort says little. The
only employee you've ever heard her thank that one time is Francis. She barely seemed to notice Iago, back-lit, at the door.

"You are welcome, Sister Comfort," he whispered. She looked.
The sun from behind him seeped into her eyes. Seated across
from her, you stared at her face.

You'd never seen this particular look in her eyes, which are dark
brown and gentle, even flat sometimes, still. Not empty, as such
—not like Ruby's—but still, like the eyes of a cow, deep and sated.
She looked up, saw Iago, and her eyes sort of flickered. Just the
hint of a hardening.

"Morring, Yaw." Her mouth full.

As you stare at her now through the wide picture window, looking
down at the garden and your cousin in her lace, you think to yourself, as you thought at the table this morning, *it's a very pretty face.*
Sort of heart-shaped and plumpish, with the cheeks of a cherub,
the long curly lashes and small, pointy chin. Her lips look like pil-

lows, some unique form of respite: top lip and bottom lip equal, together forming an O. She has Uncle's flawless skin, the same sparkle and shade as the earth after rainfall, as shea-buttered soft. The skin on her collarbones and shoulders, in particular, is impossibly smooth, with a specific effect: that calm kind of loveliness unique to flat landscapes, to uninterrupted stretches of uniform terrain. Perhaps in the absence of the absolute standard that is Auntie, you'd call Comfort beautiful.

But there she is—Auntie—fluttering from table to round table, drawing all eyes and oxygen toward her, restless Monarch. She is somewhat less witchlike when viewed through the window. Merely beautiful beyond all reason. The long jet-black hair against skin that won't tan, wide-set eyes, and the war paint of cheekbone. For a moment you wonder if it's the beauty that's aggressive, perhaps in spite of its owner, and not Auntie herself? Perhaps anyone so striking, so sharp on the outside, would appear to be hard on the inside as well?

Then Auntie stands straight and the moon gilds her up-and-down: white in a garden of color, as foreseen. As you watch from the study Auntie flutters to Comfort, who is fussing with Kwabena, her fiancé. Auntie offers her cheeks, one then the other, to his kisses. Comfort steps back, for no reason; there is space. Kwabena begins gesturing, chatting animatedly with Auntie. Comfort sips foam off her Malta, gazes away.

She isn't lovely near Auntie; you see this now, plainly. She couldn't be lovely. She is too starkly lit. It isn't that Auntie casts others in shadow, as you've often heard it said. It is the opposite. She is luminous. A floodlight on everything around it, in darkness. In an instant something lights Comfort's eyes.

It is the same thing you saw for that moment this morning, the sun slanting in thick and golden as oil. That flash, like two fireflies in Comfort's black pupils, while Iago wiped his hands on his trousers, looked down.

Francis finished crafting a blossom from an orange, then turned his focus to scalloping mango. He gave the overripe mangoes to Iago as he does, despite Auntie's weekly speech on "free lunch." You finished your pawpaw, surreptitiously watching Iago, his *chale-watas* wet still from washing the car. The pink tip of his tongue on the stringy-gold flesh, the wetness around his mouth made your stomach drop down. A feeling very similar to wetting the bed when the dream is most vivid. The dampness and all.

Iago finished the mango and tossed the pit across the kitchen. It landed in the rubbish with a clatter. *"Gooooooooooooooooal!"* Francis called out like a football announcer. You giggled. Comfort slapped at a mosquito.

"Is madame in the garden?" Iago asked, licking his fingers.

You nodded. "With the caterers."

"Bloody party," Comfort said. She considered the mosquito bite blooming on her arm. "Damn mosquitoes. Every Christmas. For what?"

"I go and come." Iago, backing away from the door. He ran down the path along the side of the kitchen.

This scraggly grass walkway runs between the house and the Boys' Quarters, the staff's modest barracks, half hidden in brush. On the other side of the house is a wide pebbled walkway that winds from the gates to the garden at the back. This is how party guests access the garden. The house staff, forbidden, use the kitchen path. It scares you for some reason. Its dark smell of dampness, the wild, winding crawlers climbing the side of the house, the low-hanging tree branches twisted together like the skinny gnarled arms of a child with lupus. And, set back in shadow behind the tangle of branches, ominous and concrete, never touched by the sun: those three huddled structures with their one concrete courtyard where the houseboys sit on beer crates and eat after dark. If you're passing the round window on the second-floor landing, you can look down and make out their shadows at night. A cooking fire flickering against the black of the sky and their laughter in bursts, muted refrains. No one's ever forbidden you to join them, to go back there. But no one's ever invited you either. They scare you: the Boys' Quarters, the trail through the thicket.

Iago disappeared down this path.

You took your plate to the sink, turned on the water to rinse it. Francis patted your head, took the plate, pushed you away. Your willingness to do housework is an oddity at Uncle's, as the notion of house staff is an oddity to you. *You* who ate leftovers at the bar with the busboys at the end of each night while your mother drank rum; who helped maids on the mornings your mother was hung-over; eating left-behind chocolates and half-rotting fruit. But Ruby doesn't need or want help with the washing. Iago will let you trail him, reciting *Othello,* across the lawn (he has memorized his part and no longer needs a script), as Kofi will abide your quiet audience. Francis will let you watch from the little wood table while he skins and chops chicken in the afternoon light. But no one will allow you to *do* what you're watching. It was Kofi who one day read from his script: "Blow, blow, thou winter wind! Thou art not so unkind as man's ingratitude." You'd been trying to hang your sheet on his line outside the kitchen. A breeze had kept billowing it up. Francis finished breakfast and arranged it on a tray. As if on cue, Ruby came into the kitchen, *chale-watas* slapping the concrete. She stopped when she saw Comfort. A small curtsy. She didn't smile. "Miss Comfort. You are very welcome home."

"Morning, Ruby."

Ruby, to Francis: "Madame already took breakfast?"

He handed her the tray. "Only tea."

"Will she eat?"

"She's fasting for the party." Comfort sucked her teeth dramatically. "That's my mother. *Bon.*" It was the briefest of glances: Ruby's eyes lifting sharply, darting quickly to Comfort, then snapping back down. Comfort didn't notice. Ruby left with Uncle's breakfast. The swinging door flapped lightly back and forth, then shut behind her.

Comfort turned to Francis, scratching the mosquito bite on her arm. "Kwabena is coming for pre-party cocktails. I told him I'd make him that *chin-chin* he likes."

*"Mais bien sûr, mademoiselle."* Francis began wiping the counter.

"Bloody bugger. Still thinks I can cook." Comfort laughed. "I haven't seen him since August. I was slimmer then, wasn't I?" She sucked at the bite as it started to bleed. She looked at you jealously. "Not like you. But still slimmer."

You shook your head, lying, "You're still the same size."

She beamed as if with delight at your very existence. Then, suddenly remembering: "I brought some books back from Boston."

"You did?"

"Yes, of course. They're in the study. Go and get them."

"Don't do that, please." Iago. Appearing at the door. He leaned in (the houseboys don't enter the house) and held out an aloe leaf to Comfort, cracked open. She looked up and frowned. The little flicker again. Confusion? Irritation? But smiled politely.

She went to the door, took the leaf from his hand. "Aloe," she said, sounding confused.

"For your arm," said Iago, backing away from the door. Suddenly shy. Disappearing. Comfort watched him go, rubbing her arm with the sap. "Has Iago gotten taller?"

*"Oui. C'est ça."*

## VI

The study is at the end of the second-floor hallway at the opposite end from your bedroom. Its one wall-length window overlooks the back garden, the three other walls lined with books. Uncle's large desk and stuffed chair face the vista, the chair with its back to the door. And the rug. Every room in the house boasts a thick Persian rug, courtesy of Auntie's (estranged) Uncle Mahmood. In the study—as in the parlor, as in the dining room, as in the drawing room—this furnishing serves to mute footfalls.

The door was half closed when you came for the books. Comfort said, "Go and get them," and you did as you were told. The swinging door clapped shut as you bounded out of the kitchen. Up the staircase to the study, skipping every other stair. You were wondering what books Comfort had brought back from Boston, whether more Edith Wharton or your new favorite, Richard Wright? The door was ajar but no sunlight spilled out of it. You approached and peered into the slim opening.

The drapes were pulled over the window, uncharacteristically. Uncle's breakfast tray, balanced at the edge of the desk. The plates were all empty, Francis's blossom destroyed. A stack of glossy paperbacks beckoned by the tray.

You assumed, perfectly logically, that Uncle had finished eating and left the tray for Kofi or Ruby to come collect. You pushed the door slightly and slipped into the slim opening, your feet sinking into the soft of the rug.

Uncle was in his chair, facing the window and drapes, gripping the edge of the desk with his fingertips. From your vantage behind him across the room in the doorway, you could barely see Ruby between his knees. She was kneeling there neatly, skinny legs folded beneath her, her hands on his knees, heart-shaped face in his lap. The sound she made reminded you of cloth sloshing in buckets, as rhythmic and functional, almost mindless, and wet. Uncle whimpered bizarrely, like the dogs before beatings. For whatever reason, you stood there transfixed by the books.

It was Ruby who saw you but Uncle who cried out, as if sustaining some cruel, unseen wound. Now you saw the trousers in a puddle around his ankles. Now he saw you, mute, at the door. He grabbed Ruby's head and pulled it away from his lap. She crumpled to the rug like a doll.

"Stupid girl!" he spat. "Get out! Get out!" Whether to you or to her, you weren't sure.

Ruby scrambled to her feet; you stumbled back out the door. She wore only her *lappa* and a tattered lace bra. She looked at you quickly as you pushed the door shut. Her almond eyes glittered with hatred.

You recognized the expression. You'd seen it once before, in the morning in Lagos with your mother and Sinclair. You'd been loitering in the kitchen waiting for the cooks to finish breakfast. Just as Francis does with Iago, they'd slip you anything spoiled: collapsed soufflé, browning fruit, crispy bacon, burned toast. The trick had been to show up after Sinclair made his rounds, shouting complaints then disappearing until dinner. The spoils that morning had been unusually abundant: enough fruit for a week, pancakes, overboiled eggs. A younger cook had set the food on a metal rolling cart and sent you up to your room in the freight elevator.

The rest you remember not as a series of events but as a single expression. A postcard. You must have inserted the keycard in the door, which would have beeped open, blinking green, making noise. But they must not have heard you. So you wheeled in the cart and just stood there, frozen, mute at the door.

That expression.

Your mother on the floor, Sinclair kneeling behind her, their moaning an inelegant music, the sweat. Her eyes open wide as she looked up and saw you, surprised that you'd returned from the kitchen so soon. And the hatred. Bright knives in the dark of her irises. Unmistakable. You'd left the cart, running.

From the study to your room.

Slamming the door, leaning against it. The sound—sloshing cloth, buckets of soap—in your ears. Your bright blue walls trembled, or seemed to, in that moment, like a suspended tsunami about to crash in. The image (not yet a memory)—of Uncle in his desk chair; of Ruby folded prayerfully on her knees between his —flashed on the backs of your eyelids like a movie whose meaning you didn't quite understand. But you saw. In that moment, as you stood there, with your back to the door and the lump in your throat and your pulse in your ears, you saw that it was *you* who were wrong and not they. You were wrong to have pitied her. Ruby. That she could make Uncle start whimpering like the dogs before beatings meant something was possible under this roof, in this house; something different from—and you wondered, was it better than? preferable to?—the thing you lived out every day. You envied Ruby something, though you didn't know what. You stood at your door trembling jealously.

Someone approached.

You heard the steps (small ones) on the other side of your door, followed by the faint sound of feet on the stairs, going down. You waited for a second then cracked the door open. No one was there. You looked down. Someone had stacked Comfort's paperback books on the threshold. Like a fetish offering. You glanced down the hall to the study; the door was open. The drapes had been drawn back to richly bright light. You picked up the books and you walked down the stairs. The meaning—whether Uncle's or Ruby's—was clear.

So you went to the garden as you would have done otherwise, had you not seen what you saw in the study just then. You said nothing to Francis, who was just starting the *chin-chin,* nor to Iago, who was making centerpieces of torch gingers as you appeared. You didn't so much as gasp when you found Comfort by the pool on her back on a towel in a bikini.

You stopped, staring down at her. She shifted, squinting up at you.

"I see you got the books," she said.

You nodded. Quietly: "Thank you."

"You're welcome." She smiled. Then closed her eyes. Without opening them: "You're in my sun."

*

Caterers swarmed the garden, unfolding round wood tables, festooning lights along the walls, ignoring Comfort by the pool. The garden half done like a woman getting ready, standing naked at the mirror in her necklace and shoes. The thick buzz of flies and the sweet smell of *chin-chin*. Not for the first time you thought about running. They were consumed with their preparations, all of the houseboys and caterers, Comfort sunning in her bikini, Iago working by the pool. You could get up now, unnoticed, leave your books, walk away. There was the door at the edge of the garden.

You'd always wondered where it led to; it was always closed and no one used it. You considered it, suddenly hopeful, not one hundred yards away. Perhaps it pushed out to some Neverland? To Nigeria? Or simply to some route to the road through the brush? You were considering the distance from the tree to the door when the thought seized you suddenly: but what if she's gone? What if they were right, and she'd run off to Abuja, with no thanks to Uncle and no thought of you? Now the breath left your chest and your heart began racing. To almost precisely the same beat, someone's hammer: *THWAP! THWAP!* Two carpenters installing the dance floor, banging nails— *THWAP! THWAP!*—while your chest refused air.

And there was Auntie.

She was standing across the garden at the door into the living room in big bug-eye sunglasses, shouting your name. The way she scanned the garden made it clear she couldn't see you where you crouched behind the veil of tree leaves, silent, trying to breathe. She was starting to go in when she saw Comfort by the pool. "For God's sake, daughter. What are you doing?"

Comfort lifted her head, shading her eyes with her hand, the flesh at her midsection folding over. "I'm sunbathing, Mother. It's good for my skin."

"You're going to get darker."

"Yes, likely."

"Don't be smart. Your husband is coming this afternoon. You need to get dressed."

"My *fiancé*." Comfort lay back down, adjusting her position on the towel. Auntie glanced at the caterers, who were observing this exchange. "What are you looking at?" Nobody answered. Auntie snapped, "Where *is* that girl?"

An inhalation at last. "I'm here, madame," you called hoarsely, stumbling out from the leaves. She glanced at you casually, as if you'd always been standing there. Then looked down at Comfort, sucked her teeth, turned away. "Kwabena is coming. You had better be decent." Over her shoulder, to you, "Ehn, let's go."

## VII

Makola Market is a thirty minutes' drive from the house. You sat in the back, silent, with Auntie. You glanced at her quickly, holding her bag in your lap, trying to interpret her vacant expression. Did she know that this morning after serving Uncle's breakfast, Ruby removed her little shirt and knelt between his knees? Would Uncle send you away if you shared this with Auntie? Would Auntie like you better if you did?

You were thinking this over when she spoke. "When I call you, you come. Do you hear me?"

"Yes, madame."

The market was crowded with Christmas returnees haggling unsuccessfully over the prices of trinkets. And the fray. The bodies pushed together in the soft rocking motions; the sellers shouting prices over heaps of yellowing fruit; the freshly caught fish laid in stacks of silvery carcasses, their eyes still open wide, as if with surprise at being dead. You pushed through the traffic to the back of the market and parked outside Mahmood the Jeweler's.

Mahmood is Auntie's uncle, one of the richest men in Accra and the nicest you've met apart from Francis. He used to call you "Habibti," as if it was actually your name, and bring you *ma'amoul* wrapped in wax when he visited. His houseboy Osekere would lug in a case of Chateau Ksara and they'd sit by the pool, drinking: Auntie, Uncle, Mahmood. Two or three bottles down, Mahmood would demand that you join them, instructing Kofi to come get you from your bedroom. Never Comfort.

He liked to tell the tale of the silkworm crisis that brought the Lebanese to Ghana. You'd lean against his stomach while he stroked your hair, talking. English Leather, fermented tobacco, citronella in your nose. The last time he visited—over a year ago, summer—you climbed into his lap as per habit. He stroked your knee gently and kissed you on the head. "Habibti." He wiped powdered sugar from the *ma'amoul* off your lip. "Have I ever told you the story of Khadijeh the silkworm?"

"No." You lied, giggling.

"Have I not?" Mahmood laughed. Uncle pulled on his cigar, his eyes twinkling in the candlelight. "Fucking silkworms."

"Watch your language," Auntie hissed.

Uncle merely laughed, ignoring Auntie, speaking louder. "Might have been silkworms that sent you damn Arabs but it was British worms who welcomed you, them and our women." He removed his cigar slowly and smiled, not kindly. "You've made whores of them. All of them—"

"Not in front of the child." Auntie glanced at you.

Laughing harder. "She's my sister's daughter," Uncle said. "She of all people understands what a whore is."

Then silence.

Their eyes grazed your face and you closed your own tightly but no sooner had you done so than the image appeared. On the backs of your eyelids where such images are stored: of Sinclair on the floor with your mother. You opened your eyes quickly but the image remained. You were sick to your stomach. There were hands at your waist.

"Don't mind them, Habibti," Mahmood whispered softly. He was squeezing your waist tightly, then kissing your cheek. His beard scratched your shoulder. His lips wet your neck. The thought was just forming: his hands are too tight. They were pressing against your ribs through your nightdress; you were nauseated. You'd eaten too many pastries—and that word in your mouth. That image in air. *Whore.* You started to speak. But heard Auntie as you opened your mouth.

"DON'T TOUCH HER!" she raged at him, leaping to her feet.

"Sit down, Khadijeh!" said Uncle, leaping to his. The gesture knocked his glass to the tile, where it smashed. The wine ran into the pool like a ribbon of blood. "You will *not* address a guest in my house in that manner."

Kofi jumped back. Auntie gasped. Mahmood chuckled.

"*Malesh*, Khadijeh. *Malesh*," he said calmly. He stood, lifting you with him, kissed your head, set you down. "Go inside, Habibti," he whispered, ruffling your hair. "Go inside. Sweet dreams. I'll see you soon."

But you haven't.

He hasn't been to the house since that night by the pool and neither Auntie nor Uncle so much as mentions him.

You trailed behind Auntie to the door to the store. A sign read: BACK AFTER LUNCH. *SHUKRAN*. She pushed the door lightly. It opened. A bell jingled. You entered. No one materialized. "Hallo?" she called out.

You lingered behind Auntie, glancing at your reflections in the mirrors. She in her sunglasses. You, shorter, in your shorts. In light like that there is something very African about Auntie. Her skin is so pale you often forget that she's half. But the set of her mouth, the slight downturn of the lips, the proud upturn of the chin betray her paternity.

Her eyes met yours suddenly. You looked away quickly. "What are you looking at?"

"I wasn't expecting you," someone said. Both you and Auntie turned to the back of the store where Mariam, Auntie's mother, stood watching her. In spite of yourself you took a little step backward. She is terrifying to you, Mariam, viscerally so. She has the same dramatic features as her daughter and brother, her skin a dark bronze from the decades in Ghana. It's the dark hooded eyes that deny her face beauty: the slope of the eyelids, the black bushy brows. They say that Mahmood would be nothing without his sister, ruthless bookkeeper; that it was she who built his business. Mariam said nothing. She just stood at the counter at the back of the store, watching Auntie. She didn't so much as look at you.

"I can't see why you wouldn't 'expect' me. We throw the same party every year." Auntie sighed. "Aren't you at least going to offer us tea?"

You stiffened. You didn't like the sound of this "us." But Mariam smiled brightly, a menacing expression. A bit like a wound beneath her nose. Her eyes traveled past Auntie and rested on you. Without irony: "May I offer you tea?"

To watch Auntie now on the dance floor with Kwabena, her seethrough lace glowing like sun-tinted ice, it doesn't seem possible, what you heard next from Mariam. It is obvious, and still seems the lie. This has less to do with Comfort—who sits sipping her Malta, watching Auntie dancing with Kwabena as the singer wails in French; and whose eyes, more like Ruby's than you'd previously appreciated, are up-lit by candles and sparkling with spite—and more to do with Auntie, who is laughing now, clapping, while the other dancers, sheep, start to laugh and clap too.

This is what jars you as you watch from the window: how impervious she appears still, impenetrable. There is anger in Auntie and you see it now, hurting. The sheen of her eyes like a lacquer, sealing grief. But the appearance is compelling, the apparition of Auntie's fortitude. Bright black-haired chimera. It wants to be believed. And you want to believe it. The lie of her majesty. That she couldn't be other than what she appears. The truth of her weakness leaves nothing to be hoped for, leaves nothing to cling to, makes everything as weak. Meaning that something is possible here in this house where you envy the housegirl but don't know for what—and it's not what you thought, which was that you were forsaken, alone. It is that all of you are.

Mariam, to you: "May I offer you tea?" How you ended up overhearing from the bathroom. You followed her up that dark, narrow back staircase to the office above the shop, which you'd never before seen. It was filthy: a cluttered office with a kitchen in the back, sticky tiles, one oily window overlooking the market. Mariam went to the kitchen and put a kettle on the stove. Auntie stood looking around as if for a mop. Finally, she perched gingerly on the arm of a desk chair. She gestured to you, impatiently. "Bring the invitation," she said.

You opened the handbag and pulled out the envelope. Mariam reappeared with two teacups. "Tea," she said. She handed you both cups, took the invitation, looked it over. Then sat at the desk, clasping her hands. You handed Auntie a teacup. There was no place to sit. You wished you had waited with Kofi in the car. You didn't dare ask now. No one moved. No one spoke.

"Keeping up appearances," Mariam said finally. "Well done." She has Auntie's clipped accent. She didn't have tea. You noticed this now, peering into your own teacup with worry. Mariam noticed your expression and chuckled. "Poison-free."

"Oh, for God's sake. Let's not start." Auntie hissed. "I'd like you to come to our party tonight. People ask questions when you don't."

"Let them ask. You've embarrassed your family. That's all there is to it."

"That's not what you said when I married him."

Mariam sneered, "This isn't about Kodjo." She said the name with contempt. "If you lie down with bush boys you get up with fleas."

"Well, you would know—"

"How *dare* you? Your father was different! An honorable Ghanaian. A *very* good man." Mariam pounded the desk with her fist on this "very," her face flushing mauve and her eyes welling up. The outburst made you start, spilling tea on your T-shirt. They both turned to look at you now.

"Please excuse me," you mumbled. You stood, glancing at Auntie. She said nothing. Mariam said, "Go," and you went. Through the kitchen into the bathroom where you closed the door quickly, then instantly wished that you hadn't. There were flies in the toilet and stains on the tiles, the stench overwhelming: urine, ammonia, mothballs. You were fumbling with the door, trying to let yourself out, when Mariam began screaming on the other side of it. "You disrespect my brother in that philanderer's home—"

And Auntie: "You can't be serious. Your little stand-off is about Mahmood?"

"*Uncle* Mahmood, kindly. After all that he's done."

"Which is what, Mother? Kindly. Do tell." Auntie laughed.

"You know bloody well that he paid for your schooling."

"For my schooling. For my *schooling?!*" Now Auntie's laughter was shrill. "Is that the going rate for a virgin in Ain Mreisseh?"

"Go to hell."

"Thank you, Mother."

"You're a liar."

"I was twelve."

"It's your husband who insults you, running around with those bush girls."

"At least they're grown women."

Mariam laughed, genuinely amused. "The daughter of a housegirl. Passed off as your child. And is she? A comfort?"

"You know why I can't."

Auntie said it very simply, in a very small voice that you'd never heard her use but could match to an image: of her standing in your doorway in pale pink sponge rollers, transfixed by the *lappa*, unbearably frail. Her words and their meaning were like a taste on your tongue, then a thickness spreading slowly across the roof of your mouth. *The daughter of a housegirl. You know why I can't.* You heaved, vomited pawpaw into the toilet.

Silence.

Now came a rustling, someone slamming a door; now the clicking of heels, growing louder, toward the bathroom. From outside the door: "What the hell are you doing?" You wiped off your T-shirt, cracked opened the door.

There was Auntie, crying quietly, fumbling for her sunglasses in her bag. She looked at you blankly and turned. "Ehn, let's go."

## VIII

You got in the car. She got in the car. Kofi glanced back at her, started the engine. She removed her bug sunglasses and wiped her eyes quickly. She put them back on. She said nothing.

Kofi pulled up to the gates and honked. George opened the gates with much clanging of locks. Kofi drove in, Benz tires crunching white pebbles. Auntie said, "Thank you," got out. You'd never heard her thank anyone for anything before. Kofi said, shocked, "Yes, madame."

You're still not sure why you followed her in. She got out on her side and you jumped out on yours. Perhaps you were waiting for instructions about something? About not saying a word to a soul or suchlike? Watching her now on the dance floor with Kwabena, it occurs to you that you didn't want to leave her alone. You needed to stay near her, you thought, trailing behind her.

So you followed her into the kitchen.

Francis was removing a tray of *chin-chin* from the oven. You entered behind Auntie, swinging door swinging shut.

"I told you to cook in the new kitchen," she said. Francis looked up, startled.

"Madame?"

"I told you to cook in the new kitchen," Auntie repeated. "Not in here. In this dump. With these flies. Do you hear?" Francis shook his head in confusion. Auntie stepped forward to stand just beneath him. "No, you don't hear me? Or no, you don't understand me? Or no, you intend to ignore me? You too?" She was laughing hysterically. He shook his head, faltering. Then Auntie reached up and slapped him. Once.

He dropped the tray of *chin-chin*, the sweets scattering across the floor. Tears sprung to your eyes.

And to his. And to hers. She stabbed the air in front of him, gasping for breath. "You do as I tell you. You do as I say."

Then walked out of the kitchen, started sobbing. You stood there with Francis, who stared at you, silent. With tears in his eyes and what else? Was it anger? You'd never seen him angry. You tried but couldn't speak. For the thickness in your mouth. All the words. The door opened suddenly and Uncle stormed in. He looked at the *chin-chin*, scattered nuggets on the floor. "Idiot." To Francis. "Clean up," as he left.

The sky seemed to darken outside the door.

Francis knelt down and picked up the tray—a long way down for such a tall man. He set it on the counter, leaving the *chin-chin* on the floor. He ducked, and walked out the door.


You waited too long.

There, dumbstruck in the kitchen. You waited too long before you followed him out. You dropped Auntie's bag and ran out the side door but you didn't find Francis so you ran down the path. You hurried through the thicket along the side of the kitchen between the house and the Boys' Quarters to the garden, crying now. The rocks and knotted roots cut through the soles of your *chale-watas* as you pushed through the low-hanging leaves. The sky was dark.

The caterers were raising a new banner above the dance floor. *Marry Christmas!* A boy was setting tea lights into bowls. No one seemed to notice you. You didn't see Francis. You saw the little door across the garden.

The door opens easily. Not to Neverland, it turns out, but to the unkempt brush of the neighbors' back lawn. Weeds, chopped-down trees, redolent dankness of earth. And Iago kissing Comfort in her bikini. She was leaning against a tree with her hands at his waist. He was cupping her breasts. He was shirtless. At the sound of the door creaking, feet crackling on twigs, Iago turned. He said, "No." Nothing else. Comfort looked also, saw you, and cried out. Iago clamped his hand over her mouth.

For the second time that day you backed out of a door, pulled it shut, and stood staring, now seeing. Four o'clock. There were your books, beneath the mango, where you'd left them. Thunder, then it started to rain.

You came up the path in the driving rain, slowly, the wet on your shoulders and face like a weight. The smell of damp earth swelling up from the ground as it does in the tropics, overpowering the air. So that all that there was for those few wretched minutes was the rain on your skin and the earth in your nose. The caterers, behind you, shouting about things getting wet, as you pushed through the low-hanging branches, then stopped.

There, through the brush, in the Boys' Quarters courtyard beneath the one shower: there was Francis, soaking wet. With the water from the shower and the downpouring rain and the soap on his face, and the cloth in his hands. And his form. You gasped to see it, that foreign landscape of muscle: the hills of the stomach, the mountain of bum, the plain of his shoulders, the tree trunk of torso, the roots of the cordons the length of his legs. In a way, it was too much to see in that moment, through the tangle of branches, nude Francis. You turned.

But the sound of the movement was loud and he heard it. He turned his head quickly and opened his eyes. He stared at you, frozen, the cloth in his hands, but not using it to cover himself, suds in his eyes. *"Regardez!"* he called out through the brush and the rain. *"Je suis un homme, n'est-ce pas?"*

Now it stopped raining, as suddenly as it had started. As if God turned a tap just once to the left. Francis stood staring at you, arms open wide. The shower still running. With rage in his eyes. You could barely see anything, for the tears welled in yours. You turned and ran into the house.

Through the kitchen.

Through the side door into the kitchen, with the oven standing open, the spilled *chin-chin* on the tiles, and Auntie's bag on the floor. To the stairs, past the washroom, where the caterers were conferring noisily about the soaking-wet linens, decrying the absence of a dryer. Up the stairs to your bedroom, where you removed your wet T-shirt, kicked off the sopping *chale-watas*, pulled on your cutoffs, a dry top. You found the slippers with the beading, beckoning cheerfully, slipped these on. You squeezed your eyes shut. But couldn't breathe. So opened your door.

Auntie was on the stairs, her eyes swollen, no makeup. She glanced toward your bedroom. You retreated too late. "Whatever are you wearing? There's a party tonight."

"I'm changing," you said softly.

"Into what?"

"A Christmas top."

"And the trousers?"

"I can press them."

"You'll do nothing of the sort. Borrow a *buba* from your cousin."

"Yes, madame."

"Your hair is wet." She continued down the stairs then paused abruptly, looking up. "And where *is* your cousin?"

"I'm right here," Comfort said.

She'd appeared at the base of the stairs in her robe, wearing Iago's *chale-watas*, many sizes too big. Auntie looked at Comfort then back up at you. Comfort looked up at you also. (And you couldn't for the life of you see how you'd missed it. Comfort looks nothing like Auntie.) Their eyes on your face, different shapes, the same pleading. Auntie turned to Comfort and pointed at her shoes. The *chale-watas* looked bizarre on Comfort's delicate feet.

"And whose are those?"

"Mine," you answered quickly.

Auntie sighed. She considered your cheerful slippers, considered Comfort, and hissed. She continued down to Comfort and lifted her chin. "We'll never bloody marry you off at this rate." She dropped Comfort's chin and walked off.

Comfort looked up, at you. "Do you not speak English? Get dressed, Mother said. There's a party tonight." But she didn't sound angry and just stood there, started crying. "Thank you," she mouthed to you.

"You're welcome," you said. She is beautiful when she smiles. It isn't often.


## IX

Enter Uncle.

He walks in behind you, saying nothing at all and not closing the door in the silvery dark. You turn round to face him. Full circle. Explaining, "I was fetching an album for Auntie. I'm sorry."

Your *buba* slides down. You start to say more but he holds up a hand, shakes his head, is not angry.

"It's nice to be away from it all. Isn't it?" He smiles.

"Yes, Uncle."

"I'll bring her the album. Relax." He joins you at the window. Ever so slightly behind you. Puts a hand on your shoulder, palm surprisingly cold. In a very gentle motion he rearranges the *buba*. "Are you happy?" The question surprises you.

"Yes, Uncle."

"What I mean is, are you happy here? Happy living here?"

"Yes, Uncle."

"And you would tell me if you weren't?"

"Yes, Uncle."

"Meaning no."

"No, Uncle."

"'No, Uncle.' Better than 'yes,' I suppose." He chuckles almost sadly. He is quiet for a moment. "Do you miss her?"

"Yes, Uncle."

He nods. "Yes, of course." Then you stare out the window, another couple at a painting. The singer is hitting a high note, clutching the mike as if for dear life. You look at the dance floor. You see Kwabena but not Auntie. The younger girls dancing with men in full suits. You look to the tables. There is Comfort, sitting stiffly. Iago, in a server's tux, approaches with drinks. He pours her more Malta; Comfort doesn't look up. You feel your breath quicken. Uncle's hand on your neck.

"You remind me so much of your mother." He leans down now. The hotness of rum and his breath on your skin. The *buba* slides off and he adjusts it again carefully. "She had this long neck. Just like yours," he says, touching. You stiffen. Not at the touch but the tense. He notices. "I frighten you," he says, sad, surprised.

"No, Uncle."

"Bloody hell. Is that all you say?" He speaks through clenched teeth. "It's a *question,* for God's sake. Do I frighten you?" You are silent, unable to move. "*Answer* me." Not gently, he turns you round. Unable to face him, you stare at your feet sinking into the carpet, toenails painted pink. But when he lifts your chin, whispering, "Look at me," you do—and don't find the anger you're expecting. None at all. You have never been this close to Uncle's face. You have never noticed its resemblance to your mother's. The dark deep-set eyes. And in them something familiar. Something you recognize. Loneliness. Loss. "I didn't frighten her," he says insistently, slurring the words. "I never frightened her. Do I frighten you?" Your chin in his hands.

You shake your head quickly. "No, Uncle," you mumble.

"I miss her so much." He cups a palm around your cheek. And when he leans down to kiss you, you know what he means. You feel his tears on your face, mixed with yours, warm; his cool. There is something sort of disgusting about the feel of his lips, as there must have been something disgusting to Auntie about Mahmood's. But you bear it for those moments, as an act of generosity (or something like it), feeling for the first time at home in his house.

Still, you can imagine how it must look from the doorway when you hear Auntie say, "How long does it take?"—then sudden silence as she sees. "Oh, God," she splutters in a horrified whisper. The only sound in the darkness. "Oh, God."

Uncle pulls away from you and looks at his wife. "Khadijeh." And there is Auntie, in the doorway. How she falls. She leans against the door frame, then slumps to the ground. She repeats the words: "Oh, God."

Close to hyperventilating. In tears. Uncle smoothes his trousers with the palms of his hands. He touches your shoulder calmly before going to the door.

"Khadijeh," he says, kneeling, but she pushes him away.

"Don't touch me. How dare you? God damn you to hell." She hits him now, desperately. "She's your *blood*. She's your *blood*."

"That's enough," he says softly, as she kicks at his shins. He grabs her by the shoulders, standing her up on her feet. She flails at him, sobbing. He slaps her. Hard. Once. "This is *my* house," he says. Walks away.

In the dark and the silence you wish you could vanish, at least crawl beneath the desk without her noticing and hide. But she barely seems conscious as she sits in the doorway, her lace like a pile of used tissues, a cloud.

And that's when it hits you. Your mother isn't coming. Wherever she's gone, it's a place without *life*. What life there was in her was choked out by hatred; whatever light in her eyes was the glint of that hate. And whom did she hate so? Her brother? Her mother? Your father? It doesn't matter. They live. She is dead.

This is what you're left with: a life with these people. This place and these women. Comfort. Ruby. Khadijeh. Who—it suddenly occurs to you, with an odd kind of clarity, as you watch from the window—mustn't be left to die too.

So you go to her, stumbling over the hem of the garment as you cross the Persian rug and she looks up, face smeared. The kohl makeup runs down her cheeks like black tears. You sit down beside her, laying your head in her lap.

"Edem," she whispers faintly.

"Yes, Auntie." You start to cry. A familiar sound, peculiar: the sound of your name. You put your arms around her waist. It is softer than you'd imagined it. You hold her very tightly, and she holds you as if for life. You wish there was something you could say, to comfort her. But what? In the peculiar hierarchy of African households, the only rung lower than motherless child is childless mother.

SHARON SOLWITZ

# *Alive*

FROM *Fifth Wednesday Journal*

SNOW WAS COMING down in fuzzed, aimless clots. He was ten; it was Saturday; Ethan was mad at him. If something good didn't happen, he would burst out of his skin.

He opened the door of his brother's room. Nate sat bent over his desk. From across the room, his head looked 100 percent bald. Up close hairs could be seen, transparent like ghost hairs.

He drifted toward Nate's bureau, on which perched a large LEGO pirate ship. He pulled off the skull and crossbones. "Nate-ster?" he said with more force than he felt. Force he wanted to feel. "Let's have a snowball fight?"

"Later. This math is a bitch."

"When's later?"

Nate shrugged.

He considered snapping the slender plastic flagpole, then stuck it onto the four-blade tail rotor of Nate's LEGO Apache attack helicopter. On the shelf below was a box of Day-Glo markers that Nate had gotten in the hospital. In Day-Glo orange he wrote ETHAN on the back of his hand, noting aimlessly that ETHAN backwards was NATE, if you lost the H.

He was trapped in a world without joy or the possibility of joy.

His mother sat at the kitchen table, drinking coffee from a mug that read around the rim: *Well-Behaved Women Rarely Make History.* Her laptop was open but the screen was dark. Her hand covered her eyes. "Where's Dad?" he said.

She sat straight up. "*Dad*—why *Dad*?" she said. "Isn't *Mom* good enough?"

It was her merry acting voice. She was in theater before she went back to school and met Dad. He looked out the window. The snow had stopped. The sky was bright blue, taunting. "I have nothing to do," he said.

"Don't whine, Dylan."

He smacked the counter. Not as hard as he could have, daring her to overlook it.

"Why don't you call Ethan?" she said.

"I hate Ethan."

"So call another friend."

He opened the refrigerator, thinking of other friends, but their homes required driving. He raised the lid of the Tupperware container of last night's dinner, greasy yellow islands floating on brown water. Prison food. Beyond the kitchen window the snow sparkled and glistened. The hedge along the back-yard fence could have been made out of sugar. "Drive me?"

"Close the fridge."

He did so, then threw his arms around his mother's neck, a gesture that had served on other occasions. "Come outside and throw snowballs at me!"

She laughed. "What, are you four years old? What's the matter with you?"

"Nothing!" he almost shrieked.

She set the mug down; he hunched against her reprimand: if he didn't learn to keep his temper, he would lose all his friends and hurt the people closest to him. "I've got an idea," she said. "How would you like to go skiing?"

He was filled, suddenly, with love for his mother so vast and profound that he was struck silent. They had skied last year once, all four of them and their cousin. Blur of white. Wind in his face. He kissed her shoulder under the cottony fabric.

"If Nate's feeling well enough," she said.

"He's well enough!"

He ran up to Nate's room, hopped up and down behind his brother, who was still, inexplicably, at his desk. "We're going skiing, Nate-ster!" He repeated the news, hopping on one foot, counting the hops, till their mother appeared. "What do you think?" she said to Nate. "Pay attention to your body."

Nate's hand went automatically to the bulge under his collar-
bone where a small box lay right under the skin. Dylan looked at
the rug. "I'm not sure your father would think this is a good idea,"
she said.

"It's a good idea!" The cry burst out like a bird taking flight.
Their father, more cautious than their mother, said no to the most
harmless of ventures. In the realm of "fun for the children," the
boys and their mother kept secrets from their father. "It's a *great*
idea!" He eyeballed Nate till he closed the book. Not without
bookmarking the page: Nate the good, Nate the nerd. But he for-
gave Nate for everything.

Alpine Valley was seventy-five or ninety minutes away from Evanston, depending on traffic and weather. They'd ski for two or three
hours, grab a snack, and be back by dinnertime. "You go *nuts* in
the winter around here if you stay in the house! And Nate's doing
so well!"

That was what their mother said into the phone, to her sister, or
a girlfriend. Their mother liked to talk and drive — had to, in fact.
If I'm not doing two things at once, I feel like I'm wasting time,
she would say. She called their father: "Monday he's going back in
— let him have fun for a change!" Clicking off, she said to Nate in
the passenger seat, "Your father." Like he was a burden she had to
bear, though both boys felt in their separate ways that she admired
him. Their father was slow to express pleasure but even slower to
anger; his pleasure in their existence, in the entity of family, discharged clouds of tenderness. He's a sage, your father, Nana had
said, and on another occasion, *Nate takes after him.* Now, alert to his
place in the family hierarchy, Dylan had to counter such remarks.
Who did *he* take after, Osama bin Laden?

Would they laugh if he said that?

Soon the car picked up speed and self-love returned. The whit-
ened streets slid by in silence, marked by stop signs with their faces
blanked, the ghosts of stop signs. Sometimes on a turn, the back
of the car spun out. "Go faster!" he cried, not that he expected his
instructions to be followed. But he liked the feeling of things not
being quite under his mother's control.

He sat in the back-seat tranquility of motion he had no control
over until roused by animated voices. Up front, his mother and
brother were discussing a movie. "It's the best film of the century,"

Nate said, and she, *"Film!"* mockingly. "So, Roger Ebert. Where did you get all that movie perspective?"

"It totally sucked," Dylan offered, which was funny, he thought, because he had no idea what movie they were talking about (and why was *he* in the back?). He tried to follow up with fabricated facts about the unidentified movie. He tried to think of a movie he'd seen that he had an opinion about. His tongue felt tired. Roger Ebert? Louder, he said, "I wish I had cancer."

Nate laughed. Their mother: "What did you say?"

He repeated the statement aggressively. The car skidded to a stop. She turned and nailed him with her eyes. "Do you know what you're saying?"

He nodded in support of himself, of his pride as a ten-year-old. Then he felt enfeebled. He knew what he'd said, the string of words that had bubbled up (not from his brain but from a spot close to his stomach). But they had floated away like balloons he'd inadvertently let go of. He maintained his ferocity for another moment or two, but there was nothing behind it. His mother's eyes flashed what looked like hatred for him.

"He didn't mean it," said Nate. "Give him a break, Thea!"

"It's *mother* to you, boy. Say it!" Laughing, she whacked at Nate, then with a cry drew her hand back. "Oh, God, your port."

"Chill," said Nate. "*Mother* dear."

Three teenagers and their jackets, caps, scarves, and gloves occupied the single bench in the rental hut. They were two boys and a girl; an electric current flowed among them, barring outsiders. Dylan, who had arrived before his brother and mother, toed off his galoshes, slid his feet into newly rented ski boots—quickly, a man who knew his business. "Where are these so-called Alps?" said the girl to her friends. "I don't see any Alps."

"There's an expert run here. A thousand yards." One of the boys pointed to a map on the wall behind them on which different-colored trails ran like veins up the mountainside. The girl bent backward on the bench and regarded the map upside down. Her hair, long, brown, straight, shining, spread out on the floor. "Ya-ards? Try *feet*. And it's just *advanced*."

"You're a cunt, Lindsey," said the other boy.

She pulled herself upright in a single swift motion, like a wave smacking the beach. Like a whip. "Watch your mouth, bitch."

Dylan cast a covert glance at the girl—Lindsey!—who didn't need to think before she spoke. Words rolled out of her the same way her hair whipped behind her. "It's called Big Thunder," she said nasally. "Let's hit Big Thunder." Yawning, she dug into her pocket and pulled out a tube of lip balm. The back of her red parka glowed in the block of light coming in the doorway. Then Nate arrived, and then their mother, regarding the scene like she wanted to improve on it.

"Uh, guys?"

It wasn't Dylan and Nate that she was addressing. Her face shone with a sour-smelling light. Dylan squirmed down inside his parka. "Would you mind," she said to the three teenagers, "moving over a little? There are other people in here who might want a seat."

Without actually acknowledging anything outside their compass, the three drifted closer to one another, leaving a small space at the end of the bench. Dylan's mother and brother regarded the space, each commanding the other to sit. Dylan edged back into a corner, as far as possible from his so-called family. His mother had a regrettable habit of not knowing the limits of her domain. Before Nate got sick, they used to joke about it. He looked toward the door; the light was blinding. With unbuckled boots he ran out into the gorgeous strangeness of not being able to see.

This was it, what he had dreamed of. The smell of wood smoke, the icy packed snow under his feet, the broad white face of the mountain. He buckled up, snapped boots onto skis, moved back and forth in front of the hut, picking up each ski and slapping it down on the snow as if leg and ski were one thing; he was born to wear these things. Last year in Minnesota, he and Nate and Cousin Jenna took a ski lesson. He remembered everything. *Schuss.* To ski straight down the mountain.

When Nate and their mother emerged at last, Dylan pushed off with his poles, knees bent as the instructor had said, to impress upon anyone who was looking the pointlessness of more instruction. His mother skied toward him, steady and quick. He admired that.

Then he saw what she had under her arm. "No way," he said.

"Oh yes."

It was a helmet, clunky and moronic, like the top of a trashcan. "*You* aren't wearing one."

"Check out your big brother."

He didn't have to look. "He's a nerd!" Trouble started in her face but he went on, "*They* aren't wearing helmets." She knew who he meant.

"They could break their necks. Wind up in a wheelchair. In a hospital bed, being fed through a tube."

"Mom," said Nate, "you're overdoing it."

Dylan felt he'd won the argument, with Nate's help, but in his mother's court of law, being right counted for nothing. Her ski came down upon the front of his skis, and he was glued in place while she situated the helmet and snapped it under his chin with a merry grin on her face. He was boxed in, cut off from the possibilities that so recently had stretched before him. No wind in his ears, and this protrusion, this *shelf,* to peer out from under. He thought of a movie (all of a sudden!) wherein the hero's entire head, front and back, was padlocked inside an iron mask, with slits for the eyes and mouth. He tried to release the helmet's clasp, couldn't manipulate the tiny plastic pieces, and in the consolidating organ of his psyche, something came loose. It was a small glitch in the system, activated when an impulse of his was checked, not invariably but once in a while. A wild dog that lived inside him had yanked free of its chain.

As if for his life, he fought the thing on his head. The strap was tight, his hands felt dead inside his fat-fingered gloves, he couldn't even feel the buckle. The poles on their wrist straps swung against his legs as if they had it in for him: Dylan against Things. With a heave of strength and will, he pulled off his gloves with his teeth, he flung off his poles. "Stupid buckle!" People cast glances. His mother shouted, "Dylan, get hold of yourself," but she seemed frightened of him, and then he too was frightened. To restore himself, he tried to turn around, turn his back on her. His skis crossed, he teetered and fell, legs entwined, at the mercy of his uncontrollable skis, and all he could do was roll onto his back, skis flailing like the broken blades of a helicopter or the legs of some mutant insect. He squeezed back tears of shame.

Then Nate was leaning over him. "Yo. Little bro." The words went by without touching him but Nate's eyes found him. Nate clicked their helmets together. "Chill, man?"

His mother on one side, Nate on the other, Dylan was raised to his feet. "I ought to knock your two heads together," she said, reclaiming maternal control of a wry, amused sort. "Now listen to me. On the slopes I want us all to stay together. Promise, wild man?"

For a while it was as if a fever had passed. They lined up at the rope tow like ducklings, Mom in front, and let the thick rope run through their gloved hands, then one-two-three, squeeze—yank—they were moving. Last year Dylan's skis kept sliding out of the ruts, and several times he fell, and they had to stop the rope and wait for him to take his place again, but he was good now. At the turnstile he let go just a little late and managed to stay upright, so pleased with his mastery that he didn't mind that the tow ended barely a third of the way up the mountain or that he remained last in the family line. Stoic in the shade of his helmet, he followed the other two down the gentle slope, veering slowly from side to side as they did, bending forward just a little to decrease wind resistance. The next time down, he straightened his skis, tucked his useless poles under his arms, and swiftly reached the base of the hill. There he raised his poles in a victory salute, for his mother and brother still midslope, traversing at snail speed, skis clumsily splayed. Nate fell; Dylan turned away in shame, thinking of yesterday at Ethan's. They were wrestling, and it was starting to be fun, when Ethan went limp and rolled out from under him: it was *wrong* when the enemy didn't even try. You're a pussy, he said to Ethan, which is exactly what the dude was and is—for quitting and for being a liar, because he had fought (he swore!) *fair;* there was no reason for Ethan's mother to send him home.

When the other two reached the bottom—finally!—his mother showed him the snowplow, as if he'd forgotten it. "I was racing," he started to say, then comprehension dawned. Again he was competing with nobody. "At least I didn't fall," he muttered.

"I fell on purpose," Nate said mildly. "To slow myself down."

If you went any slower, you'd've gone backward, Dylan said to himself but not to Nate. He fought his frustration, tilting his face up to the wind as he grasped the tow rope, snowplowing down the wide, gentle slope, back and forth, back and forth, like it didn't matter how fast he went or even where.

During lunch their mother commended Dylan's self-control. "You showed real maturity," she said. "You deserve a medal," Nate said, raising an elbow to ward off Dylan's punch. Nate didn't want to eat, though their mother coaxed him. Dylan ate his burger and most of Nate's. Snow was falling again, slanting at the picture window.

Outside the restaurant it looked like time had passed faster than inside. The swarm of skiers had thinned, though it might just be the blowing snow, into which people took a step and disappeared. It was hard to see where the tow ended, and farther up the slope, the mountain melded with the dirty white sky. Flakes were small and almost hard against his face. Fearful of being steered back to the car, Dylan grabbed his skis and poles and ran toward the tow rope. He was almost there when Nate passed him on skis, quick and strong as he had been last year. Nate swiveled, stopping dead in front of him, in a spray of stinging snow. The move looked classy. Dylan felt as always the impulse to best him. He stomped back into his bindings, stared his brother down; he was almost Nate's height. Then, maybe it was the mist thickening around them, snow settling on their twin helmets, or maybe he finally saw how futile it was to contest the advantages of age, but suddenly Nate's skills no longer agitated him. It was like losing a heavy book from his backpack. Of course Nate had skills. "Now we'll do a real hill," he said to Nate. "Right?"

Their mother approached. Dylan urged his brother toward the trails to their left, where a chairlift climbed the mountain and vanished into white. Beyond it were other lifts and trails that promised keener pleasures. "We're going *there*, Nate and me," he informed their mother, with a nod toward the white wilderness. "Want to come?"

She spoke drily. "I'm no expert. Are you?"

"It's just advanced."

"*Just?* Do you know how to parallel?"

"Yes!"

"In your dreams."

He pulled his skis together, pressed his knees together, and hopped to one side like an Olympic skier, following up with a withering look at his mother, who would never get over her need to impede him.

"I wouldn't mind us trying a long slope," she said, "but we're not going to be daredevils. Nate, how are you holding up?"

"He's fine."

"The man speaks," said Nate.

She had a trail map and she spread it out and pointed to a trail in green that was called, embarrassingly, First Adventure. According to the key, green stood for beginner. Big Thunder, three trails over, was black for advanced. "Do you think we're babies?" he said, but she wouldn't budge. "Tell her, Nate," he said, but Nate only grinned. He gave Nate a shove, Nate shoved him back, and it was like always, Nate's gloved hands against his hands, a stalemate, with Dylan suspecting he wasn't fighting his hardest.

The First Adventure lift had benches like porch swings, a substantial improvement upon the rope tow. Dylan and his mother and brother stood side by side till the seat hit the back of their knees and swooped them up, quicker and higher than Dylan expected. He sat in the middle, and inside his helmet he had to turn all the way around to see, but all his thoughts, good and bad, blew away in the gusty wind. The vista kept widening. Behind them, smaller and smaller, the bunny skiers went down the baby hill, or was it babies down the bunny hill, lurching, falling like dolls. On both sides of the lift, silvery trails snaked up the mountain through pine woods, half hidden and glimmering. Involuntarily he kicked out with his skis. The bench started swinging; he crowed with the thrill of it. "Don't *do* that!" said his mother. Bitch, he said, under his breath, almost dreamily. Heaven seemed close. And angels. Ahead, emptied of passengers, a bench clanked around the turnstile and started downward.

As soon as they reached the disembarking point, he slid down off the bench, landed squarely, and poled himself toward the ridge, where a right turn led to First Adventure and a left toward the more rigorous trails he had seen on the map, hidden in the blowing snow. He had plans. After the beginner trail, he would go right back up—no Mom, just him and Nate speeding down the silver slope as fast as thought. He opened his mouth to catch a few flakes while his heart thumped with the force of his imagining. Wind blew at him, front and back, but couldn't get inside his parka. There was wind and squeaking, crunching snow and the creaking lift, and dimly audible human voices. They enclosed him, a thicket of well-meaning sounds.

Then under the rush of wind, he became aware that one of the layers of sound was gone. He was inclined to overlook it—hardly an absence, just a thinning out, a barely perceptible dilution of the forces around him. Besides, going back to check on something, retracing his steps for any reason, subverted the proper order of things. But the silence seeped into his mind like fumes, and after a minute or two he was poling back to the lift—where he found a scattering of people stalled in confusion, and above them, perversely halted, the benches of the lift swaying a little in the wind, and below, seated in the snow, his mother and brother. Nate leaned against her, his head on her shoulder, eyes closed, while she regarded the onlookers with a stiff smile. "He'll be fine!" she kept saying. "He has to rest a few minutes."

Dylan stood on the edge of the gathering, remembering talk between his parents at the kitchen table, with him outside the door, unable not to overhear: We have to keep it normal for them. As much as we possibly can. At which he had turned and fled, from everything beyond the bounds of his parents' vision of normality for him and Nate, expanses he still had no wish to explore. He wanted to flee again, and he might have if his legs weren't so spongy. Then his mother was beckoning. "He's just tired, honey. It comes on quick sometimes. I think his count is low."

He didn't want to look at Nate, but it was hard not to. His helmet was off, their mother's plaid scarf around his head and neck. He had no eyebrows. Was this normal? Nate opened his eyes and smiled apologetically. Dylan wanted to punch him.

He punched his mother's shoulder. "Dylan, what's *wrong* with you!" she said sharply, then softened her voice. The Ski Patrol would ride Nate down on their sleigh easy as pie, like lying in bed. It was almost time to go anyway. She seemed to be talking to herself, though her words were directed at him. Could he ski down and meet them by that rental place? Go in, take off his equipment, and return it? He could do that by himself, couldn't he?

"Of course! Do you think I'm retarded?"

He moved slowly, in no willed direction, just out of his mother's sight, while snow blew at her and Nate, and people's hats and hoods and helmets and the boughs of evergreens. The lift creaked and started moving again, though many chairs were empty. The few people getting off barely paused to look around before pushing off toward their chosen slopes. The wind seemed to have intentions that weren't kind. The word *evil* came to his mind but he didn't know what to do with it.

The sky had darkened toward the gray of night when the red parka appeared on high, and the girl, Lindsey, solitary on the long bench and helmetless, hatless. She slid down onto the icy packed snow like she didn't even have to think about it, her hair bouncing behind her. For a moment their eyes met; she grinned. Then, passing, she thrust a pole in his direction as if spearing a fish, and clicked open the binding of his left ski, crowing as she flitted by.

For a moment he flailed for balance. His freed ski was sliding off, though it remained clipped to his boot by a short cord. He captured it with the sole of his boot. If she were a boy, he'd have been enraged—he'd have felt engorged with impotent hatred. But now, hearing in his mind the sound of her hilarity, he simply snapped his boot back into place and poled himself toward where she had vanished. Snow blew inside his helmet and down his neck unprotected by a scarf, but he hardly felt it, passing the turn-offs to two or three unmarked trails (there were no signs, or else the signs were covered in snow) till he arrived at the top of a hill so steep he couldn't see where it went. A shiver climbed the knobs of his spine. He had dreamed this, riding a brakeless bike down a blind hill, trying to wake before the crash while simultaneously willing himself back inside the dream, into the pure speed of the drop. Digging his poles into the feathery new snow, he crept toward the edge. He felt Lindsey here and everywhere, her skier's soul joined with his, two experts on unworthy slopes.

Then he was moving, slowly at first, then faster than he had ever gone without the shell of a vehicle around him, bent over like skiers on TV twisting through the bendy yellow flags, except that he was going straight down, past skiers traversing—no time to see faces—faster than images could be processed, faster at last than his mind could think. This was *schussing*. This was riding the wind. He wondered for a second if he should try to slow down. A voice said in his ear, Make yourself fall! But falling was what Ethan would do. Falling was Nate. Dylan leaned forward into the whoosh of his skis, the wind of his descent, as if thereby he would rise into the air like a kite.

It was his last thought before he hit. There was a crack, a flash of red. He flew backward in slow time, like the moment on Nate's sled, in the circle of his brother's arms, when, swerving around another sled, he saw a tree looming before them, and he had all the time in the world to think—*Turn, Nate! Swerve!*—and to picture the aftermath of breakage and pain, though there was no time to

say it aloud. Nate had miraculously managed to turn them; they'd
missed the tree.

When Dylan opens his eyes, he is sprawled in deep snow. The
world returns bit by bit. He tips his head back, takes a cautious sip
of air. There are things to do and things he mustn't do, so it seems.
He raises his head then sets it down. His head, inconceivably, is
lower than his feet. He's on his back, tries to turn; pain makes
him gasp and the gasp hurts the top of his belly. From somewhere
comes an outraged, teary female voice: "I'll kill him!" A chunk of
time seems gone from his brain.

Then people are bending over him as they had bent over Nate.
"It's a kid. Oh my."
"Trying to set a record, are you?"
"Kids his age don't belong here."
"Little cocksucker. I'd like to wallop him!"
"Don't move, kiddo. He shouldn't move, should he? Are you
okay?"
"Hey, bomber, what's up? Can you move your legs?"
"Let him lie still. Wait for Ski Patrol."
"I'm fine," he cries, raising his arms to prove it.
Someone taps his helmet. "Good thing you had this on. Protect
those brain cells."
Was he being insulted? "Just help me up!" he cries.
While people are unhooking his skis, unlooping the pole straps
from around his wrists, he wonders what he hit. If it was a person,
and that person was Lindsey, he didn't want to know. Someone
takes one of his arms, someone else the other; they pull him upright. Then he tries to stand, and the pain is so vast and deep, he
has to scream.

That night in the hospital where Nate was being transfused, Dylan
lay on an examining table while the doctor wound his leg in sticky
white gauze from his knee to the bottom of his foot. It was cool at
first then started heating up. He was lucky, the doctor said. It was
a greenstick fracture. He should keep it elevated when possible.
He had broken some ribs too, but they would heal on their own,
quickly, because he was young. In six weeks after moderate physical therapy he'd be back on the slopes.

His mother stood on the other side of the table, and he looked up at her to see how he was supposed to take the news. She had tears in her eyes. He felt his own tears welling, though with his pain medication he was so relaxed he could barely imagine pain. "Mom," he said tenderly, "you don't have to cry!"

"He was down to *nine,*" she said. "It's a wonder he could keep his head up."

The doctor signed a sheet of paper and left. They sat, Dylan on the table, his mother in a plastic chair in a tiny, bright, curtained-off room in the ER, where they were obliged to stay till a wheelchair came to roll him out to the car, where his father was waiting. His crutches stood in a corner; he wanted to try them but not enough to say anything. Footsteps passed but didn't enter. He was alone with his mother, which he liked though he'd never have admitted it. He liked the word *greenstick*. He didn't want to know what *nine* meant.

"It's so hard," she said.

"He's getting better," he said sternly. He sat up, kicked his good leg. "He'll be fine!"

His words sounded lame, but to his surprise her tears ceased. She put her arms around him. "Dylan," she said, "do you know how amazing you are?"

Despite himself he grinned shyly. She could stop now.

But she didn't stop. She held on to him tight. "You're alive. Alive."

Of course he was alive. She smelled of sweat and deodorant. He sat breathing her in, with a combination of joy and terror that overrode his medication. His heart thudded savagely. At her trust in him that he had to live up to—from now on, it seemed, and for the boundless rest of his life.

KATE WALBERT

## *M&M World*

FROM *The New Yorker*

GINNY HAD PROMISED to take the girls to M&M World, that ridiculous place in Times Square they had passed too often in a taxi,
Maggie scooting to press her face to the glass to watch the giant
smiling M&M scale the Empire State Building on the electronic
billboard and wave from the spire, its color dissolving yellow, then
blue, then red, then yellow again. She had promised. "Promised,"
Olivia said, her face twisted into the expression she reserved for
moments of betrayal. "Please," Olivia whined. "You said 'spring.'"

She *had* said "spring." This she remembered, and it was spring,
or almost. Spring enough. Spring advancing, the trees newly bud-
ded, the air peppery. Regardless, it felt too early to go home when
the light shone this strongly, slanting across Central Park in the
way of late March, early April; plus, the city had already collectively
sprung forward. *Spring has sprung, the grass has ris'.*

"All right," she found herself saying. "Just once. Today. Just
once. This is it." Breaking her resolution to stop qualifying—five
more minutes, this last page, one more bite—and wishing, mid-
speech, she would stop. She has tried. Just as she has tried to be
more easygoing, but when push comes to shove, as it always will,
she is not easygoing. And she qualifies. It's a verbal tic: first this
and then that. A constant negotiation—action then reward, or
promise of reward. What is it that the books say? Screw the books.

She takes the girls' hands and holds tight, changing course,
crossing Central Park West to Central Park South. The girls suddenly delighted, and delightful, straining ahead, buoyant. They
are gorgeous, bright-eyed, brilliant girls: one tall, one short, pant

legs dragging, torn leggings, sneakers that glow in the dark or light up with each step, *boom boom boom.* They break free and race across, bounding onto the sidewalk, their hands rejoined like paper cutouts, zigzagging here, zigzagging there, Maggie clutching Zoom Zoom with her free hand, choking the thing, its dangly legs and arms, its floppy, flattened ears.

Ginny follows them quickly, remembering how her heart would literally stop as Olivia—then, what? four? five?—would run to this same corner, the light not yet changed. Her daughter had only to step into traffic, to veer off the curb. She never did. Olivia climbed the stone seals at seal park in Chelsea, the bronze bears on the playground outside the Metropolitan Museum; she teetered on their heads and could so easily have slipped—she did slip once, but it was nothing. Still, Ginny had to wake her every hour that night, shake her out of her sleepy fog. "Who am I?" Ginny had said, Olivia's blue princess pajamas silky beneath her grip, Olivia's shoulders so thin. "Mommy?" Olivia said, squinting, pupils the right size, shrinking: constricting or contracting, she never knew which, but, whatever, correctly—she was fine. And then, a bit older, those other sneakers—wheelies? heelies?—and Olivia careering along the sidewalk, wheels where the heels should be, the speed! And downhill too, with nothing to hold on to, no way to stop. The pediatrician had said the most dangerous thing was trampolines, even with nets. And then the rented house that summer had one, netless, in the back yard. She had watched as the girls bounced higher and higher. She couldn't get them off, Olivia and now Maggie, just like her big sister. She had stood vigil at the window, or next to the rail in her hat and long sleeves buttoned at the wrist, the girls slathered with sunscreen. The point is, her heart stuck in her throat, always in her throat.

Ginny hurries to catch up. One has tripped the other accidentally on purpose and now the other howls as if singed with fire.

"Stop it," Ginny hisses. "Right now. Period. Stop it or no M&M World."

They stop, Olivia smiling to clear the air, though the air stinks: they're near a line of carriages and their horses.

"Please," Maggie's saying. "Please. Please." And so they circle around, petting Blackie, petting Whitey, petting Gummie with the drippy nostrils, the one the driver says loves sugar—"Yes, yes, next time we'll bring a sugar cube"—and Whinny and Happy and the other one, its long yellow teeth reminding her: she needs to bleach. Suddenly everyone's teeth are whiter than her own; they wear them like necklaces. And their faces too seem suspiciously doctored, first one line then another magically evaporating, a whole generation of women paying for erasure.

"Ouch," Maggie says. She holds one hand flat as instructed, the brown carrot there, a gift from the driver. The driver laughs. "No danger," he says. The horse roots and chews. "You're fine," Ginny says. She strokes the soft hair of the horse's muzzle, the horse nuzzling Maggie's tiny palm; it wears a hat with a feathered plume, as if it had trotted here from the stables of a fallen tsar. Ginny leans into its solid skull, and the horse stares back at her with a huge watery eye. Where am I? it wonders, or something equivalent, and she thinks of the whale in Patagonia that asked the same thing. This was years ago, before the girls were born, when she and the girls' father took a trip to Chile.

They were there for vacation; there to see animals. Animals had been promised, including whales. A center existed, manned by earnest students, young men and women from all over the world who spoke Spanish beautifully and wore thin silver bracelets with a symbol that meant something. They piloted the boats and explained to the tourists the seriousness of the venture, the need for extra donations. The tourists kept quiet, mostly, standing on the side of the boat where they'd been told to stand, given the radar and various other instruments that would determine the location of the whales—sometimes a female with a calf or two, or, rarer, a male on its own. The whales communicated over great distances, as everyone knew, but the students could intercept their communications, or decipher them: regardless, somehow the students knew what the whales were saying, or might be saying, and so could steer the boat in the right direction where, for a fee, the tourists could take pictures of the whale surfacing or of the plume of water from the blowhole, or sometimes even, if the tourists were very lucky, of a whale jumping gracefully as if showing off.

On this particular voyage, the one Ginny found herself on with the girls' father, Ginny chose to stay on the side of the boat with more shade. She was hot, she told the girls' father. He could call her if anything exciting happened. She had opened her book: *War and Peace*, a paperback edition she had picked up in the paperback exchange in Santiago, where they had stayed for a few days before heading south. She had been at a good part, a really good part, and so perhaps it took some time for the whale to get her attention. She had had, when she later thought about it, the feeling of being watched. And so she had looked up from her place in *War and Peace* and seen the whale, a female, she would learn, uncharacteristically alone, lolling before her on the surface of the water. She folded the corner of her page and stood, shading her eyes; then she walked to the boat rail to get a better look. She didn't call the girls' father; she didn't call anyone. She looked down at the whale. It lay on its side, staring with one eye straight at Ginny, drifting alone in its disappearing sea, the sun burning both of them, beaming through the torn shreds of the shredded atmosphere. They stayed like that for a while, Ginny convinced that the whale had a message to deliver, something she might translate and convey to the world. But she never figured out what, since too soon someone from the other side saw it and the whale was gone.

"Mother!" Maggie's saying.

Ginny pulls away from the solid skull of the horse and turns back to her youngest.

"You weren't listening," Maggie is saying.

"Was so," Ginny says.

"Then can I?" Maggie says.

Ginny bends down to kiss Maggie's head, the part between the plastic barrettes that Maggie repeatedly refastens each morning, wanting to look, she says, "right." Maggie's hair smells delicious.

"No," she says.

Maggie stomps her foot; she's pushed Zoom Zoom deep in her pocket, its strange face, not quite rabbit, not quite anything else —"it's extinct," Maggie once said—just above the fold.

"I love you," Ginny says. "You're beautiful."

"What about me?" Olivia says. She has been standing next to Ginny, as quiet as a stone.

"You too, sweetheart," she says, pulling her oldest in. "You too."

There are other things to fix, not just her yellow teeth. She needs some spots removed from her skin; she needs to dye her gray roots, the stubborn tuft that refuses to blend. She could use something for her posture—Pilates—and she's overdue for a mammogram, a bone scan, a colonoscopy. She needs a new coat, an elegant one like those she's seen on other mothers, something stylish to go with the other stylish clothes she means to buy, and the boots, the right boots, not just the galoshes she's slipped on every morning all winter; it's spring now, isn't it? She should pay to have her toes soaked, her feet scrubbed of dead skin. She could choose a bright color of nail polish, a hip color, a dark purple or maybe even that shade of brown. She should take a class—philosophy, religion, vegan cooking—and wear sandals there, the new kind, with the straps that wrap the ankle or twist all the way to midcalf, her brown toenails shiny smooth, as if dipped in oil. There are posters on the subway and numbers to call. She writes down the websites in the notebook she carries for such things: lists, reminders. But she is constantly out of time, losing track, forgetting. Sunday's Monday evening, then Wednesday vanishes altogether.

M&M World looms in the distance, the electronic billboard—M&M'S WORLD—as bright as a beacon. They hurry down Broadway. At Fifty-first, Olivia claims she can see the waving M&M hanging from the spire of the Empire State Building. "It's blue!" she says. "Where? Where?" Maggie says. "No, it's green!" she says. "Where?" Maggie says, hopping. She's suddenly furious. "I can't see! Lift me!"

"Be patient," Ginny says. She takes Maggie's hand and pulls her along. Olivia is in front, swimming upstream, parting the crowds. Hallelujah to the end of the hideous winter: blackened snowdrifts and dog shit and lost gloves. The city erupts, oozes, overflows; everyone is outdoors, walking quickly or standing on the corner checking phones, dialing phones, speaking on phones. "Where?" someone is saying. "You're breaking up."

"Olivia?" she yells; she doesn't see her.

Olivia has stopped in front of a store window: snow globes and hats and luggage on wheels, a rack of "I ♥ New York" T-shirts, electronic gadgets. She is suddenly taller when she turns back around, her face complicated. "I'm here, Mom," she says.

"Don't scare me."

"It's the new kind."

"I can't," Ginny says. "We've got to—"

Maggie's pulling her hand. "Mister Softee!" she's saying.

Christ, already? The truck?

"Please?" Maggie says.

"Not today," Ginny says.

"Did you see it?" Olivia's saying.

"Just a minute," she says to Maggie. "What?" she says to Olivia.

"Please? It's a special day, isn't it?" Maggie's saying. "It's spring. You said." Ginny turns to Maggie. In Maggie's smile are four missing teeth, each one saved and wrapped in tinfoil in her Tooth Fairy Box. She plans on blowing her wad all at once: fifteen teeth —or are there more?—beneath her pillow, precious little things although three have already been patched for cavities, the dentist wondering how vigilant Ginny has been about flossing, the amount of candy consumed. "Remarkably so and hardly any," Ginny had said at the last appointment. "It's a mystery."

"Next time," she says now to Maggie. "Enough's enough."

"It's the new kind," Olivia is saying.

Maggie looks up. "Please," she says, her teeth tiny pearls.

"Mom!" Olivia says.

"Oh, all right," Ginny says. "Just this once. Not again. Only because it's spring. This is it."

"Thanks, Mom," Maggie says, smiling.

"What?" Olivia says.

"Ice cream!" Maggie says. They high-five and dance around Ginny's knees.

Ginny had kept a list of the animals of Patagonia. The ones that interested her. There were the penguins, of course, an entire colony that was completely tame. They had never been hunted and it was as simple as that, the guide had said, she and the girls' father stooping, squatting to watch them furiously building their nests: the mating season had ended and now they were preparing for eggs. There were some too that were not well. Those stood outside the colonies, looking in; sometimes small crowds of other penguins gathered around them and nosed them toward the water, a not so subtle suggestion, the guide had said, that they might be better off drowned. Brutal nature, the girls' father had said. There were the lizards and the guanacos and the numerous birds, the elephant seals they'd watched from a cliff top, the males fighting over a female that lay on its side, clueless or, rather, helpless. Brutal nature, she had said, and the girls' father had laughed, and in that instant, and this is true, a rainbow had appeared—it was that kind of weather—the arc stretching from one end of the ocean to the other, and she had taken his hand and said, "Yes." She thought she was ready. Children, she had said. Dozens of them.

There are even more people farther on, in Times Square, though the cars have been blocked and so there's that, at least—one less thing. They'll finish their ice creams here before turning back toward the store, Ginny says, maneuvering the girls around the tables and chairs, the feet, the flocks of pigeons, the remnants of lunches consumed. Men and women she may or may not recognize—movie stars, rappers, models—loom above them, magnified a thousand percent, their eyes the size of swimming pools, their teeth cliff walls she could hide behind or possibly dwell in, like the Anasazi, chiseling toeholds so she might scale down at night to forage. The movie stars, rappers, and models are invariably smiling, cheerful; some sing or dance, the women with suggestive postures, the men in dark glasses and fur coats. Everyone is moving, gyrating, blinking, flashing. Tourists sit on the new risers, watching nothing or everything, looking down, from time to time, to study their guidebooks. The breeze picks up, eddying ticket stubs and wrappers and waxed paper and brown bags and plastic straws and whatever else has been left behind. Shameless, this litter: if she ran the world. Recently, a flock of plastic bags has caught in the spindly sycamore in front of their apartment, empty bags that inflate and deflate with the wind like marooned sailing ships. They are what she sees when she looks out the living room window, which, truth be told, she does more often now than she should. It's as if she was trying to remember something that she'd forgotten, as if there was someone she was supposed to call. She stands at the window and looks, the plastic bags inflating, deflating. Alive, somehow, mocking her or maybe just reminding her—a cosmological message. From whom? Of what?

"Mother!" Olivia yells. Maggie, halfway between Ginny and Olivia, is on the pavement, clutching her knee. "Mister Softee!" she's saying. "My cone!" Ginny is next to her before she knows it, pushing up Maggie's ragged leggings to expose the skin, stroking her hair. Strangers gather dumbly. "We're fine," Ginny says. "Thank you. She's fine." She blows on the scraped place, red and scratched raw but not bleeding—they were racing, they were almost tied, Olivia's explaining. Maggie's ice cream is upturned and

melting in the street, a ruination. Maggie cannot speak for sobbing. "Sweetheart," Ginny's saying, stroking her hair. "It's okay,
sweetheart. We'll find another truck. We'll get a new one. We'll
get another."

Olivia licks her cone, listening. "Then I want another one too,"
she says.

The place is jammed and loud. There are vats of brightly colored
M&M's everywhere, M&M's crammed in plastic tubes spiraling to
the ceiling. There are M&M T-shirts and M&M mugs and M&M
tote bags and stuffed M&M men, or whatever they're called (M&M
guys? M&M characters?), and M&M pillows and M&M beach towels
and M&M statues and M&M key rings and M&M snow globes and
M&M plates and M&M puzzles and M&M umbrellas. The employees, dressed in M&M colors, dance and sing along—for minimum
wage?—to a song Ginny recognizes, a song she's heard played continuously on the radio station that Olivia listens to in her room
now, the door mostly closed. It's the voice, Olivia pointed out, of
one of the men on the billboards, one of the men swathed in fur
—or maybe he was the guy in the suit. Ginny can't remember, her
head already clogged, her eyes watering. It is hot in here, the air
conditioning not yet on, the heat remembering winter. The girls
stand on either side of her, transfixed. Maggie's tears have been
wiped dry, a Band-Aid found in the deep recesses of Ginny's purse,
the wound, as Maggie called it, cleaned with a Fresh Wipe, then
kissed for good luck. Only Big Sister could do that part—wiggling
her fingers first to conjure the fairy dust that only Big Sister could
conjure. A fairy dust invisible to mothers, its healing powers a mystery, like phoenix tears, Olivia said. Or Zoom Zoom, Maggie said.

"Can we, please?" Olivia asks now. She has seen the sign direct-
ing customers up, by way of the escalator, to the second floor,
where a life-size M&M waits like Santa Claus, available for photo-
graphs.

"All right," Ginny says. "Just this once. Because we're here. But
not if there's a line."

"Yeah!" the girls say. Olivia takes Maggie's hand and leads the
way. Ginny watches them step onto the escalator with their identical ponytails, their small shoulders, their fleeces tied around their
waists. From the moment they were born, they looked like her or
they looked like their father, or sometimes they looked like a com-

bination of both: her hair and his eyes, his mouth and her nose, her chin and his smile. But from behind now they look just like little girls: sisters in a portrait, or Renoir's beauties in flat black hats, poppies sprung from their ballet shoes. They are timeless somehow, though too fast growing. "Zoom Zoom is shrinking," Maggie had said. "Wasn't Zoom Zoom once bigger?" They ascend and Ginny feels the catch of love unbearable: she never imagined this, she thinks, her heart suddenly thudding, as if stepping down a stair or two, hard, and then a pause and then another thump, or a clump, her heart clumping down the stairs—caffeine, maybe, or nerves.

She follows them up but they are already out of sight. The crowds thick, people speaking different languages, laughing, dancing with the employees. Where is she? What is this? At the top of the stairs, Olivia waits to show her. "Look!" she says, holding up a green Statue of Liberty M&M. "You pull the torch."

"Cool," Ginny says.

"Are you looking?" Olivia says. "The torch!"

"I saw," Ginny says. "It's cool."

"And they have purple ones."

"Cool."

"Can we get some?"

"Where's your sister?"

"With the guy. Can we get some?"

"What?"

"The purple ones! They're grape!"

She and the girls' father had discussed at length how to explain it to them. He had thought it best to be as honest as possible, to sit them down and simply tell them that he was moving out. "They're old enough," he had said.

They're too young, she'd said. She could barely look at him. He was all secrets; they slid around beneath his expression like tectonic plates. He was all the things he wouldn't say to her that she wanted to know, all deception and cunning. It made her crazy to look at him and so she stared at her feet, at her ubiquitous galoshes. At least she should find some more contemporary ones, the ones with the thick matching socks turned down over the top, the ones in strong solid colors that came from the British Isles or somewhere—Brittany?—and suggested other lives, lives spent

mucking stalls or milking cows, or even striding with a fishing rod
and a rough-hewn basket through streams where the trout still ran
as they once had, before, in other places, they grew strange scales
and forgot to spawn; lives spent striding and oblivious of the wet,
oblivious of the hard stones that would have pierced the soles of
lesser girls. Boots that suggested strength or, at the very least, a
day's catch.

"It's not like they don't get the concept," he had said.

She looked up at his face and squinted, and the girls were there
too: in his eyes, his eyebrows.

"Maggie!" Ginny shouts. She can't see her. The line for a photograph with the M&M is endless, and she can't see Maggie anywhere.

"What guy?" Ginny asks, turning to Olivia. "What do you mean,
'the guy'?"

"I didn't say that," Olivia said. "I don't know. She was here a
minute ago."

"Where?"

"Right here," Olivia says, and starts to cry.

"Don't," Ginny says. "We'll find her. Please. She wouldn't just
disappear. She's got to be somewhere. Maggie!"

"Maggie!" Olivia says.

"Maggie!" Ginny says.

There are too many people in M&M World. There should be
some requirements, some restrictions. She's quite sure that numerous fire codes are being broken. She plans to write a letter,
to get someone's attention—she'll call 311. There are hundreds
of people, if not thousands, in this place. How can anyone see a
thing? She looks around at the racks, the ascending columns of
stuff, the stacks and piles beneath the garish lights, and she suddenly thinks she spots Maggie, but it's not her; it's another child.
She yanks Olivia here and there. "Maggie!" she calls. She is trying to remain calm. She'll find an employee in a minute; there
must be an intercom system. "Maggie!" This must happen all the
time, as it does at Disney World and places like that. The store can
automatically lock the doors. "Maggie!" She sees an employee, a
girl no more than seventeen or eighteen in M&M green, with a
pierced nose and spiky blond hair. "My daughter," she says, breath-

less, flagging her. "She's gone." The girl's name tag says *Wendy, Kalamazoo, Michigan.* Thank God, a Midwesterner.

"I mean, she was with me. And now I don't know where she is."

"Was she here?" Wendy says.

"Yes, she was. With me. And I can't—" Ginny breaks away. "Jesus, is there someone else?"

"I'll help you find her," Wendy says.

"Is there a manager?"

"Don't panic," Wendy says.

"I've got to—"

"Barbara," Wendy is saying into some kind of apparatus she's wearing around her neck.

She and the girls' father sat across from each other at the kitchen table, the light above them harsh, the hour late. From time to time, an ambulance sirened by, or someone shouted in the street; it was the weekend. The girls slept in the other room, Olivia with the quilt wrapping her ankles—she tossed and turned—and Maggie with Zoom Zoom and her other animals positioned around her. Zoom Zoom in the doll cradle, perhaps, or tucked in a towel on the floor, its head on a pincushion or a neatly folded Kleenex.

He talked and talked. She needed a change in subject; she needed to go to bed. It was all so banal, wasn't it? So ordinary? Predictable? An intern? A true love? She looked down at her unvarnished nails: in college she had worn leather moccasins and, on occasion, feathers in her ears; she'd won a prize for her dissertation. Most days, she carried a tote bag, black, with the name of her favorite nonprofit in white.

She listened for a while, and then she did not. Then she said, "Maybe we could tell them it's like what happens when they argue about the fort. How they each want to push the other out of the fort, how there's never enough room in the fort. We could tell them you're taking a break from the fort," she said.

"All right," he said.

"This, of course, makes me the fort," she said.

"You are not the fort," he said.

"I was joking," she said.

Outside, a bottle shatters.

"But they might understand the thing about the fort," she said.

"All right," he said.

"They might," she said.

"That's good," he said.

"Maggie!" Ginny yells. She feels Wendy touch her arm, right be-hind her.

"Don't leave," Wendy says. "That's the first thing."

"What?"

"Don't go out of sight."

"*She's* out of sight," Ginny said. "My daughter. She's five years old." Olivia cries beside her. "I'm sorry," Olivia says. "It's my fault."

"It's not your fault," Ginny says. "Sweetheart, it's not your— Maggie!" Now Ginny's screaming, her voice swallowed by the wall of sound, the same song, the same rapper, repeatedly singing. Customers stop browsing, unsure what to do. They step back and multiply, as if viewing an accident.

Wendy is speaking into the gadget around her neck. She looks up. "Barbara's on her way," she says, as if delivering good news. "She was in inventory."

After the whale swam away—disappeared, really—Ginny couldn't quite explain to the girls' father why she hadn't called him im-mediately. He had promised to call her, he said, so why hadn't she called him? He had been just on the other side of the boat; he had the camera, after all. He hadn't seen a thing, he said. By the time he heard the other tourists shouting, the hubbub, the whale was gone and Ginny was standing there, red-handed. "You were red-handed," he teased her afterward. "A whale hoarder."

"Was not a whale hoarder," she'd said.

"Uh-huh," he said. "Whale hoarder."

And for a while, in the early years of their marriage, when she spent too much time reading, or rose early to walk alone in the Park or drifted off when the two were having dinner in a restau-rant, he'd kick her ankle and say it again. "Whale hoarder," he'd say. And she'd laugh and then she would not. She'd remember the whale's expression, how it lay on its side and drifted in the current, how it had been so close that she could see the raised scars of its skin, the mottled gray color of it and the sheen of evaporating water, and its massive head, how the whale's eye, onyx black, had looked directly at her, unblinking, and she had thought, If I can

stand here long enough, if I can just look hard enough, I'll understand. What, she wasn't sure, but she felt it was something she was
meant to know, something beyond the noise of everything else,
something as clear as the sounds carried across the ocean. "What?"
she had said to the whale. "What?"

It is Olivia who spots Zoom Zoom after Barbara has arrived and
the doors have been manned, after Ginny has sunk to the floor
with her head between her legs, after the tourists, English-speak-
ing and those with no idea, have come forward, rallying around
the woman with the missing child and the child that remains, a
gorgeous girl, freckled, tall, her hair loosened from its ponytail,
her face puffed with tears. It is Olivia who sees Zoom Zoom's ear,
and then Maggie's shoes, or the bottoms of them, beneath the
dressing-room curtains, Maggie covered by a heap of discarded
M&M wear, an M&M beach towel over her head. She hadn't heard
her mother or her sister, she said, howling. She thought they'd
gone too.

"Too?" Ginny says, hugging her youngest to the floor, hugging
her small arms and legs, folding her into her own arms as tightly
as she can bear. "Too?" she says, crying, laughing, pulling Olivia in
as well, so that the three form a kind of solid thing, a weight, a substance, as round as a boulder, which, for the moment, fills in the
empty space that was there just before. And suddenly everything
returns: the buzzy air, the lemony chocolate scent piped through
the store, the rapper's song, the rainbow wall of colors, the crowds.

"Let's go," Ginny whispers. The girls are sniffling, their faces
hot. She stands then, a daughter gripped in each hand. They ride
the escalator down in silence, staring out the large windows toward Broadway, toward the familiar thickening rush-hour crowd,
until they reach the bottom and step off. Ginny lets go first, leading them, pushing hard on the glass door against the wind, against
what has become more than a blustery day, because in truth it is
not yet spring, exactly; there is still the possibility of a freeze.

She squats to zip the girls' fleeces to their chins, to kiss their
cheeks—their eyes still wet with tears—then pulls them close to
her, again. How soon the whale dissolved into its darkening sea.
How soon she was left at the side of the boat, alone.

JESS WALTER

# *Anything Helps*

FROM *McSweeney's*

BIT HATES GOING to cardboard.

But he got tossed from the Jesus beds for drunk and sacrilege and has no other way to get money. So he's up behind Frankie Doodle's, flipping through broken-down produce boxes like an art buyer over a rack of prints, and when he finds a piece without stains or writing he rips it down until it's two feet square. Then he walks to the Quik Stop, where the fat checker likes him. He flirts her out of a Magic Marker and a beef stick.

The beef stick he eats right away, and cramps his gut, so he sets in on the counter while he writes on the cardboard, carefully, in block letters: *Anything Helps.* The checker says, You got good hand-writing, Bit.

The best spot, where the freeway lets off next to Dick's, is taken by some chalker Bit's never seen before: skinny, dirty pants, hollow eyes. The kid's sign reads *Homeless Hungry.* Bit yells, *Homeless Hungry?* Dude, I *invented* Homeless Hungry. The kid just waves.

Bit walks on, west toward his other spot. There are a few others out, stupid crankers—faces stupid, signs stupid: some fifty-year-old baker with *Vietnam Vet,* too dumb to know he wasn't born in time for the war, and a coke ghost with tiny writing—*Can You Help Me Feed My Children Please.* They're at stupid intersections too, with synced lights so the cars never stop.

Bit's headed to his unsynced corner—fewer cars, but at least they have to brake. Streamers off the freeway, working people, South Hill kids, ladies on their way to lunch. When he gets there he grabs the light pole and sits back against it, eyes down—non-threatening, pathetic. It feels weird; more than a year since he's had to do this. You think you're through with some things.

He hears a window hum and gets up, walks to the car without making eye contact. Gets a buck. Thank you. Minute later, another car, another window, another buck. Bless you.

Good luck, the people always say.

For the next hour, it's a tough go. Cars come off the hill, hit the light, stop, look, leave. A woman who looks at first like Julie glances over and mouths, I'm sorry. Bit mouths back: Me too. Most people stare straight ahead, avoid eye contact.

After a while a black car stops, and Bit stands. But when the windows come down it's just some boys in baseball caps. Worst kind of people are boys in baseball caps. Bit should just be quiet, but—

Get a job, you stinking drunk.

That's good advice, Bit says. Thanks.

A couple of dimes fly out the window and skitter against the curb; the boys yell some more. Bit waits until they drive away to get the coins, carefully. He's heard of kids heating pennies in their cigarette lighters. But the dimes are cool to the touch. Bit sits against his pole. A slick creeps down his back.

Then a guy in a gold convertible Mercedes almost makes the light but has to skid to a halt.

I think you could've made it, Bit says.

The guy looks him over. Says, You look healthy enough to work.

Thanks. So do you.

Let me guess—veteran?

Yep. War of 1812.

The guy laughs. Then what, you lost your house?

Misplaced it.

You're a funny fucker. Hey, tell you what. I'll give you twenty bucks if you tell me what you're gonna buy with it.

The light changes but the guy just sits there. A car goes around. Bit shields his eyes from the sun.

You'll give me twenty bucks?

Yeah, but you can't bullshit me. If I give you a twenty, honestly, what're you gonna get?

The new Harry Potter book.

You are one funny fucker.

Thanks. You too.

No. Tell me *exactly* what you're going to drink or smoke or whatever and I'll give you twenty. But it's gotta be the truth.

The truth. Why does everybody always want that? He looks at the guy in his gold convertible. Back at the Jesus beds they'll be gathering for group about now, trying to talk each other out of this very thing, this reverie. Truth.

Vodka, Bit says, because it fucks you up fastest. I'll get it at the store over on Second, whatever cheap stuff they got, plastic bottle in case I drop it. And I'll get a bag of nuts or pretzels. Something solid to shit later. Whatever money's left—Bit's mouth is dry—I'll put in municipal bonds.

After the guy drives off, Bit looks down at the twenty-dollar bill in his hand. Maybe he is a funny fucker.

Bit slides the book forward. *Harry Potter and the Deathly Hallows.*

What's a *hallow,* anyway? he asks.

The clerk takes the book and runs it through the scanner.

I guess it's British for *hollow.* I don't read those books.

I read the first one. It was pretty good. Bit looks around Auntie's Bookstore: big and open, a few soft chairs between the shelves. So what do *you* read?

Palahniuk. That'll be twenty-eight fifty-six.

Bit whistles. Counts out the money and sets it on the counter. Shit, he thinks, seventy cents short.

The clerk has those big loopy earrings that stretch out your lobes. He moves his mouth as he counts the money.

How big are you gonna make those holes in your ears?

Maybe like quarter size. Hey, you're a little short. You got a discount card?

Bit pats himself down. Hmm. In my other pants.

Be right back, the kid says, and leaves with the book.

I'm kind of in a hurry, Bit says to the kid's back.

He needs to stop by the Jesus beds, although he knows Cater might not let him in. He likes Cater, in spite of the guy's mean-Jesus rules and intense, mean-Jesus eyes. It's a shame what happened, because Bit had been doing so good, going to group almost every day, working dinner shifts and in the yard. Cater has this pay system at the Jesus beds—you serve meals or clean or do yard work and get back these vouchers you can redeem for snacks and shit at the little store they run. Keeps everything kind of in-house and gets people used to spending their money on something other than getting fucked up. Of course, there's a side market in the vouchers, dime on the dollar, so over time people save enough to get stewed, but Bit's been keeping that under control too, almost like a civilian. No crank for more than a year, just a beer or two once a month, occasionally a split bottle of wine.

Then last weekend happened. At group on Thursday, Fat Danny was bragging again about the time he OD'ed, and that made Bit think of Julie, the way her foot kept twitching after she stopped breathing, so after group he took a couple bucks from his stash —the hollow rail of his bed—and had a beer. In a tavern. Like a real person, leaned up against the bar watching baseball. And it was great. Hell, he didn't even drink all of it; it was more about the bar than the beer.

But it tasted so good he broke down on Friday and got two for-ties at the Quik Stop. And when he came back to the Jesus beds, Wallace ran off to Cater and told him Bit sold his vouchers for booze money.

Consequences, Cater is always saying.

I feel shitty, Bit's always saying.

Let's talk about *you,* Andrea the social worker is always saying.

When you sober up come see me, the fat checker at the Quik Stop is always saying.

Funny fucker, the guy in the gold convertible is always saying.

The bookstore kid finally comes back. He's got a little card, like a driver's license, and he gives it to Bit with a pen. There, now you have a discount card, the kid says. On the little piece of cardboard, where it says *Name,* Bit writes, *Funny Fucker.* Where it says *Address,* Bit writes: *Anything Helps.*

Bit starts walking again, downtown along the river. For a while he and Julie camped farther down the bank, where the water turns and flattens out. They'd smoke and she'd lie back and mumble about getting their shit together.

Bit tried to tell Cater that. Yes, he'd fucked up, but he'd actually been selling his vouchers to buy this *book,* to get his shit together. But Cater was suspicious, asked a bunch of questions, and then Wallace piped in with *He's lying* and Bit lunged at Wallace and Cater pulled him off—rough about it too—Bit yelling *God damn this* and *God damn that,* making it three-for-three (1: No drinking, 2: No fighting, 3: No taking the Lord's, etc.), so that Cater had no choice, he said, rules being rules.

Then I got no choice either, Bit said, pacing outside the Jesus beds, pissed off.

Sure you do, Cater said. You always have a choice.

Of course, Cater was right. But out of spite or self-pity, or just thirst, Bit went and blew half his book money on a fifth, spent a couple of nights on the street, and then shot the rest of the money on another. You think you're through with some things: picking up smokes off the street, shitting in alleys. He woke this morning in a parking lot above the river, behind a humming heat pump. Looked down at the water and could practically see Julie lying back in the grass. *When we gonna get our shit together, Wayne?*

Bit walks past brick apartments and empty warehouses. Spokane's a donut city, downtown a hole, civilians all in the suburbs. *Donut City* is part of Bit's *unified urban theory,* like the part about how every failing downtown tries the same stupid fixes: hang a vertical sign on an empty warehouse announcing LUXURY LOFTS!, buy buses that look like trolley cars, open a shitty farmers' market.

Very interesting, Andrea says whenever Bit talks about his theory. But we talk about *ourselves* at group, Bit. Let's talk about *you.*

But what if this *is* me? Bit asked once. Why can't we be the things we see and think? Why do we always have to be these sad stories, like Fat Danny pretending he's sorry he screwed up his life when we all know he's really just bragging about how much coke he used to do? Why can't we talk about what we *think* instead of just all the stupid shit we've *done?*

Okay, Wayne, she said—what do you think?

I think I've done some real stupid shit.

Andrea likes him, always laughs at his jokes, treats him smarter than the rest of the group, which he is. She even flirts with him, a little.

Where's your nickname come from? she asked him one time.

It's because that's all a woman can take of my wand, he said. Just a bit. Plus I chewed a man to death once. Bit right through his larynx.

It's his last name is all, said Wallace. Bittinger.

That's true, Bit said, although I did bite a guy's larynx once.

You think you're so smart, Wallace is always saying.

And do you want to talk about Julie? Andrea's always saying.

Not so much, Bit's always saying.

We're all children before God, Cater's always saying.

But Cater isn't even at the Jesus beds when Bit stops there. He's at his kid's soccer game. Kenny the intake guy leans out the window and says he can't let Bit in the door till he clears it with Cater.

Sure, Bit says, just do me a favor. He takes the book from the bag. Tell him I showed you this.


Bit walks past brick storefronts and apartments, through nicer neighborhoods with green lawns. The book's heavy under his arm.

Another part of Bit's unified urban theory is sprinklers, that you can gauge a neighborhood's wealth by the way people water. If every single house has an automatic system, you're looking at a six-figure mean. If the majority lug hoses around, it's more lower middle class. And if they don't bother with the lawns . . . well, that's the sort of shit-burg where Bit and Julie always lived, except for that little place they rented in Wenatchee the summer Bit worked at the orchard. He sometimes thinks back to that time and imagines what it would be like if he could undo everything that came after it, like standing up a line of dominoes. All the way back to Nate.

Bit breathes deeply, looks around at the houses to get his mind off it, at the sidewalks and the garden bricks and the homemade mailboxes. It isn't a bad walk. The Molsons live in a neighborhood between arterials, maybe ten square blocks of '50s and '60s ranchers and ramblers, decent-sized edged yards, clean, the sort of block Julie always liked—nice but not overreaching. Bit pulls out the postcard, reads the address again, even though he remembers the place from last time. Two more blocks.

It's getting cool now, heavy clouds settling down like a blanket over a kid. It'll rain later. Bit puts this neighborhood at about 40 percent sprinkler systems, 25 percent two-car garages, lots of rock gardens, and lined sidewalks. The Molsons have the biggest house on the block, gray, two-story, with a big addition in back. Two little boys—one black, one white, both littler than Nate—are in the front yard, behind a big cyclone fence, bent over something. A bug, if Bit had to bet.

Hullo, Bit says from his side of the fence. You young gentlemen know if Nate's around?

He's downstairs playing Ping-Pong, says one of the boys, and
the other grabs the kid's arm, no doubt heeding a warning about
stranger-talk.

Maybe you could tell Mr. or Mrs. Molson that Wayne Bittinger's
outside. Here to see Nate for one-half a second is all.

The boys are gone awhile. Bit clears his throat. Shifts his weight.
Listens for police. He looks around the neighborhood and it
makes him sad that it's not nicer, that Nate didn't get some South
Hill fosters, a doctor or something. Stupid thought; he's embarrassed for having it.

Mrs. Molson looks heavier than the last time he stopped by, in
the spring—has it been that long? More than half a year? She's
shaped like a bowling pin, with a tuft of side-swooped hair and big
round glasses. A saint, though, she and her husband both, for taking in all these kids.

She frowns. Mr. Bittinger—

Please, call me Wayne.

Mr. Bittinger, I told you before, you can't just stop by here.

No, I know that, Mrs. Molson. I'm supposed to go through the
guardian *ad litem*. I know. I just . . . his birthday got away from me.
I wanted to give him a book. Then I swear, I'll—

What book? She holds out her hands. Bit hands it over. She
opens the bag and looks in without taking the book out, like it
might be infected.

Mr. Bittinger, you *know* how Mr. Molson and I feel about these
books. She tries to hand it back to him, but Bit won't take it.

No, I know, Mrs. Molson. He pats the postcard in his back
pocket—picture of a lake and a campground. It was mailed to
their old apartment. Bit's old landlord, Gayle, brought it down to
the Jesus beds for him, what, a month ago—or was it three months
now?

Dad—I'm at camp and we're supposed to write our parents and I'm
kind of mad (not really just a little) at the Molsons for taking away
my Harry Potter books which they think are Satanic. I did archery
here which was fun. I hope you're doing good too. Nate.

I respect your beliefs, Bit tells Mrs. Molson. I do. It's probably
why you and Mr. Molson are such good people, to open your home
up like this. But Nate, he loves them Harry Potter books. And after

all he's been through, me being such a fuckup—Jesus, why did he say that—I'm sorry, pardon my . . . and losing his mother, I just . . . I mean . . . Bit can feel his face flushing.

Mrs. Molson glances back at the house. For what it's worth, we don't push our beliefs on the boys, Mr. Bittinger, she says. It's all about rules. Everyone here goes to church and everyone spends an hour on homework and we keep a close eye on what they read and watch. We have the same rules for all the boys. Otherwise it doesn't work. Not with eight of them.

No, I could see that, Bit says. I could.

Bit read the first Harry Potter to Nate when he was only six, even doing a British accent sometimes. Julie read him the second one, no accent, but cuddled up in the hotel bed where they were crashing. They got the books from the library. After the second one, Nate started reading them himself. Bit kind of wishes he'd kept up, before the dominoes started going: before CPS came, before Julie got so hopeless and strung out, before . . .

We've been doing this a long time, Mrs. Molson is saying. We've had upwards of forty foster kids and we've found that this is what works: adherence to rules.

Yep, that's how we saw things too, and I can't tell you how much I appreciate him having a stable home like this. I really do. My wife and I, we did our best, and we always figured that once we got everything back together, that, uh . . . but of course . . .

Mrs. Molson looks down at her shoes.

This wasn't what he meant to do, this self-pity. He wanted to talk like real people, but Bit feels himself fading. It's like trying to speak another language—conversational suburban—and it tires him out the way group does: everybody crying out their bullshit about the choices they've made and the clarity they've found. And he's worse than any of them, wanting so bad for Andrea to like him, to think he's fixed, when all he really wants is a pinch. Or a pint.

Bit clears his throat.

It's just . . . you know, this one thing. I don't know.

Mr. Bittinger—

Finally, Bit smiles, and rasps: Anything helps.

She looks up at him with what must be pity, although he can't quite make it out. Then she sighs and looks down at the book again. I guess . . . I could put it away for him. For later. He can have it when you can take him again . . . or when he's on his own, or with some other—

Thank you. I'd appreciate that. Bit clears his throat. But before you put it away, could you show it to him? Tell him his old man brought it for his birthday?

Sure, Mrs. Molson says, and then she gets hard again. But Mr. Bittinger, you can't come by here.

I know that, he says.

Next time I'll call the police.

He begins backing away. Won't be a next time.

You said that last spring.

Backing away: I know. I'm sorry.

Call Mr. Gandor and I'm sure he'll set up a visitation.

I will. Thank you, Mrs. Molson.

She turns and goes inside. Bit stands where he's backed up to, middle of the street, feels like he's about to burst open, a water balloon or a sack of fluid, gush out onto the pavement and trickle down to the curb. *When are we gonna get our shit together?*

Quickly, Bit begins walking toward downtown. He imagines the curtains parting in the houses around him. *Think you're so smart. Let's talk about you.* Jesus he wants something. He stowed his cardboard back behind Frankie Doodle's; instead of going to the Jesus beds and pleading with Cater, maybe he'll go get it. Hit that corner again. Tear it up one more night, like he and Julie used to do. Maybe the guy in the gold convertible will come by and give him another twenty. He tries to think of something good. Imagines the guy pulling up and Bit spinning his sign and it reading *Funny Fucker* and the guy laughing and Bit jumping into the car and them going to get totally fucked up in Reno or someplace. *Anything helps funny fucker! Funny fucker helps anything! You want to talk about Julie? Fuck funny anything helps! How long you been saving for that book, Bit? Anything funny helps fuck*

Dad!

Bit turns and there's Nate, stand-pedaling a little BMX bike up the street, its frame swinging beneath his size. Jeez, he's big, and he's got a bike? Of course he does. What thirteen-year-old doesn't have a bike? He remembers Julie waking up once, saying, We gotta get Nate a bike. Even fucked-up Bit knew that not having a bike was the least of the kid's problems.

He tries to focus. The kid's hair is so short, like a military cut. Julie would hate that. There's something else—his teeth. He's got braces on. When he pulls up, Bit sees he's got the book in its brown bag under his arm.

I can't take this, Dad.

No, it's okay, Bit says. I talked to Mrs. Molson and she said—

I read it at camp. This kid in my cabin had it. It was good. But you should take it back.

Bit closes his eyes against a wave of dizziness. No, Nate, I want you to have it.

Really, he says, I can't. I'm sorry. And he holds it out, making direct eye contact, like a cop. Jesus, Bit thinks, the kid's different in every way—taller and so . . . awake.

Take it, Nate says. Please.

Bit takes it.

I shouldn't have wrote that in my postcard, Nate says. I was mad they wouldn't let me read the book, but I understand it now. I was being stupid.

No, Bit says, I was glad you sent that card. You have a good birthday?

It seems to take a minute for Nate to recall his birthday. Oh. Yeah. It was cool. We went to the water slides.

And school starts . . .

Three weeks ago.

Oh. Sure, Bit says, but he can't believe it. It's not like time passes anymore; it leaks, it seeps. He wants to say something about the grade, just so Nate knows he *knows*. He counts years in his head: one after they took Nate, one after Julie, and one he's been trying to get better in the Jesus beds—a little more than three years the Molsons have had him. Jesus.

So . . . you nervous about eighth grade?

Nah. I was more nervous last year.

Yeah. Bit can barely take this steady eye contact. It reminds him of Cater.

Consequences, Cater's always saying.

I was more nervous last year, Nate's always saying.

I don't feel good, Julie's always saying.

Yeah, Bit says, no need to be nervous. He's still in danger of bursting, bleeding over the street.

You okay, Dad?

Sure. Just glad I got to see you. That *ad litem* business . . . I'm not good at planning ahead.

It's okay. Nate smiles. Looks back over his shoulder. Well . . . I should—

Yeah, Bit says. He moves to hug the boy or shake his hand or something, but it's like the kid's a mile away. Hey, good luck with school, and everything.

Thanks.

Then Nate pedals away. He looks back once, and is gone.

Bit breathes. He stands on the street. Feels the curtains fluttering. What if Julie didn't die? What if she got herself one of these houses and she's watching him now? *You ever gonna get your shit together, Bit? You gonna get Nate back? Or you goin' back to cardboard?*

Bit looks down at the book in his hands.

At the Jesus beds last weekend, after Bit explained to Cater how he was only a couple dollars short of buying this book for his kid, Cater stared at him in the most pathetic way.

What? Bit asked.

Cater said, How long you been saving for that book, Bit?

What do you mean?

I mean, ask yourself, how long you been a couple dollars short?

He supposes that's why he went crazy, Cater always looking at him like he's kidding himself. Like he's always thinking, How long has it been since you saw your kid, anyway?

Bit stands outside Auntie's Bookstore holding a twenty-eight-dollar book. Holding twenty-eight dollars. Holding a few fifths of vodka. Holding nine forty-ounce beers. Holding five bottles of fortified wine. Holding his boy. Civilians go into the store and come out carrying books in little brown bags just like the one he's got in his hands.

Here's why at the Jesus beds they can only talk about all the stupid shit they've done—because that's all they are now, all they're ever gonna be, a twitching bunch of memories and mistakes. Regrets. Jesus, Bit thinks. I should've had the decency to go when Julie did.

Back at his corner, Bit eases against the light pole. You think you're through with some things. But you aren't.

It's about to rain; the cars coming off the freeway have their windows up. It's fine, though. Bit likes the cool, wet air. The very first car pauses at the bottom of the hill and its driver, a woman, glances over. Bit looks away, opens the thick book, and begins reading.

*The two men appeared out of nowhere, a few yards apart in the narrow, moonlit lane. For a second they stood quite still, wands pointing at each other's chests . . .*

The light changes but the woman doesn't go. Raindrops have started to dapple the page, so Bit pulls his jacket over his head, to shield the book. And when he goes back to reading, this time it's with the accent and everything.

ADAM WILSON

# *What's Important Is Feeling*

FROM *Paris Review*

WE'D BEEN SHOOTING for two weeks already, melting. Most of the crew had chiggers bad. Chiggers, we were told, crawl in and lay eggs beneath your skin. They attack ankles and genitals. The cure is nail polish. A good coating will smother them to death. We wore the clear stuff so it wouldn't show.

Only the L.A. people got them. The Texans wore sulfur in their socks to keep the chiggers out. They didn't mention this trick to us. Nathaniel and I sat on our opposing motel beds—AC on, anchorman singing box scores in soothing Texas twang—examining the bumps around our sock and jock lines. My body was a morgue; chigger corpses floated through my veins, suffocated under my skin.

"Tonight I plan to dream about Monica Bradley," said Nathaniel. "Her dream self will meet my dream self somewhere in the depths of my unconscious, and we'll talk until sunrise."

Monica was the film's female lead. Older than us, but looked five years younger with non-hips and blonde fuzz on her pale arms. Monica's character was meant to be seventeen. There was something deeply erotic in the way her smoke-seasoned voice slipped into teenybop squawk-talk when the cameras came on.

"She's sexy," I said. "Definitely."

"But her personality, I mean. She's great, right? That joke she told about her mom and the albino. Was that a joke? It might have been a true story. Man, what an interesting life."

I was distracted by nail polish; I daintily painted. I like its bleachy smell and the way it slowly hardened on my blistered skin and shined.

"I just feel so alive when I'm around her. Like I want to stop time and spend seven years in medical school so I can save her life if she happens to get stung and goes into anaphylactic shock." Monica had a bee-sting allergy.

"Sure," I said. "Save her life."

Nathaniel had gotten me the gig. He was savvier than me, pluckier, bigger in the biceps. Had a surfer thing going on. Not bleached blond in a mimbo way, just tan and easy. Same patchy beard all the hip ones had, hints of amber in the chin hairs. Two years below me in film school, but he'd caught up careerwise. His résumé was up on all the job boards. Had a website with built-in Flash and a slick montage. I was shitty at self-promoting. Sent my thesis screenplay around in manila envelopes awaiting return.

"I should probably get an EpiPen and carry it on me. Just in case."

"I thought Felix would be here by now."

We knew Felix was coming, but we didn't know when. He'd written the script and was associate producer. He'd been nominated for an Academy Award. Some people said Felix was a genius. We (the L.A. people) had read the new script. It was good, better than good. Better than the other crap we worked on: thirty-second spots for regional fast-food chains, student shorts, overfunded indie twee. Nathaniel had even done a blockbuster, some sci-fi thing in Death Valley, CGI spaceships crop-dusting the desert. It was a fact Nathaniel never let me forget. He said craft service served Kobe beef and goat-cheese sliders. The food may have been good, but the picture certainly wasn't.

Felix's script was different: sexy, savage, utterly bleak. In short: Art. We imagined being thanked in the acceptance speech ("I'd just like to thank the wonderful crew, whose hard work really made this movie come to life"). We imagined our résumés, our next jobs, moving up in the industry, moving out of our tiny apartments, buying new cars, using those cars to convince women to have sex with us.

We wanted a movie that might one day be called a "film," that we could refer to at a dinner party ten years down the line, light a cigarette, and say, "We were naive kids. We thought we were taking the world by storm."

There were problems. The director and the star hated each other; everyone hated the first AD; the first AD was a cokehead and running out of coke; the star had fucked the costar, then her assistant; the production was out of money; the DP had also fucked the star's assistant; the dailies looked amateur; the food was shit; the Texans thought the L.A. folks were homosexuals; the L.A. folks were mostly homosexuals and took umbrage.

By the time Felix showed up, hope was lost. The director, Andrew Solstice, had lost interest. He spent most of his time trying on cowboy hats, posing in the hair/makeup mirrors, and blowing residue from his finger gun.

It was the day we had the rain machine. Solstice wanted it for the scene in the car when Francisco tells Monica he killed her boyfriend. A bad idea—too soap opera for a subtle picture like this one. In my imagining of the film, the sun beats like a tanning-bed light, providing alien glow, almost x-ray vision to their emaciated torsos.

I stood twenty yards away, doing lockup. In a city like Los Angeles this generally meant blocking off a major street corner, stopping pedestrians from barging into your shot. Here there were no pedestrians, only sand and weedy fields. It was just past dawn. In the distance was the Corpus Christi coast, pink sky interrupted by oil rigs. Fake rain fell heavy on the picture car, a rusted blue Mustang.

I didn't know what to make of Francisco, the talent. He'd been a child star of the Mexican stage, and later the hunky adulterer on a popular telenovela. His mother was an opera singer, and his father handcrafted violins. Rumor had it his maternal grandfather had made his nut in munitions.

Francisco played seven instruments and was fluent in as many languages. He'd grown up in a fenced-off estate with verandas outside Mexico City, Ferraris, and armed guards—all the gaudy signifiers of cartel superwealth. Still, he played himself off as a man of the people, spoke Spanish with the Mexican grips and electricians, kicked the soccer ball between takes, smiled a humble, punchable smile at everyone he passed. His acting was iffy, but his face was an exemplar of symmetry and composition. My jealousy was undermined by my interest in star fucking. I had hoped to befriend him, swill tequila by the motel pool. I wanted to ask about the queeny Argentine director who'd kicked him off set for being three pounds overweight. But I was rarely close to the cast members. They ate at different hours. Some nights though, Francisco would sit with his eyes closed on the motel's shared balcony and pluck a nylon-stringed guitar. The insomniacs among us would come out of our rooms, slowly at first, lingering in our doorways, then gradually getting closer until we'd formed an impromptu audience. Francisco would open his eyes, blush, and apologize for waking us. We'd all say nah and urge him on—as he knew we would—and he'd close his eyes again, allowing just the hint of a smile to cross his lips as he moved into another song.

"What is this cock shit?" someone behind me said.

I turned. Felix wore camo pants and a sleeveless tee. Hair long and greasy, facial features exaggerated: comically oversized mouth and nose. Like late-career Bogart: rheumy-eyed, beyond saving.

"It's raining," I said.

"It's fucking Texas," he said, stormed past me, headed for set, where he grabbed Solstice by his mullet tail, pulled him under the rain machine, threatened to remove his genitals if he didn't first remove the rain machine.

I was approached by first AD Mark Tipplehorn.

"You idiot," he said. "You were supposed to be locking up."

"He was like a bull," I said.

"You idiot," he said again, and wiped his forearm across his face.

Tipplehorn's uniform was all white every day: sneakers, socks, shorts, shirt, visor. He was going for "asshole from L.A. stranded in small town." He wore reflective aviators, scratched chigger bumps.

"Towel me," he said.

I pulled his towel from my pocket and tossed it over.

"I've got a new job for you anyway. I need an ounce of weed as fast as you can get it."

Tipplehorn had worked with Felix before. Felix thought he had say over what happened on set.

"Weed's the only way to calm him down," Tipplehorn explained. "Also someone to give him a haircut; he likes to have his hair cut on location."

The haircut would be easier to get than the weed, but he wanted the weed first so he could be stoned during the haircut. For the weed I had to approach a Texan. The Texans hated us, but some hated us less than others. Luckily, a kind woman bummed a cigarette off me, called me "sweetheart," and agreed to help with both my tasks. Her name was Kathleen, and she was the on-set hairdresser.

Kathleen didn't give a shit about the higher-ups like Tipplehorn. Just did her thing in the hair trailer, smoking bats and talking on speakerphone to her teenage daughter who was spending the summer at an arts camp outside Denton. When they said goodbye, Kathleen waved her hand as if her daughter could see her from the other end of the line. She said, "Girl," and her daughter said, "Bye now," and Kathleen looked in the mirror and saw me behind her, squint-eyed in the barber's chair, finally sun-shaded, almost asleep.

"Now about that marijuana," she said.

"You got any nail-polish remover?" I said.

We sat on the edge of Felix's bed, facing the television, which was playing dailies. Francisco drove across the bridge into sunset.

"You can imagine the lush strings," Felix said, and threw the remote against the wall. Batteries fell to the floor, rolled to opposite corners of the room. I handed him the blunt.

"Straight men smoke blunts," he said. "Instead of sucking big black cocks."

"Oh?"

"That's why you'll never see a fag smoke a blunt. Their cravings are satisfied. They smoke little joints and prance around thinking about all those beautiful pricks shooting cum like shooting stars across the galaxy of their faces."

"Poetic," I said.

"I want to show you something," Felix said, fast-forwarding the tape.

The scene where the dog runs into the road and Francisco doesn't stop the car until Monica screams and grabs the wheel. We'd spent four hours on it because the dog kept running the wrong way.

"This fucking dog—too pretty. Of course he wants to run it

over. Who doesn't want to crush that smug bitch? Dog's not even running right. This is supposed to be suicide. We need an ugly dog, some kind of mutt, runt of the litter, nothing to live for. I want him lingering on the shoulder, contemplating, then dashing out. Francisco sees the trajectory of the dog's life, refuses to alter its course. It's an act of mercy. An act of love."

"I could love a dog," I said.

"The thing that worries me isn't the dog," Felix said. "It's not the dog at all. What worries me is that if they fucked up the dog, how are they going to deal with the cat?"

Felix took a deep pull, ashed on the carpet.

"The cat is the whole picture; the way he moves through the house at the end. If they get the cat right, then maybe this thing can work."

He passed me the blunt.

"Promise me something," he said. "Promise me you won't let them fuck up the cat."

"I'll do my best," I said.

"I like this guy," Felix said to the TV.

We sat stoned in the hair trailer after an afternoon of me making and remaking iced coffee for Solstice—"more milk," "less milk," "soy milk"—and Felix yelling at Tipplehorn, and Tipplehorn rubbing his nose and saying, "Felix, baby, listen," and Felix throwing his coffee on the ground and kicking the Styrofoam, and then Tipplehorn making me pick up the kicked Styrofoam. Finally the haircut. I sat next to him, watched Kathleen's breasts bob as she moved the clippers, feet dancing in tiny increments, eighth steps in time with the half notes, Patsy Cline crooning sweet and solemn, something about three cigarettes in an ashtray.

"The thing about the cat," Felix said.

Kathleen ran a hand through his hair, said, "Don't worry your pretty head."

She shaved it all off. Felix was ready for battle. I was off to battle with him. In a moment of camaraderie, I'd shaved my head too. He appointed me his assistant, carrier of his marijuana, lieutenant in our army of three (Kathleen was also a lieutenant).

Monica was in her trailer, not coming out. The chiggers had gotten to her, and it was too hot to work. Her assistant stood by the camera truck, sobbing into her own cleavage. Mascara, mixed with sweat, dripped black down her chest and neck. Francisco was there, stroked her hair, called her "sweet pea."

Solstice knocked on Monica's door, said, "The camera never sees your ankles."

"That's not the problem," Nathaniel whispered. "She doesn't want to work with Francisco anymore, ever since he fucked her assistant."

"How do you know?"

"I fucked Monica last night."

He was grinning big, but must have been joking. If he'd slept with Monica, it meant the death of the hierarchy. Not that she gave unattainable vibes. Monica was fairly normal—for an actress, anyway. She had a B.A. in psych with a minor in French. Bumped Brooklyn indie pop from the speaker dock in her trailer. Liked football, the Food Network, and books by Bret Easton Ellis. Hailed from the Carolinas, still sent handwritten checks to her mom and sister. Seemed shy and overwhelmed by the attention. Chain-smoked Parliaments between takes, flipping glossy mags or checking her cell while Kathleen reset her hair. This was supposed to be Monica's break. Next year she'd be up on billboards, airbrushed, overlooking highway traffic.

"I'll talk to her," Felix said, removed his shirt, tied it around his head like a bandanna.

"Be my guest," Solstice said.

Felix stepped up, knocked softly.

"Baby girl," he said. "It's just me, Felix. Let's just talk for a minute. I just want to chat."

The door opened. Felix entered. The rest of us stood waiting outside the trailer. Tipplehorn looked at me, mouthed the word *coffee.*

When I came back, Felix and Monica were walking arm in arm. Monica laughed, smiled, leaned into Felix.

Here's how I imagine it: Felix sits on the bed. He begins to roll a blunt. "Mind if I smoke?" he says. Monica is crying. Wordless, Felix takes a bottle of clear nail polish from the top of her dresser and applies it to Monica's ankles. "Men are scum," he says. He slowly lifts her dress above her waist. He runs the nail brush over the bumps around her bikini line. He hands her the blunt.

Monica stops crying. She looks at Felix. He tells her that her role in this film is important, the most important. He tells her to channel her hatred of Francisco into hatred of his character. He tells her this scene, the scene they are about to shoot, it came to him in a dream after his mother died. In his grief he imagined a girl —Monica's character—sitting in a diner booth, sipping soda, making origami birds with the paper place mats.

The scene came out okay. When I told Tipplehorn that I was now Felix's assistant, Tipplehorn said, "No, you're not." People said, "What's with the haircut?"

The thing about night shoots is they go until morning. Now it was 6 A.M. We were dumping raspberry Emergen-C into our coffees. Monica had retired to the motel. We were shooting just Francisco now, burying the body. Even with cameras and crew, the place felt desolate: a six-foot hole in soft earth, surrounded by marshland, mosquitoes hovering.

The scene was tough to shoot because the body couldn't breathe while being buried. The body was Phil, another actor. He lay naked and tried to stretch his penis with his hand between takes.

"Got a fluffer around here?" Phil said.

"Dead men have hard-ons," Felix said.

Solstice pretended not to hear. If you want an R rating you can't show an erection. Besides, according to the film's time line the body had been dead for hours. I wasn't sure how long dead men stayed aroused.

"Years," Felix said. "Being dead's like being on permanent Viagra. There's no distractions; all you can think about is pussy."

"I didn't know you could think while dead," I said.

"Thinking's overrated," Felix said. "What's important is feeling."

Felix handed me a pen.

"What I want you to do is take the pen, shove it as hard as you can into my leg."

He rolled up his shorts, exposed a swath of hairy thigh.

"Just stab me with the pen. Maybe it's filled with special ink. Maybe it will inspire me."

"Are you sure?"

"Even better idea," Felix said. "Don't stab me."

"I prefer this idea."

"Stab Francisco instead. Next time he walks by, take that pen and jam it up his ass. Maybe then he'll feel something. Maybe he'll learn to act."

"I doubt it," I said.

"Me too," Felix said.

We finished when the sun came up, rose over the rigs, glistened on the oil-slick sand. The oilers were already out, already sweating. They walked across the beach with their hard hats and paper-bag lunches in hand. Silence in the van back to the motel. Kathleen tried to sleep, cheek pressed against the window. Mike Michaels, the wardrobe guy, puked into a plastic bag on the rocky coastal road. I was alive and awake. All that coffee coursing through me, plus the vitamin C.

"I think we really nailed that burial scene," I said. "Really captured the light and the feeling."

"Shh . . ." Kathleen said.

"Things are looking up," I said. "Now that Felix is here. As long as the cat works out, I think it will be okay. I think things are really looking up."

I heard a couple of grunts. Nathaniel told me to shut up. We passed the local bar. I imagined the inside, lit only by a prism of light from the one tiny window.

Back at the motel everything was bright: the awning, the cars in the parking lot, the glare from the turned-off television. Our AC sputtered and died. I blew dust from the ancient window, willed in a breeze.

"Yo, Nat," I said. "Let's get out of this shit hole, find a diner or something. I feel like eggs."

"Sorry, brah," he said. "Other plans."

Nathaniel claimed he was going to Monica's room to have sex with her. I followed him into the hall, watched while he knocked on her door. She opened, stood framed by the doorway, wrapped in a black bathrobe, hair wet, hanging, impossibly clean. She pulled him in.

Felix had to stay up and watch dailies. I imagine him pacing his room, blinds drawn, take after take rolling across the screen, room heavy with blunt smoke. Phone is ringing. It rings and rings. Eventually Felix unplugs the phone and throws it against the wall.

\*

Gil Broome, the on-set animal wrangler, wore the biggest belt buckles I've ever seen. Different buckle every day. He had a bull buckle, a horse buckle, a cowboy-boot buckle, and one with a diamond-studded state of Texas.

Gil had been in Los Angeles for a short while, a city that didn't suit him. Too many cars, not enough horses. Homesick for animals, he offered to walk a neighbor's dog. Each morning he'd take the dog to the dog park among the actresses and their purse poodles. One day he met another walker, a man of about his own age. The man wore floral-print shirts, but had a deep, kind voice and knew enough about the racetrack. They walked together each morning. Do you like music? the man asked Gil. Gil replied that he did enjoy music, mostly country, like Merle Haggard and of course Johnny Cash. Have you ever heard of Neil Diamond? the man asked. I believe I recognize the name, Gil said, but for the life of me I can't place it. Well, I'm Neil Diamond, the man said. He changed the subject. Do you like drinking, Gil? Yes, sir, I do, Gil said.

He told a story about his Navy SEAL days on the cleanup crew for the space shuttle *Challenger*. He described the debris, the unrecognizable metal, the smell that might have been the smell of space, the intact finger he claimed he'd found and kept for a souvenir.

Gil gave me his card, invited me to visit his ranch in West Texas. We could ride horses across his acres and drink whiskey under the stars. When the film was over I could show up at Gil's ranch, backpack slung over my shoulder. I'd be his apprentice, learn the trade; my skin would darken; we'd cook baked beans over an open fire. A neighbor girl wore cutoff denim skirts, no shoes. Never met a Jew before. Neil Diamond would visit. We'd sit on the porch and sing "Sweet Caroline."

Felix hated Gil from the moment he saw him.

"You," Felix said, "you there with the mustache."

"Yes, sir," Gil said. "Gil Broome, hombre."

"Gil Broome," Felix said. "I want to talk to you, Gil Broome."

Gil was standing, eating eggs off a paper plate. He was on set today because of chickens; Francisco kills a chicken in front of Monica. They didn't really need Gil because the special-effects people were in charge of the fake chicken and its head. Gil was there to judge authenticity and to keep track of the real chickens that wandered through the background.

"No one cares about the dog," Felix said. "I care about the dog, but the dog's not what we're talking about."

Felix placed an arm on Gil's shoulder.

"Fuck the chickens too," he said. "This scene wasn't in the script anyway."

"No chickens," Gil said. "Got it."

"Yes chickens," Felix said. "Just fuck them. You see what I'm saying?"

Gil looked perplexed. He took a bite of his eggs.

Felix pointed at the eggs. "All that chickens are good for."

Gil smiled.

"What we're talking about is the cat," Felix said.

"What cat?"

"What cat? I like this guy. What cat? The cat that walks through the burning house in the final shot. The death cat. The beautiful agony black cat."

"Beautiful agony?"

"Look. You fucked up the dog. Wrong dog, ran the wrong way. I'm over the dog. But it can't happen again. The cat has to be beautiful. Small green eyes. Completely black. It's got to move slowly up the stairs. It's got to look around, smell death. Can you promise me that, Gil, can you promise me the cat will smell death? That when it says in the script, 'Cat walks up the stairs,' the cat will dance through that house like he's Mikhail fucking Baryshnikov?"

Gil put his plate down on a bench, as if, like a cat, he sensed the threat of physical danger.

"Cat can't read your script," Gil said. "Cat can't read."

Felix's face went scarily still. Only his eyes moved. He scanned from Gil's nose to his own clenched fist. Knuckles bubbled and shifted beneath the stretched skin. Felix flexed his biceps; they were tried-and-true weapons for getting his way. I took a step back, but Gil didn't budge, coughed out a laugh.

"You, Gil Broome, you can read my script. That's the thing. That's what we're paying you for. To read the script and then whisper some Doctor Dolittle whatever the fuck into the cat's ear so he'll do what it says in the script."

"Cat's not an actor," Gil said. "Cat doesn't take notes."

"So let me get this straight," Felix said. "Your job title, right, you're a wrangler, an animal wrangler? Am I correct that that is the title of your job, that on the call sheet it says 'Gil Broome, Animal Wrangler'?"

"Yes, sir, that is correct."

"Because as far as I can tell, Gil, Gil Broome, as far as I can tell, you're just a fucking pet owner. You're just a guy with a cat."

"Cat can't read," Gil said.

Tipplehorn approached. He was good at his job; he knew when to break up a conversation. "Gil, you're needed on set."

I was supposed to hold an umbrella over Monica, shield her from the sun. Her assistant had been fired, sent back to L.A. with a half-decent story, waiting for a call from Francisco that never comes. Monica didn't need me, but there was protocol. Her skin was gold from an adolescence spent sitting shotgun in drop-tops, joyriding the Outer Banks. Now she was someone and sat in my shade. A website had spotted her finger-picking from the salad bar at Whole Foods in West Hollywood. A true coronation.

"I'm sorry you have to do this," Monica said. "I know it's incredibly degrading."

"That's nice of you to say," I said, but she was already back to ignoring my existence. Stared at the script pages, her highlighted lines. I could hear her mumbling. My arm ached. It had only been a minute.

"I could practice with you if you want?" I said.

Monica turned, assessed. I could see my reflection in her oversized shades: peeling nose and stubbly dome, the glop of excess sunscreen on my chin.

"Sure," she said. "I guess. You do Francisco."

I read: *Baby don't, baby don't cry, c'mon.*

She read: *Oh, fuck off.*

*Baby don't* . . . I read, and leaned in like the stage directions said. Smelled lavender, honey blossom, a thin strain of uterine blood. My nose against her neck fuzz. My shallow breathing.

"What the fuck are you doing?" Monica said.

"Acting?"

"Jesus Christ," she said, stood, sauntered off, left me holding the umbrella over nothing.

*

That night, the storm. One of those passing tropical numbers.
Black clouds like Mexican chimney smoke rising up the Gulf, covering the coastline. They get one every summer. Felix didn't want
to shoot in the rain for the same reason that Solstice did—melo-
drama. Tipplehorn had a more convincing argument—money
—and he won. Felix was angry and took it out on the wardrobe
guy, who didn't have shoes the right color for Little Brother. Little Brother was in sneakers, was supposed to be in dress shoes,
church shoes. Felix tried to color the white sneakers with black
marker. Because everything was wet, the marker wouldn't ad-
here. Felix threw the sneakers in the mud. I had to retrieve the
sneakers, give them back to the kid who now had to wear wet
shoes.

According to Nathaniel, Tipplehorn had run out of cocaine.
"I want him off my set," he said, referring to Felix. He told me
to get the DV cam from the camera truck. Tell Felix, he told me,
that you're shooting a behind-the-scenes documentary. Take him
under the craft-service tent and interview him for as long as he'll
let you.

I didn't like deceiving Felix but told myself they might actually
use the footage when they saw how Felix opened up to me.

We marched to the craft-service tent, a culinary oasis where
Darrell the craft-service chief presided over the cast's unreason-
able requests: Vermont maple syrup, organic soy milk, fair-trade
Colombian coffee, and other things you couldn't get in Corpus.

I struggled with my tripod, which was sinking in the mud. The
truck drivers laughed at me from their own tent. They were Texan
and in the Teamsters union. Got paid time and a half when it
rained. Plus overtime. I couldn't steady the camera on the sinking
tripod, so I just said fuck it and went handheld.

Felix said, "Do you have an agent? You don't have an agent, why
would you have an agent? I have an agent, and I have a manager,
and my agent has an assistant, and my manager has an assistant,
and right at this moment they're poring over scripts asking, Is this
the next Felix? Is that the next Felix? Because Felix is done and
we've got money to spend, all this fucking money, and we need
an army of Felixes marching the streets of Los Angeles with their
Final Draft printouts, their Terrence Malick–inspired voice-overs,
their hunger."

I'd managed to focus but was having trouble getting him in frame. He moved, paced, grabbed handfuls of candy corn and stuffed his face.

"And all these assistants have meetings," he said, still chewing. "And they meet with the higher-ups, like my agent and manager, and they all wear shirts unbuttoned at the collar, like one fucking button too many, just so they can say I have hair on my chest, I do not have breasts, in this shell of a body there is something animal that still exists, that is ruthless, that will ruin other men, and supply my office with a mini fridge and excellent air conditioning. I'm not allowed in the meetings, but I know what goes on: they sit around, and he's Geppetto. You remember Geppetto?"

The rain came now in sulfuric sheets. Others arrived around us, edged in on our shelter, chomped cheese balls, tortilla chips. Nathaniel had taken over umbrella duty. He escorted Monica to her trailer. Her nipples were visible through her soaked summer dress. Big nipples that took up most of her little breasts. Nathaniel had a hand on the small of her back, but she was a step ahead, almost running. When Nathaniel tried to follow her into the trailer, Monica gave a small shove and said something I couldn't hear. She shut the door. Nathaniel stood shocked for a moment. The soundtrack in his head played maudlin classical. The camera caught a tear coming down his cheek. The audience empathized. Nathaniel looked out at the horizon before remembering real life and that he was soaking and still on the clock.

My camera kept rolling. Others talked, drowned him out. Tipplehorn, in rain goggles and a white Gore-Tex shell, saying, "What I'd give right now for a soy chai latte."

Felix didn't notice. He said, "I'm this little fucking doll, and I'm surrounded by Geppettos, and each one has a different string and they're pulling my strings, my limbs are flopping everywhere, and they're saying who's going to direct? What kind of box office? Maybe if we change the ending?" Nathaniel sidled up to me, clearly still in disbelief. But he was playing it cool. He said, "I'm thinking this thing with Monica wasn't such a good idea. Actresses . . ."

I shushed him, nodded at Felix.

Nathaniel said, "You wanna get out of here? They're calling

the shoot anyway. Equipment's too wet. Let's ditch this and find a couple beers. We can hide out in the hair trailer while they pack."

"I'm busy," I said.

The cat wouldn't go up the stairs. One of the grips had to rush home and get his cat, a gray cat, not even the right color. I put a tin of sardines at the top of the staircase and the grip's cat got it right. The scene was completed. Solstice said that's a wrap, and we took cold beers out of picnic coolers and patted each other on the back. We returned to the motel, watched the sun lazily emerge. Day after the rain and everything smelled like wet oil and ragweed. Francisco had his guitar out by the pool, and Kathleen did her best Loretta Lynn.

When it went to DVD, Nathaniel and I were in Brooklyn, sharing the ground floor of a freestanding Victorian in Ditmas Park. We had hardwood floors and original molding, and we got a grand feeling eating cereal under our twelve-arm chandelier. New York was nice; everything was expensive, but you didn't need money. You could take a girl to the nearest dive, drink cheap pitchers, and tell her about your brush with Francisco Gomez, the way he closed his eyes when he played guitar. The girl would grab your wrist. Then you'd lean in close to talk over the DJ, say something like, "I've got a record player and some beers back at my place," and let her ride sidesaddle on your single-speed bike through the falling snow.

We were finding work, or Nathaniel was anyway. I liked the cold nights, smoking out my cracked window, staring at the empty yellow cabs that lined our block. Off-duty drivers speaking loudly on cell phones in Cantonese and Arabic and Staten Island English.

People came over for the screening—Nathaniel's idea. Put out cheese and hummus, a jug of Rossi. Crowded onto the couch. Nathaniel was wearing a cowboy hat. The girls appreciated irony; they'd gone to art school. Gwen, Nathaniel's latest thing, had stringy hair, a shrill laugh, and fingers pink at the joints from New York winter. She wrote for a weekly paper that published blind items about people we knew, or at least that we were friends with on Facebook. Nathaniel had his arm around her. Gwen's friend Anne sat to Nathaniel's left, her fishnet legs up on the coffee table. She said the phrase "Shit, man" at all possible instances—when she saw the chandelier, when she saw the TV, when she saw Nathaniel's Texas-flag tattoo.

Two girls I didn't know sat cross-legged on the floor. One was beautiful but kept checking her cell phone, awaiting better plans. The other had eaten Adderall and blew gum bubbles she then poked with a mechanical pencil. "Roll tape," she said, then said it again. "Action," she said, and Nathaniel dimmed the lights.

Title screen, then open on an empty beach, littered with foil and aluminum, cigarette cellophane blowing in the wind. Pan across to the oil rigs. Long-muscled men, like evolved primates, hang from the machinery's rungs. And there I am in my brief appearance as an extra. They'd needed people to swell out the crowd. I look ridiculous as a roughneck, draped in too-large Carhartt, hard hat in hand. The camera sees me for only a second. I'm sweating and blotchy, and my shaved head has a bull's-eye sunburn.

Everyone laughed, and I felt myself blush.

"You look like a dork," Gwen said. Nathaniel agreed. The other blew a confirmative bubble. But Anne looked over, gave a nod of recognition, said, "Shit, man."

It was all wrong. What I wanted was the action just offscreen. I wanted Tipplehorn screaming indecipherable instructions across all walkie frequencies; Solstice silly in boots and unnecessary spurs; Kathleen on speakerphone in the hair trailer, oblivious to outside commotion; Nathaniel hidden behind a garbage can, whispering "Cut" to a featured extra.

I looked at Nathaniel when Monica made her debut. They'd given her entrance music, some too-obvious C&W ballad about lost innocence. Monica stands on the porch, watches Francisco watch her from his parked Mustang. Nathaniel's face didn't move, but I saw him ball a fist around a skinny hipster hand.

Then the house is on fire, flames reaching up into Texas night. They'd got the colors right, a hundred shades of orange, gray, and blue. We were coming to the cat's coda, the feline waltz that Felix had dreamed about. I hoped Solstice hadn't screwed it up in editing. I wanted Felix to have that victory. Anne got up, stretched, shook her curly hair from its bun, and bent to tie a shoelace. She walked toward the kitchen, asked if I wanted another beer. The cat did its thing, but I wasn't watching. I was in another movie, myself the star, Anne lit by the headlights of a passing cab.

*Contributors' Notes*

*Other Distinguished Stories*
*of 2011*

*Editorial Addresses of American*
*and Canadian Magazines*
*Publishing Short Stories*

# Contributors' Notes

CAROL ANSHAW is the author of the novels *Carry the One, Aquamarine, Seven Moves,* and *Lucky in the Corner.* Her fiction has appeared in *Story, Tin House, NOR,* and *Granta Online,* and has been included twice before in this series. Anshaw is a past fellow of the NEA. For her book criticism she was awarded the NBCC Citation for Excellence in Reviewing. She teaches in the MFA in Writing program at the School of the Art Institute of Chicago and divides her time between Chicago and Amsterdam.

• I set out to write a story that was agile and speedy, with shorthanded exposition. As soon as I started working on it, though, all my writerly planning turned out to be beside the point. The whole thing was a gift. It's as though I opened a box and inside was this story. All I had to do was unpack it and perform some light assembly. This rarely happens for me, but it does occasionally, and I've come to think these are pieces I've already written in my imagination, carried around in bits and pieces without realizing it, until I have gathered up everything and begin to place it on the page.

TAYLOR ANTRIM is the author of a novel, *The Headmaster Ritual,* and a senior editor at *Vogue.* His short fiction has appeared in journals including *Terminus, Phoebe,* and *Black Warrior Review,* and online at *FiveChapters.com* and *Esquire.com.* Born in Richmond, Virginia, he lives in Brooklyn, New York, with his wife and daughter.

• The year was 1998 and jobs in San Francisco were easy to find—even for an English major like me. A college friend, Jonah, invited me to join him and three others at an Internet startup. No thanks, I said breezily, having just been offered an editorial position at a magazine called *Wine and Spirits.* The pay: $24,000, no benefits. "Not bad," my dad, back in Virginia, said on the phone.

Jonah was a multimillionaire within six months. He was also my roommate, so I tagged along to his company's lavish dot-com parties, let him treat me to sushi, and sampled a bit of his weed. My job had perks too, of course: as much free wine as I could drink and good tables at restaurants all over town. Sounds nice to me now. But I was stirred up and unsatisfied most of the time. What was I missing out on? Shouldn't I be living in New York? I was twenty-four.

The Noe Valley apartment Jonah and I shared wasn't much—a cramped place with beige wall-to-wall carpeting and an ant infestation. But the building was perched high and we had a balcony with a view that stretched over the city to the bay. The balcony was so narrow that you couldn't do anything on it except stand there, but the panorama had a quieting effect on me.

"Pilgrim Life" starts with that calming view, that apartment, my millionaire roommate, my wine magazine job. The rest of it I entirely made up (I swear) over a three-month stretch in the midst of the worst financial crisis I've ever lived through. Jobs were not easy to find in 2009, and I had recently lost mine. Going back to a charmed year in San Francisco felt like a tonic.

NATHAN ENGLANDER is the author of two story collections, *What We Talk About When We Talk About Anne Frank* (2012) and *For the Relief of Unbearable Urges* (1999), and the novel *The Ministry of Special Cases*. His translation of the *New American Haggadah*, edited by Jonathan Safran Foer, and a co-translation of Etgar Keret's *Suddenly a Knock on the Door* were also published in 2012. His play, *The Twenty-Seventh Man*, will premiere at the Public Theater in November 2012.

▪ This story is based on a game that—until the story's publication—I thought was played only in my house. You can call it the Who Will Hide Me? game or the Righteous Gentile game, or, most troubling of all, the Anne Frank game. If it's not already clear, the rules are quite simple: you sit around and wonder who would hide you in the event of a second Holocaust.

In truth, my sister and I have played the game forever and ever. It was maybe twenty years ago when it dawned on me that it wasn't a game at all. The highest compliment we'd give to certain friends was to say something like "Yes, Nicole would hide me. She really would." The story started to take form when we were talking about a couple we were both friendly with, and my sister said, "He would hide us, and she—she would turn us in." And I knew in my heart that my sister was right. And I got to thinking about what it is to know that, or believe that, about certain people. And, in the story, I take the idea to its extreme.

As for its connection to Raymond Carver's legendary story "What We Talk About When We Talk About Love": I really can't tell you how long ago

I first read the Carver, but I'll bet it had been fifteen years since I'd last sat down with his story when I started drafting mine. I actively avoided revisiting his masterpiece until I was well into the writing. I say that because the model I wanted to use was not Carver's story as written, but my memory of it. I first wanted to work with the picture that had formed over the years in my mind's eye—this sort of faceless visual of two couples at a table with a bottle between them, talking through the changing light of day. Only later did I go back and open Carver's collection and decide that I wanted to give my story that same entrance, to really bind those worlds, with the narrator saying, "And people from there think it gives them the right."

MARY GAITSKILL is the author of the novels *Two Girls, Fat and Thin* and *Veronica,* as well as the story collections *Bad Behavior, Because They Wanted To,* and *Don't Cry.* Her stories and essays have appeared in *The New Yorker, Harper's Magazine, Granta, The Best American Short Stories,* and *The O. Henry Prize Stories.* Last year she was a Cullman Fellow at the New York Public Library, where she was doing research for a novel. She is currently teaching writing at the Eugene Lang College at the New School in New York City.

• I wrote "The Other Place" for a very simple reason. I was afraid. I was living alone in a flimsy fishbowl house on a college campus that, as far as I was concerned, was a pervert magnet. The climactic scene of the story came to me before I had any intention of writing a story; I think it appeared in my mind because I wanted to imagine killer and victim coming right up to the crucial moment and then both walking away unharmed. At some point after that, the story formed.

ROXANE GAY's writing appears or is forthcoming in *New Stories from the Midwest 2011* and *2012, Best Sex Writing 2012,* Salon.com, *NOON, American Short Fiction, Indiana Review, Cream City Review, Black Warrior Review, Brevity, The Rumpus,* and many others. She is the co-editor of *PANK* and an *HTMLGIANT* contributor. She is also the author of the collection *Ayiti.*

• I moved to Michigan's Upper Peninsula to pursue a Ph.D. and realized I had moved into a different world, one where it was cold and snowy and where nothing made sense. Everyone kept asking me if I was from Detroit, and it was confusing and irritating because I had never been asked such a thing in my life. I'm from Nebraska. Finally, a few months into my tour of duty, which would last five years, I realized, oh, right, the only black people they know are from Detroit. Then it became a game to see who would ask the question, how often, and how I might answer it. My responses got creative. In my fourth year, I met a logger who would do strange things like take me into the woods and bring me dead deer. I started to realize there was a lot more complexity and beauty to the U.P. than I had realized, so I wrote a story about it—a love letter to the North Country.

JENNIFER HAIGH is a 2002 graduate of the Iowa Writers' Workshop. Since then she has written four novels: *Faith, The Condition, Baker Towers,* and *Mrs. Kimble.* Her books have won both the PEN/Hemingway Award for debut fiction and the PEN/L. L. Winship Award for outstanding book by a New England author, and have been published in sixteen languages. Her short stories have appeared widely, in *The Atlantic, Granta, Ploughshares,* and many other publications. A collection is forthcoming.

• A few years ago, a friend of mine was honored with a lifetime achievement award in his field. I attended the tribute and found it unsettling to hear his life and career summed up in retrospective fashion, as though no one had noticed that he was still very much alive. That odd situation, and the feeling of dissonance it created, led me to write "Paramour." Like all my stories, it is in some sense a mash-up of several things that interest me intensely—in this case, other people's marriages, sex and innocence, the theater, fathers and daughters, and Ukrainians.

MIKE MEGINNIS studied creative writing at Butler University and New Mexico State University. He has published fiction in *Hobart, The Collagist, Lifted Brow, Sycamore Review, PANK, SmokeLong Quarterly,* and many others. He serves as fiction editor for Noemi Press and co-edits the magazine *Uncanny Valley* with his wife, Tracy Rae Bowling.

• It feels like I spent most of my childhood playing Nintendo. The best games were those I couldn't play alone. These were adventures like *The Legend of Zelda* and *Metroid;* my father and I would play them together, making maps, sharing codes and secrets. The key mechanic in both games is the slow accumulation of new equipment and abilities. Your character grows progressively stronger and more capable until a final, game-ending triumph. These games tell a comforting story: You Get Better. This story makes a lot of sense when you're very young; it makes less sense as you get older. "Navigators" began with the idea of a game that tells a different, more likely story: You Get Worse. In some ways, this felt more organic to *Metroid,* which has a hostile, cryptic, and often flatly un-fun design. The structure of *Legend of Silence* borrows heavily from *Metroid,* though it is superficially an inversion.

My real father shares the story's fictional father's belief that a video game is best approached with the help of a navigator: someone who can help you better see the game and your place in it. Apart from that similarity, I am happy to report that "Navigators" bears little resemblance to my life. The mother's absence is necessary to the protagonist's decline, but I hope it also resonates with the experience of being a little boy playing video games as he slowly discovers the differences between the sexes. So often you are searching for a woman. When you find her, the game is over.

All of your problems are solved. In *Metroid,* brilliantly, the woman you find is yourself: only in the game's ending do you discover that your avatar, previously obscured by a spacesuit, is the beautiful Samus Aran.

I wrote "Navigators" during the second year of my MFA program, between semesters. My wife helped me with the second draft. *Hobart* editor Aaron Burch guided me through to the last.

STEVEN MILLHAUSER is the author of twelve works of fiction. His most recent collection, *We Others: New and Selected Stories,* includes stories written over the past thirty years. His story "Eisenheim the Illusionist" was the basis of the film *The Illusionist* (2006). He was born in Brooklyn, grew up in Connecticut, and now lives in Saratoga Springs, New York.

• I was seized by the desire to write a mirror story, but that was as far as things went. Every possibility seemed boring or frivolous. I turned my attention to something else. One day it came to me: the mirror shouldn't be the gateway to a fantastic world, but should behave very quietly. This thought, or instinct, propelled me into the story.

ALICE MUNRO grew up in Wingham, Ontario, and attended the University of Western Ontario. She has published twelve collections of new stories —*Dance of the Happy Shades; Something I've Been Meaning to Tell You; The Beggar Maid; The Moons of Jupiter; The Progress of Love; Friend of My Youth; Open Secrets; The Love of a Good Woman; Hateship, Friendship, Courtship, Loveship, Marriage; Runaway; The View from Castle Rock; Too Much Happiness;* and two volumes of selected stories, *Selected Stories* and *Carried Away*—as well as a novel, *Lives of Girls and Women.* Her thirteenth collection, *Dear Life,* is forthcoming in November 2012. During her distinguished career she has been the recipient of many awards and prizes, including three of Canada's Governor General's Literary Awards and two of its Giller Prizes, the Rea Award for the Short Story, the Lannan Literary Award, England's W. H. Smith Book Award, the U.S. National Book Critics Circle Award, the Edward MacDowell Medal in literature, and the Man Booker International Prize. Her stories have appeared in *The New Yorker, Harper's Magazine, The Atlantic, Granta, Paris Review,* and many other publications, and her collections have been translated into thirteen languages. Alice Munro lives in Clinton, Ontario, near Lake Huron.

• "Axis" was written with the question of whether a person can ever escape the ancient confines of her own history—or gender, for that matter. Grace and Avie, farm girls who go off to study history at university, attempt to use sex in order to manufacture love. On his escape from Grace, Royce is questioned about his goals in life. He sees an escarpment—new life growing from a crack in a massive rock—and understands all that he needs to do.

LAWRENCE OSBORNE is the author of several works of travel journalism, including *Bangkok Days,* published in 2009. His novel *The Forgiven* will be published this fall.

• I wrote the story some years after attending a lucid dreaming class at Kalani in Hawaii, where I failed to have any dreams. I was actually on a small island in Sicily called Favignana, waiting for an annual tuna hunt called the Mattanza, and the nightmarish atmosphere of the island during this time (I was trapped there with only a bicycle) for some reason reminded me of this place on the Big Island of Hawaii, where I had stayed before. For some reason islands always fill me with dread.

JULIE OTSUKA is the author of two novels, *The Buddha in the Attic,* which won the PEN/Faulkner Award and was a finalist for the National Book Award and the Los Angeles Times Book Prize, and *When the Emperor Was Divine,* which won the Asian American Literary Award and the American Library Association Alex Award and was long-listed for the UK's Orange Prize. Her fiction has been published in *Granta* and *Harper's Magazine.* A recipient of a Guggenheim fellowship and an Arts and Letters Award in Literature from the American Academy of Arts and Letters, she lives in New York City.

• "Diem Perdidi" is probably the most personal and the emotionally "truest" (though fictional) story I have written. It came to me very slowly—over many years—and then, once I began writing it—over the course of several months—very quickly. I had been collecting notes for it—jottings on torn scraps of paper, the backs of envelopes, napkins, ATM receipts—ever since my mother was first diagnosed with fronto-temporal dementia in 2003. But for the longest time, I could not make myself sit down to write it. I wasn't sure that I felt comfortable writing about my mother, or myself, or that dementia, as a story *(She was here, she forgot she was here, she died),* or whether it was even that interesting. Maybe, I thought, I would just go on collecting those scraps of paper forever. Or stuff them into a box and forget about them.

But once I got the idea for the structure ("She remembers," "She does not remember") and found the right voice (using the second-person narrator addressed to the "me" stand-in seemed vastly preferable to writing about myself in the first person), the story began to write itself and seemed to take on a life of its own. So much so that I took three months off the novel I was working on to finish it. I remember, at times, feeling almost euphoric and wishing that the story would never end. Writing it, I suppose, was my way of keeping my mother with me in the world, a way of being with her even as she was slipping away.

EDITH PEARLMAN is the recipient of the 2011 PEN/Malamud Award for excellence in short fiction, honoring her four collections of stories: *Va-*

*quita, Love Among the Greats, How to Fall,* and *Binocular Vision.* In 2011 the latter received the National Book Critics Circle Award in fiction and was a finalist for the National Book Award in fiction, the Story Prize, and the Los Angeles Times Book Award in fiction. *Binocular Vision* also received the Edward Lewis Wallant Award, presented annually to an American writer whose published creative work of fiction is considered to have significance for the American Jew.

• While I was digging in the loose soil of a new story (that's Jhumpa Lahiri's unbeatable phrasing), *Orion* wrote to request some fiction (it had published a short essay of mine about beetles). The story I was just beginning was to be about a triangle. Each member had my sympathy—the mistress, the wife, and the man between them. There was also a girl who didn't like to eat. But for *Orion* the lovers and the would-be anorexic would have to be vigorously involved in the natural world. And so, digging further, I encountered suicidal ants; more beetles, including the honeydew-making Coccidae; and the moth grub called *bicho de taquara,* which, ground up and mixed with water, produces an ecstatic sleep. Thanks to *Orion* for asking for a story; thanks to my characters for requiring me to do entomological research; thanks to powdered *bicho de taquara* for revealing itself in a scientific journal. I mean to try it as soon as I find a supplier.

ANGELA PNEUMAN is the author of a story collection (*Home Remedies,* 2007) and a forthcoming novel (2014). She teaches writing at Stanford and works as a copywriter in the California wine industry.

• Twenty years ago I graduated from college, married, and moved from rural Kentucky to Indianapolis. I took a grim, windowless job near the airport with a temp service—a yearlong position supporting wastewater-treatment-plant inspectors for the Indiana Department of Water. During this time, I often drove home to the west side's ugliest apartment complex for lunch. As I remember, I was trying to make a go of the Slim-Fast diet plan. One day at lunch I caught a television interview with a man whose nose, arms, and legs had been eaten away by a type of strep that he believed he'd picked up through a paper cut at his office. This was a lonely, impressionable period of my life. I felt far away from home, unsure of my choices, and overwhelmed by what seemed the inevitability of their consequences and their distance from my dreams. I couldn't stop thinking of bacteria—its relentlessness, its omnipresence—and how the people I worked with struggled to harness its covert operations. I couldn't stop thinking about the unfortunate man on television. During this time I began writing in earnest. I had a feeling I would write about bacteria someday, and I remain grateful for the way this detail and others hovered patiently around my consciousness, like narrative portals. I began this story a lifetime later, while living in San Francisco after finishing the Stegner

Fellowship at Stanford. The series of drafts that became "Occupational Hazard" hung around for a few years as the piece tried to work itself out. Finally I gave the main character a job as a wastewater-treatment-plant inspector. I gave him a name that means something to me, I "remembered" some of his childhood habits, and I set him in a place I know well. Only then did the story coalesce around my preoccupations and begin to make sense.

ERIC PUCHNER is the author of the story collection *Music Through the Floor* and the novel *Model Home,* which was a finalist for the PEN/Faulkner Award and won a California Book Award. His work has appeared in *GQ, Tin House, Zoetrope: All-Story, Glimmer Train,* and *Best New American Voices.* He has received a Pushcart Prize and a National Endowment for the Arts fellowship. He lives in Los Angeles and teaches at Claremont McKenna College.

• This story was a real departure for me. I'm not a big reader of science fiction, though the first stories I fell in love with as a boy were Ray Bradbury's magical Martian creep-outs. I honestly don't remember where the idea came from. The opening image—of a man showing up in a boy's yard one morning, as exotic as Bigfoot—floated around in my head for a long time before I dared to sit down at the computer and get it out there. (The short stories I end up being most proud of are generally the ones I thought I couldn't—or perhaps shouldn't—write.) My interest in the story never had to do with divining the future; it was always much more about capturing what it means to have a parent, about distilling the entire emotional arc of having a father into twenty pages. The "girl" was less of a presence in the first draft—it wasn't until I showed it to some very smart friends, and they encouraged me to push the premise to its logical extreme, that I nudged the story into darker waters. I'd like to thank these friends, and also the folks at *Tin House* for convincing me that the original title, "Neverland," showed my hand too early. I think of "Beautiful Monsters" as a fable more than anything else: a stranger-comes-to-town story, in which the stranger is death.

GEORGE SAUNDERS, a 2006 MacArthur Fellow, teaches at Syracuse University and is the author of the short story collections *CivilWarLand in Bad Decline, Pastoralia,* and *In Persuasion Nation.* "Tenth of December" is the title story of a new collection, to be published early in 2013.

• Sometimes a story comes from a little lonely moment of unwilled, spontaneous fantasy. For example, I once wrote a story called "The End of FIRPO in the World" that came out of seeing this miserable little boy standing right on the curb of a busy street, and then thinking, What would I do or say if that kid got hit and I happened to be the first responder?

"Tenth of December" was kind of like that. One day, just minding my own business, it hit me—really hit me—that I would die someday, and that it would happen via a series of actual events for which I'd have to be present: I'd get the news on a certain day, gradually start to weaken, etc., etc. Horrifying. And in next split second I revolted against this idea, thinking, Argh, no way, I'm not doing that; how do I get out of it? Embarrassingly, my solution was this: I know, I'd go freeze myself in a forest somewhere. That way, no fuss, no pain, no trouble for my family. Then all of those thoughts fell away, and I was back to "normal," that is, realizing that I would never die, and that if by chance I did, there would be nothing horrid or ignoble about it—it would be fast, cool, and heroic. So that was a relief. But I was left with the seed of this story: a guy with a fatal illness decides to kill himself via freezing. I didn't start writing right away but for over a year just kept that conceptual seed in my head, adding bits to it as they naturally arose. So: *guy tries to kill himself by freezing . . . and meets a kid . . . a kid in white . . . who saves him, or doesn't . . . or maybe he saves the kid, or doesn't. Saves the kid from what? Freezing? Drowning? The kid falls through the ice of a pond?* And then at some point I started sketching things out, trying to get the physicality straight (who follows whom into the forest?) and trying to find out *which* dying man and *which* little boy. And that, of course, was where all the real fun started, and when the real meanings started to unveil themselves.

TAIYE SELASI was born in London and raised in Massachusetts. She holds a B.A. in American studies from Yale and an M.Phil. in international relations from Oxford. Selasi made her fiction debut in *Granta* with "The Sex Lives of African Girls." Her first novel, *Ghana Must Go,* will be published in 2013. She lives in Rome.

 • "The Sex Lives of African Girls" was written under duress. In 2005 I was eight years into a grave case of writer's block. Incapable of finishing a piece of fiction, I abandoned the form to write scripts. *Winston Light,* my only play, ran for a week that spring. Our executive producer was Avery Willis, Toni Morrison's niece. When her aunt came to receive an honorary degree from Oxford (where we were grad students), Avery kindly invited me to come to the reception. So it was that I found myself at the side of my literary hero, confessing my lifelong love of prose and newfound refusal to write it.

The most magical thing happened next. I happened to be spending that summer in Lawrenceville, where my beloved ex-stepfather teaches. A few weeks after I returned from Oxford, Professor Morrison invited me to see her. Over a glass of wine, she patiently listened as I explained my predicament: fear of failure had replaced the joy I'd always found in fiction. This was June 2005. By December 2006 I still didn't have a single coherent piece of work to show her. At Christmastime my mum and sister came with me to Princeton. Professor Morrison came straight to the point. "I'll have finished my next novel in November," she said, "and will then have time to read yours. Send me a manuscript by the end of next year." With our families as witnesses, we shook on it. Deal.

I had a year. But no story. For two months I stared at my MacBook screen, willing words to come. They didn't. Tears did. I didn't sleep that March. I considered requesting an extension. One day in April—in the shower at noon—I heard, as if remembering it, "The sex lives of African girls begin, inevitably, with Uncle." A bit like a song I'd heard somewhere, the bridge of which I'd forgotten. "There you are, eleven, alone in the study in the dark," the song went on without music. I raced to the laptop, still dripping wet, and wrote—or wrote down—the stanza. "'You,'" I thought. "Okay. Second person. Really? Try. Worked for McInerney. "Alone in the study." Okay. Why alone? Where are you? Who are you?"

A story.

On December 31, 2007, as per our agreement, I sent Professor Morrison the first piece of fiction I'd finished since 1997. I was in Ethiopia for New Year's; it was already 2008 in Addis. Electricity was spotty in the Internet café there; I was advised to type fast and be brief. Afraid that we'd lose power (or more to the point: that I'd lose nerve), I typed just two words —*thank you*—and sent off these thirteen thousand.

SHARON SOLWITZ's stories, published in such magazines as *TriQuarterly, Ploughshares,* and *Mademoiselle,* have received awards including the Push-cart Prize, the Nelson Algren Award, and the Katherine Ann Porter prize. Her collection *Blood and Milk* received the Carl Sandburg Literary Award and the Midland Authors Award and was a finalist for the National Jewish Book Award. The story appearing in this volume is from her current work in progress, a collection of interrelated stories. She teaches fiction writing at Purdue University and lives in Chicago with her husband, the poet Barry Silesky.

 • A couple of years ago I read a story about a new widow whose friends and acquaintances, highly verbal and educated, are tongue-tied in the face of her grief. As I recall, one friend actually crosses the street to avoid the social awkwardness of having to find words for what there are no words for. *It's so embarrassing.*

When my almost-fourteen-year-old son died of cancer, there was nothing anyone could say to assuage me. Still, it helped when my grief was recognized. One feels so alone in bereavement that mere recognition does something useful and good. There were times when I wanted to shriek at people, at strangers: *World, weep for Jesse.* And, however weird it may seem, acknowledgment of my grief by other people helped pull me back, bit by bit, to the world of people who hadn't lost their children.

"Alive" is part of a collection of stories about a family with a son who has cancer, a collection that shrieks, as I did not, *Weep, world.* It is also the result of my irrational wish to breathe life back into Jesse and into the part of us that we lost with his death. Still, the work isn't memoir or autobiography. The situation is what we went through, but the characters are purposefully, purposely different from us. Only thus I could write with less pain than pleasure — the deep pleasure of invention converting pain and grief into something like fuel.

The events in "Alive" are largely factual. One snowy Saturday when Jesse and his chemo were in sync, I drove him and his brother to Alpine Valley, only the second time either of my children had put on skis. Jesse took no risks, but his brother, Seth, went down a steep slope and broke his thumb. Writing the story as fiction, my chief discovery was this brother's voice. Wonderful, to romp in the mind of the invented younger brother, whose anger, pride, shrewdness, and vulnerability kept surprising me.

KATE WALBERT is the author of *A Short History of Women,* chosen by the *New York Times Book Review* as one of the ten best books of 2009; *Our Kind,* a finalist for the National Book Award; *The Gardens of Kyoto;* and *Where She Went.* Her short fiction has been published in *The New Yorker, The Paris Review, The Best American Short Stories 2007,* and *The O. Henry Prize Stories,* among other magazines and journals. From 2011 to 2012 she was the Rona Jaffe Foundation Fellow at the Dorothy and Lewis B. Cullman Center for Writers and Scholars at the New York Public Library. She lives in New York City with her family.

• Years ago, in Patagonia, I found myself on a small boat and, in my memory, alone (although I'm sure there were throngs of tourists around me) staring into the scaly, impenetrable eye of a right whale. I was reminded of that moment as I worked on "M&M World," a story I'd been kicking around for a long time and one that was no doubt inspired, and complicated, by the fact that I'd never been to the place. (Its existence loomed large. When they were little, my children would beg to stop every time we drove by the M&M guy waving from the top of the Empire State Building, until the repeated promise of "some other day" became a running joke in the family.) I could say that the resonance of the whale's eye, the stillness at the center of it, seemed the right counterweight to the craziness of Times Square, but that's suggesting too much understanding of what I'm writing as I write it. I only know that the whale gave the story a momentum I hadn't been able to find, a momentum that made Maggie's disappearance, and delivery, seem inevitable.

JESS WALTER is the author of six novels, most recently *Beautiful Ruins* (2012). He was a finalist for the 2006 National Book Award for *The Zero* and winner of the 2005 Edgar Allan Poe Award for best novel for *Citizen Vince*. His short fiction and essays have appeared in *Harper's Magazine, Mc-Sweeney's, Playboy,* and many other publications. His story collection, *The New Frontier,* is forthcoming early in 2013. He lives in his hometown of Spokane, Washington.

• My city is poor. Over the past few years it has seemed as if a homeless person with a cardboard sign has staked out every downtown corner. At the best corners, they wait their turns like workers expecting a shift change. Sometimes I give money. Sometimes I don't. I don't have a coherent policy. Sometimes I don't even see the person until I drive away; they are part of the landscape. Sometimes they have a story about what happened to them. These stories rarely seem true (Vietnam War vets in their forties, former bank executives without teeth). So I do what people do: I make assumptions. I crunch the numbers. Before I give money, I engage in the calculus of need: *Isn't he young enough to work? Is she a meth addict? Will my money just go for booze?* The political and corporate right in this country would have us believe that someone's hard times are an affront to our own hard work, that we should blame the poor for their own poverty. I think this is like hitting a pedestrian with your car and then blaming him for the dent.

A few years ago, a panhandling woman asked my wife and me for money to buy food for her three children. It was clear to us both that she was lying; she probably didn't even have kids. She seemed drunk and there was a liquor store nearby. Still, I gave her ten dollars. Later, we saw her walking with a couple of grocery bags. Three little kids were walking behind her. I suppose that's what sparked "Anything Helps": plain old empathy and shame.

ADAM WILSON is the author of the novel *Flatscreen* (2012). His short stories have appeared in many publications, including *The Paris Review, The Literary Review, New York Tyrant, Washington Square Review, Meridian, Coffin Factory,* and the anthology *Promised Lands: New Jewish Fiction on Longing and Belonging.* He is the 2012 recipient of the Terry Southern Prize, which recognizes "wit, panache, and sprezzatura in work published by *Paris Review*." He teaches creative writing at NYU and lives in Brooklyn.

• After college I moved to Austin, Texas, to become a character in my own imaginary movie. Until that time I'd never lived outside of my home state of Massachusetts. College had given me the romantic notion that to be a real writer one must wade through the American South, working menial jobs and staring at horizons. Austin rhymed with Boston, so it seemed like as good a place as any. Also, I'd watched a lot of movies about high school football in Texas and knew that former cheerleaders often fell in love with mysterious strangers freshly landed from the East and sizzling with irony. The first job I got in Austin was as an assistant on a movie set not unlike the one in "What's Important Is Feeling." Part of the film was shot in Corpus Christi, where the story takes place. I couldn't get over the strange sight of a tourist beach covered in oil rigs. Among many other things, my experience working on the film helped dispel the idea that screenwriting was a worthwhile venture. I had front-row tickets to the film's screenwriter's slow psychic meltdown as he watched his artistic vision turned into something other and unrecognizable. This story is my attempt to capture that meltdown, both comically and sympathetically. After that gig I had one more movie job, doing catering on an indie horror flick. I was fired about halfway through the film and followed it with a long period of unemployment. Eventually I got a job holding up a giant orange arrow at a highway exit ramp. Then my car got stolen and I moved to New York with the insurance money.

# Other Distinguished Stories
# of 2011

DONOVAN, GERARD
  Holiday. *Zoetrope: All-Story*, vol. 14,
    no. 4.
DORFMAN, ARIEL
  Where He Fell. *McSweeney's*, no. 38.
DRURY, TOM
  Joan Comes Home. *A Public Space*,
    no. 12.
DUBOIS, JENNIFER
  Wolf. *The Kenyon Review*, vol. 33,
    no. 3.
DUVAL, PETE
  I, Budgie. *Witness*, vol. 24.

EDWARDS, MELODIE
  The Bird Lady. *Prairie Schooner*, vol.
    85, no. 2.
EPSTEIN, JOSEPH
  Arnheim and Sons. *Commentary*,
    January.
EVANHOE, REBECCA
  Snake. *Harper's Magazine*,
    November.

FRANZEN, JONATHAN
  Ambition. *McSweeney's*, no. 37.

GIRALDI, WILLIAM
  Hold the Dark. *Ploughshares*, vol. 37,
    no. 4.
GREENFELD, KARL TARO
  Even the Gargoyle Is Frightened.
    *Missouri Review*, vol. 33, no. 4.

HAIGH, JENNIFER
  Thrift. *Five Points*, vol. 14, no. 1.
HART, BRIAN
  Horseshoe Bend. *Alaska Quarterly
    Review*, vol. 28, nos. 1 and 2.
HEMENWAY, ARNA BONTEMPS
  Elegy on Kinderklavier. *Seattle
    Review*, vol. 4, no. 2.
HOLLADAY, CARY
  Seven Sons. *Hudson Review*, vol. 64,
    no 3.
HORROCKS, CAITLIN
  Sun City. *The New Yorker*, October
    24.

HUDDLE, DAVID
  Doubt Administration. *Green
    Mountains Review*, vol. 24, no. 1.
HUNT, SAMANTHA
  Wampum. *HOW*, no. 8.

JOHNSTON, BRET ANTHONY
  Paradeability. *American Short Fiction*,
    vol. 14, no. 53.

KADISH, RACHEL
  The Governess and the Tree.
    *Ploughshares*, vol. 37, no. 4.
KAPLAN, HESTER
  The Aerialist. *Salamander*, vol. 17,
    no. 1.
  Natural Wonder. *Ploughshares*, vol.
    37, no. 1.
KARDOS, MICHAEL
  A Story with Strong, Graceful
    Hands. *Harvard Review*, no.
    41.

LAMBERT, SHAENA
  The War Between the Men and the
    Women. *Ploughshares*, vol. 37,
    no. 1.
LANCELOTTA, VICTORIA
  A Good Woman. *Idaho Review*, vols.
    11–12.
LANDERS, SCOTT
  The Age of Heroes. *New England
    Review*, vol. 32, no. 2.
LEARY, ANN
  Safety. *Ploughshares*, vol. 37, no. 4.
LEPUCKI, EDAN
  Take Care of That Rage Problem.
    *McSweeney's*, no. 37.
LIPSYTE, SAM
  The Climber Room. *The New Yorker*,
    November 21.

LOMBREGLIA, RALPH
  Mountain People. *American Scholar
    Online*.
LONG, DAVID
  Oubliette. *The New Yorker*, October
    10.

LUNSTRUM, KIRSTEN SUNDBERG
The Remainder Salvaged. *Willow Springs*, no. 68.

MAKKAI, REBECCA
The Way You Hold Your Knife. *Ecotone*, no. 11.

MARRA, ANTHONY
The Palace of the People. *Narrative Magazine*, Winter.

MAXWELL, ABI
Giant of the Sea. *McSweeney's*, no. 39.

McGUANE, THOMAS
The Good Samaritan. *The New Yorker*, April 25.

MEANS, DAVID
The Butler's Lament. *Zoetrope: All-Story*, vol. 15, no. 1.

MILLHAUSER, STEVEN
Rapunzel. *McSweeney's*, no. 38.

MOFFETT, KEVIN
English Made Easy. *American Short Fiction*, vol. 14, no. 52.
Lugo in Normal Time. *McSweeney's*, no. 37.

MOSES, JENNIFER ANNE
Angels of the Lake. *Nimrod*, vol. 54, no. 2.

MOSLEY, WALTER
Familiar Music. *Tin House*, vol. 12, no. 4.

MUNRO, ALICE
Gravel. *The New Yorker*, June 27.
Leaving Maverley. *The New Yorker*, November 28.

MURPHY, YANNICK
Secret Language. *McSweeney's*, no. 39.

ORNER, PETER
Plaza Revolution, Mexico City, 6 A.M. *Witness*, vol. 24.
You Can't Say Dallas Doesn't Love You. *A Public Space*, no. 14.

PANCAKE, ANN
Mouseskull. *Georgia Review*, vol. 65, no. 4.

PEARLMAN, EDITH
Tenderfoot. *Idaho Review*, vol. 11, no. 12.

PERCY, BENJAMIN
Writs of Possession. *Virginia Quarterly Review*, vol. 87, no. 2.

PENKOV, MIROSLAV
The Letter. *A Public Space*, no. 13.

PETERSON, ADAM
It Goes Without Saying. *Camera Obscura*, vol. 3.

PIERCE, GREG
Later That Night. *New England Review*, vol. 32, no. 2.

PITT, MATTHEW
Where You Get Ahead of Yourself. *Epoch*, vol. 60, no. 2.

PRINCE, ADAM
Action Figures. *Southern Review*, vol. 47, no. 1.

RASH, RON
The Trusty. *The New Yorker*, May 23.

REA, A. R.
The Silver Bullet. *Missouri Review*, vol. 34, no. 2.

RICH, NATHANIEL
The Northeast Kingdom. *McSweeney's*, no. 38.

ROWELL, DAVID
The Piñata. *American Scholar Online*.

RUSSELL, KAREN
The Hox River Window. *Zoetrope: All-Story*, vol. 15, no. 3.

RYAN, PATRICK
Which Way to the Osterling Cloud? *Tin House*, vol. 12, no. 4.

SAUNDERS, GEORGE
Home. *The New Yorker*, June 13 and 20.

SHEPARD, JIM
HMS Terror. *Zoetrope: All-Story*, vol. 15, no. 3.

SHEPARD, KAREN
Don't Know Where, Don't Know When. *Tin House*, vol. 12, no. 4.
Girls Only. *One Story*, no. 157.

# Editorial Addresses of American and Canadian Magazines Publishing Short Stories

Able Muse Review
467 Saratoga Ave. #602
San Jose, CA 95129
*$22, Nina Schyler*

African American Review
http://aar.expressacademic.org
*$40, Nathan Grant*

Agni Magazine
Boston University Writing Program
Boston University
236 Bay State Rd.
Boston, MA 02115
*$20, Sven Birkerts*

Alaska Quarterly Review
University of Alaska, Anchorage
3211 Providence Dr.
Anchorage, AK 99508
*$18, Ronald Spatz*

Alimentum
P.O. Box 776
New York, NY 10163
*$18, Paulette Licitra*

Alligator Juniper
http://www.prescott.edu/alligator_juniper/
*$15, Melanie Bishop*

American Letters and Commentary
Department of English
University of Texas at San Antonio
1 UTSA Blvd.
San Antonio, TX 78249
*$10, David Ray Vance, Catherine Kasper*

American Scholar
1606 New Hampshire Ave. NW
Washington, DC 20009
*$24, Robert Wilson*

American Short Fiction
P.O. Box 302678
Austin, TX 78703
*$30, Stacey Swann*

Amoskeag
Southern New Hampshire University
2500 North River Rd.
Manchester, NH 03106
*$7, Michael J. Brien*

Anderbo.com
anderbo.com
*Rick Rofihe*

Annalemma
annalemma.net
*Chris Heavener*

Antioch Review
Antioch University
P.O. Box 148
Yellow Springs, OH 45387
*$40, Robert S. Fogerty*

Apalachee Review
P.O. Box 10469
Tallahassee, FL 32302
*$15, Michael Trammell*

Arcadia
9616 Nichols Rd.
Oklahoma City, OK 73120
*$24, Noah Milligan*

Arkansas Review
P.O. Box 1890
Arkansas State University
State University, AR 72467
*$20, Janelle Collins*

Armchair/Shotgun
377 Flatbush Ave. # 3
Brooklyn, NY 11238

Arroyo Literary Review
Department of English
California State University, East Bay
25800 Carlos Bee Blvd.
Hayward, CA 94542

Arts and Letters
Campus Box 89
Georgia College and State University
Milledgeville, GA 31061
*$15, Martin Lammon*

Ascent
English Department

Concordia College
readthebestwriting.com
*W. Scott Olsen*

Asian American Literary Review
www.aalrmag.org
*$28, Lawrence-Minh Bùi Davis*

At Length
atlengthmag.com
*Jeremy Keehn*

Atlantic Monthly
600 New Hampshire Ave. NW
Washington, DC 20037
*$39.95, C. Michael Curtis*

Bayou
Department of English
University of New Orleans
2000 Lakeshore Dr.
New Orleans, LA 70148
*$15, Joanna Leake*

The Believer
849 Valencia St.
San Francisco, CA 94110
*Heidi Julavits*

Bellevue Literary Review
Department of Medicine
New York University School of
Medicine
550 First Ave.
New York, NY 10016
*$15, Danielle Ofri*

Bellingham Review
MS-9053
Western Washington University
Bellingham, WA 98225
*$12, Brenda Miller*

Bellowing Ark
P.O. Box 55564
Shoreline, WA 98155
*$20, Robert Ward*

Blackbird
Department of English
Virginia Commonwealth University
P.O. Box 843082
Richmond, VA 23284-3082
*Gregory Donovan, Mary Flinn*

Black Warrior Review
P.O. Box 862936
Tuscaloosa, AL 35486-0027
*$16, Farren Stanley*

Blue Mesa Review
Creative Writing Program
University of New Mexico
MSC03-2170
Albuquerque, NM 87131
*Samantha Tetangco*

Bomb
New Art Publications
80 Hanson Pl.
Brooklyn, NY 11217
*$22, Betsy Sussler*

Boston Review
35 Medford St., Suite 302
Somerville, MA 02143
*$25, Joshua Cohen, Deborah Chasman*

Bosque
http://www.abqwriterscoop.com/
bosque.html
*Lisa Lenard-Cook*

Boulevard
PMB 325
6614 Clayton Rd.
Richmond Heights, MO 63117
*$20, Richard Burgin*

Brain, Child: The Magazine for
Thinking Mothers
P.O. Box 714
Lexington, VA 24450-0714
*$22, Jennifer Niesslein, Stephanie
Wilkinson*

Briar Cliff Review
3303 Rebecca St.
P.O. Box 2100
Sioux City, IA 51104-2100
*$10, Tricia Currans-Sheehan*

Callaloo
MS 4212
Texas A&M University
College Station, TX 77843-4212
*$50, Charles H. Rowell*

Camera Obscura
obscurajournal.com
*M. E. Parker*

Carolina Quarterly
Greenlaw Hall
CB #3520
University of North Carolina
Chapel Hill, NC 27599
*$24, the editors*

Cerise Press
P.O. Box 241187
Omaha, NE 68124
*Karen Rigby*

Chattahoochee Review
555 North Indian Creek Dr.
Clarkson, GA 30021
*Anna Schachner*

Chautauqua
Department of Creative Writing
University of North Carolina, Wil-
mington
601 South College Rd.
Wilmington, NC 28403
*$14.95, Jill and Philip Gerard*

Chicago Review
5801 South Kenwood
University of Chicago
Chicago, IL 60637
*$25, P. Genesius Durica*

Chicago Quarterly Review
517 Sherman Ave.
Evanston, IL 60202
*$17, S. Afzal Haider*

Cimarron Review
205 Morrill Hall
Oklahoma State University
Stillwater, OK 74078-4069
*$32, E. P. Walkiewicz*

Cincinnati Review
Department of English
McMicken Hall, Room 369
P.O. Box 210069
Cincinnati, OH 45221
*$15, Michael Griffith*

Colorado Review
Department of English
Colorado State University
Fort Collins, CO 80523
*$24, Stephanie G'Schwind*

Columbia
Columbia University Alumni Center
622 West 113th St.
MC4521
New York, NY 10025
*$50, Michael B. Sharleson*

Commentary
165 East 56th St.
New York, NY 10022
*$45, Neal Kozody*

The Common
Frost Library
Amherst College
Amherst, MA 01002
*$20, Jennifer Acker*

Confrontation
English Department
C. W. Post College of Long Island
University
Greenvale, NY 11548
*$10, Martin Tucker*

Conjunctions
21 East 10th St., Suite 3E
New York, NY 10003
*$18, Bradford Morrow*

Crab Orchard Review
Department of English
Southern Illinois University at
Carbondale
Carbondale, IL 62901
*$20, Carolyn Alessio*

Crazyhorse
Department of English
College of Charleston
66 George St.
Charleston, SC 29424
*$16, Anthony Varallo*

Cream City Review
Department of English
University of Wisconsin, Milwaukee
Box 413
Milwaukee, WI 53201
*$22, Jay Johnson*

Crucible
Barton Collge
P.O. Box 5000
Wilson, NC 27893
*$16, Terrence L. Grimes*

Cutbank
Department of English
University of Montana
Missoula, MT 59812
*$12, Lauren Hamlin*

Daedalus
136 Irving St., Suite 100
Cambridge, MA 02138
*$41, Phyllis S. Bendell*

Denver Quarterly
University of Denver
Denver, CO 80208
*$20, Bin Ramke*

Descant
P.O. Box 314
Station P
Toronto, Ontario M5S 2S8
*$28, Karen Mulhallen*

descant
Department of English
Texas Christian University
TCU Box 297270
Fort Worth, TX 76129
*$12, Dave Kuhne*

Ecotone
Department of Creative Writing
University of North Carolina,
Wilmington
601 South College Rd.
Wilmington, NC 28403
*$16.95, David Gessner*

Epiphany
www.epiphanyzine.com
*$18, Willard Cook*

Epoch
251 Goldwin Smith Hall
Cornell University
Ithaca, NY 14853-3201
*$11, Michael Koch*

Esquire
300 West 57th St., 21st Floor
New York, NY 10019
*$17.94, Fiction Editor*

Event
Douglas College
P.O. Box 2503
New Westminster,
British Columbia V3L 5B2
*$29.95, Elizabeth Bachinsky*

Fantasy and Science Fiction
P.O. Box 3447
Hoboken, NJ 07030
*$39, Gordon Van Gelder*

Farallon Review
1017 L Street #348
Sacramento, CA 95814
*$10, the editors*

Fiction
Department of English
The City College of New York
Convent Ave. at 138th St.
New York, NY 10031
*$38, Mark Jay Mirsky*

Fiction International
Department of English and
Comparative Literature
5500 Campanile Dr.
San Diego State University
San Diego, CA 92182
*$18, Harold Jaffe*

The Fiddlehead
Campus House
11 Garland Ct.
UNB P.O. Box 4400
Fredericton,
New Brunswick E3B 5A3
*$55, Mark Anthony Jarman*

Fifth Wednesday
www.fifthwednesdayjournal.org
*$20, Vern Miller*

Five Points
Georgia State University
P.O. Box 3999
Atlanta, GA 30302
*$21, David Bottoms and Megan Sexton*

Fjords Review
www.fjordsreview.com
*John Gosslee*

Florida Review
Department of English
P.O. Box 161346
University of Central Florida
Orlando, FL 32816
*$15, Jocelyn Bartkevicius*

Flyway
206 Ross Hall
Department of English
Iowa State University
Ames, IA 50011
*$24, David DeFina*

Fourteen Hills
Department of Creative Writing
San Francisco State University
1600 Halloway Ave.
San Francisco, CA 94132-1722
*$15, Holly Hardy*

Fugue
uidaho.edu/fugue
*$18, Mary Morgan*

Gargoyle
3819 North 13th St.
Arlington, VA 22201
*$30, Lucinda Ebersole, Richard Peabody*

Georgetown Review
400 East College St.
Box 227
Georgetown, KY 40324
*$5, Steven Carter*

Georgia Review
Gilbert Hall
University of Georgia
Athens, GA 30602
*$35, Stephen Corey*

Gettysburg Review
Gettysburg College
300 North Washington St.
Gettysburg, PA 17325
*$28, Peter Stitt*

Ghost Town/Pacific Review
Department of English
California State University, San Bernadino
5500 University Pwy.
San Bernadino, CA 92407
*Gina Hanson*

Glimmer Train
1211 Northwest Glisan St., Suite 207
Portland, OR 97209
*$36, Susan Burmeister-Brown, Linda Swanson-Davies*

Good Housekeeping
300 West 57th St.
New York, NY 10019
*Laura Matthews*

Grain
Box 67
Saskatoon, Saskatchewan 57K 3K9
*$35, Sylvia Legns*

Granta
841 Broadway, 4th Floor
New York, NY 10019-3780
*$39.95, John Freeman*

Green Mountains Review
Box A58
Johnson State College
Johnson, VT 05656
*$15, Jacob White*

Greensboro Review
3302 Hall for Humanities
and Research Administration
University of North Carolina
Greensboro, NC 27402
*$14, Jim Clark*

Grey Sparrow
P.O. Box 211664
St. Paul, MN 55121
*Diane Smith*

Gulf Coast
Department of English
University of Houston
Houston, TX 77204-3012
*$16, Ian Stansel*

Hanging Loose
231 Wyckoff St.

Brooklyn, NY 11217
*$22, group*

Harper's Magazine
666 Broadway
New York, NY 10012
*$21, Ben Metcalf*

Harpur Palate
Department of English
Binghamton University
P.O. Box 6000
Binghamton, NY 13902
*$16, Barrett Bowlin*

Harvard Review
Lamont Library
Harvard University
Cambridge, MA 02138
*$20, Christina Thompson*

Hawaii Review
Department of English
University of Hawaii at Manoa
P.O. Box 11674
Honolulu, HI 96828
*$20, Donovan Colleps*

Hayden's Ferry Review
Box 875002
Arizona State University
Tempe, AZ 85287
*$25, Cameron Fielder*

H.O.W.—Helping Orphans Worldwide
12 Desbrosses St.
New York, NY 10013
*Alison Weaver*

High Desert Journal
P.O. Box 7647
Bend, OR 97708
*$16, Elizabeth Quinn*

Hobart
P.O. Box 11658
Ann Arbor, MI 48106
*$18, Aaron Burch*

Hotel Amerika
Columbia College
English Department
600 South Michigan Ave.
Chicago, IL 60657
*$18, David Lazar*

Hudson Review
684 Park Ave.
New York, NY 10065
*$36, Paula Deitz*

Hunger Mountain
www.hungermountain.org
*$12, Barrry Wightman*

Idaho Review
Boise State University
1910 University Dr.
Boise, ID 83725
*$10, Mitch Wieland*

Image
Center for Religious Humanism
3307 Third Ave. West
Seattle, WA 98119
*$39.95, Gregory Wolfe*

Indiana Review
Ballantine Hall 465
1020 East Kirkwood Ave.
Bloomington, IN 47405-7103
*$17, Kurian Johnson*

Inkwell
Manhattanville College
2900 Purchase St.
Purchase, NY 10577
*$18, Tanya Beltram*

Iowa Review
Department of English
University of Iowa
308 EPB
Iowa City, IA 52242
*$25, Russell Scott Valentino*

Iron Horse Literary Review
Department of English
Texas Tech University
Box 43091
Lubbock, TX 79409-3091
*$15, Leslie Jill Patterson*

Italian Americana
University of Rhode Island
Providence Campus
80 Washington St.
Providence, RI 02903
*$20, Carol Bonomo Albright*

Jabberwock Review
Department of English
Drawer E
Mississippi State University
Mississippi State, MS 39762
*$15, Michael P. Kardos*

Jewish Currents
45 East 33rd St.
New York, NY 10016-5335
*$25, Editorial board*

The Journal
Ohio State University
Department of English
164 West 17th Ave.
Columbus, OH 43210
*$15, Kathy Fagon*

The Journal
info@thejournalinc.com
*Julia Dippelhofer, Katherine Bernard*

Joyland
joylandmagazine.com
*Emily Schultz*

Juked
110 Westridge Dr.
Tallahassee, FL 32304
*$10, J. W. Wang*

Kenyon Review
www.kenyonreview.org
*$30, the editors*

Lady Churchill's Rosebud Wristlet
Small Beer Press
150 Pleasant St.
Easthampton, MA 01027
*$20, Kelly Link*

Lake Effect
Penn State Erie
4951 College Dr.
Erie, PA 16563-1501
*$6, George Looney*

Lalitamba
110 West 86th St., Suite 5D
New York, NY 10024
*Florence Homolka*

Literary Review
Fairleigh Dickinson University
285 Madison Ave.
Madison, NJ 07940
*$24, Minna Proctor*

The Literarian
www.centerforfiction.org
*Dawn Raffel*

Los Angeles Review
redhen.org/losangelesreview
*Kate Gale*

Louisiana Literature
SLU-10792
Southeastern Louisiana University
Hammond, LA 70402
*$12, Jack B. Bedell*

Louisville Review
Spalding University
851 South Fourth St.
Louisville, KY 40203
*$14, Sena Jeter Naslund*

Madison Review
University of Wisconsin
Department of English
H. C. White Hall
600 North Park St.
Madison, WI 53706
*$25, Elzbieta Beck*

Make
www.makemag.com
*Sarah Dodson*

Mānoa
English Department
University of Hawaii
Honolulu, HI 96822
*$30, Frank Stewart*

Mary
www.maryjournal.org
dpd2@stmarys-ca.edu
*Paul Barrett*

Massachusetts Review
South College
University of Massachusetts
Amherst, MA 01003
*$27, Ellen Dore Watson*

McSweeney's
826 Valencia St.
San Francisco, CA 94110
*$55, Dave Eggers*

Meridian
Department of English
P.O. Box 400145
University of Virginia
Charlottesville, VA 22904-4145
*$12, Hannah Holtzman*

Michigan Quarterly Review
0576 Rackham Building
915 East Washington St.
University of Michigan
Ann Arbor, MI 48109
*$25, Johnathan Freedman*

Mid-American Review
Department of English
Bowling Green State University
Bowling Green, OH 43403
*$12, Michael Czyzniejewski*

Minnesota Review
ASPECT Virginia Tech
202 Major Williams Hall (0192)
Blacksburg, VA 24061
*$30, Janell Watson*

Minnetonka Review
P.O. Box 386
Spring Park, MN 55384
*$17, Troy Ehlers*

Mississippi Review
University of Southern Mississippi
118 College Dr. #5144
Hattiesburg, MS 39406-5144
*$15, Julia Johnson*

Missouri Review
357 McReynolds Hall
University of Missouri
Columbia, MO 65211
*$24, Speer Morgan*

Mythium
1428 North Forbes Rd.
Lexington, KY 40511
*$20, Ronald Davis*

n + 1
68 Jay St. #405
Brooklyn, NY 11201
*$30, Keith Gessen, Mark Greif*

Narrative magazine
narrativemagazine.com
*the editors*

Nashville Review
331 Benson Hall
Vanderbilt University
Nashville, TN 37203
*Matthew Maker*

Natural Bridge
Department of English
University of Missouri, St. Louis
St. Louis, MO 63121
*$10, Mary Troy*

New England Review
Middlebury College
Middlebury, VT 05753
*$30, Stephen Donadio*

New Letters
University of Missouri
5101 Rockhill Rd.
Kansas City, MO 64110
*$22, Robert Stewart*

New Madrid
www.newmadridjournal.org
*$15, Ann Neelon*

New Ohio Review
English Department
360 Ellis Hall
Ohio University
Athens, OH 45701
*$20, John Bullock*

New Orphic Review
706 Mill St.
Nelson, British Columbia V1L 4S5
*$30, Ernest Hekkanen*

New Quarterly
Saint Jerome's University
290 Westmount Rd.
North Waterloo, Ontario N2L 3G3
*$36, Kim Jernigan*

The New Yorker
www.newyorker.com
*the editors*

Nimrod International Journal
Arts and Humanities Council of Tulsa
600 South College Ave.
Tulsa, OK 74104
*$17.50, Francine Ringold*

Ninth Letter
Department of English
University of Illinois
608 South Wright St.
Urbana, IL 61801
*$21.95, Jodee Rubins*

Noon
1324 Lexington Ave.
PMB 298
New York, NY 10128
*$12, Diane Williams*

Normal School
5245 North Backer Ave.
M/S PB 98
California State University
Fresno, CA 93470
*$5, Sophie Beck*

North American Review
University of Northern Iowa
1222 West 27th St.
Cedar Falls, IA 50614
*$22, Grant Tracey*

North Carolina Literary Review
Department of English
555 English
East Carolina University
Greenville, NC 27858-4353
*$25, Margaret Bauer*

North Dakota Quarterly
University of North Dakota
Merrifield Hall, Room 110
276 Centennial Dr. Stop 27209
Grand Forks, ND 58202
*$25, Robert Lewis*

Northwest Review
5243 University of Oregon
Eugene, OR 97403
*$20, Ehud Havazelet*

Notre Dame Review
840 Flanner Hall
Department of English

University of Notre Dame
Notre Dame, IN 46556
*$15, John Matthias, William O'Rourke*

One Story
232 Third St. # A111
Brooklyn, NY 11215
*$21, Maribeth Batcha, Hannah Tinti*

Open City
270 Lafayette St., Suite 1412
New York, NY 10012
*$30, Thomas Beller, Joanna Yas*

Orion
187 Main St.
Great Barrington, MA 01230
*$35, the editors*

Oxford American
201 Donaghey Ave., Main 107
Conway, AR 72035
*$24.95, Marc Smirnoff*

Pak N Treger
National Yiddish Book Center
Harry and Jeanette Weinberg Building
1021 West St.
Amherst, MA 01002
*$36, Aaron Lansky*

Paris Review
62 White St.
New York, NY 10013
*$34, Lorin Stein*

PEN America
PEN America Center
588 Broadway, Suite 303
New York, NY 10012
*$10, M. Mark*

Phoebe
MSN 2C5
George Mason University
4400 University Dr.
Fairax, VA 22030
*$12, Kathy Goodkin*

The Pinch
Department of English
University of Memphis
Memphis, TN 38152
*$22, Kristen Iverson*

Playboy
730 Fifth Ave.
New York, NY 10019

Pleiades
Department of English and
Philosophy
University of Central Missouri
Warrensburg, MO 64093
*$16, Wayne Miller, Phong Nguyen*

Ploughshares
Emerson College
120 Boylston St.
Boston, MA 02116
*$30, Ladette Randolph*

PoemMemoirStory
HB 217
1530 Third Ave. South
Birmingham, AL 35294
*$7, Kerry Madden*

Post Road
postroadmag.com
*$18, Rebecca Boyd*

Potomac Review
Montgomery College
51 Mannakee St.
Rockville, MD 20850
*$20, Julie Wakeman-Linn*

Prairie Fire
423-100 Arthur St.
Winnipeg, Manitoba R3B 1H3
*$30, Andris Taskans*

Prairie Schooner
201 Andrews Hall
University of Nebraska

Lincoln, NE 68588-0334
*$28, Kwame Dawes*

Prism International
Department of Creative Writing
University of British Columbia
Buchanan E-462
Vancouver, British Columbia V6T 1Z1
*$28, Cara Woodruff*

A Public Space
323 Dean St.
Brooklyn, NY 11217
*$36, Brigid Hughes*

Puerto del Sol
MSC 3E
New Mexico State University
P.O. Box 30001
Las Cruces, NM 88003
*$20, Evan Lavender-Smith*

Redivider
Emerson College
120 Boylston St.
Boston, MA 02116
*$10, Matt Salesses*

Red Rock Review
English Department, J2A
Community College of Southern
Nevada
3200 East Cheyenne Ave.
North Las Vegas, NV 89030
*$9.50, Richard Logsdon*

River Oak Review
Elmhurst College
190 Prospect Ave.
Box 2633
Elmhurst, IL 60126
*$12, Ron Wiginton*

River Styx
3547 Olive St., Suite 107
St. Louis, MO 63103-1014
*$20, Richard Newman*

Roanoke Review
221 College Ln.
Salem, VA 24153
*$5, Mary Crockett Hill*

Room Magazine
P.O. Box 46160
Station D
Vancouver, British Columbia V6J 5G5
*$10, Clélie Rich*

Ruminate
140 North Roosevelt Ave.
Fort Collins, CO 80521
*$28, Brianna Van Dyke*

Salamander
Suffolk University
English Department
41 Temple St.
Boston, MA 02114
*$23, Jennifer Barber*

Salmagundi
Skidmore College
Saratoga Springs, NY 12866
*$20, Robert Boyers*

Salt Hill
salthilljournal.com
*$20, Kayla Blatchley*

Santa Clara Review
Santa Clara University
500 El Camino Rd., Box 3212
Santa Clara, CA 95053
*$16, Nick Sanchez*

Santa Monica Review
1900 Pico Blvd.
Santa Monica, CA 90405
*$12, Andrew Tonkovich*

Seattle Review
P.O. Box 354330
University of Washington
Seattle, WA 98195
*$20, Andrew Feld*

Sewanee Review
735 University Ave.
Sewanee, TN 37383
*$53, George Core*

Shenandoah
Mattingly House
2 Lee Ave.
Washington and Lee University
Lexington, VA 24450-2116
*$25, R. T. Smith, Lynn Leech*

Slake
P.O. Box 385
2658 Griffith Park Blvd.
Los Angeles, CA 90039
*$60, Joe Donnelly*

Sonora Review
Department of English
University of Arizona
Tucson, AZ 85721
*$16, Astrid Duffy*

South Dakota Review
University of South Dakota
414 East Clark St.
Vermilion, SD 57069
*$30, Brian Bedard*

Southeast Review
Department of English
Florida State University
Tallahassee, FL 32306
*$15, Katie Cortese*

Southern Humanities Review
9088 Haley Center
Auburn University
Auburn, AL 36849
*$18, Dan R. Latimer*

Southern Indiana Review
College of Liberal Arts
University of Southern Indiana
8600 University Blvd.
Evansville, IN 47712
*$20, Ron Mitchell*

Southern Review
3390 West Lakeshore Dr.
Baton Rouge, LA 70808
*$40, Cara Blue Adams*

Southwest Review
Southern Methodist University
P.O. Box 750374
Dallas, TX 75275
*$30, Willard Spiegelman*

Subtropics
Department of English
University of Florida
P.O. Box 112075
Gainesville, FL 32611-2075
*$24, David Leavitt*

The Sun
107 North Roberson St.
Chapel Hill, NC 27516
*$39, Sy Safransky*

Sycamore Review
Department of English
500 Oval Dr.
Purdue University
West Lafayette, IN 47907
*$14, Anthony Cook*

Tampa Review
The University of Tampa
401 West Kennedy Blvd.
Tampa, FL 33606
*$22, Richard Mathews*

Third Coast
Department of English
Western Michigan University
Kalamazoo, MI 49008
*$16, Emily J. Stinson*

Threepenny Review
2163 Vine St.
Berkeley, CA 94709
*$25, Wendy Lesser*

Timber Creek Review
8969 UNCG Station
Greensboro, NC 27413
*$17, John Freiermuth*

Tin House
P.O. Box 10500
Portland, OR 97296-0500
*$24.95, Rob Spillman*

TriQuarterly
629 Noyes St.
Evanston, IL 60208
*$24, Susan Firestone Hahn*

Unstuck
4505 Duval St. #204
Austin, TX 78751
*Matt Williamson*

Upstreet
P.O. Box 105
Richmond, MA 01254
*$10, Vivian Dorsel*

Vermont Literary Review
Department of English
Castleton State College
Castleton, VT 05735
*Flo Keyes*

Virginia Quarterly Review
1 West Range
P.O. Box 400223
Charlottesville, VA 22903
*$32, Ted Genoways*

War, Literature, and the Arts
Department of English and Fine Arts
2354 Fairchild Dr., Suite 6D45
USAF Academy, CO 80840-6242
*$10, Donald Anderson*

Water-Stone Review
Graduate School of Liberal Studies
Hamline University, MS-A1730
1536 Hewitt Ave.

Saint Paul, MN 55104
*$32, the editors*

Weber Studies
Weber State University
1405 University Circle
Ogden, UT 84408-1214
*$20, Michael Wutz*

West Branch
Bucknell Hall
Bucknell University
Lewisburg, PA 17837
*$10, Paula Closson Buck*

Western Humanities Review
University of Utah
255 South Central Campus Dr.
Room 3500
Salt Lake City, UT 84112
*$16, Barry Weller*

Willow Springs
Eastern Washington University
501 North Riverpoint Blvd.
Spokane, WA 99201
*$18, Samuel Ligon*

Witness
Black Mountain Institute
University of Nevada
Las Vegas, NV 89154
*$10, the editors*

World Literature Today
University of Oklahoma
630 Parrington Oval, Suite 110
Norman, OK 73019
*Daniel Simon*

Yale Review
P.O. Box 208243
New Haven, CT 06520-8243
*$34, J. D. McClatchy*

Zoetrope: All-Story
Sentinel Building

916 Kearney St.
San Francisco, CA 94133
*$24, Michael Ray*

Zone 3
APSU
Box 4565
Clarksville, TN 37044
*$10, Amy Wright*

Zyzzyva
466 Geary St. #401
San Francisco, CA 94102
*$40, Laura Cogan*